Deniable

DENIABLE

DAVID EDGERLY

Copyright © 2025 David Edgerly

The moral right of the author has been asserted.

Apart from any fair dealing for the purposes of research or private study, or criticism or review, as permitted under the Copyright, Designs and Patents Act 1988, this publication may only be reproduced, stored or transmitted, in any form or by any means, with the prior permission in writing of the publishers, or in the case of reprographic reproduction in accordance with the terms of licences issued by the Copyright Licensing Agency. Enquiries concerning reproduction outside those terms should be sent to the publishers.

The manufacturer's authorised representative in the EU for product safety is Authorised Rep Compliance Ltd, 71 Lower Baggot Street, Dublin D02 P593 Ireland (www.arccompliance.com)

This is a work of fiction. Names, characters, businesses, places, events and incidents are either the products of the author's imagination or used in a fictitious manner. Any resemblance to actual persons, living or dead, or actual events is purely coincidental.

Troubador Publishing Ltd
Unit E2 Airfield Business Park,
Harrison Road, Market Harborough,
Leicestershire. LE16 7UL
Tel: 0116 2792299
Email: books@troubador.co.uk
Web: www.troubador.co.uk

ISBN 9781836283607

British Library Cataloguing in Publication Data.
A catalogue record for this book is available from the British Library.

Printed and bound by CPI Group (UK) Ltd, Croydon, CR0 4YY
Typeset in 11pt Minion Pro by Troubador Publishing Ltd, Leicester, UK

To my beloved daughter Hannah

CHAPTER 1

Southern Syria, near the Jordanian border, March 2018

Walid peered out from the opening of the crude cement and stone structure he called home to face another day of blistering heat. The wooden door and the lone window frame had long since disintegrated. Occasionally, he had to share the dwelling with a few goats seeking shelter. The only furniture to speak of was a rough, flea-bitten blanket that served as both a bed and a coat when the cold winter winds swept across this part of southern Syria near the Jordanian border. He blinked in the bright sunlight, relieved that the sky was clear of the government fighter planes that weren't above using shepherds as target practice. Then he scratched his wafer-thin physique in a futile effort to get rid of lice and other bugs and hobbled outside to the ditch that served as a toilet. His ablutions done, he cleaned his hands in the sand and dirt before going back inside to unroll the small bundle that held some bread and cheese his sister had given him a few days before. He didn't own a watch. His daily routine didn't really call for one. After his meager breakfast, he left to tend his brother-in-law's goats which wandered over the barren landscape looking for anything to eat. He was a little nervous today because the original group of 14 goats was now down to 12 after the herd had wandered too close to the border, and a couple of them stepped on mines placed there by the Syrians to discourage smuggling. He was afraid his brother-in-law Farhan would be furious and take away his few possessions. Farhan was a fervent supporter of the Bashar al-Assad regime, and his loyalty had been rewarded with the Mazda dealership in nearby Tal Shihab. That particular dealership had become available when the previous owner had, somewhat foolishly, joined an anti-regime demonstration a few years previously. The remains of those demonstrators were now covered by a low mound just outside the town. Farhan kept the goats mainly as a favor to his wife to give her idiot brother something to do.

Walid took his job seriously and hustled as fast as he could in his old flip-flops to make sure none of the remaining goats had strayed too far. He could see a small cloud of dust in the distance as a truck sped away toward the town, and he wondered idly what was going on. That much activity in this backwater was unusual, and he only hoped that no one had stolen any of the goats. As he scurried after the goats, he couldn't help noticing the ground was covered by more than the usual dried rat droppings. He didn't think anything of it when he stepped on one pile of these droppings, setting off the usual cloud of dust that covered him from head to toe. It happened all time. And he took a few futile swipes of his hand to wipe the dust off his torn and filthy shirt.

To his great relief, he ultimately found all 12 goats gathered around a small patch of grass. Then he sat down to pass the rest of the day watching them to make sure none got lost.

***

This was his routine until about a week later when he tried to get up one morning and discovered he was too weak to stand. He felt cold, his head ached like nothing he'd ever experienced, and he threw up what little was in his stomach. Finally, he managed to stand up by leaning against the wall and pushing himself up slowly, but after one or two steps, he fell down again and then dragged his emaciated body halfway out the door. Every muscle in his body was screaming. His head was spinning, even when he crawled into a fetal position. He didn't know it, but his blood pressure was dropping sharply.

Later that afternoon, his sister showed up with her weekly offering of food and was shocked to find him almost unconscious. She hauled him into the car and drove quickly to what passed for a clinic in Tal Shihab. The so-called "doctor"—another regime supporter whose brother was a pharmacist in Damascus—could only give Walid a few antibiotics in hopes that the condition would pass. Given all the parasites and worms already in Walid's system, it would have taken someone very, very skilled to figure out that Walid was being victimized by a virus—not bacteria.

***

A couple of days later, Walid unfortunately went into shock, caused by his steadily dropping blood pressure. Within a few hours, he was dead. There was a lot of death in Syria those days, and no one made a big deal about an illiterate shepherd dying from what seemed like natural causes. It was just fate; nothing you could do about it. He was unceremoniously buried the next day.

More unfortunately for the village, the "doctor" had nicked himself when trying to treat Walid and was now infected with the same virus. Within two weeks, he developed the same symptoms, started to panic, and took every pill in his limited medicine cabinet. By the time he realized none of these were going to work, he too had died, but not before vomiting all over several people who were trying to help him.

In due course, the unknown disease spread to much of the town. More and more people died. The authorities were no help—they were more concerned about getting as far away from the village as possible before they suffered the same fate. Some of the more astute villagers, including Farhan and Walid's sister, decided to join the stream of refugees heading into Jordan. There perhaps, they might get some relief.

***

Late the next afternoon, a tired and dusty Colonel Hisham Turkeri was sitting nervously in front of one of the most feared men in Syria. The colonel had just returned from the Crusader castle of Crac des Chevaliers, and he had to report to Ziad Duwaji, the member of the Assad clan who ran the family's personal security office. Like most things in Syria, power was displayed publicly by medal-bedecked senior officers ostentatiously reviewing troops or marching in state parades. Then there was the real power wielded by people who don't need military rank and who remain far from the public view and—equally importantly—far from any would-be assassins.

Although not an outwardly cruel man like so many of his thuggish contemporaries, who seemed to think that merely having a terrifying, snarling appearance would get results, Duwaji preferred a more subtle approach—one that almost seemed to be sympathizing with the victim as great pain was inflicted on them to get the information he wanted. Being tall, slim and favoring elegantly tailored suits of lightweight linen and silk, he appeared more like a successful banker than one of the most feared people in the Middle East. With an ascetic face dominated by cold, black eyes set above an aquiline nose and thin, bloodless lips, he could command unspeakable terror in a suspect with a mere flick of one of his long fingers or a skeptical lift of an eyebrow.

After clearing several layers of security, Colonel Turkeri tried vainly to brush the road dust off his uniform before entering Duwaji's office several floors below ground. As the colonel went inside, Duwaji came around from his desk, smiled thinly, and gestured that the colonel should take one of the comfortable chairs arranged around a small table inlaid with delicate mother of pearl—a Syrian specialty. With a brisk snap of his fingers, he ordered two coffees from his assistant. When they had been placed on the table and the door firmly closed behind the rapidly retreating assistant, he took a sip and turned to Turkeri.

"Successful trip, Hisham?" he asked mildly.

"Very. The effects were even better than we'd hoped. Almost the entire population of a small village became infected and died."

"So the biochemist we"—he waved his hand gently as if searching for exactly the right word—"*rented* did his job. Any side effects I should know about?"

"Only that it's very potent material and as dangerous to the handlers as it is to the enemy."

"That's good to hear." He raised his delicate cup slowly and took another sip. "Any complaints from the North Korean biochemist and his team?"

"Not really, sir."

Duwaji pulled a pack of Marlboros from his jacket pocket and carefully took out a cigarette. He was about to put it in his mouth when—almost as an afterthought—he offered one to the colonel, who was wise enough to turn down the offer rather than assume equality with the likes of Ziad Duwaji, who held the cigarette and a gold lighter in one hand while he asked the colonel one final question.

"And when do they say there will be enough of the virus to unleash major attacks?"

"About six to eight weeks."

"That long?" he questioned. He rose from his chair and moved behind the almost empty desk.

The colonel took this as a sign that the meeting was over and got up himself. He was about to leave when Duwaji gestured that he should stay for a minute more.

"One more thing, colonel. And not a word of this effort to anyone, understand?"

The colonel quickly nodded his understanding.

"Not even to the army and certainly not to our *allies*—the Russians. Nothing must leak out. For the time being, it must be kept between just us two"—he pointed a finger at the colonel and then back at himself—"and a very few family members. The world will find out soon enough. Even the idiots we have on guard at the fortress don't really know what's going on. Now get back there and make sure the program stays on track."

With that instruction, Colonel Turkeri did as he was asked. Once outside, he blinked in the strong sunlight and patted his coat pocket, feeling for a thin, rectangular device about the size of a cigarette case. Indeed, if anyone had bothered to look, they would have found an engraved silver case containing a few cigarettes. However, they wouldn't see the very thin transmitting device inserted in the small space between the back of the case and the tray containing the cigarettes. Reassured, he looked around and headed for a small, narrow side street lined with buildings whose overhanging balconies blocked out most of the sun. After glancing cautiously around him, he ambled toward the end of the street and chose a coffee house with a row of hanging beads serving as a door. Once inside, he stood for a moment as his eyes adjusted to the gloom of the space, which was lit by a single bare, low-wattage bulb dangling from a thin, frayed cord. The owner of the shop took one look at his uniform and almost snapped to attention as he offered the colonel the best table by the door. With a smile and a shake of his head, Colonel Turkeri said he preferred something quieter, toward the rear. The owner knew enough never to question someone in an officer's uniform, and he showed the colonel to a table separated from the others and tucked into a corner.

The colonel ordered a medium-sweet coffee and reached across the table to pull over the ashtray that, once upon a time, had been the bottom half of a tin can of green beans. After the nervous waiter had delivered the coffee, the colonel pulled out his cigarette case and opened it ostentatiously to take out and light a thin cigarette filled mainly with the pungent Syrian *latakia* tobacco. He pressed down carefully, unobtrusively, on one corner of the case to activate the transmitter and held it loosely between his thumb and forefinger as he rotated it while gently—almost absentmindedly—tapping the table. As he drank his coffee and smiled benignly, no one noticed that he was tapping in Morse code—which the clever device in the bottom of the cigarette case would scramble and send out in short bursts that no counter-surveillance could pick up.

A few months previously, a man with a very plain, easily forgotten face had approached him on a street on the outskirts of Damascus. The man had done his research and learned that, while the colonel was an Alawite like the Assad family, he was from a different clan and had very limited chances for advancement. More importantly, the plain man had learned that the colonel's sexual tastes ran more to men than woman—something that would most likely get him executed. The colonel recoiled in horror when the plain man first approached him as he was leaving the apartment of his low-level-government-employee partner. No, he almost screamed, there was no way he'd betray the government. That was sheer suicide. The plain man merely smiled and mentioned that the colonel's fate—and that of his family, as well as his partner—would be the same if certain pictures were ever posted online.

It didn't take the colonel very long to make up his mind. He didn't know exactly who was getting his information, but after receiving the very advanced miniature transmitter, he'd made a pretty good guess. The deposit of several thousand U.S. dollars in an offshore account and promise of escape also helped persuade him. He was correct in his general assumption that the Israelis had supplied the equipment. He was wrong in assuming that all Israelis were the same. He would never have guessed that his information was going to a small, very secret, private group with close ties to certain elements of the Israeli military, security and government apparatus—elements that had no interest at all in making peace with anyone in the Arab or Persian worlds.

***

The group in Jerusalem quickly forwarded the information to a company called Cougar—a very private military contractor based just outside Washington, D.C.

When the encrypted message came through, an excited junior executive called his boss, Brigadier General Stanley Meadows (ret.), over: "Holy shit! General, you gotta see this. That stuff actually works."

Meadows rushed to the computer and grinned widely when he read the message. He clapped the young man on the back. "Son of bitch! That's it, son," he barked. "That's what we've been waiting for. Those damn rats are going to lead us into a nice war. Yessir, a very nice war. We'll take care of them ragheads once and for all."

CHAPTER 2

Darfur region of southern Sudan

The sun was just peeking above the flat horizon to the east. There wasn't a cloud in the pale-blue sky, which was going to get even paler as the glaring sun burned all the color out of it. The spirals of heat rising off the hard-baked ground were curling gently, almost acrobatically, into the sky. With the exception of a few empty reed shacks and scrawny trees huddled around a trickle of water, nothing disturbed the solitude, the emptiness, which extended for hundreds of miles in all directions. Scraggy, undernourished goats bleated softly as they scratched around for whatever bits of food they could find. They provided the only sound in the vast desolation of the landscape.

"Another shitty day in paradise," murmured Viktor Lipsky as he peered over the top of the well-made foxhole at the flat, waterless landscape of the West Darfur region of Sudan. He wiped his brow with a sodden handkerchief in a futile effort to keep the sweat out of his eyes. He looked at the goats and shook his head. "You poor fuckers are about to become breakfast if you don't get the hell out of there," he muttered to no one in particular as he rolled his thick shoulders to get the kinks out.

The short, wiry, desert-camo-attired figure of his partner, Ricky Davies—a former sergeant in the specialist Delta Force of the U.S. Army—reclined casually against the side of the foxhole. His face, the color of well-seasoned mahogany and drawn tightly over his cheek bones, was almost hidden beneath a floppy, wide-brimmed hat and a pair of wraparound Bollé sunglasses. In his hands, a small Bible was open to one of the psalms. He recited the timeless words patiently and silently, in the same way he'd been doing before every combat action in his more than 20 years with the U.S. Army. He saw no need to alter his devotions just because he'd left the army and was working privately.

Lipsky pushed his sunglasses on to the top of his head and looked over at his partner. By now, he was used to Davies's reading habits. "What is it this time?" Although he privately thought Karl Marx had a point when he referred to religion as "the opiate of the people," he respected Davies's deeply held beliefs that had been hammered—sometimes literally—into him at an early age in southern Georgia, where his father was a fervent, evangelical Baptist preacher.

"Psalm 16," Davies answered. "*Preserve me, O God: For in thee do I put my trust.*" He closed the Bible carefully over the bookmark and put it into one of his shirt pockets, being sure to close the button securely to keep it from falling out. "Not a bad thought before the shit hits the fan." He glanced at the perfectly cleaned and oiled Heckler & Koch HK 416 weapon, which was wrapped loosely inside a cotton cloth, and brushed off an imaginary dust mote. Then he reflexively and needlessly checked all his spare ammunition magazines laid neatly, ready for instant use. It didn't take long for a 30-round magazine to run out. Fumbling for a replacement could be a deadly mistake. He leaned back against the side of the foxhole and closed his eyes, as if he were taking a nap on his veranda back in Addis Ababa.

Davies's wiry frame contrasted sharply with Lipsky's bulk. At 6'3" and weighing more than 210 lbs, Lipsky had the build of the American football player he used to be. His thick, black hair was swept back off his high forehead and tumbled loosely almost to his shoulders. With sharp, angular features, eyes the deep-black color of anthracite coal, and thin lips, he would almost be considered handsome—if it weren't for a sharp nose that had a slight bend and the vivid scar that ran from the bottom of his left ear to the corner of his mouth. The expression on his well-defined face was inscrutable—revealing absolutely nothing. Davies didn't have to teach Lipsky much. His mind already had the uncanny ability to calculate, assess, and evaluate the situation in front of him—separating the important from the irrelevant—and then transmit signals to his muscles in nanoseconds. His focus on the immediate problem in front of him was uncanny. While others were often distracted by the noise, dust, muscle-constricting fear, and general confusion of battle, Viktor radiated calm determination. Many soldiers were so scared they forgot to take the safety off and never even fired their weapons. Opposing soldiers were terrified of this large figure with long, waving hair walking calmly toward them firing in deadly controlled bursts. By the time the enemy perceived what was happening, they were either dead or retreating rapidly.

He'd learned at a very early age never to reveal what was behind those eyes. That only risked exposing a weakness. A certain type of women found him attractive—the kind drawn to sharply hewn brawn with a hint of deeply hidden mystery. They made it their goal to pry the mystery out of those almost-hypnotic eyes. It never worked. It wasn't that he didn't like women. He did. It was simply that he didn't like women who thought he was a laboratory specimen to be analyzed. He loved the stunned expression on their faces when he asked them their opinion on Heisenberg's uncertainty principle or what they thought Dostoyevsky was really trying to say in *Notes from Underground*. They blinked once or twice at the disconnect between the words that belonged in the Harvard faculty club and the body that belonged in a boxing ring. They soon retreated in search of easier prey. When he smiled, which wasn't often, he had the sort of lopsided grin that caused most people to swallow nervously a couple of times.

He took a drink from his canteen and looked at his watch. "Shouldn't be long now."

Davies had been relaxing against the side of the foxhole, his eyes closed behind the sunglasses. "Don't be in such a hurry, Viktor," he said without moving. "No need to go lookin' for trouble. Them boys will be along soon enough. We'll hear 'em long before we see 'em. They ain't 'xactly strategic geniuses and never vary their routine."

At that point, his earpiece crackled into life: "Just a comms check, Sarge. Ain't nuthin' goin' down yet."

"I hear y'all good, Bubba. Folks know what they're supposed to do?"

"Oh yeah." Bubba chuckled. "Them boys is as happy as pigs in shit. They ain't never had real guns before. Whoever they pray to just delivered big time."

"OK, make sure they stay outta sight till I give the word." Davies clicked off and turned to Viktor. "By the way, where did you get all this shit? You brought all sorts this time."

"Balko," Viktor answered tersely.

"That sumbitch again? He try to screw you like the last time?"

"He tried." Viktor didn't take his eyes off the eastern skies.

"Asshole never learns, does he? I take it you persuaded him to stick to his deal?"

"After a little discussion. As usual he wanted more money. Four RPGs [rocket-propelled grenades] aimed at his plane and a shotgun aimed at his balls helped him remember the original deal." Viktor recalled with a grim smile the scene at the dusty, remote airfield where the heavily loaded twin-engine Soviet-era

Antonov thumped down on the ground made hard by months of no rain...

***

The scrawny figure of Ivan Balko—wanted in numerous countries for gunrunning and violations of what are quaintly called the "rules of warfare"—had edged cautiously down the ramp and headed toward Viktor, who had stood unmoving and unsmiling about 50 yards from the plane with two large bags by his feet. Then two heavily armed and tattooed men had walked down the ramp behind Balko and stood guard, forming a rough semicircle with Balko included.

There had been a weak smile on Balko's face, with his arms outstretched in a "what can we do?" gesture as he had approached. He had tried to plead that some unnamed bureaucrats were demanding more money.

Viktor hadn't budged. He had merely pointed to the plane. "The merchandise, Ivan; the merchandise. I assume you have it," he said in Russian, their one common language. Viktor had leaned down and picked up one of the heavy satchels. He had opened it in front of Balko to show thick bricks of used $100 bills. "This is it, Ivan. This is all you're getting. What was agreed."

The smile had disappeared from Balko's face. "This isn't smart, Viktor. Why don't we just take the money and leave you standing here holding nothing but your pecker?"

Then it had been Viktor's turn to smile. "OK, OK. Ivan, you win." He had reached into another satchel as if to pull out more money. Instead, he had extracted a short-barreled 12-gauge shotgun and pushed it into Balko's groin as he pulled both hammers back with a loud click.

Balko's eyes had widened in horror as he tried to pull away.

But Viktor's strong left hand had grabbed the front of his

shirt and pulled him close. "Now, Ivan. The merchandise. Tell your goons to get it out of the plane."

Balko had regained some of his composure and snarled at Viktor: "You're making a big mistake, Lipsky. My guys"—he nodded toward the guards around the plane, who were getting nervous at the delay—"can put a lot of holes in you before you pull that trigger."

"Maybe, maybe not. You want to find out?" Viktor gestured across the small landing strip with his chin.

Four small, dusty figures had popped up from the surrounding shrubbery, hoisted RPGs onto their shoulders, and aimed them directly at the plane's cockpit. The pilots had started to wail loudly and yelled for the guards to get the boxes off the plane before they were all incinerated.

"About those holes, Ivan. Seems we have a bit of a Mexican standoff here. We can all do our business and go home, or we can all stay here in small pieces. The choice is yours."

"Fuck you, Lipsky," Balko had spat out in English.

"Glad to see your language skills are improving, Ivan. What's your choice? I have to say I never figured you for choosing martyrdom over cold cash."

Balko had angrily barked an order to his men to take the boxes of weapons and ammunition off the plane.

"You satisfied, asshole?" Balko had asked. "Now can we get the hell out of this shithole?"

After checking the boxes thoroughly, Viktor had shoved Balko away and gestured for him and his crew to get back on the plane. "Have a good flight, Ivan. Don't forget to fasten your seat belt."

Balko had turned around with one final outburst. "You'll fucking pay for this, Lipsky. No one fucks with Ivan Balko and gets away with it. There's no place on this earth for you to hide."

***

Back in the foxhole, Davies laughed at the thought of Balko being forced to stick to a deal. "Well, that prick should be happy those things are in good hands now. The locals were happy as hell to get them. They got guts, I'll say that. Didn't take long to teach them how to use the AKs. Shit, just aim and pull the trigger. Ain't real hard. Anyways, they're primed and ready to go. At least we've evened the odds a bit. They ain't exactly crack shots. But, hell, it don't matter. They'll make enough noise to scare the good Lord hisself."

"Where are the rest of the villagers?"

Davies nodded off to the southwest. "Over yonder a couple of klicks. Hidden down in a wadi with a bunch of the powdered-milk crowd," he said, referring to the NGO representatives. "They weren't thrilled about fighting back, but when I explained the alternative of getting sliced up, raped, and left for dead, they got the point."

"By the way, where'd the money come from this time?"

"Avram."

"Him again?"

"Yeah. His people hate that son of a bitch al-Bashir who runs Sudan. They'll do anything to put sand in his gears—especially if their fingerprints aren't all over the deed. They figure this deal is cheap at twice the price."

Davies laughed. "Shit, Viktor. We gotta review our price list. We're sellin' ourselves too cheap."

Right then, they heard the throbbing noise of an overloaded prop plane heading their way. Even at 5,000 feet, it made a lot of noise.

Viktor looked at Davies. "Show time, Ricky. The boys all set?" he asked rhetorically.

Davies scoffed at the thought that his boys would be anything but "all set." "Damn it, Viktor, you know my boys are the best there is. Smart, tough, and mean as hungry rattlesnakes. Don't you worry. They know what to do and when to do it. Trained them myself on things the U.S. Army left out of their training."

They could barely see the plane circling lazily in the distance as someone lowered the ramp and 42-gallon oil barrels started falling out in a haphazard fashion.

"Barrel bombs. Nasty fuckers," Davies said disgustedly. "No fuckin' idea where they're gonna land, but they make a helluva bang."

The plane stayed over the settlement just long enough to push all the barrels out. Then it did a sharp U-turn and headed back toward Khartoum. The barrels left scorched earth and a lot of holes in the ground but did little serious damage. The main intention was to terrorize the local population. Viktor and Davies watched the plane pull away, but they didn't leave the relative safety of the foxhole.

Davies checked his watch and clicked on the comms mic strapped around his neck. "Bubba, hold 'em tight. That was only the opening act; the second one should come along shortly."

"Copy that, but these boys are getting anxious to start playing with their new toys."

"Sit on 'em if you have to. Just make sure they keep their heads down." He clicked off his mic and carefully picked up his own weapon.

Viktor did the same and bent his head slightly as the faint *thup, thup* of three low-flying helicopter gunships filled the early morning sky. They watched impassively as the aircraft, with machine guns blazing away, slowly circled what was left of the burning settlement.

Davies grabbed Viktor by the arm. "There, look—at your 9 o'clock. Isn't that sumbitch Balko standing in the door of that chopper?" He started to raise a weapon, but Viktor put out a restraining hand.

"Not now, Ricky. Nice as it would be, we need to wait for the third act. They're the real target."

Davies reluctantly put down his shoulder-held missile. "For now, Viktor; for now."

The helicopters stayed for less than 10 minutes and then swung back the way they came from.

"OK, now it's our turn," Viktor murmured.

They climbed out of the foxhole and whistled for the others to come out from hiding and take up positions in front of the empty settlement. Ten obvious military types led 30 rail-thin, poorly clad figures into shallow defensive trenches that had been prepared the previous day. The villagers wore grim expressions and clutched automatic weapons. Each of the soldiers took three villagers to their positions and emphasized once again the need to hold their fire until they heard the order to shoot.

They didn't have to wait long. First, they saw the rapidly moving dust clouds coming out of the sun right at them. Then the whine of over-revved engines and the thump of suspension systems bouncing over the rough ground broke the silence. Finally, the crackling sounds of AK 47s firing wildly into the air reached them.

"Stupid fucks never change, do they?" Viktor said.

"Never." Davies was disgusted, his professional pride offended by the amateur tactics of his enemies. "Whatever, we're in business now. Tell me again what they call these assholes."

"Janjaweed," Viktor answered. "Man with a gun on a horse."

"Well, them fuckers got one less horse now." Davies laughed as the first of the trucks hit a land mine his men had placed the previous night.

The battered Toyota pickup flew high in the air while the others circled wide around it, their drivers suddenly nervous. Viktor counted nine remaining trucks, each with a mounted machine gun and about six men—boys really—in the back. One boy was shoved roughly out of each truck and ordered to jog along ahead to make sure there were no more mines. Every gun on the truck was aimed at his back in case he thought of changing course. For the first 10 yards, everything was fine. Then one of the boys stepped on a mine and let out a blood-curdling scream as his shattered limbs flew back toward the trucks. The remaining fighters could no longer restrain themselves. They leaped out of the trucks and raced toward the shacks, screaming their revenge while firing their ancient AK 47s and waving vicious long knives. They never paid attention to what was immediately in front of them. They never even had time to register surprise as the ground rose up and started firing at them. Like many firefights, it was over in a matter of minutes—seconds really. The stench of cordite; the loud, deadly clatter of automatic weapons; the crump of exploding land mines; and the screams of maimed and dying boys were quickly replaced by the stillness of the ancient, barren landscape. Only the buzz of hungry insects disturbed the silence. A few wisps of smoke and dust trailed lazily up into the vast, empty sky. The scattered remains of the young Janjaweeds lay over the ground, bent into unnatural positions. In death, they'd lost their fearsome expressions and looked more like schoolboys astonished at being caught doing something they shouldn't be doing.

The relieved villagers were equally astonished—but alive. They were all grins and laughter as they went around picking up weapons for further use.

Davies, however, was furious at the carnage. "Ain't no fuckin' need for this, Viktor; no need at all. Just look at those poor fuckin' kids. Never knew what hit them. It's that asshole Balko and the people behind him that set these kids up. They give 'em a little weed to chew, some piece-of-shit gun, and a knife, fill them full of bullshit and turn 'em loose." He turned to Viktor, deadly serious. "Mark my words, next time I'm takin' that fucker down."

"He's all yours, Ricky. He's all yours."

Viktor took a satellite phone from his backpack and punched in a long series of numbers. After several rings it was finally answered. "Merchandise worked, Avram," he said simply.

"You OK? You don't sound too good."

"I'm fine. Not a scratch. I'm just getting tired of this shit."

"I know. It's a dirty business. Think that al-Bashir learned a lesson?"

"Not a chance. People like him never learn."

"That's what I'm afraid of. We'll probably be at this again fairly soon." He paused for a moment. "Take some time off, Viktor. Go back to your island. And be sure to thank Davies and his team. They do good work. We'll put something extra in their accounts."

After ending the call, Viktor walked toward Davies, who was back in instructor mode, showing the villagers how to take advantage of their new-found arsenal. Viktor tapped him on the shoulder and pulled him aside. "I'm out of here. Let me know the next time Desta finds a cause that needs saving."

Davies, knowing all about post-combat fatigue, understood that words were mostly useless. He merely nodded his agreement and told Viktor to take one of the jeeps back to an airfield where a plane with no markings was waiting. "Take your time, Viktor. I'm heading back to Addis to see how many other groups Desta thinks need saving."

***

Addis Ababa, ten days later

The intense, rhythmic Gospel notes from the choir of the evangelical Holy Savior Church in Addis Ababa, Ethiopia, rang through the open doors and windows of the packed church on a hot Sunday morning in April. Ricky Davies, the son of a traveling Baptist minister from southern Georgia, lent his loud, deep bass support from the middle of the congregation.

When the choir stopped, the preacher shouted, "*Praise the Lord,*" as he waved his arms in front of him.

The congregation picked up the chant with arms waving joyfully in the air: "*Praise the Lord! Praise be to Him!*"

"And don't forget to pass the damn ammunition," Davies added softly.

His wife Desta poked him sharply in the ribs. "Behave yourself, Richard," she commanded.

Davies smiled in mock surrender as he looked up at his wife, who was almost three inches taller than him and had the regal bearing of many of the people from the Amhara region of Ethiopia. Although she was a proud member of the Orthodox Church of Ethiopia, she took a tolerant, somewhat bemused view of her husband's religious roots and often joined him in those somewhat alien services—especially after he'd just returned safely from a mission to save one of the many groups she deemed vulnerable to the ravages of warlords and other genocidal maniacs that dominate so much of East Africa.

Later they joined other parishioners at long, heavily laden picnic tables set up under the eucalyptus trees behind the church. Davies and his wife passed slowly down the table greeting other parishioners as they loaded their plates with steaming meat and vegetables. Davies looked slightly puzzled as Desta led them to a small table slightly removed from the others.

"This ain't like you, Desta, movin' away from everyone else. Why do I have the feeling you got something on your mind?" He started to eat while Desta pushed her food around on her plate.

"How is Viktor these days?" she asked.

Davies shrugged, wondering what was behind this sudden interest in Viktor. "Viktor is, well, you know, Viktor. Reliable, tough, mean in a fight. Damn glad he's on my side. Oh, and one other thing. He's probably the smartest damn person I ever did meet. That man just knows stuff. Know what I mean? God knows how many languages he speaks. You should hear him jabber away in Russian—like a goddamned native." He hoped this would satisfy Desta. He was wrong.

"That's not what I mean, Richard," she shot back sharply. "I mean how *is* he? He seldom says anything and always seems angry at something. Is he happy, sad, lonely?"

Davies pushed his plate away and rubbed a hand over his face. "Well, now, these ain't subjects you really bring up with someone like Viktor. After 20 years in the army, you learn somethin' 'bout men—what's important for the job at hand, and what's best left alone. A man's private life is simply that—private. He shows up for work, keeps his weapons clean, and keeps his mouth shut—well, that's enough for me."

"And this island of his," Desta continued, oblivious to Davies's comments, "where in Greece is it? What does he do there?"

"Now look here," Davies snapped, "I got no idea where his bolt hole is. It's his business, not mine. When he's good and ready, he'll tell me—maybe. I suggest you let Viktor's private life remain his affair."

"Well, I'm afraid it's gone beyond that."

"What do you mean?" Davies was alarmed at Viktor's possible reaction to interference in his life.

"There's someone I'd like him to meet. Someone who needs his help on a matter that doesn't concern anything in Africa." She held up her hand to forestall Davies's reaction. "Let me explain. There's a volunteer in a camp west of here, not far from South Sudan—"

Davies winced. "You mean the one where a drone wiped out some jeeps packed with really bad *jihadis* a couple of weeks ago?"

Desta waved away any possible connection. "Yes. Somewhere near there. Anyway, this woman, Sarah Huntington, came up to me at an aid conference last month. She knew some of what you and Viktor do, and she asked if she could meet him. She said there was a serious problem with her brother somewhere in the Middle East." She took a deep breath. "To cut a long story short,

I said I didn't know exactly where Viktor lived, but that it might be on an island somewhere near Turkey."

"How in God's name do you know that?" Davies exploded.

"I overheard him once in our house making travel arrangements that involved a ferry from the island of Rhodes. He was speaking Greek," she added in explanation. "I'm Greek Orthodox, remember? I understood just enough to figure out what he was doing."

"You know he ain't gonna take kindly to intruders. This woman'll be lucky if she don't get shot."

Desta smiled. "That would be a shame. She might be good for him. She's really quite beautiful. And Viktor can be quite nice sometimes."

"When he ain't shootin' people in the head."

CHAPTER 3

Greek island of Telos, Aegean Sea

Viktor tipped the rickety chair back against the whitewashed wall of his stone house and gazed contentedly at the sun rising over the brilliant-blue Aegean Sea surrounding the small Greek island of Telos. The chair creaked and groaned from the pressure of his bulky frame, but so far, it was holding together due to the bits of wire reinforcement he'd wound around the legs.

A perfect refuge and place to decompress, he thought.

He was drinking coffee on the wide veranda overlooking the harbor, with a pergola of grapevines protecting him from the sun, which could be fierce even in April. The only sounds were coming from the never-ending cicadas and the bells of goats wandering around his 10 acres, with its olive trees and orange grove. The olive trees were bare of fruit at this time of year, and the oranges were almost finished, but he still had plenty of his own freshly pressed olive oil and frozen juice he'd squeezed from the oranges.

Best of all, he mused, *no one is shooting at me.*

He had liked the isolated, slightly decrepit house the moment he'd laid eyes on it a few years previously. He'd been searching for a place that was remote, but not too remote. Off the beaten path, but not completely inaccessible. A place that only very few people knew about. After looking at several locations, he'd finally settled on Telos and this old house. The roof was sagging, and the windows and doors really didn't fit too well, but the stone walls were at least a yard thick and looked as if they could withstand a few direct hits. Details like that were important to him. The location was perfect. The old Greeks knew what they were doing. Placed on a slight rise to catch the breeze off the sea, even on the hottest August days, the house had an unobstructed view of the small town and harbor. The three eucalyptus trees around the sides and rear shaded it from the worst of the sun. He also liked the way the sound of the church bells rolled gently up the hill on Sundays and the numerous saint's days.

The locals weren't quite sure who this new guy was or why he was wasting his time on this wreck of an old house and its surrounding orchards. But they quickly buried whatever questions they had when he paid over the odds for the property. His funds—in cash—also made sure there were no problems with the building permits. Then he found a small team of Albanians whose families had been living on the island for decades to do the restoration work. These skilled stone masons showed up on time every day and stayed late—encouraged perhaps by the fact that they were paid every week. This was important at a time when many people in Greece could barely come up with the money for food and clothes. Belonging to a race of hard men, the Albanians also knew enough to say nothing about the large storage area they dug out under the floorboards, which they lined with cement and coated with waterproof sealant. The storage area also contained several gun racks and a large safe built into the wall. The workmen simply nodded their approval. Sometimes these things are necessary.

Viktor added a couple of rooms, installed modern plumbing and electricity, and found enough furniture in the town to make it comfortable. He also found some old bookcases to take care of all the books he ordered online. The cleaning lady who came once a week could barely read Greek, let alone all the other languages that seemed to be represented in his house. An Italian artist on the island—who was probably a descendant of the Italian soldiers who were more or less stranded there during World War II—provided the wall decoration and sometimes spent the night there admiring her handiwork.

He liked the way the house overlooked the small village that was organized around the port. Small, whitewashed houses stretched along the three roads radiating from the square. Each house was neat, with flowers in the windows and its paths swept clean every morning. House proud, these people were. Small shops—including a butcher, greengrocer, and all-purpose grocery store—surrounded the square. There was a pension on one of the side streets for the occasional tourist who wandered off the ferry. He enjoyed taking in the village scene while he was having his coffee.

Some store owners were sweeping in front of their shops. Others were lowering their awnings as the sun started to beat down on the white marble paving stones. A couple of fishermen were sitting by the port, mending their nets, with last night's catch spread out on trays. It wasn't a rich town. No ship owners had built mansions here over the years. No diaspora Greeks had built fancy summer homes for their annual migration to the land their grandparents or great-grandparents had left in despair. It was simply an ordinary small island town. Ordinary people doing ordinary things. The kind of place he'd been seeking for a long time.

While they appreciated the money he spent, the villagers were still curious about him. His arrival was the biggest news since one of the ferries had run aground ten years earlier. *Who is he? Is he American, German, or English? Costa, the police chief, says he has a Greek passport, but these days, who really knows?*

What does he do for money? He certainly doesn't look Greek; he's much too serious. And look at the size of him! And that scar! Mother of God! He looks like one of the old bandits in the hills. How come he speaks such good Greek? Is he even a Christian? Surely, he must be running away from his wife and family—or the law?

Viktor was aware of their questions, but he never volunteered any information. It wasn't that he was rude. He just gave a slight smile and gently waved away any speculation.

After a few months when nothing bad had happened to the island because of his arrival, he began to be accepted simply as the *"xeno"*—the foreigner. A little strange maybe, but certainly no threat. The questions were also stilled by mysterious, anonymous donations to the school and the church. Every school child received a new computer, and the bell tower of the church was finally repaired after an earthquake 15 years ago had cracked it badly. Even the police station got a new roof.

One time, an old widow was trapped in her house when a heavy limb of a cypress tree fell through the roof in a big storm. It would take days to get the right rescue equipment from Rhodes. A crowd had gathered to stare at the sight and loudly offer useless advice. The stranger—the *xeno*—was passing by and saw the crowd. He came over to investigate and rapidly realized something had to be done quickly. The crowd gaped as he squatted under the tree, gritted his teeth, and lifted it just enough for someone to pull the old woman out. The people were briefly speechless. Then they rapidly started clapping and offering the *xeno* multiple cups of coffee with sweet pastries. He merely smiled as best he could and then walked slowly home. After that, the questions ceased. He may be a scary-looking and huge *xeno*, but he was now *their* scary-looking and huge *xeno*.

Every so often, he'd disappear for a few weeks. Some of the local women thought he looked a little haggard after these trips, but they never said anything—at least to him. The only thing was that his cleaning lady noticed the clothes in his bag were usually filthy when he returned. They were often covered with the same kind of reddish sand that strong northerly winds from across the Mediterranean sometimes dumped on the island in a heavy rainstorm. One time, she even thought she detected blood stains, but after crossing herself several times, she convinced herself they were just rust stains. Occasionally, one of the concerned women would make the journey to the house with a bowl of her own boiled greens—an ancient recipe for restoring energy. He'd smile his thanks and accept the greens graciously. He always made sure the bowl was washed clean before placing it on the porch, from where it would be picked up.

However, the concept of *"parea"*—a group of friends or company—is a key part of Greek life. His lack of *parea*, apart from the Italian woman, was a constant source of speculation. No one could figure out how he could appear to be so content with just himself for company—but, equally, no one could muster the necessary courage to discuss it with him.

***

Alex Kalistos—Aleco to the locals—was the name he used on the island. There was no need to make it easy for anyone trying to find Viktor Lipsky. In fact, he had a different name for each of the five passports he carried. But for now, Alex Kalistos was enough. His real name had been shortened from the original Lipchinsky when his great-grandfather emigrated to the United States from Russia in the 1930s and wound up in the iron-ore country near Ishpeming on the Upper Peninsula of northern Michigan, right across the frigid Lake Superior from the Canadian province of Ontario. Young Viktor grew up doing pretty much what everyone else did in that part of the United States: play football, drink beer, hunt, fish, and, ultimately, work in the iron-ore mines.

The one Lipsky family tradition not shared by his childhood friends was the Russian passion for chess. He remembered his grandfather sitting hunched over a chessboard for hours, playing and replaying famous games as the pieces glided over the 64-squares of the board: sometimes attacking, sometimes feinting, and sometimes lying in ambush, waiting for an unwary move. His grandfather and father reacted violently when young Viktor called chess a "game."

"This is not a game, you silly boy!" his grandfather chided. "This is life. Learn it and you might begin to understand something. How your opponent plays says more about his character than anything he might tell you."

And Viktor did learn. Slowly at first, gradually, the endless variations began to make sense, and in a few years, he could at least extend a game to 30 moves. Sometimes, he even played his father to a draw. He also learned that his grandfather was right. The lessons learned on the chessboard served him well over the course of his life.

Where he grew up was an area of tough kids—very tough kids. What passed as normal comforts of life in other areas were scoured off by the bitter, harsh environment. What remained was a very hard, durable core—a survivor's core. You never, ever turned the other cheek. Forget cold servings: revenge was dispensed immediately and violently with fists and stout boots. Viktor survived and stood out just enough to promise a somewhat different future. Being over six feet tall, he had the powerful shoulders and quick feet that football coaches notice. He had another trait the coaches valued highly: he seemed impervious to physical pain. Slam him down, and he just got up and slammed you harder. Put him on defense as a linebacker, and he could deliver a crippling blow to a runner or crush a receiver dumb enough to come anywhere near him. Nothing fazed him. Scouts from Michigan State University loved him and signed him up for a football scholarship. After two outstanding seasons, with visions of a professional career looming, he blew out his knee while sacking the Purdue quarterback one rainy Saturday afternoon in East Lansing.

Faced with the prospect of dropping out of school or instead undergoing lengthy rehab and keeping his scholarship, he wisely chose to do the rehab and stay in school. Knowing that his serious football days were over, he not only stayed in school but also studied hard. The thought of returning to a life in iron-ore country, with its disappearing jobs, was enough to keep him studying. To his surprise, he found he was far better than average in two subjects: history and languages. To be fair, he had an advantage in having learned to speak Russian at home. Like many immigrant groups, the Russians almost never married outside their own community. With both his parents and his grandparents speaking Russian at home, it was natural that he was fluent at an early age.

***

Viktor checked his battered €20 watch to make sure he got to the town square before the ferry came in. He felt safe on the island, but it never hurt to double-check to see if anyone out of place got off the ferry from Rhodes. After his run-in with Ivan Balko, he was even more on his guard. He picked up a thick book on the origins of World War I and a pair of military-spec binoculars, which he added to his backpack. Then he stepped outside into the bright sun and adjusted his wraparound sunglasses. The ferry was just a dot on the cloudless horizon, and if he hustled, he'd have time for a coffee and a few pages of his book before studying the passengers getting off. With that in mind, he hurried off toward his destination.

As he reached the small coffee shop and restaurant in the town square and sat under the large awning, Maria, its owner, smiled at him and had his medium-sweet Greek coffee and a glass of water ready for him.

"Am I that predictable?" he queried with a laugh.

She leaned over and gave him a motherly pat on the shoulder. "Only on days when the ferry comes in. It's almost like you're waiting for someone—or perhaps hoping someone doesn't get off the boat. Some poor woman you left behind, maybe?" She gave him another pat on the shoulder and a knowing wink before heading back inside.

Maria's words were playful, but they reminded Viktor that people on the island didn't miss very much. One small mistake could bring his carefully constructed refuge down on his head.

Very few people—not even Davies and his wife, Desta, back in Addis Ababa—knew exactly where he was. They had a rough idea, but that was all. He had no real friends to keep in contact with, and he took elaborate precautions to cover his movements. One of the things he liked about the island was that the ferry from Rhodes on three days a week was the only way onto it. There was no airport. Perhaps a helicopter could land in the town square, but you would hear one of those things coming for miles. Private motor yachts didn't like the usually rough seas, and he was pretty sure that none of his "business acquaintances" would have a clue how to pilot a sailboat. However, after years of dealing in a business where deceit, betrayal and violence were standard operating procedures, he'd learned that a little bit of paranoia wasn't a bad thing.

On the days the ferry arrived, he still managed to show up at the coffee house opposite the pier just as it came in. Telos wasn't really on the tourist trail, and most people on board were headed further up the line to Kos or Patmos. Usually, the only people who got off were locals returning from Rhodes or the occasional sunburned backpacker who thought the island looked like a good place to stop. Some of the islanders thought more tourism development would be a good thing, but most of them thought it was more trouble than it was worth. Every time they came back from the tourist magnet of Rhodes, they recoiled in horror at the thought of a string of souvlaki joints, discos with thumping techno music, and drunken tourists descending on their quiet island. Viktor was happy with the island just as it was. And a little of his cash in the right hands made sure it stayed that way.

As the latest ferry docked and disgorged it's complement of passengers, from his table obscured by the pergola jutting out from the coffee house, he still assiduously scanned them all, looking for the out-of-place traveler—someone who didn't fit into the normal pattern. Most days, after checking them out, he just finished his coffee, paid the €2, left a tip, and walked back up the hill to his house. Other times, when he wasn't quite sure, he'd slip out the back door of the café and take a roundabout route home. Once here, he'd grab the binoculars and carefully watch the stranger as he made his way across the square to the one and only pension on the island. Then he'd make a quick call to his cop buddy, who'd casually stroll over to—very politely—check the passport of the new arrival. Costa, the cop, might have thought this routine was a little bizarre, but the extra cash in his pocket quickly banished those thoughts. Once satisfied that the new arrival was indeed just an innocent tourist, Viktor would replace the binoculars in their case and resume his daily routine.

CHAPTER 4

He was to remember this particular day—Tuesday, April 3rd—as the day when his life took a sudden and dramatic turn. It had started off normally when he was gazing over the sea and could just make out that the ferry from Rhodes was about three miles away and beginning to slow down as it approached the port. This was the ferry that would make its way slowly up the Dodecanese chain of islands to Patmos, wait for a couple of hours, and then begin the return trip in the early evening. He sipped the same medium-sweet Greek coffee with a glass of water and watched as the ferry went through its usual maneuvers of lowering the car ramp halfway, dropping the anchor, using the bow and stern thrusters to spin around, and then reversing gently back to the pier, at which point thin lead lines were thrown to handlers on shore who hauled the thick mooring lines onto the pier and slipped them over huge bollards. Finally, the ramp slammed down on the stone pier, and the passengers started to get off.

 He watched closely as the usual assortment of black-clad elderly ladies carrying bulging plastic bags made their way slowly down the ramp in front of the few cars waiting impatiently. He also noted old Vassilis, who'd gone to Rhodes to visit his grandson who ran a decent fish restaurant inside the old fort. Then he sat up suddenly and looked closely at the next person getting off the boat. This one was different. Viktor's well-developed threat antennae started vibrating as he saw a tall, athletic-looking woman with the deep tan that comes only from long hours spent in a hot climate stride confidently down the steep ramp. Maybe it was her air of self-confidence. Maybe it was her clothes—from the well-worn khaki shirt with military-style epaulets and buttons for rolled-up sleeves to the hiking shorts and specialist lightweight hiking boots—that alerted him. Or perhaps it was her striking features, which were revealed when she pushed her sunglasses onto her well-shaped forehead: the almost Slavic cheekbones, the aquiline nose, and the slim, determined mouth. Most of all, he noticed the raven-dark hair and the startling blue eyes.

"Nice combination," he muttered to himself.

Her long hair was tied back in a single loose braid, and she impatiently shook her head to get the braid out of her way while she consulted a small notepad. A slight nod indicated she was satisfied with the information on the pad, and she stuck it back into one of the many pockets of her shirt. Then she casually picked up the large backpack, slung it over one shoulder, and headed over to the pension. She certainly wasn't a Greek woman—or even Italian, for that matter. No, this kind of confidence and boldness could only come from North America or possibly Australia.

Either way it spelled trouble—serious trouble. Viktor had seen that look before. The best of the NGO women had it. Confident, fearless, and with that rare combination of efficiency and compassion. Seemingly hopeless causes were their specialty. Desta loved these people. Viktor thought they were a huge pain in the ass. The people they were helping would have been better off heading out of town—fast. But no, led by these Wonder Women with bags of flour and powdered milk, they wanted to stay on their "ancestral" bit of waterless, barren wasteland, despite the roving gangs of machine-gun-toting, drugged-up thugs trying to drive them off. He had to admit that such groups were his best market—in fact, the only market that Desta would allow him and Davies to serve. But convincing them they had to fight fire with fire was very, very hard. The NGO women were against guns and violence. They refused to leave even when the pickup trucks with machine guns started circling the ragged settlements. More than once, Viktor had to physically carry them, kicking and screaming, to safety.

And now one of them was on Telos. Shit. Shit. Shit. It was time to exit quietly out of the rear door, head home, and give Costa a call.

He carefully put the coffee cup back on the table and was about to leave when he caught sight of the last two people getting off the ferry. He froze momentarily as two tough-looking guys strolled down the ramp with their eyes firmly fixed on the NGO woman. He thought he recognized them, but he couldn't immediately remember where from. He certainly knew the type. Their occupation was clear. From their bulging muscles and their flat eyes staring out of hard, scarred faces to the camo pants tucked into their combat boots, they looked like the mercenaries he saw all over Africa. He also doubted that the large satchels they carried contained just a bathing suit and a few T-shirts. But why would a couple of heavily armed mercs suddenly descend on this little island? Why were they following the NGO woman?

Then it suddenly dawned on him. He remembered where he'd seen these two. At the last arms dump where Ivan Balko was screaming about his revenge on Viktor, they were guarding the merchandise. Now it was beginning to make sense. They were here for him. But how the hell had they found him? Were they just guessing? Or did they really know he was here?

"Son of a bitch," he muttered. "It's the bloody NGO woman. They're following her in the hope she'll lead them to me."

Hidden behind the pergola, Viktor followed their scans as they spotted the NGO woman and set out to follow her. Betrayal and revenge were always high on Balko's agenda. If he had to butcher several people in a small island town to get that revenge, well, that was just part of the price of messing with Ivan Balko. He had a reputation to uphold after all.

Viktor wasn't sure how the girl fit into this scenario. He'd never seen her before, so why were they assuming she might lead them to him? He watched her stride across the square and enter the small pension. The two thugs sat down at a *kafeneion* on the other side of the square where they could watch the entrance of the pension. They scowled at a waiter and gestured crudely for coffee and beer. Their satchels were carefully placed within easy reach. The larger one had pulled out his cell phone and started to make a call when the smaller one grabbed it away.

"What the fuck are you doing?" he asked in loud, angry Russian.

"I was just going to call Ivan and tell him we probably found Lipsky," the shorter one said.

"No. Wait until we're sure. All he knows is that we're on a well-deserved break in Rhodes. He doesn't know we saw this broad waiting for a ferry. She's our best lead to Lipsky. We do this on our own. We don't need no advice from Balko. We'll tell him after. Don't worry. The bitch will lead us to Lipsky. When we're done, we'll take a picture of both of them laid out nice and dead, and then send the picture to Balko. Maybe then we'll get the respect we deserve. I'm getting sick of being treated like some fucking servant."

This was all Viktor needed to hear before retreating behind the small greengrocer signaling for the owner not to say anything. Once out of sight, he ran as fast as he could back to his house. There was only one person who might know what was going on. He grabbed his satellite phone and punched one of the few speed-dial buttons.

When the call was answered, the mellifluous voice of Desta floated over the airwaves. At first, he'd badly underestimated Desta's influence on operations. Once she saw Davies's plans could actually save people she cared about, she became an active part of the team. All projects had to pass her sensitive "smell" test. In other words, the odds—as they usually were—had to be stacked against the weak and powerless. Then she'd give her approval, and Davies and Viktor would start the wheels rolling.

"Why, Viktor, how nice to hear from you. I was going to call you. I was just talking to Richard about a wonderful young woman who's looking for you."

"Let me guess, Desta. The call was gonna warn me about one of 'your people' or 'your projects' mysteriously arriving on my little island refuge."

"Exactly," she said excitedly. "Have you had a chance to meet her yet? She's an amazing person. Her name is Sarah Huntington."

"I'm sure she is, Desta. But, no, I haven't met her yet. I recently saw her get off the ferry—followed, unfortunately, by two of Ivan Balko's goons. I'm guessing they're using her as bait to get to me."

He heard her gasp at the thought that she'd pushed this woman into a trap. "My God, Viktor! You must protect her."

He quickly bit back a reply about protecting himself first. Sarcasm never got far with people like Desta. "Let's back up a minute. Before we get to that point, exactly how did she get here and how did those two guys get on her trail?"

She took a deep breath. "It's a bit of story. She was working for an NGO not far from one of 'our' villages—one of the ones you and Ricky helped. I met her at a conference recently. It turns out she'd heard of the work you and Ricky do, and she needed your help with something. To cut a long story short, she said she has a brother who's also working for an NGO and who's got lost—possibly kidnapped—somewhere in Syria. She's afraid they took him to some place called Crac des Chevaliers, and she wanted to talk with you to see if there was anything you could do."

Viktor groaned. "There's nothing, absolutely nothing, I can do for the guy. Syria is one place I won't go near. It makes Africa look like Switzerland. And the Crac des Chevaliers you mentioned? The place is impregnable. The Crusaders who built it back in the 12th century knew what they were doing. It has thick walls and several levels carved out of the rock. No. I'm sorry, but if he's inside the Crac, there's not a damn thing I or anyone else can do."

"I know, I know. I told her as much. But she was very insistent and wanted to know how to contact you personally. I couldn't tell her exactly *where* you are because even I don't know. I just said it was some Greek island…"

"Greece has a lot of islands, Desta."

"I'm aware of that, thank you, Viktor," she replied testily. "I simply said it was an island somewhere close to the Turkish coast and left it at that. I guess she's just going from island to island seeing if she can find you."

"OK, so how did she attract the two guys following her?"

"That I don't know. I can only guess that word leaked out when she told her colleagues she was going away for a while. She might even have mentioned your name to the person who runs that particular NGO. One thing led to another, people started talking about her trip, and word must have slipped out to one of Balko's people who are always in the markets. Evidently, he must have heard about it and decided Sarah might be able to lead his people to you."

Viktor thought about that possibility for a minute or two. It could be the way it had worked. People talking carelessly, not understanding the risks. Maybe. Or maybe not. Either way, he needed to be careful.

"OK, I'll try to contact your Sarah Huntington without causing World War III on this little island. Tell Ricky what's happening if you want, but there's nothing he can do. This will be over one way or another long before he can get here."

He closed the satellite phone, picked up the local one, and called Costa, his friendly cop.

Before he could say anything, Costa was complaining about the two "tourists" who were scaring everyone in town. "I've never seen anything like it, Aleco. These guys don't speak a word of any known language except 'beer'. Even I get that one. They've got scars and tattoos all over them, and they look like they could tear everyone in the village apart. What the hell are they doing here, and more importantly, what can we do about them?"

He tried to calm his friend down. "Look, Costa, I'm sure they'll be gone on the night boat. They obviously got off on the wrong island and are just killing time. If I have time, I'll have a word with them."

"Just make sure they don't kill anything other than time. Look, I don't care what you tell them. Just get them out of here."

"OK. Now I need you to do something for me."

"What do you have in mind?" he answered suspiciously.

"Nothing dangerous. Did you see that woman who got off the boat?"

"Are you kidding? The whole town saw her and placed bets on who'd be the first to go and meet her."

"This is your lucky day. I need you to go to the pension and give her a message from me. Tell her—and her alone—that I have information on the person she's looking for. Send her up to my house."

"You're a sly one, Aleco. Who's she looking for? You?"

"No," he said, glad Costa couldn't see his face. "She has no interest in Aleco Kallistos. Don't worry about the two mugs in the square. They'll be gone soon."

"I don't really understand, but I'll be happy to see the last of them. But Aleco," he added, unexpectedly cautious, "I have a feeling there's a lot more going on here than I understand. That's

OK, but just make sure there's no blowback. I want them on the boat tonight."

"Don't worry, Costa. One way or another, they'll be off the island by tonight. Now please give the message to the woman."

Once he'd ended the call, he peeled back the *kilim* on the floor and stepped on one of the floorboards to release a catch for the trapdoor leading to the storage area the Albanians had built for him. They were right. Sometimes these things *are* necessary. He climbed down the six steep steps and switched on the light to reveal his own collection of tools. He settled for a Czech-made 9 mm pistol with a 15-round magazine. He picked up a silencer and looked at the knives. The rugged Ka-Bar knife was good, but he preferred the slim, lethal throwing blade that Davies had introduced him to. He probably wouldn't need it, but it never hurt to have a little extra. He took it off the rack, pulled it from the thin leather sheath, and laid it gently on his fingers, where he could feel its fine balance. The razor-sharp blade glistened in the bright light. All it took was a flick of the wrist and this blade would fly straight and true, cutting right through the thickest jacket to bury itself deep in some unfortunate's torso.

He smiled as he remembered Davies's lesson: *"No need to get fancy. No point in aiming for small targets like necks or legs. Just go for the bulk, the mass. Fucker will go down like a sack of shit when this little baby hits him. Then you shoot him in the head. Just to make sure."* He pulled out a couple of extra magazines, just in case. Again, he remembered Davies's words about the lethal "stupidity" of running out of ammunition: *"The worst goddamned sound in the world, Viktor, is that gun goin' click on an empty chamber."* Then he climbed back up to the living room, replacing the door and carpet carefully before setting about arranging things for his visitors.

He went into the small kitchen and brought out his good Ethiopian coffee, squeezed some of his oranges, and laid out a plate of fresh bread and black olives, which he pulled out of a large earthenware jug filled with olive oil, sliced lemons, and wild thyme. After laying the food on a small table just inside the door, he went back into the kitchen, where he opened the rear door. Just to be sure, he grabbed a can of WD-40 and squirted some on the hinges to make sure the door would swing quietly. Another Davies lesson: *"It's the little things that'll kill you. A jammed weapon, a reflection off your scope, or makin' too damned much noise. Little shit like that. Take care of them things, and the rest is easy. Or,"* he corrected himself, *"at least you got a chance."*

He didn't have long to wait before he heard light footsteps on the gravel path leading to the veranda. The visitor paused briefly in front of the house before climbing the few steps and knocking tentatively on the screen door.

"Hello. Is anyone here?" the NGO woman asked somewhat peevishly.

Viktor got up and opened the door cautiously as he looked casually back down the path. He nodded for her to come in and sit at the table.

"Am I in the right place? You don't make things easy, do you? You are Viktor Lipsky, aren't you?" She glanced over at the side table and noticed the array of weapons laid out neatly. "Jesus Christ," she exploded. "Who were you expecting? All I wanted to do was talk with Viktor Lipsky, not wipe out half the island." She held her hands high. "See, I don't have anything that could be dangerous."

Except your mouth, he was about to add. Instead, he merely motioned that she should help herself to the food. She tucked into the food and the fresh orange juice, smiling in spite of herself at the quality. "You make quite a host—when you're not shooting anyone."

He casually picked up his cell phone and snapped her picture as she was eating.

"What was that for?" she asked.

"Souvenir. It's not every day a pretty woman comes into my house. You're looking for Viktor Lipsky," he said simply. "He doesn't live here. Never has. Aleco Kallistos does. Remember that. Now"—he sat down—"who are you? What do you want? And why did you lead two goons up to my house?"

"The first part is easy; I'll get to that. I have no idea why those guys are following me. They're not subtle. I picked them up in town. Are they after me or you?"

"Both of us. Mainly me," he corrected, "but they can't afford to leave you alive."

He was impressed that she didn't panic, didn't flap about, and didn't start babbling about how much she didn't want to die. This was no ordinary NGO woman.

She nodded toward the weapons. "Thus the arsenal. What's your plan? Is this the Alamo? Or do we get out of here alive?"

Before he could answer there was a loud Russian shout from outside: "*Lipsky, we know you're inside. We won't kill the girl if you come out now.*" A volley of silenced shots bounced off the thick walls to reinforce the message.

Viktor grabbed the woman and pulled her down below the window. He put a finger to his mouth, signaling that she should remain quiet. Then he slid over to the table, grabbed the weapons, and started to crawl toward the rear door. She started to follow him, but he gestured that she should stay put. She nodded in agreement and then surprised him by pulling a small .25 pistol from one of the pockets of her cargo pants.

"I lied," she mouthed as she held the pistol professionally in both hands.

More shots hit the wall and shattered a few windows as Viktor made it to the rear door, which swung open soundlessly. He headed for the irrigation ditch that ran behind the house and curved through the orchard toward the front. He crawled along the ditch until he got behind the two Russians, who were creeping slowly toward the front door with their guns still spitting bullets into walls and windows. After inching deliberately out of the ditch, he crawled from tree to tree until he was within about 20 feet of the two assassins, who were so intent on getting into the house that they never looked behind themselves.

His first shot hit the leader high in the back and drove him onto the porch in a heap. His gun dropped next to him, and he was gasping for breath. The second one whipped around, startled, and began firing wildly in the direction of Viktor's shot. The bullets destroyed a few of the remaining oranges, but they missed Viktor, who'd rolled over to the next tree. While the Russian changed magazines, Viktor took advantage of the momentary lull to stand and aim carefully. By the time the Russian was ready to fire again, he looked up with resignation written all over his face just before Viktor calmly put three shots in the middle of his chest.

Viktor sighed deeply, put the gun back in his belt, and started to walk over to the two would-be assassins. The one he had just shot was slumped against one of the porch pillars. Viktor glanced at him to make sure he was dead and then turned toward the steps.

Right then, the first one lurched over onto his back, grabbed his pistol, and aimed squarely at Viktor. "Fuck you, Lipsky," he gurgled, with blood spilling out of his mouth.

Before he could pull the trigger, the door slammed open, and his head exploded from two well-placed rounds from the NGO woman's pistol.

"Well," she said as she clicked the safety back on, "I guess that settles the question of your identity."

"Indeed," Viktor admitted with a smile. "In addition to increasing my appreciation of 'powdered-milk ladies,' this little…" he stumbled looking for the right word as he nudged one of the dead gunmen with his foot, "…incident raises the even more interesting question of your identity. Most NGOs I know don't include firearms in their training."

"Perhaps later. Right now, what do we do with these two losers?"

He motioned for her to wait a minute while he made a call to the Albanians who'd restored his house. He closed the phone and told her help was on the way.

A few minutes later, a battered panel truck made its way up the track and pulled up in front of Viktor. Three of the Albanian workmen climbed out and smiled broadly at the sight of Viktor and his "guest" standing over two dead bodies.

"These the Russians you mentioned?" one of them asked.

Viktor nodded, and one of the Albanians walked over to deliver vicious kicks to both the dead men.

"Mother-fucking Russians," he spat out, "Bad as the Serbs. Killed half my family in Kosovo." He looked at Viktor with renewed admiration. "Good work."

"It wasn't just me." Viktor laughed and nodded toward the woman, who was just putting the small pistol into one of the many pockets of her cargo pants.

The Albanians all laughed loudly.

"Son of a bitch!" their leader exclaimed. "Some woman you found, Aleco. Keep this one! You sure she's not one of us? Now how can we help?"

Viktor asked if they could dispose of the bodies.

"Gladly," the leader said. "We'll take them fishing tonight."

Before they could pick up the bodies, Viktor pulled out the cell phone of one of the Russians. Then he went into the house and climbed back down into the storage area, where he opened the safe and pulled out a thick wad of €100 notes. He returned upstairs and tried to give them to the Albanians' leader, who merely peeled off one of the bills and handed the rest back.

"This is pleasure, not business." The man smiled wickedly. "We'll come back tomorrow to fix your house."

By then the truck had been loaded with the bodies, and as it pulled away, Viktor and the woman sat on the veranda.

"Now, where were we? Oh yes, your name. Desta says you're someone named Sarah Huntington whom she met in one of the refugee camps in East Africa. That bear any relation to the truth?"

"More or less."

Viktor snorted skeptically. "Glad to hear it. Why don't you go back to the pension and pretend nothing happened up here? We're too far away for anyone to have heard the racket. Simply smile at everyone, keep your gun out of sight, and be especially nice to Costa the cop. He may be a little curious, but I don't think he's about to push it. I'll clean up here and meet you for dinner in a couple of hours. Then we can continue this discussion. Remember," he cautioned her, "I'm Aleco Kallistos here."

She nodded in agreement and took her leave.

After she'd left, he pulled out the Russian's cell phone he'd taken and checked the contact list. There was only one name: Balko. Nothing surprising there. He thought briefly about sending Balko a smart message, but then he decided that little act of revenge could wait. He had more important things to do now.

CHAPTER 5

After cleaning up the broken class and wiping up the worst of the blood from the veranda, Viktor surveyed his orchard and thought idly that it was time to check the olive and orange trees for pruning. If he waited any longer, buds would appear, and then it would be too late for any pruning. It was odd, perhaps, to think of something so mundane after fighting for his life just a few minutes earlier. But that was how he decompressed and stayed sane: compartmentalizing events. When one task is over, it's over. No sense worrying about it. There's time enough to worry about the consequences later.

When he first came to the island, he thought of it as merely short-term R&R—a place to recharge his batteries before heading back into the snake pit of arms dealing. After a few years, he found he actually liked living in a place with settled rhythms of daily life and calmly accepted that life out of the so-called "mainstream" was fine. He noted that the people here lived to a ripe old age and had probably never heard of hypertension—or cholesterol, for that matter. Violent deaths were almost unheard of. The same circle of old men who'd known each other since birth gathered every day outside the same coffee house their fathers and grandfathers had used. They most likely sat in the same creaking chairs. Essentially, they had the same conversations:

the weather, the quality of the food, the fools in Athens, and the activities of their children, grandchildren, and in some cases, their great-grandchildren. Occasionally, one of them would pass away, and his chair would be presented, almost formally, to the next in line who was deemed worthy—or old enough—to join the morning discussion. One of them might have had a cell phone, but they'd probably forgotten how to use it. Besides, who was going to call? At first, he'd thought they were just doddering old men who'd been living on their meager pensions for decades. Then he learned that several of them—far from being the yokels he'd imagined—had retired from prestigious positions as judges or senior civil servants in Athens. They'd returned to the island of their birth, where they swiftly and happily slipped into the old local patterns. It didn't take Viktor long to realize that those old patterns—and those old, familiar relationships—offered the solid touchstone that was missing in his own life.

He remembered a recent conversation with one shrewd old chess player, a former judge, who realized that the person he knew as Aleco was more than he seemed.

"Your Greek is very good," the judge said casually and quietly one day in the coffee house as he replaced the pieces after losing yet another game to Viktor. Left unsaid, but understood, in the statement about Viktor's Greek was the phrase *"for someone who isn't Greek."*

Viktor's heart stopped for moment, but then he recovered, thanked the judge for his praise, and said his accent might seem strange because he'd lived in several different countries for years before returning to Greece.

"Yes, it's almost like the Greek Americans we see from time to time who come 'home' and tell us the errors of our ways. But"—the judge smiled as he patted Viktor on the knee—"you very kindly spare us the lectures and seem to accept us as we are. Although"—he laughed—"you play chess like a Russian. You mass your attack and show no mercy at all. You were kind, however. You could have check-mated me in about 20 moves, but you kept me in the game. Interesting, no?"

He sat back in his chair and pulled out a pack of cigarettes. He extracted a cigarette, put it in his mouth, and patted his pockets looking for matches. Viktor offered his lighter, the cigarette was lit, and the old man blissfully inhaled a lungful of smoke and nicotine.

He smiled as he held the cigarette at arm's length and examined it closely. "This is one of life's little pleasures that comes with age. I mean, what are they doing to do to me now? I've lived 85 years, and I can die happily with a cigarette in my hand. Who knows? St. Peter may even have an ashtray and a book of matches in his waiting room."

At that moment, then a woman's querulous voice came booming over the square.

The judge pushed on his cane and got to his feet as quickly as he could. He winked at Viktor. "We must continue this fascinating discussion. I'm sure I have much to learn. But now my wife is calling—*ordering* really—me home for lunch." He carefully put out the cigarette and placed the unsmoked portion in his shirt pocket before hobbling over to the sparkling, white house where his apron-clad wife was sweeping an already spotless front step.

It'd be a shame to give this up, Viktor thought. *This really could be nice.* Then he shook his head and got back to the problem in front of him.

His first call was to Sergei in Liechtenstein, and he asked him to do a little research on Russians in Syria. "Do you know any of them? Are they bent?"

"Every Russian is bent," Sergei retorted.

"No, Sergei, this isn't the usual sort of *bent*. I'm looking for someone who can give me a little information about Syria, particularly a place called the Crac des Chevaliers—an old Crusader castle in the part of Syria that the Russians control. This has nothing to do with the Russians themselves. I really don't care what they're up to. I have no intention of expanding our operations to that dump."

"OK, give me a couple of days. I'll see what I can do."

Viktor's next call went to Zurab. He wasn't quite sure exactly where Zurab was at any given time, but his calls usually bounced around several countries then reached Zurab eventually. Once again, he explained that his request had nothing to do with current or planned operations. "I need you to check on someone—an American who calls herself Sarah Huntington. Maybe she really is Sarah Huntington. Or maybe not. Either way, I need to know. I'll be sending an encrypted email with her picture and fingerprints."

A few minutes passed in nervous silence.

"OK. I've got them. Pretty girl. Your standards are improving. Judging from the background you're on your island. Now what do you want me to do with these?" Zurab questioned.

"Is there anyone you know who can check her out to find out if she is who she says she is?"

Zurab thought for a minute and then laughed. "There's a guy in Washington: Sidney Hurwitz. Completely fucking nuts, but a genius at this sort of stuff. Used to be with the Agency [the CIA] a long time ago. Now he works on his own and seldom leaves his fortress at the top of some old warehouse. He actually believes all the crackpot conspiracy theories that flood the web."

Viktor was doubtful. "You sure this such a good idea? Can we trust this guy?"

"Actually, yes. Very good at keeping his mouth shut. Several times, people from places such as the Agency or the NSA have threatened him with all kinds of shit if he doesn't cooperate. He hates them with a passion. Wouldn't give them the time of day. And," Zurab added, "he has enough money to hire the best lawyers in the country. No, Sidney is safe. Tell him you want this information to bust the Agency's chops, and he'll probably do it for free. Give me a couple of hours, and I'll see what I get for you."

CHAPTER 6

He put the phone down, leaned back in his chair, and recalled with a rueful grin how his whole venture into arms dealing began after a chance meeting with both Zurab and Sergei several years ago. No, it had really begun when the CIA recruited him straight out of Michigan State. He'd had no idea what he wanted to do, other than to avoid working in the iron-ore pits. The CIA, however, had known exactly what they wanted to do with him. A professor of his had notified the Agency that he might have a candidate. It had turned out the CIA loved him. He was exactly what they'd been looking for: a tough kid who spoke Russian like a native, could look after himself, and maybe, just maybe, could get some information on precisely what was happening in Chechnya.

No one had told him in so many words, but it hadn't taken him long to understand what *they* had in store. They'd wanted someone on the ground in the cesspit of the Caucasus and Chechnya to figure out what the hell was going on. This was the time of the so-called "Second Chechen War"—a war that never seemed to end. Who was butchering whom? Who was winning? And should we give a fuck? Other than to achieve the standard goal of pissing off the Russians, that is, which is always good sport. Satellites can't do it. Electronic intelligence was useless with these Stone Age people who still used goddamned carrier pigeons instead of cell phones. They'd tried, but it's tough to kidnap a carrier pigeon.

The problem was that alleged "human intelligence" didn't always work out well—especially for the human involved. One guy had come home in small pieces. The last one had dropped off the radar more than six months ago. No one was terribly optimistic about his fate. So they'd needed someone out there. Now.

Viktor had gotten the strong sense that they weren't going to waste too much time training him. First, they had no idea exactly what he was going to face, so how could they really prepare him? Second—and most important to Viktor—was that they believed his relatively short life expectancy didn't merit all that much training. Why waste all that time on someone who wasn't going to be there by Christmas? No hard feelings, kid; this is just the reality of the situation. He was to report what he could and then get the hell out. If he could.

Within a few months, Viktor had found himself on a plane for Tbilisi, Georgia—the jumping off point for trips into Chechnya. The only real information he'd been given was that he was to meet with some guy named Lev in a bar called The Caucuses. The Agency's background on the Chechen conflict was slim. He'd read it in less than 10 minutes. Basically, it was round two in the current fighting, and the Russians were really pissed this time. They were going to level the whole miserable place. They couldn't stand the Muslims. And they sure as hell couldn't stand anyone messing with their oil supplies from the Caspian Sea. On the one side, there were the Russians and their puppets. On the other side, there was a bunch that weren't much better. But for better or worse, they were causing problems for the Russians. He was not to be put off by the Islamic horseshit. As long as they were hassling the Russians, they were his new best friends.

His contact in Tbilisi, named Lev, had turned out to be a useless drunk still waiting for a CIA paycheck. His brandy-slurred English had been good enough to tell Viktor to "*Fuck off. Fuck Chechens. Fuck Russians. You want get killed? Be my guest.*" With that, his head had dropped onto the bar with a thud, and he passed out.

Rather than using this as an excuse to retreat empty-handed as fast as possible, Viktor had simply been sitting in the bar, considering his slim list of options, when he had felt a tap on his shoulder. He had turned around to face a thin-faced young man with long, greasy hair and prominent, crooked teeth. His joyless black eyes had been sunk deep into his skull.

He'd spoken to Viktor in Russian. "So you want to go to Grozny," he'd said simply.

Viktor had nodded slightly and gestured for the newcomer to take the bar stool next to him. He'd picked up his glass of beer, taken a swig, and replaced the glass gently on the bar. "Maybe," he'd replied quietly.

The newcomer had breathed out heavily and looked steadily at Viktor. "Maybe not such a good idea. Very confused situation. Always has been. Not clear who's good and who's bad."

"Thanks for the history lesson, but I've read Tolstoy—*Hadji Murad*. The modern-day version of Sheikh Shamil probably lives not far from here."

"Then you know all you need to know about Chechnya. Betrayal and deceit. Bad for everyone."

Viktor had waggled his hand back and forth. "Maybe yes. Maybe no."

"What do you mean?" the newcomer had asked.

"It really all depends on who is the betrayer and who is the betrayed. Two sides of the same coin."

The Georgian had said nothing for a minute. Then he'd slapped his hand hard on the bar and laughed loudly. "Fuck, you really are Russian. Glad the Agency finally sent someone who understands those assholes."

Viktor had sighed. This was getting him nowhere. "OK.

Enough of the foreplay, Socrates. If you got something to say, say it. Otherwise, let someone else buy your drinks." Viktor had turned back to the bar and started to drink his beer.

The guy hadn't gone anywhere, but he'd sat there patiently.

"Fuck it," Viktor had said to himself. "May as well get this over with." He'd swung around on the stool to face the newcomer. "Let's start with a name. You got a name, right?"

"Zurab."

Viktor had nodded slowly. "Who do you work for? Who sent you? You got a last name?"

Holding out his hands in innocence, Zurab had smiled broadly. "You could never pronounce my last name. Let's leave it at Zurab. I don't work for anyone. I'm what you might call an 'entrepreneur'. You know, like Steve Jobs." He'd motioned with his head that they should move to a table in the far corner.

Viktor had looked carefully around him to make sure this wasn't a trap and then cautiously followed him to the table. *Like in* The Godfather, he'd thought as he pulled out a chipped chair and sat with his back to the wall.

After having inched his chair closer to the table, Zurab had leaned over to speak softly. "I'll tell you what—instead of risking your neck for no good reason, why don't I bring Chechnya to you? And a chance to make some real money."

"Exactly what are you talking about?" Viktor had looked at him, puzzled.

Without another word, Zurab had slid off the chair and walked around to the other side of the bar. When he came back, he was holding the arm of a short, thin man whose narrow face bore a striking resemblance to a startled field mouse. The image wasn't being helped much by the thick glasses that kept slipping down his long nose every time his prominent Adam's apple bobbed up and down.

Viktor had almost laughed. "And this is?"

"This is Sergei, late of the great Russian army. After having spent the last 18 months in that shithole, he knows a great deal about Chechnya. And, also like Steve Jobs, he has a very promising idea." He poked Sergei in the back. "Don't you, Sergei?"

Sergei merely gave a slight, nervous nod in return.

"What's more important is that some of the information he has—very interesting information—has led directly to his presence here." Zurab had guided the nervous Russian to a chair and then had gone to the bar to get three glasses of Georgian brandy, handing one to each man on his return.

Sergei had thrown his down in one gulp, coughed, and begun to breathe a little easier.

Viktor remained skeptical. "OK, so exactly what's this member of the great patriotic Russian army—the victors of Stalingrad and Berlin—doing in a dump of a bar in Tbilisi that I imagine is a long way from his assigned post?"

"Liechtenstein; Vaduz, actually. I was in Vaduz." Sergei had coughed, still gagging on the brandy. "I'm not really a soldier. I mean, I *was* in the army, but I'm an accountant. Not a real soldier."

Viktor had shaken his head in disbelief as Zurab had motioned for Sergei to continue.

"My colonel is a pig. A very greedy, fat pig. But a shrewd, greedy, fat pig. Stupid-shit Sergei was checking the accounts one day and found some problems. Seems our colonel was selling weapons—shitty old weapons from our own arsenal—to the guerrillas. All done through fairly well-disguised third-party cutouts. Dumb fucks never know the real source of the weapons. Then he wipes out these same guerrillas with modern weapons, takes the old ones back, and resells them to some other group of assholes. Nice business."

Viktor's jaw had dropped. "You're shitting me!"

"No, is true."

"And the guerrillas? Where did they get the money to buy the weapons?"

Sergei had laughed loudly. "Easy. Crazy, very rich Arabs love to give money to these groups. Proves to their own nutcases that they're on the side of Allah. Keeps the nutcases off their backs."

"Profitable business, then, this selling weapons?" Viktor had asked ingenuously.

"Very. That's why I'm here. One day stupid-shit Sergei confronts this colonel with proof of what he's doing. Piggy colonel just laughs and laughs. Says I now have two options: I can lead a small patrol deep into the woods where these fanatics are based, or I can arrange to put his money into a safe bank that doesn't ask too many questions. Obviously, I chose the second option and went to Vaduz with some heavy bags of cash. The one thing those people in Liechtenstein don't do is ask questions. I stopped off here on the way back to Grozny and decided to stay. No way am I going back there."

Viktor had given a small smile of admiration for the enterprising colonel and for Sergei, who was smart enough to catch the scam and then get the hell out. He had thought about the possibilities this opened up: forget Chechnya and the guerrillas; if he played this right, there was some serious money to be made. He'd patted Sergei on the back and told the man he'd be in touch. Meanwhile, he was going nowhere near Chechnya.

Sergei had laughed nervously. "Don't even think it! Are you out of your mind? I'm never, ever going back there."

CHAPTER 7

On the long trip back to Washington, D.C., Viktor had thought about how to play this situation. *The key element,* he thought, *is a little seed money to prime the pump. And who better to provide that than the CIA itself?* After having been sent on what was going to be a suicide mission, his institutional loyalty was a little weakened. Fuck 'em. It had been time to turn the tables. He simply needed to convince them that the way to the hearts and minds of the anti-Russian guerrillas was through their arsenals. Why should fanatical Arabs be the main source of funds to buy weapons? Why shouldn't the CIA step in and gain some control by providing those funds? And there would have to be middlemen in the form of Viktor, Zurab and Sergei, of course. Middlemen who, understandably, would have to be paid a healthy percentage of whatever funds the CIA provided to the guerrillas. Sergei had immediately grasped the potential and was already sketching a pyramid of shell companies to protect their gains from nosey government officials. Zurab, knowing he'd be the one actually talking to the guerrillas, had been a bit more cautious. But as long as he could arrange those contacts without ever setting foot in Chechnya, he was happy. It was Viktor's job to sell this plan to his bosses at the CIA.

Once back in Washington, the sales job had been easier than he dreamed. For much of the CIA, terms such as "good" and "bad" or "fair" and "unfair" simply didn't seem relevant. His bosses had a hard time in hiding their admiration of the Russian colonel. "Son of a bitch has a pair of balls on him. I'll give him that much," summed up the general attitude. They laughed out loud when Viktor presented his plan for the CIA to replace the Arab funding.

"This is beautiful. It keeps those crazy fuckers messing with the Russians forever. And it gets better. We give them just enough to cause problems, and we don't have to worry about what happens if they ever win. How much is this going to cost, kid?" his boss asked.

Viktor and Sergei had thought this through meticulously: too much, and they might get concerned about accounting for it; too little, and they wouldn't take him seriously.

Viktor had shrugged his shoulders as if it really didn't matter. "About $5 million should do," he ventured.

Again, his boss had chuckled. "Shit, that isn't even lunch money. Fucking bean counters won't see a thing."

It hadn't taken them long to determine that Viktor was the perfect person—the only person—who could pull the pieces of this operation together. The basic principle was the same. Maybe it works. Maybe it doesn't. If it blows up, it's too bad for the kid—but there's no strings back to us. The one concession Viktor had gotten was time to learn all he could about the arms trade before he tried to convince the *jihadis* that he knew what he was talking about.

***

It had taken Viktor about three months to trawl through the undergrowth of the world's arms trade—both legal and illegal. He'd tracked down tired and worn-out agents from most major intelligence services, salesmen from just about every weapon-producing country in the world, local warlords, mercenaries, and local and national "leaders" who differed only in the amount of money it took to buy—or rent—them. When boiled down to its finest points, the information was pretty consistent. Arms dealing was in fact a very profitable business. Very risky, but very profitable. Despite periodic interruptions caused by overzealous United Nations (UN) officials and infrequent outbreaks of peace, demand had grown steadily.

Viktor had absorbed all this information quicker than a blotter absorbs water. Any potential moral scruples had easily been rationalized away. Barring a complete change in human nature, there was always going to be a need—and somebody had to fill it. Why not him? It didn't take him long to get familiar with the major products such as the basic AK47, the Uzi, its Czech look-alike the Skorpion, the very handy RPG and all its variations, the more sophisticated Swedish AT4, the very effective shoulder-held Russian anti-aircraft missile Igla, or the American Stinger.

Nairobi was going to be the last stop on his whirlwind tour to learn about warlords, pirates, and the other self-proclaimed leaders of "popular" revolutionary movements. To some, they were nothing more than vicious thugs. To Viktor, they were potential clients, noted conscientiously in the small notebook he carried with him. He'd also met with the usual swarm of intelligence operatives from just about every possible agency in the U.S. government, barring perhaps the Agriculture Department. Most useful were the soldiers—the tough Delta Force guys who did the real work. The ones he'd met in a small Kenyan settlement near the Somalian border had been typical. In the camp, dust-covered tents had been neatly arrayed and the smell of unwashed bodies had pervaded the air. Weary, suspicious eyes had peered at him over long, brown scarves wrapped around the soldiers' necks and mouths; and the assorted lightweight clothing they wore had almost been hidden under belts of ammunition, water bottles, first aid kits, and hand grenades. Two items were extremely well cared for: their boots and their weapons. The latter were oiled and ready for instant action. Viktor wondered how these guys were ever going fit into the lives they'd left at home. They probably won't, he concluded.

As he'd said his farewells, the sergeant had pulled him aside and given him some more advice: "You really want to learn about this shit—the weapons, the logistics, all of that? One guy knows more than anyone you ever will meet: Ricky Davies. He's probably the best damn Delta I ever did see. Saved my ass several times. He was here longer than anyone. Somalia, Chad, Sudan, and a whole bunch of places we ain't supposed to have been in. The guy's seen it all. Done it all."

"Where can I find him?" Viktor had been excited about finally cutting through all the theory and getting to the real story.

"Up around Addis Ababa somewhere. He put in his 20, found a beautiful woman, filed his papers, and as far as I know, is settin' on his ass collecting his pension. After all he did, the man deserves it. Ain't none of us gonna get old in this business."

Viktor had eventually found Davies sitting on the porch of an immaculate bungalow high in the Entoto Hills above the city of Addis Ababa. Davies had waved him onto the veranda—which was made out of thick, well-seasoned eucalyptus planks—and motioned that he should take a seat. The veranda was spotless. There wasn't a dust mote, crumpled paper, or empty beer bottle in sight, just four comfortable wood and leather chairs arrayed neatly around a low table that comprised an elaborately decorated copper tray set on four short legs. Davies had the perfect Delta Force body: about 5'8" of pure muscle and gristle, with not an ounce of fat. He was more or less a tightly coiled spring. But it was his eyes that had drawn Viktor's attention. They were hard, calculating, and set deep in his skull. These eyes had seen the worst that humans can do to each other and now held very low expectations for anything different.

Davies had noticed Viktor looking at the neat surroundings. "Ain't my doin'. My wife, she likes things real neat and tidy. Won't let me drop nuthin' on the floors." He chuckled. "Inside is just the same. Not a damn thing outta place. She's as tough as some old drill sergeant about this house." He had paused for a minute. "Heard you was lookin' for me."

Davies had laughed at the surprise on Viktor's face. "Jungle drums, son; jungle drums. Did you really think you could start askin' some of my men about me without them givin' me a heads-up? No, sir. We look after each other. Now what can I do for you? Let me get a couple of beers, and then we can do a little debriefing."

After having ducked briefly inside, Davies had come out of the house with two cold bottles of the local St. George beer and put them on the table. They each had taken a couple of drinks from the bottle and, like most beer drinkers who can't find much to say, started picking at the label on the bottle. Viktor had been about to ask just how Davies wound up on a hill in Addis Ababa when the door had opened and the most beautiful woman he'd ever seen had come out carrying a tray with small dishes of appetizers and two glasses. Tall with coffee-colored skin, she'd had the elegant, regal carriage that would put any member of European royalty to shame. Her smooth skin was stretched over a fine-boned face that featured a thin nose and dancing, dark eyes. She'd been dressed in a simple but elegant white Amhara tribal dress decorated with intricate embroidery, and her only jewelry was a thick Orthodox cross that hung around her neck.

She'd smiled as she'd carefully placed the tray on the table and pointedly put the glasses in front of each man. She'd turned to Viktor, almost apologizing for Davies's lack of manners. "I keep telling Richard that he's no longer in the army. He doesn't have to drink like an uncouth soldier." With that, she'd giggled and swept back into the house.

Viktor's mouth had hung open as he looked at Davies and then back to where the woman had been. Something didn't add up. *Richard? Where did that come from?*

Davies had laughed and come to his rescue. "You're wonderin' how an old cracker like me wound up with somethin' like her. I ask myself the same thing every damn day. I gotta blink and make sure it ain't some dream that's goin' away when I wake up."

He'd dutifully started to pour his beer into the glass, and Viktor did the same rather than disappoint that gorgeous woman.

"Her name's Desta," Davies had said. He'd gone one to explain that he'd met her at a UN camp that was supposed to distribute food evenly over the entire region. This particular UN commander, however, was basically stealing the food and selling it on the black market in Eritrea or South Sudan. When Davies and his men had showed up, they'd found Desta protesting vainly to the UN bureaucrat.

"Anyways," he continued, "we was just sorta standin' around when I heard a real shoutin' match inside the command tent. I went to take a look and saw the most beautiful woman I ever did see standing up to some fat UN commander and telling him his actions were '*sinful*'—she actually used the word '*sinful*.'" He'd spat on the lawn. "I gotta tell you that '*sinful*' ain't the first word I woulda used." He shook his head in amazement at what came next. "I dunno. Maybe it was the heat and dust, maybe it was bein' real sick and tired of seeing the same shit every goddamned day, or maybe it was just the thought of helping a real pretty woman. Now, we ain't supposed to get involved in local hassles. Ain't our business, *they* say. But I looked at the boys, and they just nodded that they was with me." Davies smiled at the recollection. "We all cocked our weapons, nice and loud, at the same time. Sorta a conversation stopper. When that fat UN bastard saw a platoon of dusty, tired, heavily armed Deltas walk into his command post, he sort of changed his mind real quick. It was beautiful. Didn't have to say a word or fire a shot. It's one thing blowin' off a real nice, polite woman, but it's somethin' else tryin' to blow us off. Amazin' how quick that food got to the Amhara villages. You know, it felt real good to do somethin' *decent* for once."

Davies had started to peel to peel more of the label off the bottle, but then he'd remembered his wife's request and poured the cold beer into the glass. "Well, one thing sorta led to another. And here we are. I put in my 20 years, got my pension, and did the smartest thing I ever did—married Desta."

Viktor had sensed there was a lot more to the story, but he knew he'd get it only when Davies was ready to give it to him. "And your men, where are they right now?" Viktor had suddenly perked up.

"Most of them are still with the army. Ain't nuthin' better waitin' back in the States. See, we get 'em right after high school when they're real dumb shits. Don't know nuthin'. Then we train 'em real good and send 'em to places God hisself has forgotten about. Then, after what they seen and done, we expect 'em to go home and run a forklift at Walmart or sing in the church choir? Ain't gonna happen."

Viktor had gotten the feeling that this was one of the longest speeches Ricky Davies had ever made.

He had been thinking fast. All the pieces had seemed to be falling into place. All he'd needed to do was nudge them in the right direction. What had seemed like a crazy idea back in Tbilisi was suddenly seeming not so nuts after all.

He'd explained how the Chechen guerrillas raised funds from willing supporters and gave the funds to a middleman, who—through several well-disguised cutouts—paid the Russian for the weapons. He'd also detailed that the CIA thought it would be a good idea if the Americans replaced some of the funding sources and gained some degree of control over the guerrillas. He'd said they didn't mind experimenting with $4–$5 million of Agency money.

Davies could only shake his head in disbelief. "You gotta be shittin' me." Viktor was about to reassure him that the story was true when Davies stopped him: "No, no. I do believe the bit about the fundin' for the weapons. What I don't get is that the assholes in Washington actually think that funding will buy them some control over the guerrillas. Don't work that way." He'd looked suspiciously at Viktor. "You can really get that money from the Agency?"

"Yeah. The guy said it was no problem."

"Look," Davies had continued, interested but cautious, "you really don't know what the hell you're doin', but you seem smart enough. And there's a chance you can learn enough to keep your ass from gettin' blown away." He'd looked Viktor directly in the eye. "I'll give you a hand, but ain't nuthin' in this world for free. In return, you gotta do some things for me. You understand?"

Viktor hadn't been sure he did understand, but he also didn't know what choice he had. "OK. Exactly what do I have to do in return?"

Davies had hitched forward in his chair and lowered his voice. "Listen, that $4–$5 million you was talkin' about? You only need about a million to keep them Chechen loonies happy, right?"

Viktor had been beginning to see where this conversation was leading. "Yeah. That should keep them going for a while."

"And the rest? What exactly you plannin' to do with the rest?"

"I thought I'd help the Russian colonel expand his market and find new customers. From what I've seen in the last couple of months, there's a shitload of people who want more and more weapons."

Davies had snorted. "You got that right. Now here's the deal. You don't know shit about this business, but I'll help you get started if some of that money finds its way to some folks who need them guns." He turned to make sure his wife wasn't nearby. "Fact is, Desta don't wanna go down this route. She figures the UN or some other useless agency will keep her people here in

Sudan or South Sudan from gettin' blown to hell or wherever they're plannin' on goin." He'd laughed at the thought of international agencies doing anything.

For the next two hours, Viktor had gotten a cram course in arms dealing: logistics, payment, types of weapons, delivery points across Africa, contacts, and—crucially—protection.

"Most important, Viktor, this ain't no one-man operation. You need a team. A small team, but good people. People you can trust. Once you get goin', somewhere along the line, everyone else is gonna try to cheat, rob, betray, and probably kill you. You absolutely gotta find a few people you can really trust. Trust like your life depends on it. Cuz it does." Davies had taken a swig of beer and munched on a fat chicken leg. He'd stared directly at Viktor, "Ain't many of 'em. Think you can find 'em? If not, forget the whole idea and go sell used cars."

"I've got a couple of guys who might help, but that's not enough. No way could they provide the muscle required for this line of work." Viktor had taken a deep breath. "How'd you feel about teaming up? Maybe get some of your Delta boys who are sick of nursemaiding real assholes? Given what you said about the competition, it wouldn't take us long to build a rep as the 'honest' arms dealers—if that's not too much of a contradiction. The point is we need to be pretty choosey about our customers. No genocidal warlords, no religious fanatics, no drug dealers…"

Davies had let out hoots of laughter. "Not that I don't agree with you, but you just damn near eliminated about 60% of the market. No, make that 80%."

Right as he'd finally calmed down and reached for his beer, Desta had rushed out onto the terrace to see what was going on. "Richard! What are you boys up to?" She'd stood over Davies, shaking her finger at him as he'd smiled and held up his hands in a peace-making gesture.

"Nuthin'. Nuthin' at all. We're just figurin' out how to do the

Lord's work and put our thumbs on the scale. Maybe a little more directly than your average priest or NGO, but more effective. Trust me, Desta, we're on the side of the angels."

"Not much chance of that," she humphed. "You just make sure my people don't pay the price for whatever you two have cooked up."

Davies had abruptly gotten serious. "Desta, hon, you can be sure of one thing: your people are done payin' any price for just bein' who they are or goin' wherever they wanna go. Me and Viktor here are gonna make damn sure of that." He'd turned to a slightly puzzled Viktor. "Ain't we, Viktor?"

"Uh, yeah. A-absolutely," he stammered out. He'd felt Desta's glare on him and started fumbling with the beer bottle.

"Mr. Lipsky," she'd said quietly, staring at him hard, "understand one thing: you be sure to bring Richard back here in one piece. Got that?"

Viktor had felt it couldn't be clearer if she'd nailed the message to his heart. "I'll do my very best, ma'am."

"You'll do better than that, Mr. Lipsky," she'd concluded fiercely before heading back into the house.

Neither of the men had said anything for a few minutes. Finally, Davies broke the silence: "Well, that sure as hell reduced our market even more. What was I sayin', 60–80%? Now, son, we've just eliminated 95% of the market." Then he'd chuckled. "Well, hell, that's OK. Still enough out there to make some money while doin' God's work. Ain't a bad deal."

Viktor hadn't been convinced. "But I'm not sure how much God pays. The people you and Desta are talking about have trouble scrounging a decent meal. Forget about paying for a plane load of weapons. Maybe we can do this once—just once. Courtesy of the CIA and a greedy Russian colonel. But then what? I can't see the CIA falling for the same story again."

Davies had said nothing for a while. He'd merely peered out into the darkness surrounding his bungalow, letting his gaze swing languidly from left to right, checking how the moonlight played on the trees and shrubs.

He'd abruptly broken out of his reverie. "Actually, Viktor," he'd said softly. "Don't need the CIA after this one. The reality of this business is that there are so many groups out there"—he waved his arm in a broad arc, almost taking in the entire world—"that generally hate each other—wanna slaughter each other—that I'm sure we can find a paymaster somewhere. Sad but true.

"Say we find some group like Desta's people. Wrong place, wrong time, wrong religion, wrong color—it don't matter. Just some poor sumbitches in the way of some big pain in the ass who wants to wipe 'em out. Happens all the time. That's all it takes. One day, you're down by the river catchin' fish. Next day, bits of you are feedin' the fish. Don't pay to look for reasons. There ain't any. Good news for us is that, somewhere out there, there's also someone who really don't like the bad guys any more than we do. Look at the big players like the Chinese. All they want is easy access to all the raw materials around here. They don't give a shit about anythin' else, but they'll pay any amount to anybody so long as they can rip up some more ground without gettin' shot. Anyone gets in the way of that is toast. Nuthin' but toast. Israelis can always be counted on. A lotta folks around here don't like 'em too much. Israelis would do just about anythin' to encourage someone, anyone, to cause a few problems around here. Don't give a rat's ass about the people we're tryin' to protect, but they're willin' to pay to cause the other bunch problems."

"Makes sense, but even with you, we need more people," Viktor stated.

"Don't get me wrong, we ain't gonna do most of the heavy lifting. Maybe some of my boys will have to show the folks how these things work. But don't worry. Once they get the hang of it, they'll *wanna* do the work. Don't underestimate the power of revenge. Give 'em the right tools, and they'll do the job. We may not be God's army, but ain't nuthin' stoppin' us from being God's arsenal." Davies giggled at his play on words. "And don't you worry about findin' the paymaster. Once this first deal goes down, they'll find you. Word travels real fast in this business. You'd be surprised how many people wanna unload a mess o' weapons. You'd also be surprised how many people are willin' to pay for those weapons to be used against enemies of their enemies. Thankfully for our business, ain't no shortage of very rich people with a lotta enemies. Somewhere, there's a niche for us."

CHAPTER 8

While sitting on the veranda of his house on Telos several years later, Viktor had to admit that Davies had been right. There certainly was a niche for their "services," and that niche just kept growing no matter how hard they tried to stay beneath everyone's radar.

Sergei had proved to be a very, very smart accountant with many thick files of damaging information about senior Soviet Army officers, which helped keep initial supplies of "surplus" Russian weapons flowing freely. He agreed to move to Liechtenstein and set up a small office on the condition that he never, ever got anywhere near where the weapons were used. He was also delighted to learn that certain officers from NATO, China, and Pakistan had similar appetites to his Russian contacts, which enabled him to expand the supply chain. All the funds they received over the years went through a complicated system of bank accounts that Sergei had established around the world. By the time Viktor's share got to his account in Zurich, it looked as if it had come as a consulting fee from a Danish dairy-food producer.

As for Zurab, Viktor never did a straight answer about who else he might be working for, but in the end, it didn't really matter. He'd proved to be an absolute genius at matching demand from some of the most godforsaken places on the planet with people—sometimes even governments—willing to fund that particular group for whatever reason. As long as the cash came through, he really didn't care about the reasons.

And as for Viktor? Well, there had been enough cash left over from the Chechen deal to buy enough AK 47s and RPGs—together with sufficient ammunition—to support a strong defense effort for a lot of people caught *in the wrong place at the wrong time.* Viktor had originally thought his deal with the Russian colonel and the CIA would give him a nice little nest egg to do whatever he wanted with. He hadn't planned on staying in the business, but things hadn't quite worked out that way. It turned out there was an almost endless supply of helpless groups that, for one reason or another, were in the way of a bunch of thugs with guns and machetes. And there was no shortage of people willing to sell weapons, lots of weapons, to the thugs who happened to control much of the area's natural resources and could pay top dollar.

He showered and changed into fresh clothes before heading down to the square to meet the alleged Sarah Huntington for dinner. The night ferry was just leaving, and the crowd that always gathered for every arrival and departure was gradually making its way home. He sniggered when he saw that much of that crowd had managed to move from the pier to gather around her table outside the pension and Maria's restaurant. By the time he'd elbowed his way through the crowd, he saw Costa seated opposite her, struggling to keep a conversation going in his broken English.

The cop jumped to his feet as Viktor tapped him on the shoulder, and he graciously held out a chair. "Don't blow this one Aleco," he warned. "She's the best thing to hit this island in a long time." He turned away and motioned for the other onlookers to scatter. Then he turned back and, with a nod toward the departing ferry, whispered, "Those other two? Are they off the island?"

"Don't worry. They're definitely off the island."

"Good." Costa was relieved at the news. "Enjoy your evening."

Viktor turned back to Sarah Huntington and noticed that she too had freshened up. The pistol-carrying cargo pants had been replaced with elegant slacks, and a white silk blouse had replaced the shapeless, military-style shirt.

"Very nice." He smiled. "Although I don't see where you could stuff a .25 automatic in that outfit."

"That's why you're here. To protect me," she responded with a laugh.

Just then, Maria came over and told them what was for dinner. They settled for a collection of *mezes*, followed by *barbunya* (red mullet) for her and Maria's *suzukaikia* (special meatballs loaded with island herbs and spices) for him. They both decided on *ouzo* to drink. Viktor was impressed. Not every foreign woman appreciated this strong anise-flavored drink that requires water—and maybe some ice—to make it palatable. A single glass, diluted frequently with a bit of water, can last for an entire meal. The *meze* soon arrived, and they began to eat.

"Now," he began after they'd finished the meal in a companionable silence and then ordered coffee, "tell me more about this lost brother of yours. Desta gave me the quick version and said he'd been kidnapped somewhere in Syria and is now in the Crac des Chevaliers."

She looked deeply into her glass of *ouzo*, trying to gather her thoughts. "Yes, well, Neil was working with Syrian refugees in Jordan when he disappeared suddenly. We heard the Syrians had nabbed him, called him something like *jasus*, and shipped him to that castle you mentioned. I'd really like to know what's going on and whether there's any chance of getting him out."

Viktor took a deep breath and started to tell her the same thing he'd told Desta; he concluded by saying her brother was in deep trouble because the word "*jasus*" means spy. At that moment, his satellite phone buzzed. He excused himself as he pulled out the cumbersome receiver. The caller list showed it was Zurab.

"What's up?" Viktor asked.

"We've got a problem."

"OK. What happened?"

"I'm afraid your Sarah Huntington isn't quite who she says she is. It didn't take Hurwitz long to find out that the real Sarah Huntington died in a car crash in 1992 at the age of 12."

"Why am I not surprised?" he declared, gazing across the table. "That explains a few things."

"Hang on. It gets worse—or better, depending on your point of view. Those prints and the picture you sent me? Drove Hurwitz nuts. He couldn't find anything. I mean nothing. All the standard databases had absolutely no record that such a human being has ever existed. Either she just landed from outer space or was deeply—*very* deeply—hidden. Then he went into the really dark part of the web and eventually found a way into the NSA's own database. Guess who pops up? Our own Sarah Huntington or, rather, Emily Wilkins. She was born in 1985 in Portland, Maine, and did in fact go to Yale. By the way, she's an only child. No brothers or sisters. Here's the interesting thing: her father was on one of the suicide planes on 9/11. Apparently, she's not the type to forgive or forget. She finished Yale early—*summa cum laude*—and went straight into the NSA. They loved her brains and commitment. She made it her business to go after *jihadis* around the world and made sure they were on the wrong end of a drone strike." He paused to catch his breath. "You know about her NGO work in Africa, right?"

"Yeah, sort of."

"Well, when she wasn't passing out condensed milk, she was targeting some very bad people in East Africa. Some of the big *jihadi* names got erased. Interesting when you correlate the locations of her NGO activities and some very effective drone strikes. Almost a perfect match." He paused again. "Gotta hand it to her. Very effective indeed." The line went quiet for a few minutes while both of them tried to work out the implications of Hurwitz's discoveries.

At last, Zurab chuckled. "By the way, she scored in the top two percentiles in target shooting…"

"Yeah, I witnessed some of that." *That figures,* Viktor thought. This was, after all, a woman who just shot someone in the head a couple of hours ago without blinking an eye. No tears. No remorse. Very professional. He didn't know whether to be pissed or very, very impressed.

"Sounds like your kind of girl, Viktor. Christ, I'd hate to see your children. But be careful. One wrong move, and your little island paradise could wind up with a big, red dot over it."

Viktor didn't say anything for a few minutes.

"Viktor, you still there?" Zurab almost yelled down the phone.

"Yeah, yeah. I'm still here. I'm thinking about how to play this. What's really going on?"

"Haven't got a clue, man. But be careful. This broad sounds like trouble. Stay in touch."

Viktor clicked the end-call button and simply sat there for a few minutes, idly tapping his chin while looking suspiciously at his dinner companion.

She could tell something had happened, but she didn't know what. "Interesting call?" she asked innocently.

"Yeah, you could say that… Ms. Wilkins."

She was about to drink the coffee when she stopped and placed the cup carefully back on the small saucer. She didn't seem embarrassed or particularly surprised that she'd been found out. "That didn't take long. Guess you're as good as they say you are. What tipped you off?"

"Well," he drawled in his best hillbilly imitation, "maybe we didn't all go to Yale and graduate *summa cum laude,* but we ain't complete hicks…"

"Oh my, we have a chip on our shoulder, do we?" she snapped back.

"Only when people like you take us for fools," he answered sharply. "Did you really think I wouldn't check your very, very thin story?" Then he leaned back and smiled. "Actually, I prefer it this way. It's always easier dealing with straightforward liars, cheats, and murdering thugs than it is putting up with fools trying to save the world."

She dismissed his dyspeptic view of the world with a weary wave of her hand as if to say she'd heard it all before. "So that's why you took my picture and picked up the orange-juice glass yesterday. Still," she continued, "all those trails were supposed to have been erased. How did you find out?"

"Let's just say that people at the NSA aren't the only ones who know how to use a computer."

"There are only a very small handful of people who could penetrate our system. And we know them all," she added menacingly.

"Oh please," he said in an exasperated tone. "I thought you were smarter than that. One stupid move from your bosses, and they'll find all their supposedly ultra-classified top-secret emails clogging the inboxes of every major news organization and social media outlet from here to Beijing. Now smarten up. Let's get to the main point: What the hell are you trying to do? Why bother with that half-assed story? Inasmuch as you have no brothers or sisters, I assume that *"Neil"* you talked so passionately about doesn't exist."

She sat back and held up her hands in surrender. The pretense of the guileless NGO girl out to save the world was swiftly replaced by the very skilled, very professional intelligence agent. "OK, OK. I get your point. You're right. There is no *Neil*. That part of the story was a fabrication, and not a very good one at that. I can assure you that no one would like to be WikiLeaked. First of all, like most misinformation, the story isn't complete bullshit. Some of it's true—only the plan the geniuses back at Fort Meade designed now seems a little screwed up."

"I take it this isn't the first time their 'plans' didn't quite work out."

"Spare me the lectures about government incompetence; I've heard and seen them all. Seems I spend a lot of time cleaning up after those *geniuses,* as you call them. The solution may be a little fucked up, but the problem seems real enough. The trouble is we don't know for sure, and we certainly don't know how to deal with it."

This got Viktor's attention. The fact that there was a potential problem—but no one could define that problem— was interesting to say the least.

"OK, enlighten me."

She sighed. "We've all heard of Assad's chemical weapons, right? We've seen the results. We've even developed some protection against most of that stuff. But now it seems he's gone one step further—namely, biological weapons. Very deadly biological weapons. Viruses against which there's no known vaccine or effective treatment." She paused for a minute as if to collect her thoughts.

"What gets me is that none of this crap is new. The Romans used dead animals to foul their enemies' water supply. Russians used plague-infected corpses against the Swedes in 1710. A little later, during the French and Indian wars, the British used to wrap smallpox victims in blankets. Then they gave those blankets to hostile Indian tribes. And on, and on, and on. Not surprisingly, biological weapons are known as the 'poor man's atom bomb.'"

Again, Viktor didn't respond immediately. His lack of obvious concern began to rattle Emily.

"Well," she finally blurted out, "doesn't any of this stuff interest you?"

"You know"—he turned slowly to face her—"if people spent more time thinking and less time talking, we might all be better off."

"*Jesus Christ,*" she exploded, "I came all the way to this dinky little island to hear the 'sage of the olive trees' give me his thought for the day? I can find that in a Chinese fortune cookie. What the hell do I have to do to get through to you? Drop my knickers and jump your bones?"

He smiled wickedly. "It's a thought."

"Don't get your hopes up."

"Look, you want instant analysis and answers, yet you haven't answered some very basic questions. First" —he held up one finger—"how do you know any of this? What gives you a clue that Assad even has this stuff? If he does, where did he get it? Can he manufacture it, or does he have to import it? From what I know of basic chemistry and biology, a lot of these biological weapons don't travel very well. The cultures are all fairly fragile. So what are we dealing with exactly? Big scale? Small scale? Deadly? Or all of the above?"

"Alright," she conceded, "you've made your point." She hitched her chair forward and rested her elbows on the table. "The first indication we got was from a Jordanian who has a relative in one of the Syrian villages close to the border. Suddenly, this relative tells him that people have started getting sick, really sick, and many are dying. Apparently, what starts as a bad flu rapidly gets worse, with intense headaches, back and abdominal pain, fever, nausea, etc. The local medics haven't got a clue what's going on. None of their dwindling supplies of medicine seem to help at all."

Then she smiled. Unexpectedly, that hard, serious, professional front broke into something appealing, almost vulnerable. Something that could admit that events had a way of unfolding that even the "geniuses" have yet to control.

"Actually," she admitted almost ruefully, "we caught a break—a couple of huge breaks. One of those villagers managed to get into Jordan, and someone had the wit to call a doctor. Fortunately, his doctor in turn recognized he was dealing with something way above his skill level that wouldn't respond to his limited supply of antibiotics. Several more calls finally resulted in a senior Ministry of Health official contacting our embassy for help. The embassy doctor is a marginal alcoholic waiting for his pension, and he quite happily passed this on to the U.S. Army.

"Here, we struck pay dirt. One of the senior medics had recently completed his residency in Los Angeles in—guess what?—immunology. This very bright young captain realized quickly he was dealing with something very nasty called 'hemorrhagic fever.' Basically, it causes multiple organ failures, then you go into shock and die. There are lots of varieties of this beauty, and our captain didn't have the equipment to discover which particular strain the poor man was suffering from. So he took some blood from the villager, who by this time was on the verge of going into shock from various organ failures, and sends it immediately to the Centers for Disease Control in Atlanta. That's the good news.

"The really bad news, according to the captain, is that even if the CDC can pinpoint the exact hemorrhagic fever, there's no cure. No vaccine. Your body either has the strength to resist—or you die. Unfortunately, our villager wasn't in the best of health to start with. His internal organs started failing one by one, and he died in a matter of days."

"So what happened? What did the CDC have to say?"

"Oh, the guy was indeed suffering from hemorrhagic fever. The only problem was this was a relatively new, mutated strain. Got the folks in Atlanta all excited."

"OK, villagers get sick and die. Unfortunately, this isn't exactly news. Happens all over the world. So what's special about this? More to the point, what does it have to do with me?"

She held out her palms, trying to calm him down. "Give me a minute. How do you think people pick up this particular virus?"

Viktor shrugged his shoulders. "No idea."

"Rat shit is one of the more effective ways. Or more precisely, rodent shit. Works like an aerosol spray. Step on the dried shit of an infected rodent, breathe in some of the dust, and *bingo!* You become a very sick person with very little chance of surviving."

"Look, I'm sorry. I still don't get it. Syria is filled with rats. What's so special about these particular rats?"

"Ah, this is where it gets *very* interesting. Where do you think the virus that infected these particular rats is usually found?"

Viktor held up his hands in surrender. "OK, you win. Where?"

"Korea. More to the point, North Korea."

This bit of information stunned even Viktor, who—after a decade of gunrunning—was fairly immune to being stunned by anything. "You're shitting me, right? How the hell does a deadly virus found only in Korea wind up in a nothing little Syrian village?" He stopped in mid-flow and rubbed the bridge of his nose with the fingers of his left hand. "Are you telling me that fat, little toad in North Korea is somehow involved in this? Nuclear weapons aren't enough for him?"

"We think that 'fat, little toad,' as you so accurately describe him, is directly involved." She paused for a few minutes to finish what was left of the bread covered with sesame seeds. Viktor may have lost his appetite, but there was nothing wrong with hers. After neatly wiping the crumbs off her mouth, she continued. "Remember what I said about this stuff being a 'poor man's nuclear weapon'? Well, that's just what this is. As you, more than most people, may know, it's not easy to move nuclear weapons."

Viktor only nodded without conceding the point.

Without commenting on his reaction, she continued, "Anyway, moving infected rats around is a hell of lot easier—and cheaper. The Syrians wanted to experiment with a few and the fat, little toad was only too happy to grant their wish. You saw the effect on one particular village, which was perhaps chosen because it was relatively isolated. Then some bright lad in Damascus says that infected rats are very nice, but learning how to make the culture is even nicer. Then they can infect as many rodents as they want. Think what you could do with a simple aerosol can filled with the dust from infected rat shit."

"It can't be that simple." Viktor shook his head.

"It's not. But our friend in Pyongyang is eager to add to his very short list of friends. So he agrees to 'lend' a couple of very, very smart scientists to the Syrian leadership to show them how to cultivate the virus. We think these scientists are working in the Crac and testing the results in remote parts of the country." She sat back in her chair and steepled her fingers under her chin. "Unlike many viruses we know about, this one has no vaccine, no known cure. Once started, its distribution is utterly random. In addition, it mutates very quickly into new forms. As soon as you analyze one batch, another different strain comes along. What might be going on in Syria right now takes this problem to a new dimension."

"Look, I grant you this all very bad news. Apparently, this stuff can make the Black Plague look like a weekend flu. But I'm still at a loss. How did we, the Americans, get involved? And more specifically, why are you here? What exactly do you want?"

She smiled sweetly. "Don't underestimate yourself." She went into her teacher mode. "How did we get involved? The Russians—"

"The Russians," Viktor blurted out. "Since when did they do us any favors?"

"As I was saying," she said, slightly annoyed at the interruption, "the Russians, for their very own reasons, decided to break the habit of a lifetime and very quietly ask for our help. You see, they don't like the fat, little toad any more than we do. The thought of him dragging everyone into World War III scares them shitless. China, they can more or less deal with. But this little psycho is off the scale. Furthermore, their position in Syria is—to put it mildly—a bit complicated. Yes, they're helping Assad, but the last thing they want to see is the country so badly destroyed that the only survivors are the *jihadis*." She looked at him pointedly. "You should know this from your days in Chechnya. Right now, there are so many factions in Syria that even the Russians have trouble telling them apart. And," she added while demurely checking her immaculate fingernails, "in the first place, we told them about the virus that killed so many villagers. They had no idea what was going on. They were very annoyed at their 'ally' going behind their backs like that."

"You what?" Viktor was incredulous. "What the hell did you hope to accomplish with that little maneuver?"

"Assad may be the Russians' so-called 'ally,' but that doesn't mean they trust each other. The Russians think he's using them for his own ends and doesn't really give a damn about what they think. The Russians have no interest at all in fighting Israel, and that's where they think Assad is headed—once he's used them to help clean up what's left of Syria. Right now, the Russians feel they're trapped with Assad, and they don't like it. Information about that virus was news—very bad news—to them."

"So what's the big deal? Surely they can just tell him, order him, to stop that shit. If that fails, they can send in the Spetsnaz and kick some ass."

"You guys are all the same," she exploded disgustedly. "Nothing but testosterone. Kick some ass! Send in the Spetsnaz! Whatever happened to *nuances* or *subtlety*?"

"They're usually the first to fall when the real shooting begins."

"Look," she almost pleaded, "I realize shooting is what you specialize in, but we're hoping to deal with this without lighting up the skies with bombs and missiles. Most sane people don't want to see the entire region from Iran to the Med go up in a mushroom cloud. As I said, the Russians are in a slightly delicate position in Syria. They can't be seen to go against Assad directly.

For that matter, neither can we. Body bags filled with American soldiers don't play well in Washington."

"What about the Israelis?"

"Even worse. They don't do subtle when it comes to Syria. Look, we've got a very small window to deal with this threat. We get one shot, as it were. If that doesn't work, then inevitably, Israel and some other regional players will hear about it. Then all hell breaks loose."

Viktor laughed. "Don't kid yourself. I'm willing to bet you the finest dinner in Paris that the Israelis already know exactly what's going on and are waiting to see what, if anything, you do about it. Trust me, they know when Assad farts."

She looked at him warmly. "I'll hold you to that dinner. I have the perfect place in mind. I hope your credit card isn't maxed out. In the meantime, however, *we* have a problem."

"What's this '*we*' shit?"

"Don't be dense, Viktor. I happen to know that your IQ is way, way up there."

"Bet you even know my inseam measurement."

"That too. But as I was saying, *we* have a problem. We *and* the Russians would like this little problem solved; eliminated, in other words. But we both need what's usually called 'deniability'. Neither our fingerprints nor the Russians' can be anywhere near this operation. They may want this operation shut down, but they sure as hell don't want to be *seen* cooperating with us. No, all we've got from them is a vague promise not to tell Assad we know what he's up to. In other words, their position is 'Try something if you want, but don't tell us. If you're caught, we know nothing. We won't be able to save you from the consequences of capture.'"

"Ah, the light begins to dawn." He opened his arms wide in exaggerated understanding. "Now I get it. Let me guess where this is going. This is where you want me to come in. Not to put too fine a point on it, I'm the one who's *deniable*. Shit hits the fan, and Viktor is shown on prime-time TV as a 'tool of the perfidious West.' He becomes target number 1 for every *jihadi* between here and Kabul. Meanwhile, those same Western 'leaders' are denying any knowledge of me. I can just hear them now: *'Viktor Lipsky? Never heard of him. Checked all our files. Nothing there. Too bad about his head rolling off like that. Wonder what he was doing over there in the first place?'* Nice try, sweetheart. Let the geniuses who created this mess in one way or another get us out of it."

Now it was her turn to get up and look out over the small village square toward the sea. She could see various people going about their routine daily chores: shopping, working on their fishing boats, meeting old friends for coffee, or cleaning a couple of fish to cook for some other customer in the case of a chef.

Then she turned back to Viktor. "Look," she said soothingly, "this rat program is real."

"How can you be so sure?" he snapped.

"Because we heard it from the horse's mouth. It seems a certain colonel in Assad's army—a former colonel, actually—reported on the progress of this program to a real charmer named Ziyad Duwaji, the member of the Assad clan responsible for the regime's security. This colonel—Hisham Turkeri—says his sexual preferences have made him a marked man in Syria. We think there's more to it than that, but right now, that's not important. What *is* important is that our colonel fled to Istanbul in the hope of escaping from Assad's justice. While there, he contacted one of our people and said he had something to trade. In return for some serious cash, he gave us proof of the rat program."

"And what happened to the colonel?"

"Haven't got a clue. If he's smart, he's used the cash to get as far from the Middle East as possible. But," she added with a hint of sadness, "I don't think he's that smart. He says he likes Istanbul."

Viktor almost laughed aloud. "A huge city. More people than all of Greece. On top of that, there must be thousands of Syrian refugees there. Maybe he's right. Maybe he can hide in a crowd." He shrugged his shoulders. "Doubt it, but's there's always a first."

"Look, you don't have to do this. You can stay here in your little paradise and occasionally go back to Africa to fight the good fight and earn a pot full of money. We can't match the pay. But think about this: if that program is real and if it actually takes off, then all of this"—she waved her arms toward the square—"is threatened. Make no mistake. Those rats could spark a war that would quickly spread from the Middle East. How far is it from Syria to Cyprus, to Crete, to Rhodes? Not far."

"OK, I get the picture. What can be done about it?"

She smiled thinly. "That's tomorrow's lesson."

"I can understand why you don't want anything to do with this. You don't owe anyone in any government any favors. And in all honesty, this little adventure could end in total failure and death—your death. But, again, in all honesty, the threat of death is something you've dealt with for a long time. You don't win a lot of friends doing what you do. Quite a few people would be delighted to hear of your demise." She extended her arms like a late-night talk-show host introducing a special guest. "Yet here you are, basking in this beautiful peace and solitude. You're recognized as a key member, supporter, of this little community. Very safe it is too. In return for some generous 'gifts,' you've set up a very effective early warning system. If anyone gets off that boat who doesn't look right, you get notified. And if, by any chance, the wrong sort do make it off the boat undetected, you have quite an arsenal to deal with them. No, Viktor Lipsky has indeed found his little paradise."

She sat down and polished off what was left of the dinner. Viktor just sat there, wondering where this was going.

"OK," he said finally. "I'm not committing to anything, but if I do, how much freedom of action do I have without some of your friends stomping over everything with their size 15 shoes?"

"Complete. We can help most by staying out of your way. Our experts can tell you exactly what to look for, how to avoid contamination, and how to destroy the cultures. Remember, they're the target. How you do it is your business."

"That's it? No medals, no money?" he asked half-seriously.

Then she made a mistake. "How about *all sins forgiven*?" she said in a wry, almost coquettish tone of voice.

"Sins? What *sins*?" Viktor shot back, suddenly very alert to the danger of dealing with any government. "What the hell are you talking about?"

"Well, sunshine, let's just say you're not exactly regarded as Mother Theresa by some parts of the U.S. government. People keep score. Remember that initial $5 million several years ago? Some people wonder where it really went. Right now, your ledger is just about evenly balanced. There are those who want to shut you down immediately. Others are not so rash; they see some merit in letting you and your Merry Men raise hell in certain quarters. But," she cautioned in a more serious tone of voice, "don't think you can stay beneath the radar forever. If I can find your little island retreat, think what some less benign government minion might do."

"That's bullshit, and you know it. I haven't broken any American laws."

She rolled her hand back and forth. "Maybe, maybe not. But the reality—whatever that is—is completely irrelevant. What's important is how certain people think you *help* or *hinder* their pet projects. Right now, I wouldn't take a bet either way. The zealots in this new day and age can easily create their own set of 'facts' to build a narrative that helps them. You don't really want to find out how nasty and powerful they can be. You may not know it, but the U.S. Treasury, to cite one example, wields a much bigger stick than the Pentagon in these matters. People listen when they put their finger on the scales. All those nice bank accounts that your buddy Sergei has set up can suddenly be frozen, or worse yet, disappear." She snapped her fingers. "Just like that, you return to ranks of the unemployed."

This got Viktor's back up; he didn't like being threatened. "Look, lady," he snarled, "let's get one thing straight. It's people like you who create problems like this—not me. So back off. It's just a little rich hearing lectures about 'gunrunning' from an agent of the biggest gunrunner in the world—the U.S. government. This is *your* problem to solve, not mine." He sat back, grinned wickedly, and spread his arms in innocence. "Me, I like life simple. I don't wake up every day trying to figure out how to make the world safe for Uncle Sam. Actually, every day that I wake up without a tag on my toe I count as a good day. See, it's people like you who screw things up for those of us who actually enjoy a *simple life*."

"All right, all right," she conceded. She wasn't actually backing down, but she was smart enough to realize that when one approach doesn't work, it's time to try another one. "Calm down, for Christ's sake. I'm not threatening anything—"

"Bullshit," Viktor spat out.

Now it was her turn to get exasperated. "Will you just listen for a minute?"

He nodded slightly.

"Good. Now, as I was saying, the Syrian threat with the rats is real. We can deal with it in a couple of ways: by creating an even bigger mess, which as we've seen again and again, doesn't really work all that well; or we can try to be a little more subtle." Before he could jump back in with some crack about "subtle" governments, she retreated—a little. "I know, I know. We don't really do subtle very well either. You and your friends, however, can do subtle very well. So, I'm *asking*—not threatening—for your help. Will you at least consider it?"

Viktor thought about it for a long time. He knew he'd lose

any serious fight with the U.S. Treasury, and that might cost him the very life he'd worked so hard to create on this little island. "OK," he said grudgingly. "You win. We'll at least take a look at it. But how sure can I be that what others see as my 'sins' will in fact be forgiven? Can you really keep those assholes off my back?"

"Let's just say that, if you pull this off, your account with the U.S. government will be so far in the black that no one will dare come after you. I can guarantee that much. There might even be some cash involved."

"And if I don't pull it off, I'll probably be dead." He chuckled. "So, one way or another, the *problem* of Viktor Lipsky is solved. Nice work you do. But I'll need something. Saving *paradise* isn't cheap. And please don't ask for receipts."

"I'll see what I can do. Now where do we start?"

"*We* start by you returning to the pension. I'll let you know by tomorrow morning if I think I can do anything. First, I need to see if there are any Russians in Syria who might be willing to help."

"By the way," she said as she got up from the table, "as you saw today, we're not the only people trying to find you."

"You mean those two clowns? They got lucky by following you. They're Balko's men, but I'm not sure he knew about their freelancing."

"Maybe, but he's let it be known he'll pay a great deal of money to learn your whereabouts."

"And just how do you know so much about Ivan Balko?"

She looked at him pityingly. "We're the NSA, Viktor. There's not a hell of a lot we don't know about. Anyway, he's pissed about some deal in Sudan where he says you screwed him. Now, he's out for blood—your blood."

"Nothing new in that, but thanks for the heads-up."

She reached out and put her hand on his arm. "We need you in one piece, Viktor. Please don't try to settle personal scores right now. There will be plenty of time for that later. We'll do what we can to watch your back by tracking his movements and letting you know."

Viktor gave a short laugh, remembering what Ricky Davies had to say about Balko. "It's not me you have to worry about. I've promised him to Desta's husband."

"OK, where do we go from here?"

"Before we even think about going to Syria, we need to learn a lot more about that fortress. I might know someone who can help."

He pulled out his phone and punched in a long series of numbers. When it was answered, Emily noticed that he smiled warmly before speaking rapidly in fluent, idiomatic French.

"What was all that about?" she inquired when the call was finished.

"Paul Deschamps. He wrote books and prepared diagrams about the Crac."

Emily smiled excitedly. "Great! When can we meet him?"

"We can't. He died about 45 years ago."

"Wonderful. You got any more bright ideas?"

Viktor laughed. "Relax, for Christ's sake. I didn't say there was no information. One of his students carried on most of the work and still has the original plans. He lives near Bordeaux, and some friends can arrange a visit."

Emily nodded her agreement and then made her own call to Washington to speak with her boss, John Shepherd, at the NSA. She told him that Viktor had reluctantly agreed to help and they were off to France to get more information about the fortress.

"Why France?" he inquired.

"Lipsky has a contact there who can get us access to a full set of plans for the place."

"OK. But Emily," he cautioned, "be careful. There are some people here who really don't want you to succeed. They're looking for a chance to unleash a major war. And these rats may be just the trigger for that war." Then he added in his dry, understated way, "They won't appreciate your efforts."

***

Jerusalem, Israel

Uri Abramov carried an armful of newspapers and wore a big smile on his face as he strode into the small third-floor office on Ze'ev Jabotinsky Street in Jerusalem. The headlines—some sensational, some reasoned, and some angry—all referred to more Palestinian protests against the increasing number of Jewish settlements in the West Bank. Bricks and stones were thrown, shots were fired, and some construction trailers were burned. In the northern part of the country, missiles were fired from mobile Hezbollah launchers supplied by Iran. Even the Syrians across the Golan Heights were staging tank maneuvers in hopes of one day thundering down the slopes and across the fertile plains of Israel. The time was getting ripe for their move.

He took off his jacket and turned to his zealous young colleague, Myer Hirschon. "Any more news from the Syrian project?"

"There's one slight issue," Hirschon warned.

"What *now*?" Abramov almost yelled in frustration.

"Our people are also picking up noise about other American interest in the Syrian project…"

"What the hell happened? Who talked?" Abramov demanded.

"Relax. No one talked. It's just that one of the Syrian villagers hit by the virus made it into Jordan, where he wound up at the U.S. embassy when the Jordanians couldn't figure out what happened to him. A U.S. Army doctor we don't control is a smart fucker and figured out what disease the guy had. He sent blood samples to the CDC in Atlanta. They confirmed it but said there's no known vaccine. I've also heard the NSA is on the case."

Abramov reached for his secure phone. "It's far from simple, Hirschon. Once those pricks start investigating, this whole thing could unravel—and quickly."

Abramov picked up the phone and called an office in Alexandria, Virginia.

"Uri, good to hear from you," a gruff voice answered. "Everything OK on your end?"

"We may have a problem."

General Meadows sat up straighter and gripped the phone hard. Problems weren't supposed to happen on his watch. His voice took on the edge of irritated command. "What problem? It's a little late in the day to start fuckin' around. We got people lined up over here ready to push the button. Now what the hell's goin' on at your end?"

"It's not my end, General."

"What the hell are you talkin' about? Nuthin's wrong over here."

"Maybe not in your group, but someone's asking questions that really shouldn't be asked right now." He went on to explain about the sick Jordanian making it to the U.S. embassy, where the army doctor got involved and sent samples to the CDC. "I've also heard the NSA has gotten involved."

"Son of a bitch!" the general exclaimed. "I'll have that dickhead treatin' the Taliban for the clap if he don't learn to keep his goddamned mouth shut." Then he took a couple of deep breaths and thought about the problem. "OK. Look, Uri, this really ain't a big deal. We've got some people close to the CDC and can get them to forget all about that particular blood analysis. And we'll make damn sure no one from the fuckin' NSA pokes his nose where it don't belong. You leave that to me. Those fuckin' rats will generate the shitstorm we've been waitin' for. Then you boys may just create Greater Israel all the way to the Fertile Crescent." The general hung up and drummed his fingers on the desk. It was time for action, he decided. He'd nip this bullshit in the bud.

He picked up the phone once more and called his contact at the NSA. "What the fuck's goin' on over there, Harry? Why's someone pokin' around in business that don't concern them?"

When he heard that an NSA analyst was on her way to France to learn more about the fortress of Crac des Chevaliers from an archaeologist who lived near Bordeaux, he slammed his fist on the desk in frustration. "*What the fuck do I pay you boys for? This ain't supposed to happen, you dimwit.*" He took a few deep breaths to calm down. "OK, OK. Didn't mean to yell. You just keep your head down and don't say nuthin' to nobody. I got a couple of guys in France who can deal with this shit."

His next call was to one of his mercenaries in France. "You get your ass to Bordeaux and make sure she don't cause no problems."

CHAPTER 9

Bordeaux and Cap Ferret, France

A few days later, the Aegean Airlines flight from Athens was descending gently over the low, rolling wine country of Bordeaux on its way to Mérignac Airport. Viktor could see the spires and narrow, winding streets of medieval towns surrounded by some of the most expensive vineyards in the world. Soon, the plane made a sweeping left-hand turn over the broad Gironde Estuary, and the rich Médoc region spread beneath him. It was a glorious sunlit day. As the Airbus 320 lined up for its approach, he could just make out Arcachon Bay and the waves of the Atlantic Ocean lapping at the long beach that ran all the way to the mouth of the Gironde.

The plane bumped down on the runway and started its taxi to the gate. Emily laughed and coyly put her arm through his. "And you, my handsome new best friend, what persona are you taking: Viktor or Alex?"

"Going through passport control, I'm Alex Kalistos with a Greek passport. I can zip through passport control as an EU citizen. You, on the other hand, with your American passport, will have to wait in line. I'll meet you outside the arrivals gate."

"Where are you going in such a rush? Car rental?"

"No. It's been arranged."

"When?"

He smiled as they made their way out of the plane and down to passport control with their small carry-on bags. "All will be revealed."

"Bastard," she muttered at his back as he disappeared swiftly beyond passport control, through the crowds waiting around the baggage carousels, and out the automatic sliding doors.

She was in a foul mood when she finally emerged from passport control after her passport was flagged as belonging to an American security officer. This involved a few phone calls to Paris to see what was going on. Why was an American security officer making an unannounced visit to Bordeaux? They finally decided that she posed no harm to the republic and was allowed through with a polite nod, apologies for the delay, and a polite request to let the French know if she found something that might interest them.

Her mood wasn't made any better when she saw Viktor standing with one of those distinguished couples who look as if they belong on the cover of a glamour magazine. The man was as tall as Viktor, slender, and with short, dark hair graying at the temples. He had a patch over his right eye and a broad smile on his thin lips as he clasped Viktor strongly by the shoulders. His wife was one of those women who make all other women feel dumpy, as if they've just stepped out of a Breughel painting, dressed in a sack, and wearing wooden clogs on their feet.

"Christ," Emily muttered irritably to herself, "do all French women come out of the womb looking like this?"

The woman wasn't quite as tall as her husband and had the kind of aristocratic bearing and facial features that take centuries to perfect. A pleated, navy silk skirt fell to a little below her knees without hiding her perfect legs. The lightweight, beige suede jacket and white pure-Pima-cotton shirt displayed just enough of her elegant figure to attract a second glance from any man with a pulse. And her rich-golden hair fell in gentle waves to a long, slender neck adorned with a simple gold chain. She too was smiling warmly at Viktor. Emily felt like crawling into the nearest garbage can. Why didn't that son of a bitch warn her about this? She swallowed her anger and walked up to the group.

Viktor introduced her: "Emily, I'd like you to meet two very old friends: Phillipe and Suzanne de Villers. Phillipe and I came across each other in Africa, and they were kind enough to invite me to their home near here several times."

Suzanne de Villers regarded Emily warmly and said any friend of Viktor's was a friend of theirs. The two men went off to get the car, and Emily noticed Phillipe carried a cane and walked with a stiff right leg. Suzanne caught the glance and suggested they have a coffee while waiting for the men. They headed for a nearby café, placed their orders, and found a small table to sit at.

"How much do you know about Viktor?" Suzanne asked once the coffees arrived.

"We're working on a project together, but I don't really know him all that well."

"Well, let me tell you something. If it weren't for Viktor, my husband would never have returned alive from that horrible country Chad. He was a colonel in a parachute regiment of the Foreign Legion. They were ambushed one day and caught in a vicious crossfire. Viktor and some of his friends were nearby and heard the calls for help on the radio. They raced over and helped push back the attackers. Many of Phillipe's men were killed, and he was badly wounded. They were still under fire when Viktor picked him up and carried him more than three kilometers to where a helicopter could pick up the survivors. I'm sure there's more to the story, but this is all they told me." She paused and ran a long, elegant finger along her jaw. "Viktor's scar? That's when that happened. Apparently, Viktor stopped a sharp machete aimed at Phillipe. It almost took his face off. So you see, we owe him twice." She studied Emily closely. "But you should know that the Foreign Legion remembers these things. We've remained close personal friends ever since." Then she paused for a minute as if reflecting on something. "It's important, I think, for Viktor because he strikes me as the kind of person who doesn't have very many friends. Don't you agree?"

Emily gagged a little, trying desperately to think of something to say. "I don't really know. You see, we recently met on this project. I haven't spent that much time with him."

"Perhaps." Suzanne's elegant Gallic shrug indicated polite disbelief. "But something tells me there's more going on than a nice little holiday in France." She laughed lightly. "I'm not sure Viktor understands the concept of holidays, but a couple of days in Cap Ferret could be good for both of you, no?" Then she looked sharply at Emily. "But I have to tell you, we'd be *very* upset if anything were to happen to Viktor. Now, I realize you're on your way to see Henri Duclos in Cap Ferret…"

Emily stammered and tried to come up with a non-committal response.

Suzanne simply laughed again and patted Emily on the arm. "Bordeaux is a small place, my dear. Everyone knows everything. You see, it was my grandfather who helped fund Paul Deschamps' research in the first place, so you must be interested in the Crac des Chevaliers. We have a bit of a family connection because one of my ancestors was actually a *chevalier* when that fort was built. I, however, have absolutely no interest in going there. As Phillipe would say, '*Putain Guerre, Putain Pays.*'" She glanced out of the large windows and saw the cars pulling up outside the door. "Ah, they've arrived. We mustn't keep them waiting."

The two women got up from the table and left the terminal.

Once outside, Suzanne gave Viktor a big hug and commanded him to stay with them the next time he was in France. She touched his scar gently. "We'll get that fixed one day, Viktor." Then she turned to Emily and kissed her on both cheeks. "Take care of him," she whispered into Emily's ear.

"I'll do my best," Emily replied, slightly surprised at her changing view of Viktor.

Then Phillipe and Suzanne climbed into an old Land Rover and roared off.

Emily was startled to see that the ride she'd share with Viktor was a new, shiny, black Citroen DS5. "Where the hell did this come from?"

"Phillipe," Viktor confirmed, almost embarrassed. "It's their town car. He insisted we take it."

Emily ran her hands over the luxurious leather seats. "Nice ride." She nodded back toward the terminal. "What was all that about? How come your friends know so much about what we're doing? That elegant woman just told me to take very good care of you."

"Don't believe everything you hear," he snorted, trying to deflect the questioning. "It was a long time ago."

Emily merely smiled and patted him lightly on the arm.

With that, they got into the car and Viktor drove off. The car came with a satnav system, but he never really trusted them. He was busy navigating the roundabouts that the French love so much while looking for the D213, which would lead them to the coast. He found it on the third roundabout and let out a small grunt of satisfaction.

Once safely on the right road, he explained to Emily. "They're nice people. Phillipe was pretty banged up after Africa, and they came back here. Suzanne's family has owned a vineyard not far from here for a very long time. It was going straight downhill until they took it over. They restored the vines and the chateau. I caught a glimpse of the chateau as we descended over the Médoc on the way to the airport."

"So," Emily said snidely, "we're dealing with the lords and ladies of the manor, are we?"

"Don't kid yourself. They work like hell. Running a vineyard is hard agricultural work, much of which you do yourself if you really care about the grapes. And they care. The chateau was falling down when they took over, and over the years, they've managed to repair about a third of it."

He smiled at the power of the big car as he eased out into the left lane to fly past a huge IKEA truck. "This baby really moves," he noted with a chuckle.

"Boys and their toys." She rolled her eyes. "So how come this hard-working, elegant French couple know so much about our interest in Syria?"

"How do you think we got to see Henri Duclos? It was a call to Phillipe, who in turn called his good friend Henri, who in turn agreed to cooperate fully with us. Plus, of course, a case of Phillipe's very good 2013 vintage sealed the deal."

"All very cozy. And here I was thinking that those Yankees from New England were the masters at the Ivy League old-boy network." She turned in her seat to face him. "Before we get to Duclos, did you find a potentially helpful Russian in Syria?"

"Maybe. Sergei is working on it and might have a name in a day or two."

As they neared the coast, Viktor kept looking in the rear-view mirror.

"Anything wrong?" Emily asked.

"A black Renault has been keeping the same distance from us for the last several miles."

Emily sniggered. "Viktor, this is France. There are a lot of black Renaults, and this is the only road to the coast."

"Maybe," he said doubtfully. "We'll just see what happens when we get into the towns."

About an hour later, they were winding around the small streets of Cap Ferret, which is situated at the end of a long, sandy peninsula stretching down to the Bay of Biscay. The black Renault had turned off a few streets earlier, and Viktor let out a sigh of relief. The town was a summer resort for wealthy Bordelais, and the houses were a wild mix of styles, shapes, and colors. Many were semi-hidden in the dense pine groves that dotted the area.

Viktor pulled over to consult the instructions from Phillipe. "Go to the lighthouse," he muttered, "then go south of the lighthouse toward the restaurant Chez Hortense and look for Avenue Belleville. Then look for a large, green wooden house on the right-hand side as you head toward Arcachon Bay."

After several frustrating wrong turns, they finally stumbled upon the restaurant, backtracked to the right street, and found the large, green wooden house, which had a wide covered veranda with three steps leading to the stone walkway. Viktor carefully pulled the car onto the sandy edge of the narrow road, leaving plenty of room for other cars to pass without scratching Phillipe's car. They sat there for a few minutes, listening to the ticks in the engine as it cooled down.

Finally, Viktor climbed out and motioned for Emily to come with him while he approached the house. At the last minute, he remembered something and reached into the back seat to haul out a case of Phillipe's wine. Thus armed, he walked up to the front porch, set the case of wine carefully on a chair, and then knocked politely on the door.

The door was answered quickly, as if Viktor had been expected. His first impression of Henri Duclos was of a smiling basketball, topped with a thatch of white hair and ringed with a white beard. He was almost like one of those characters children draw—a round head, no neck, and a round body with short arms and legs. What separated him from the cartoon characters were his wide smile and piercing, blue eyes topped with bushy eyebrows.

"Ah, you must be the Viktor that Phillipe mentioned. The one interested in the Crac des Chevaliers. For what reason, he did not tell me," he said in a tone that indicated he was somewhat put out by that slight, "but that does not matter." Then he noticed Emily and was transformed instantly into a gallant

French chevalier of yesteryear. "But he did not say you would be accompanied by a vision of loveliness. All his sins are forgiven." He gestured grandly for them to enter the house. "My dear, you're most welcome." He gave the best bow his round stomach would allow. Then he spied the case of wine sitting on the chair. "And, of course, my dear Phillipe remembered perhaps the most important thing: this lovely case of his treasured 2013." He turned to Viktor and Emily. "This should go very well with studying dusty old documents and maps, don't you think?"

Viktor and Emily glanced at each other in a way that questioned exactly what they'd gotten themselves into. He nodded to show she should go before him and follow Duclos into the house.

Their initial impression of Duclos as a somewhat bumbling dilettante living off his professor's hard work changed instantly once they were inside. While the porch and bookshelf-lined front room were shaded by the tall pine trees, the entire back of the house was bathed in the bright light shining through large windows. Arcachon Bay opened up in front of them, and they could see the enormous Dune du Pilat across the narrow opening. Sailboats were darting about the bay in the strong breeze. The back room was clearly the main work center and was dominated by a large table holding a powerful Mac, plus several old maps and architectural drawings. There were more drawings pinned to huge pegboards on the white walls. Any empty wall space was taken up with floor-to-ceiling bookcases. The only sign of a woman was a small, silver-framed picture on his desk. The woman had a friendly, smiling face and was squinting into the sun. Viktor could just make out the bay in the background.

Duclos noticed him looking at the picture. "My wife," he said, all trace of the bumbling professor gone. "She died three years ago. She left a big hole in my life that I try to fill with work. But"—he gave a shrug with upturned palms— it only partially works." Then he brightened. "You didn't come all this way to listen to me reminisce. Let's have some coffee and get to work."

He bustled off into a very modern kitchen and soon came back with three small cups of dark coffee, which he carried on a tray over to a round table with a delicate mother of pearl inlay. "One of the professor's favorite purchases, that table. He brought it back here in 1935 from Damascus."

They finished their coffees speedily and followed him around to the other side of the big table covered with maps.

"Phillipe said you were interested in ways to get into the fortress. Undetected ways to get into the fortress." Henri studied them closely over a pair of half-moon reading glasses. "I assume this isn't for preparing a new touristic guidebook. I also assume that whatever you plan on doing will in no way endanger France."

Emily, in perfect Parisian French, answered him: "You assume correctly, M. Duclos. We need to stop a certain potentially very dangerous operation that's going on in the fortress. Nothing we do will in any way endanger France. In fact, if we succeed, the people of France and many other countries will be able to sleep more soundly in their beds."

Duclos nodded his understanding. "I enjoy sleeping soundly, as you put it. So I wish you good fortune. Now, M. Lipsky, I know a little about through Phillipe. But you, *mademoiselle*, are a bit of a puzzle. Am I to once more assume that you are more than a tour guide?"

"That would be a good assumption, but why don't we leave it at that?"

"As you wish. I've known a few such 'tour guides' in my time. But I have to warn you that Crac des Chevaliers isn't a pleasant place right now for anyone, let alone a beautiful woman." He gave a little "Humph," making it clear he didn't completely accept their comment but was willing to let it go for the moment. *If they want to undertake some foolish, hopeless mission, who am I to stop them? Besides,* he rationalized, *they look as if they can take care of themselves.*

"Come, let us take a look at what you'll be facing." He unrolled one of the large maps on the table and put glass weights on the four corners. The map was covered with spidery drawings depicting various parts of the fortress in detail. Duclos explained these were some of the earliest sketches from the restoration in the 1930s. The drawings showed the exquisite detail of the brickwork, Gothic arches, colonnades, and columns. They also detailed a large central hall on the ground floor. Duclos said it must have been the main ceremonial hall for the knights, with its huge fireplace, long table, and walls adorned with shields, massive two-handed swords, and other weapons of the day. There was a separate drawing of the entrance and its U-turn, designed to herd any attackers into a killing zone where they'd be massacred by stones, boiling oil, arrows, or anything else the defenders could find.

Viktor let out a low whistle. "This place really is impregnable."

"Yes, and no," Duclos answered enigmatically. He then rolled up the first map and fetched another one from a large pile. He opened this one, laid it on the table, and once again weighted the four corners.

Viktor and Emily studied the new drawings, unsure what they were looking at.

"These particular sets of drawings show the lower levels of the fortress." Duclos pointed out the faint lines indicating where the stone staircases would have been. "See, this is how you descended to this series of interconnected rooms." He looked up at them. "It's a real rabbit warren. Some hallways lead nowhere. Others lead to the next room. It's easy to get completely lost, which is what they had in mind should any invader succeed in getting this far." He searched through the pile of papers and came to a slightly smaller one, which he unfolded and placed on top of the previous one. "Now we go one floor down to the sub-basement, as it were." He outlined the rooms with his chubby index finger. "Here, you see that the rooms are much smaller. If you look closely at the entrances, you can still identify the holes where gates were installed." He leaned back and stretched his back. "The professor wasn't sure what these rooms were used for, probably storage of some sort, but," he added ominously, "They could just as easily have been prison cells."

Viktor and Emily peered closely at this drawing, both convinced it was precisely in these small, well-protected rooms with many feet of stone and brick between them and the surface where any laboratories would be placed. Viktor shook his head at the difficulty of what they were planning. Even if they got into the fortress, their odds of getting two levels down undetected were almost impossible.

Duclos noticed their discouraged looks and allowed himself a little smile. Once again, he rummaged through the pile of drawings. "Now I'll show you something very interesting." This drawing seemed to show a hole, almost like a tunnel, spiraling down and away from the fortress. He leaned his back against the table and assumed his professorial manner. "Those very traits that make a fortress like Crac des Chevaliers impregnable for attackers also make things difficult for the defenders."

Viktor and Emily both appeared suitably puzzled.

Duclos was delighted to present something that these bright young Americans didn't know. He raised two fingers in the air. "What two things must defenders of any fort have access to?"

"Food and water," Emily ventured, not quite sure where this line of inquiry was headed.

"Partially right." Duclos chortled. "Food, they could stockpile for months. Remember, sieges did not happen overnight. You had plenty of warning about what was coming. But water was another thing. This they needed constant access to." He turned back to the table and unfolded the first drawing. "Note that the Crac is on a high hill, with a river flowing at the bottom. Now it is just a trickle going through the village, but in the days of the *chevaliers*, it was a real river." Then he reshuffled the drawings and put the final one back on the table. He pointed to the mysterious circle. "That's precisely what this circle represents. It was the opening of a tunnel leading down to the river."

"Now," he continued in his lecture-hall tone, "what else did the defenders need?"

Viktor thought for a minute. "A way out. A back door just in case the attackers ever got through the various lines of defense."

"Absolutely." Duclos beamed at this particularly bright pupil. "Not everyone was willing to get slaughtered like those fools at the Battle of Hattin. What idiots they were, Reynald and Guy," he almost spat the names out. Like many history professors, he thought what happened almost 1,000 years ago was more vivid than anything in the current world.

"Battle of Hattin? Reynald? Guy?" Emily asked, confused by the reference. *What the hell is the old boy talking about?*

"To cut a long story short," Viktor answered, "the Crusaders led by Guy de Lusignan and Reynald de Chatillon overplayed their hand. They left the safety of defensive positions in Jerusalem that had plenty of water and marched into the arid wasteland in heat of the day near Tiberias in modern Israel. Saladin and his army of about 30,000 slaughtered most of the 20,000 knights and soldiers on July 4th, 1187. A few months later, he took Jerusalem."

"Of course, how could I have missed that?" Emily said with a laugh.

Duclos, on the other hand, nodded with pleasure. "Impressive. Glad to see that not everyone has forgotten history. Now you see why, a few years later, more-intelligent Crusaders had learned their lesson and made sure they had plenty of water—and a back door. The professor was very interested in this and prepared a special drawing of this multipurpose tunnel." He pulled out a smaller, square drawing from the pile and put it on the table. This time, he needed something finer than his finger and picked up a thin pencil. "You see how the tunnel begins just outside this particular cell," he said, pointing to a cell in the far corner of the sub-basement. From there, he traced the faint lines that went down at a steep angle. Deschamps had also drawn the village that existed in his time.

Viktor could see the tunnel ended in what appeared to be an empty field, or maybe a rubbish dump. "That's it," he said to Emily. "That's our way in—and out."

"If it's still there," she added skeptically.

Duclos made them copies of the old plans and then led them back out to the front porch. They assured him they'd let him know as much as they could about what might happen at the fortress and climbed into the car.

"What now?" Emily asked.

"Food," Viktor answered simply. "I'm starved."

***

They drove along the small, sandy road until they came to a row of shacks along the edge of the bay. Viktor was looking for one in particular, and he gave a grunt of satisfaction when he found one with a red, white, and blue pole out front.

Emily took a jaundiced look at the weathered old building. "You really know how to treat a girl. Do you take all your dates to such high-class places?"

"Only ones with big mouths. Wait a minute. You might actually like this."

He parked the car in the shade of some large pine trees, and they got out. He looked around casually and thought he saw the black Renault that had been behind them on the road from Bordeaux. He couldn't see inside the car, but he made a mental note to check it after lunch.

They entered the shack and were immediately confronted by

a large, florid woman who bustled out from behind a counter, carrying a huge tray filled with fresh oysters. She put the tray down and grabbed a startled Emily by the arms. "You must be the ones Suzanne called about. She said there was a beautiful woman and a large man. Follow me," she commanded, and she led them onto the patio that jutted over a shallow inlet.

Emily blushed deeply, and Viktor just smiled as they sat at an old wooden table under a large umbrella. There was no menu, and the lunch of a dozen fresh oysters, a huge lump of local pâté, hot crusty bread, and a carafe of chilled dry white wine was placed in front of them. Neither of them was very good at social chitchat, and so they ate in a companionable silence while looking at the boats darting around Arcachon Bay.

Viktor found that, somewhat to his surprise, he actually was beginning to like being with Emily. Yes, she had a very sharp tongue from time to time and wasn't above blackmail, but she also had some useful skills. And—he had to admit—she was pleasant to look at.

Emily was also revising her early opinion that Viktor was just another Rambo wannabe. *At least,* she mused, smiling to herself, *he's a Rambo who can read without moving his lips and speaks at least five languages. Most of all, he's showed no signs of being needy or clingy. God, I hate that.* "I'm not your mother," she'd wanted to scream in some earlier unsuccessful relationships. 'Need' was simply not part of her vocabulary. She may *want* something, but she'd steeled herself never, ever to need *anyone* or *anything.* She had an agenda and intensity that didn't lend themselves to cute little tennis outfits or sipping margaritas at 5 p.m. Viktor might not be exactly the doctor or lawyer type her mother had in mind, but, still, he wasn't bad.

She usually hated to be touched, but after they'd paid the bill, she didn't mind at all when Viktor guided her gently by the elbow back to the car. He even opened her door and was heading around to his side when her cell phone fell to the ground under the engine. As she kneeled down to pick it up, she noticed a thin wire hanging loosely from just behind the radiator. She rapidly discarded innocent implications of the wire. Good cars like this simply don't have loose wires hanging down from the engine block. By then, Viktor had settled in his seat and was about to start the car.

She stood up swiftly and shouted, "*Get out of the car! Do not turn the key!*"

Viktor sensed the urgency in her voice and didn't argue. He got out, raced around to her side, and peered under the car. "Son of a bitch. You're right," he said calmly. "Good catch. Someone must have rigged this when we were eating. Thank God they were sloppy."

He moved around to the front of the car and was about to open the hood when Emily put a restraining hand on his arm. "For Christ's sake, Viktor, be careful. Let's try not to incinerate the entire neighborhood—not to mention ourselves."

He eased the hood up gently and peered at the engine. Jammed next to the battery was enough explosive wired to the starter motor to destroy several cars. His mind quickly cycled through all possibilities and just as quickly discarded most of them. "Crude but effective," he concluded. "They really didn't want to leave any traces."

"What now? Do you know anything about bomb disposal?"

"We're in luck. There's nothing sophisticated. No sign of a timer or cell phone connection. If there were," he added nonchalantly, "bits of us would be on their way to Spain by now. They were rushed. It's simply wires hooked up to the starter motor. Should be simple to disarm."

"*Should?* Only should?"

"Relax, for God's sake. We're good." He took out the multipurpose knife he always carried, opened one of the blades, and carefully pried the wires apart. A few nervous moments later, he found the connection and then disconnected the wires from the starter motor. He cautiously lifted out the bomb and held it in one of his hands. "Look at this," he scoffed, almost offended by such shoddy work. "Amateur hour. Still, it would have done the job if you hadn't spotted that wire. At least Phillipe gets his car back in one piece. The question now is who put the damn thing in there?" He looked around, but he couldn't see any trace of the black Renault that was there before lunch.

"The black Renault?"

"Good guess. The place is pretty empty, and no one would have spotted him messing with our car. He's probably long gone by now. His boss won't be happy. Clearly, someone doesn't like us poking around the Crac."

"John Shepherd, my boss," Emily explained, "warned me there were people who definitely *do not* want questions asked about the fortress. I didn't think they'd go this far. I'll follow it up when I'm back in Washington. Shepherd may have some ideas."

"I sure as hell hope so. This goes way beyond Ivan Balko. The Syrians are one thing, but dealing with people we can't even see is something else. We're going to need help. I've got to figure out how to get into that damn place and—more important—get out alive."

***

They headed to the airport so Emily could catch a flight to Paris in time to make the late connection to Washington. She gave Viktor a quick kiss on the cheek before running into the terminal. "Take care of yourself, Viktor. I'll let you know what happens in Washington. Call me if Sergei gives you a name."

***

Viktor spent the night with Phillipe and Suzanne before returning to Greece the following day. As he traveled, he spent much of the time on the phone with Davies and Sergei, filling them in on developments. Sergei said he'd see if he could find a Russian in Syria who might help.

Davies's only reaction was caution.

"Look, Viktor, that bomber may have been amateur, but he must have some powerful people behind him. How the hell did he know you were gonna be in France? Don't get me wrong, I ain't against this move, but we gotta think about this one real good. This here is the big leagues. We ain't goin' up against little shitheads in pickup trucks. No, this time we got some big fuckers with big fuckin' guns. I never did like suicide missions, and I sure as hell ain't about to start now. We got some plannin' to do if we wanna keep our asses in one piece."

Viktor agreed and said he'd be in touch when he was back on the island. He shook his head at the speed of developments. If infected rats and car bombs weren't enough, he now had to deal with the fact that Emily was beginning to crack his wall of self-containment. Simple gunrunning was never this complicated.

CHAPTER 10

Telos, Aegean Sea

It took Viktor two days to get back to the island, and he was just making coffee one morning when his phone buzzed with a message. He looked at the small screen. Sergei.

He rang the Liechtenstein number.

Sergei answered on the first ring. "Viktor," he said without any preamble, "I might have found someone for you."

"Who?"

"I'll send more detail, but very quickly, this guy Oleg Yushenko is a former *starshiy leytenant* in Syria who has a couple of problems—big problems that you might be able solve."

Viktor sighed. "Sergei, how in hell can I solve a problem for a senior lieutenant of the Russian army—?"

"Let me finish. This guy is a *former starshiy leytenant* for a very good reason. He's a native Ukrainian—a large and powerful native Ukrainian. One bright day his senior officer— who was actually a contractor—said something very rude about Ukrainians in general and Ukrainians serving the in Russian army in particular. *Especially* rude about a Ukrainian who married a Syrian woman, albeit a Christian. Our Oleg took exception and belted the officer. Broke his jaw in two places. Needless to say, that was the end of Oleg's career in the Russian army, but it isn't the end of the story."

"And this helps us how?" Viktor asked.

"Very simple really. Before his dust-up with the *podpolkovnik*, our Yushenko had been assigned to work in southern Syria as a liaison with Assad's troops stationed near the Crac des Chevaliers. His wife's family lives in the village near the Crac. Yushenko was supposed to be training them in the real craft of warfare, rather than the simple looting and pillaging they were used to. Being married to a Christian Syrian woman and speaking fluent Arabic, he was uniquely qualified. But after getting booted out of the army, he had a major problem.

"He was allowed to stay in Syria, but he had to scrabble around for work. That's your problem—and your opportunity. He and his wife have a son, one who unfortunately inherited the wrong sort of genes from his parents. Don't ask me to go into medical details because I'm not really sure how this works. Anyway, the kid has cystic fibrosis—"

Viktor let out a low whistle. "Poor kid is screwed."

"Unfortunately, yes. Hard to argue with that conclusion. But this is precisely where you come in—if your girlfriend's agency is willing to help. As you may know, people with cystic fibrosis require a regimen of about 50 pills every day: enzymes to help the pancreas do its job, and medication to clear up mucus that forms in the lungs. These drugs aren't cheap or readily available in Syria. And no one is rushing to help Oleg by sending him back to Russia, where they might get some help. Oleg has a little savings, and his wife comes from a family with some money. But that, as you can imagine, is drying up fairly fast. As it stands now, Oleg goes to Larnaca in Cyprus once a month to load up on these pills."

"Ah, I see where this is heading."

"Smart man. Larnaca is where you get a chance to meet

Oleg. And if the Americans are willing to help, offer him a deal. A way out of Syria and a way to pay for all those expensive medications. In return, you'll learn all there is to know about the current setup at the Crac: possible ways in; information about any suspicious workshops; laboratories he might know about; and most important, guard rotations and ways out of there. Without him, I doubt there's much chance of getting anywhere near the place where they might be trying to create that culture. With him, there's a chance. A small chance, but still a chance. Helping him and his family seems a cheap price to pay for that."

"Sounds reasonable. When's his next trip to Cyprus?"

"Next week. Thursday, I think."

Viktor checked the calendar on his phone. "OK. That gives me enough time to make some arrangements. One other thing: where in Larnaca can I find him? The place is crawling with Russians."

"My source says he always go to the Church of St. Lazarus. Seems appropriate when you have a kid with cystic fibrosis."

Viktor thanked Sergei, said he'd let him know what happened, and ended the call. He checked his watch. It was only about 5 a.m. in Washington. Early, but with the jet lag, she should be up. Anyway, she needed to hear this before she met with her boss.

The phone rang several times before Emily picked up. "Well, if it isn't the sage of the olive trees? How are things in paradise?"

"Peaceful, so far. I'd like to keep it that way. How did you know it was me?"

"I don't get many calls routed through places like Turkmenistan. What's up?"

"Got a call from Sergei with information about a Russian officer—a former Russian officer—in Syria who might be willing to help."

She perked up immediately. "Great. How do we get in touch?"

"Slow down. There are some issues. Some things your boss can help with."

"Shit," she groaned, "The NSA isn't exactly your neighborhood Welcome Wagon for Russian officers—even former Russian officers."

"Listen will you," he snapped. "If you're serious about stopping those rats, this may be our only chance." He quickly filled her in on his call with Sergei.

"OK, I get the point," she said. "I have no idea what his answer will be, but I'll ask him. God knows the NSA spends enough money on really bad ideas. Maybe this time they'll open their wallets for something good. I'll call you later this afternoon, our time. Try not to shoot anyone in the meantime," she ended with a chuckle.

***

Fort Meade, Maryland

Emily sat in a small, sterile third-floor meeting room in the NSA headquarters in Fort Meade, Maryland, staring out the window at the constant drizzle that seems to envelope the mid-Atlantic region every spring. The walls of the room were bare. There wasn't even a picture of the current president. She grinned inwardly at the absence of the picture. It probably reflects the image of Jedi knights that people in the intelligence agencies have cultivated about themselves. The smartest people in town. Above all the political riffraff. Who needs a president? For just a moment, she allowed her thoughts to wander back to Telos with its sun, warmth, and relaxed tempo. There was absolutely nothing relaxed, warm, or sunny anywhere near Washington, D.C., these days.

She couldn't help thinking the whole idea about the rats and the fortress was nuts. It was bound to end in disaster. But then she thought of Viktor, smiled, and thought, *Maybe, just maybe, we can pull this off.* The main thing she remembered was his grin and light touch as he guided her out of the restaurant. Not a possessive I-own-you touch, but a soft, almost intimate gesture. *Very deft for a big man,* she supposed.

Her thoughts were pulled sharply back to the present when the door clicked open and her immediate boss, John Shepherd, walked in carrying a thick file and a cup of coffee that had gone cold long ago. There had been no time to get a fresh one. A packet of credentials hung from a lanyard around his neck. The sleeves of his white shirt with its slightly frayed collar were rolled up, and the knot of his tie hung a few inches below his neck. His slight frame was topped with short, brown hair speckled with lots of gray. His face was tightly drawn and featured a prominent jaw. His eyes were deep-set and ringed with dark circles. He was only about 45, but his pale face and air of general weariness gave him the expression of someone much older who hadn't slept in about four days.

Probably not a bad estimate, Emily thought.

He slumped down into a chair, dropped the file on the table, gave Emily an appraising look, and started slowly and absent-mindedly twisting his thin gold wedding ring. She'd learned that this was the one sure tell that he was thinking very carefully what to say. He'd picked her out of several candidates in an incoming class of recruits to become his mentee. All the recruits were smart, but there was something about her intensity and her questioning of assumptions that appealed to him. Most recruits would simply do what you told them. Not Emily. She'd question everything. You really had to convince her that what you wanted made sense. These traits didn't make her an easy employee, and many of Shepherd's colleagues found her irritating and a real pain in the ass to work with. Not Shepherd. He loved her sheer brain power and almost uncanny ability to link unconnected events into a smooth pattern that few others saw. By the time she'd left for her African assignments, their relationship had evolved into the type of honesty that's rare in any office—let alone in one of the most high-powered outfits in the country.

He took a sip of coffee, grimaced, and set the cup aside. "One of these days, I'll get a real coffee machine," he muttered.

Somehow, Emily doubted that. He didn't seem like the kind of guy who'd decorate his office with a shiny Italian coffee machine.

He flicked through the file in front of him and then focused on Emily. There was no chitchat; he got right to the main point. "Good to see you back in one piece, Emily. Got your message about meeting Lipsky." He looked up for a minute. "Tell me, how in the hell did he crack your cover so quickly?"

Emily blushed at the memory of just how easily her cover became uncovered. "A friend of someone in Viktor's network—some guy in Washington—cracked our network."

He didn't miss the reference to *Viktor*. *Be careful Emily*, he thought, *don't mix business with pleasure*. Shepherd laughed. "That little prick Sidney Hurwitz, I'll bet. The guy's a genius with a warped sense of humor. Made his name hacking into the Fed chairman's computer and charging a shitload of stuff to the man's credit card. Poor bastard didn't notice until his PA asked him how he liked his new 56" TV with surround sound. I'm not surprised he was able to get into our system." He glanced back at the file to double-check a name. "And this guy Yushenko, Oleg Yushenko, how did you find out about him? What's your impression?"

She recognized this was about as much of prompt as she was going to get. "Another one of Viktor's contacts—apparently, a former Russian soldier—came up with his name." She paused for a few seconds. "Sounds like the real deal. Got screwed by the Russian army, wife is a Syrian Christian, and they still live in Syria. But his real problem is with his son, who suffers from cystic fibrosis. He just might help us if we help him. He wants to get out of Syria and into a place where his son can get decent medical care. I need to check him out myself."

"Seems a long shot at best, but then again"—he pointed to the thick file in front of him—"Lipsky and this Yushenko just might be up to it. Other options don't jump off the page. I tend to agree that the threat of a huge pandemic is real. Exactly the kind of last resort Assad would use."

She raised her eyebrows in surprise at the size of the file.

Shepherd caught the glance and chuckled. "Oh yes, we have quite a file on Mr. Viktor Lipsky, or any of the several other names he tends to use. Busy guy, our Viktor. What did he tell you about his work?"

"Not much. Seems to focus mainly on the fundraising and organization for the arms deals. Mostly small stuff going to endangered groups all over Africa."

Shepherd grinned at this understatement and opened the file. "All true enough, but it doesn't begin to explain how he's been keeping busy for the last several years." He flicked through a few pages. "Chad, Southern Sudan, Somalia—all the hellholes of Africa. Our boy has been busy, and not just organizing. Oh yes, he has some powerful and well-funded contacts in various unlikely places. But he's also spent time at the sharp end—the very sharp end. It started with the CIA, who sent him on what was basically a suicide mission. He understandably didn't appreciate that very much. He turned the tables, took a bit of their money, and moved on rather smartly. So he's no dope." He scanned through another couple of pages. "He's even helped us from time to time." He closed the file and tapped his pen on top of it. "Basically, he's kept his nose clean, as far as I'm concerned. Unlike some of our more ideological colleagues, I tend to view Lipsky as an asset. Maybe an asset with an asterisk, but still an asset."

Emily breathed a silent sigh of relief.

They spent the next half hour reviewing the meeting in France and the one planned in Cyprus. Shepherd spread copies of the drawings of Crac des Chevaliers in front of him and examined them closely. "So you really think that the North Koreans are working in these deep underground cells trying to make the culture?"

"Everything points to it."

"Christ!" Shepherd exclaimed. "Fucking infected rats. Nuclear weapons, I can just about understand. But diseased rats? Once they're out, they're out, and they multiply rapidly. And who's to say they'll go where you want them go? Little bastards can go anywhere." He shook his head. "And you really think this scheme of yours will actually work? It sounds harebrained on the face of it."

"I'm aware of that, but unless someone comes up with a better idea, this'll have to do. Besides," she said cheerfully, "if it all goes belly-up, there's nothing to associate us with this. We can put our hands on our hearts and deny any connection. As far as we're concerned, it was just a crazy scheme dreamed up by some loony toons."

"You think anyone is going to believe that fairy tale?"

"Doesn't really matter what they think. As long as they have no proof of anything else, there's nothing they can do."

Shepherd rubbed his hands over his face and stood to leave. "Glad to see you've developed some useful cynicism, Emily." He looked at his watch. "Christ, I've gotta go to another firefighting session." He was about to open the door when he stopped and drummed his fingers on the wall. He turned abruptly back toward Emily. "Enough of this crap," he said sharply. "You know, we sometimes simply overanalyze things. We can tell you what some stupid son of bitch might do. Maybe even figure out when. But"—pent-up anger was seeping into his voice—"too often, we don't *do* a damn thing about it in time to make a difference. We don't recognize that some things simply need to be stopped— pure and simple. And this is one of those times. You get to Cyprus. Meet with this Yushenko guy and find out if he's real.

Then get back here, and we'll decide exactly what to do. If you think he's willing to help us, we'll get his son the best treatment anywhere in the world he wants to go.

"But," he cautioned, "be very careful, Emily. As I've told you before, not everyone in this agency or even in the White House agrees with what you're doing. There are some who'd be only too happy to see Assad succeed with his rats." He sat back down when he saw that Emily was about to erupt. "Look, it's no secret that parts of our so-called 'intelligence community' and our political masters are just looking for an excuse to start a war—a war that, in their minds, would *settle* the Middle East issue once and for all."

"*Have they lost their minds? Wasn't Iraq enough of a fiasco?*" Emily exploded.

Shepherd waved his hands gently in a calming motion. "For the most part, these groups have been kept on the fringe, but now I'm hearing things that indicate they could be moving into the mainstream." He pulled out his phone and looked at the calendar. "I'm due to testify before the Senate Intelligence Committee early next week. This is a closed session, and I certainly intend to bring up problem of non-official actors creating problems for us."

He got back up and had started to open the door when he turned back. "One more thing: watch your back. Lipsky can help with the dangers in front of you, but I'm more worried about the ones behind you. Deal only with me. By the way, do me one last favor," he said wearily, "try to keep the Israelis out of it. Things tend to get a little heated and complicated when squadrons of IDF [Israel Defense Forces] paratroopers descend on a place."

CHAPTER 11

Larnaca, Cyprus

About a week later, Viktor was sitting under an umbrella in front of some place called Ammos, one of the indistinguishable bars/restaurants that lined Mackenzie Beach just outside the main town of Larnaca. He stared out at the flat, empty Mediterranean Sea, wondering what the hell he'd signed up for. He hated places like this, which were filled with wannabe Eurotrash and Russians looking desperately for some place to hide their money from Putin and the tax authorities of most Western countries. For one thing, he felt desperately overdressed in his beige chinos, baggy white T-shirt, and boat shoes. All he could see around him were men in their mankinis, most of which were hidden under bulging stomachs that drooped down almost to their balls. Their well-toned women were dressed in bits of string or nothing at all. A bored, snooty waiter finally arrived with his Diet Coke, which was delivered with the sarcastic flourish of someone who feels it's beneath his dignity to serve such a lowly drink. Viktor told him he could keep the pink umbrella and straw that came with the drink.

It was hot, much hotter than Telos at this time of year. The air was still, without a breath of wind. The usual tantalizing scents of a Mediterranean island were overpowered with the cloying smells of various suntan lotions and the thick clouds of big, powerful cigars smoked by the chubby, balding men as they balanced their "nieces" on their knees. Viktor wondered why in hell he'd agreed to meet Emily here, of all places. Viktor's mood wasn't improving as he sipped his rapidly warming Diet Coke while getting a headache from the loud *thump, thump* of the techno music and the incessant buzzing of the endless stream of motor scooters buzzing up and down Piale Pasha. He wondered how many of the sunbathers even recognized the irony of frolicking beside a major road named after the Ottoman admiral who conquered Cyprus back in 1570. The thought of a few of their heads impaled and displayed on Ottoman spears brought a wicked smile to his face. A light tap on his shoulder brought him out of this semi-trance, and he whirled around ready for hostile action. His eyes opened wide and his fist stayed half-cocked as he stared at what was in front of him.

"Sweet Jesus!" he exclaimed. "What happened to you?"

The Emily Wilkins in front of him had been transformed from the eager agent dressed in oversized cargo pants and loose denim shirts to something that had just emerged languidly from the sea as the drops of water flowed down and around her generous curves.

"Viktor," she declared with a giggle, "you have to get out more. Haven't you ever seen a woman in a bikini before?" She pulled up a lounger next to him and wiggled provocatively onto it, placing a small shoulder bag next to her.

The overweight Russian in the next lounger unceremoniously dumped his niece on the sand as he turned and stared open-mouthed at Emily, a cigar balanced delicately on his lower lip. This time the waiter hustled over without delay. He took her order for a frappé cappuccino with a big smile.

"Well, I'll give you this much: you certainly know how to make an entrance. Any minute now, that poor bastard next to us is going to have a heart attack." Viktor's smirk spread wider at the thought.

She leaned over quickly, grabbed his arm, and gave him a warm kiss on the cheek. "Then I guess I'll have let him know I'm already spoken for," she said coyly.

"Bad choice." Viktor laughed. "I'm sure he can pay more than I can."

"Bastard. I'm going for a swim. Aren't you coming? It's boiling."

He merely held out his baggy T-shirt. "Awkward. My friend Walther is with me."

"Walter? Who the hell is Walter?" Then it dawned on her. "Oh, *that* Walther. Size 38, I take it."

He merely nodded.

"Isn't that overdoing it just a little?"

"This is Cyprus," he said simply. "Operating territory for just about every spook, arms dealer, crook, traitor, terrorist, and mercenary in the world. Think of it as sort of a terrorist R&R retreat. Even they need to take a break from the *jihadi* front from time to time. Cypriots turn a blind eye as long as they keep the faltering Cypriot banks full. Discreet assassinations are OK, but mass murder is frowned upon. If things get hot, just hop over to the Turkish side where there's no extradition." He patted her playfully on her well-formed ass and told her to go for her swim. "Put the Russian out of his misery. Let him ogle you going into the water and coming out like Ursula Andress in *Dr. No*."

***

Later, while lying under the oversized umbrella, she brought up the subject he'd been hoping she'd skip. She turned on her side and inched her lounger slightly closer to him. "Tell me, something, Viktor. Don't mind me; I'm just curious. Did you leave Michigan State planning to become a big deal international arms merchant? Or did you sort of fall of into it?"

Christ, he hated these questions. What was important for him was the here and now—what was in front of him, not behind him. That was gone, etched in the pages of history. The last thing he needed or wanted was some half-baked analysis. *That fucking Freud has a lot to answer for.*

"The dental plan," he answered simply.

Emily sat up sharply. "The what? You set up an international arms dealing company because of the *dental plan*? Get serious."

"Why don't you tell the whole world," he snapped as her sharp tones carried down the beach. "Look, it just sort of happened, OK?" Then he gave her the edited version of meeting with Davies and his wife, and how one thing led to another.

Emily wouldn't be brushed off so easily. "So what exactly do you do? Do you actually use these weapons you provide? That's got to be pretty hairy."

He laughed at this. "No, no. I leave most of that to Ricky and his crew. They know what they're doing. I'd only be a drag. I just sort of make sure the cash gets where it's supposed to go." He picked up his glass and finished off the last of the by-now lukewarm Diet Coke. "So, you see, this is nothing special. No running around firing off AK-47s; no dramatic rescue missions. More bookkeeping really."

Emily snorted. She knew there was more to it than that. He didn't get those nicks and scars sitting in small meeting rooms, but she also knew he wasn't going to say much more right now. So she changed the subject: "Assuming Assad's people really are using the Crac des Chevaliers as a factory to make that culture, have you come up with any brilliant insights about how to stop them, and how to get in and destroy their little lab?"

"You mean insights that involve me getting out again in one piece?"

"Of course," she answered a little too quickly. "We're not planning a suicide mission."

Viktor raised his eyebrows in response. "No, of course not," he said sarcastically. "Sergei sent over a ton of stuff about the Crac, but right now, I don't have any brilliant plans. I can list a lot of problems, but I'm not sure of the answers. I'm hoping Yushenko can provide some of them." He counted off on his fingers. "The normal entrance is impossible. An air assault won't work for a lot of reasons, and we have no idea exactly where this lab is. We also have to do all this without Assad ever knowing who really screwed up his little Armageddon. Plus," he added as an afterthought, "we also can't expect any help from your new best friends—the Russians. And I wouldn't bet the house on there being full support from the American side either. Right now, our main hope is Yushenko. Without his agreement and help, this is all fantasy."

"Speaking of Yushenko, any ideas how we find him?"

"Church of St. Lazarus." Viktor glanced at his watch. "He goes there every day around 2 p.m. when he's in Cyprus." He nodded his head behind them. "We should get going. It's just over a mile east of here."

She reached into her bag and pulled out a pair of cargo pants and the familiar denim shirt, which she shimmied into. Then she carefully zipped the bag and slipped into a pair of sandals. "Walking or riding?"

"Walking. It's easier to keep an eye on anyone showing too much interest."

***

About half an hour later, they showed up at the wide square in front of the Byzantine-era church. After cautiously surveying the surrounding coffee houses and tourist shops filled with plastic Chinese-made souvenirs of the Virgin Mary and Baby Jesus, they approached the entrance, where they could smell the incense filtering out from inside the church.

The interior of the church was cool, and a sand-filled brass container resting on a stand had several thin, still-burning votive candles stuck in it. There was no sound except for the constant buzz of motor scooters muted by the thick walls. A ray of sunlight reflected off the gold-plated iconostasis, and dust motes danced in the soft beams of light that played gently over the center of the church. Viktor and Emily stood quietly at the back, letting their eyes adjust to the dim light as they surveyed the interior. Then they each dropped a euro into the slot, took a candle from the rack, put it into the container, and lit the small wick. There was no sense standing out any more than they already did. A black-clad elderly woman was kneeling painfully on her arthritic knees in front of the iconostasis, apparently asking for blessings for long-departed friends and family. Finally, Viktor raised his chin in the direction of the far corner. There, almost hidden in the shadows, a solitary man was sitting in one of the church chairs, which was much too small for him. His head was bowed, and his hands resting on the back of the chair in front of him were tightly clasped in prayer. His black hair was closely cropped, and a thin leather jacket was stretched tight across his bulky shoulders.

Viktor leaned close to Emily. "Must be our man," he said softly.

She nodded and gestured that they should wait by the main door. "Give him his peace. There's no rush," she whispered.

They waited behind one of the pillars until the man got up, crossed himself, and started toward the main door.

Viktor took one look at him and noticed the heavy, dark bags under his eyes. He nodded at Emily and stepped from behind the pillar as the man passed. "Lieutenant Yushenko," he said softly but clearly in Russian.

Yushenko whirled around ready for a fight. His black eyes were blazing with fury at this intrusion into his moment of solitude—this last, almost forlorn hope for his son. "Who the fuck are you?" he snarled. "Did that asshole Rostov send you?"

he asked, referring to the colonel whose jaw he'd broken. He looked like he was about to do the same to Viktor, who took a step back and raised his hands in surrender.

"No, no. Nothing like that," Viktor tried to assure him. "We think we might be able to help you if you give us a minute." He gestured to one of the nearby coffee shops and suggested they might want to head over there for a cup of coffee.

Yushenko looked at him warily, and then seemed to notice Emily standing next to him. He calculated that Viktor was unlikely to do anything in public, especially with this woman next to him. He inclined his head slightly, indicating he'd at least listen to them.

They went across to the nearest coffee shop, sat down, ordered their coffees, and waited for the server to disappear. Emily looked closely at the two men while waiting for the coffee. They were so alike in many ways: large, fit, and with the same rugged Slavic faces with high cheek bones, black eyes, and black hair. The only difference was that Yushenko's hair was cropped short in military fashion, while Viktor's was long and thick—hanging almost to his collar. Yushenko's eyes were also burdened with sizable bags, while Viktor's skin was taut over his prominent facial bones. But then Viktor wasn't unemployed and didn't have a child with cystic fibrosis. She could sense the men weighing each other up, and quietly but alertly waiting for the other to make the opening move. Any fight would be pretty much an even match. Yushenko was sitting with slightly belligerent body language, wondering just what he was doing there. Trying to judge just how far to go with this conversation, Viktor seemed completely relaxed. She was about to break the silence with some smart remark, but then she remembered a bit of advice from her training course: *Don't be in a hurry. Don't break the silence. You don't always have to show that you're the smartest kid in class.*

Finally, Yushenko ended the stalemate. "First question: who

are you? You Russian? What do you want with the *ex*-senior lieutenant Oleg Yushenko?"

"I'm Viktor. And no, I'm not Russian," he confirmed simply.

"But you speak Russian. Israeli? That's it! That's all I need to have the fucking Israelis on my back."

Again, Viktor merely shook his head.

Then the coffees arrived with a small dish of pastries, and all conversation ceased until the server disappeared again.

Yushenko sipped the thick coffee, nibbled at the pastries, and then snapped his fingers. "I get it." He smiled mirthlessly. "You're goddamned Americans. CIA." He was about to head off into a tirade about how he was still a good soldier, would never, ever work with the CIA, and would never, ever betray his men, when Viktor held up his hand to stop him in mid-stride.

Viktor neatly side-stepped the nationality issue. "Relax, I'm not with any American agency. I'm on my own. I have no intention of working against any of your comrades," he tried to reassure Yushenko and hunched forward over the table. "But I *am* in a position to help you and your family."

Yushenko jerked his head up. "What are you talking about?" he barked. "What do you know about my family?" He got up and was about to leave.

Viktor put his hand on Yushenko's arm. "Sit down and hear us out. *How* we know about your son's illness isn't important. What *is* important is that we can help. We may be able to get you and your family out of Syria and put you in a place with the right kind of care for your son. Now do you want that help or not?"

Yushenko grudgingly sat back down. He needed this help. Where it came from was less important than the assistance itself. He nodded toward Emily. "Who's the bimbo? Why bring her along?"

Viktor felt Emily bristle. Before she could hit the roof, he quickly intervened. "This is Emily, and she's the one who's going to deliver the help your son needs. Be nice."

Their coffees had gotten cold by the time Viktor finished explaining what they'd learned about Assad's efforts in biological warfare. Emily called the waiter and ordered some more coffee and an extra helping of the pastries. Yushenko didn't say anything during the recitation, but he let out a low whistle when they came to the effect of the infected rats.

"They wanted to test the cultures in a place far removed from major population centers. We're guessing they loaded up a truck with a lot of infected rats and drove it far away from where they were making the cultures. The southern part of the country fit the bill perfectly. If some of the rats made their way into Jordan or, better yet, Israel, so much the better," Viktor explained.

Then the new round of coffee came, and Viktor interrupted the narrative while the young waiter carefully put the small cups and plates of pastries on the round table. The kid had heard enough Russian during a normal day to understand they were speaking Russian, but he couldn't really understand too much. His uncle who owned the coffee shop had drilled into his head the importance of becoming part of the background and ignoring what customers were saying.

"Trust me, Niko," he told his nephew, "On this island, it never pays to know too much. Just keep your head down, keep your mouth shut, and do your job."

When Viktor had finished his explanation they all sat back and drank some coffee.

Yushenko picked up the conversation. "Given what I saw in the area during the last few months I was there, what you say makes some sense. Assad's people wouldn't let anyone near the Crac—not even us, their so-called 'allies.' My wife's family lives in the village near the fortress. One day, her father said that certain parts of the town right under the fort were suddenly placed off limits. No explanation. Just a lot of guards.

"If what you say is true, this is very bad stuff. Assad has clearly slipped his leash and is into something that will cause the war to spread all over this already volatile region. But I'm not quite sure why you're telling me. What can I do about it?"

"It might be possible to help each other," Emily answered. "How much of a risk are you willing to take to get out of Syria with your family? You see, this must be solved without the world and its mother learning about it. The only people we want to get the message are Assad and the guy in North Korea. Your Russian mates know about it, but they don't want to be part of the solution." When she saw Yushenko start to back off she moved quickly to reassure him. "Actually, you don't really have to do much at all. Even if you could convince your former employers, I doubt very much they'd move in time—even if they wanted to move at all. No, we need your help at the right time to get Viktor, here, into Syria undetected. We also need any information you can get about manpower at the fort. How many guards? What's their rotation? Are they any good?"

Yushenko scoffed at the idea. "You don't ask much, do you? With the war, it's not easy getting into the country, let alone out of it. Yeah, maybe somewhere along the Turkish or Iraqi border, but that would involve a lot of different groups, most of whom don't speak to each other. And those options are a long way from the Crac."

"Actually, we were thinking of Damascus."

Yushenko sputtered and nearly choked on his coffee. "Are you shitting me? Damascus airport isn't exactly flooded with foreign passengers these days. He'll stand out like a beacon announcing that he's an American spy."

"Not if he's with you, wearing the uniform of a senior Russian officer with all the right papers."

"You're out of your mind, lady. Where's he going to get exactly the right uniform with exactly the right badges and insignia of rank saying he is who he says he is and that he has the right to be in Damascus?"

Emily gave him her sweetest smile. "That, my friend, is up

to you. The next time you come back to Cyprus, you bring one of the uniforms of a Russian unit in Syria. He has to look real."

"Not with that hair," Yushenko grinned, pointing at Viktor's nonmilitary haircut.

"OK, the hair goes."

Viktor winced at the thought of becoming essentially bald.

"Even with a haircut and the right uniform, it's not easy getting past the VP."

"VP?" Emily asked. "What the hell is the VP?"

"*Voennaya politsiya*," Viktor interjected. "Russian military police."

"They're all over the place. Always checking orders and transit papers. It's not just the uniform. The real pain in the ass is that he'll need real papers, or at least as real as you can make them." Yushenko sat back and drummed his fingers on the table.

Emily was pleased that he seemed to be getting into the plan.

"Better make him navy. He could be returning from a routine trip to Cyprus and going back to the main naval base at Tartus." He looked at Emily and Viktor and shrugged his shoulders. "At least it gets him in the right direction toward the Crac."

It was Viktor's turn to drum his fingers on the table. This whole effort sounded half-assed to him. He hated loose ends, and this was nothing but a mass of loose ends. It all depended on Yushenko. He looked steadily at the former lieutenant. "Look, we need to know. Are you really going to do this or not? If you're *in,* you've got to be 100% *in*—no changing your mind halfway through. I don't need to show up in Damascus only to be arrested by your people, or worse, Assad's people. There's no harm in backing out now, but it'd be a real problem later. So, Lieutenant, what's it going to be? In? Or out?"

Yushenko said nothing for several minutes. He just played with his coffee cup and picked at the crumbs of the pastries. He really didn't want to get involved, but then he thought of his family. They were caught in a pincer. They despised Assad, but they feared the *jihadi*s and ISIS even more. As Christians who'd benefited under the Assad regime, they'd be the first casualties of a new regime. Also, he wasn't the only one being penalized for slugging his superior officer. What chance did his son now have? None in Syria, but maybe a chance in a place with a real hospital and doctors who knew what they were doing. His wife had gone from a position of some respect in the community to being almost an outcast. She had to go back to her family's home near the Crac des Chevaliers. *She's a smart woman,* he thought, *and trained as a nurse. She could adapt to life in another country—maybe even relax in a country where most of the people are at least nominally Christian.* In the end, he had no real choice. He had to go along with these people.

"OK," he said. "I'm in—*if* you can guarantee safety for my family and treatment for my son, Yuri." He stared hard at Viktor, who gestured toward Emily with a look that said *no bullshitting now. Yes or No. Binary choice.* She nodded her agreement.

"Done," she said in the definite tone of someone who can actually deliver on a promise. "We pay our debts. Pull this off and you can name your relocation country." She offered up a silent prayer that she was right.

"Fine. One step at a time. You"—Viktor nodded toward Yushenko—"go back to Syria, and we'll see you back here in a couple of weeks. Don't try to contact us," he cautioned. "Behave normally. Take no risks. You don't need to tip anyone off. We'll be here, in the same place."

"What are you going to do while I'm back in Syria?" Yushenko questioned.

"Some research to see if this whole idea just may be possible—or completely nuts."

Yushenko nodded his agreement and got up to go to a pharmacy.

Emily turned to Viktor and waggled her fingers back and forth: maybe yes, maybe no.

"You're right. Nothing is certain, but he's the best—the only—hope we have. Can your people really get him and his family out of the mess he's in?"

"I'll return to Washington and do my best. My guess is that they'll go along at least on a conditional basis. If he comes through and the lab is destroyed, then he'll get everything he wants. If not..." She shrugged at that outcome. "Let's hope it doesn't come to that." She patted his arm and got up to head back to the airport. "I'll let you know how it goes. I should know in a day or two." With that, she left.

Viktor picked up his phone and called Davies to tell him about the meeting with Yushenko.

"Guy sounds real," Davies said. "Not too early to start our planning."

Viktor agreed and suggested that Davies make his way to Telos to start the planning.

CHAPTER 12

Telos, Aegean Sea

Viktor's spirits rose the minute he stepped off the ferry ramp back onto Telos. Infected rats, impregnable medieval fortresses, and shadowy North Korean scientists all seemed a very long way away. The so-called "plan," which had seemed plausible on Cyprus, now seemed full of holes. He was determined to put it behind him until Davies arrived. Waving greetings as he walked through the square and headed up toward his house, he thought he'd have dinner at Maria's to catch up on events in town and maybe have a game of chess with the judge. He was resigned to letting him win again, but the old boy was good company.

***

Three days later, Viktor was back down in the square with his usual coffee and waiting for the ferry. This time, he smiled as the familiar figure of Ricky Davies strode down the ramp, dressed in his usual T-shirt, camo pants, and combat boots. The floppy hat and wraparound sunglasses completed the picture. Slung casually over one shoulder was a large backpack.

Viktor grabbed his friend by the shoulders and laughed. "Glad to see you're wearing your fancy traveling gear."

"Oh yeah. Desta made damn sure they was washed and ironed before I set out on this expedition about three days ago." He surveyed the surroundings with a practiced eye. "You do know how to drop off the radar. God hisself would have trouble finding this place."

The sight of a wiry, tough-looking man dressed for combat walking easily beside the known quantity of the man they knew as Aleco Kalistos caused more than a few quizzical eyebrows to be raised by the locals as the two men tramped across the square and up the path to Viktor's house. Along the way, Viktor filled Davies in on the meeting with Yushenko.

Davies merely grunted his acknowledgment and got right to the point: "Could help, but it all depends on your girlfriend."

When they got to the house, he reached down and pulled several packages of Ethiopian coffee from his backpack. "Figured you might like some of the good stuff. Why don't we go inside and have some of this while you show me some of them plans your Frenchman gave you?"

Viktor busied himself making coffee while Davies spread copies of the old Crac des Chevaliers plans across the table. Davies pulled out from a pocket a crumpled package of Ethiopian cigarettes and a lighter made from a rifle cartridge. He lit a cigarette, and as he inhaled a lungful of nicotine, he scrutinized the plans with a professional eye.

Two cigarettes later, he turned to Viktor. "I'll say this much. Them sumbitches knew what they were doing back in the day. No fuckin' way was any medieval army gonna break into that baby. Even a modern army ain't gonna find it real easy." He pointed a nicotine-stained forefinger at the drawings. "But you, you clever bastard, you found a way in, didn't you? Right up this here tunnel goin' from the fort to the water." He looked at Viktor and let out a laugh. "There's only one problem. You taken a good look at this so-called 'tunnel'? Noticed it ain't real big? If these drawings are halfway accurate, ain't no way in hell you or that big fuckin' Russian are gonna get up that thing. Look at it, man," he ordered. "You could just about fit your head in there, but then the rest of you gets stuck with your ass hanging out. You'd be lucky to get back out again. It just ain't made for big-time college football players."

Viktor took another look at the drawings. "Fuck! How could we miss that?" was all he could say. All their hopes of an easy entry had just disappeared.

Davies simply laughed. "Relax, Viktor. I didn't say it wasn't a plan. Fact is, it's the only plan I can see. You got that part right. You wanna get in there and wipe out those labs. I get that. But you ain't the one to pull that part of it off."

"OK, who is?"

Davies made a fist and pointed his thumb at his chest. "Me."

Viktor tried to hide the surprise in his voice. He failed. "You? Christ Almighty, Ricky, how do you figure that?"

"Simple. You're what, 6'3"? And must weigh about 220 lbs. No way you're getting in that tunnel. Me, I'm maybe 5'8" and a skinny 160 lbs. I can just about fit. Guess I'm the best you got to climb up that thing and do the job."

"Alone?" Viktor asked, skeptical about Davies's chances.

"Naw, I'll bring one of the boys. Figure this is something Arlo would like. Right up his alley. He's the right size. More important, he's a mean sumbitch in a fight. Good man to have at your side." He paused for a minute. "Besides, he's got another skill that's gonna be real important."

Viktor still couldn't believe that Davies was serious. Now the problem of getting him into Syria was doubled with Arlo. Just how the hell was that supposed to work?

"Look, Ricky, I don't want to get all negative here, but assuming we can get you into the place, how the hell do we get you and Arlo—along with the rest of us—out? Me and Oleg can sort of bluff our way. But you and Arlo? No way," he said, shaking his head.

Davies chortled. "Don't be such a damned pessimist, Viktor." He pulled the fortress diagrams toward Viktor. "See how nice and flat it is on the inside? Perfect helo pad. Now I'm guessing that Assad's guys use choppers to ferry their North Korean guests in and out of that place. Don't want too many people to see 'em and figure out what's goin' on deep inside."

"OK, so what? Even if you're right, how's that help us?"

Davies slapped him on the back. "Ol' Arlo is a man of many talents. I ain't bringin' him along for his good looks. He's a helluva helo pilot. Flew damn near 50 missions all over Afghanistan. Absolutely fuckin' nuts, he is. But the sumbitch can fly anything with rotors or wings. He's our ticket out of there."

"That's a hell of gamble. What if they don't use helos?"

"Well, see, that's where your girlfriend comes in again…"

Viktor opened his mouth to reassure Davies that Emily wasn't his girlfriend.

However, Davies cut him off before he could say anything: "Don't get all excited, Viktor. Just a figure of speech. She's kinda cute, though. Desta likes her, even though she's a two-faced liar." He gave Viktor an appraising look, suggesting that maybe it was time he did in fact find someone. "Anyways, I was thinkin' maybe you could get her to ask her boss—real politely—to reposition a satellite over that part of Syria. Maybe take a picture or two. Without, of course, sayin' anything about the real target. Hell, I'm damn sure they've got a sky full of satellites over that place. We just wanna borrow one for a few seconds. Should be a piece of cake," he said innocently. "Sure would be nice to get some idea of what's waitin' for me when I pop out of that damn tunnel wearin' not much more than a jockstrap and a sharp knife."

Viktor went outside and checked his watch. He saw it was just about 7 a.m. in Washington, and so Emily should be at the office. He pulled out his encrypted satellite phone and punched in her numbers.

She answered after four rings. "Figured it was you. I don't get many calls at this hour. How are things with the olives and oranges?"

"They're fine. Trees are still waiting to be pruned."

She noticed he sounded distracted. "What's up, Viktor? I'm supposed to meet with Shepherd in a couple of hours, and I don't need last-minute problems."

"No, no," he hastened to assure her. "There's just a couple of things you might be able to help us with."

"Such as?" she asked warily.

"Well, Ricky's here. After looking at the diagrams, he pointed out a couple of things we overlooked. Number one, there's no way I or Yushenko can get up that tunnel. The Crusaders were a lot smaller than we are. We'll never fit."

"Shit, oh shit! There goes that idea."

"Don't get all negative here. I didn't say it wasn't a good idea, but we're not the ones to do it. Ricky figures he and maybe one or two of his team can make it."

"This is suddenly getting much more complicated."

"Not really, but we need some more information that maybe your boss can provide. Basically, we need a look inside that fortress to see what's waiting for us. How many men? Is there a helicopter landing pad? Things a satellite could pick up easily."

Emily groaned. "A helicopter landing pad? That's your way in and out? And just where do you plan on getting a helicopter? Are you two out of your mind? And now I'm supposed to arrange a few satellite pictures. Is that all?"

"Not the whole orbit, simply a slight detour. No one will notice."

"So now my day just got more interesting. First, I have to convince my boss to give Yushenko what he wants. Second, I have to convince him to give us satellite coverage."

"Look, if you want us to deal with that lab, this is cheap at twice the price. Just get the goddamned pictures and let us do the worrying."

"All right, all right. Keep your shirt on. I'll see what I can do."

Viktor clicked off the phone and stood there for a minute looking out toward the orchard but not really seeing anything. Various scenarios were flashing instantaneously through his mind, and the more he thought about Davies's plan, the more convinced he was that they were going to need some specialized help—help they could really count on. He took a deep breath and made another call on the encrypted phone—a kind of break-the-glass-in-an-emergency call.

The man who answered the call wasn't surprised to hear from Viktor. After all, they'd done a bit of business before without any problems. He listened patiently while Viktor outlined what they *might* need. He pulled a slim fountain pen and an elegant, small notepad from the inside pocket of his handmade suit, jotted down a few figures, and said they should meet to discuss this further. There were details that were best left out of a telephone conversation. Viktor explained he was going to Cyprus soon and they could meet there. That would be fine, the man said, as long as they could find a place removed from all the intelligence agencies on the island.

Viktor ended the call, put the phone back in his pocket, and went inside.

Davies, still in front of the bookcase, raised his eyebrows in a question.

Viktor waggled his hand back and forth. "Emily's going to call back with an answer. Look, Ricky, even if we get satellite coverage, we'll still have a few problems. Like how do we get you and Arlo into Syria? And how do we deal with the guards? You know, a few things like that."

"Workin' on it, Viktor; workin' on it. As Desta keeps tellin' me, the Lord will provide."

"Let's hope He's not busy with other projects."

***

Two hours later, Viktor's phone buzzed. He swiftly pulled it out of his pocket and pushed the accept-call button.

It was Emily. "You're in luck, Viktor. First, we can assure Yushenko he'll get the help he needs. Second, it turns out we already had a bird over the area. It wasn't a big deal to shift it a few degrees west to get a shot of your fortress. There's one problem, though."

"And what problem would that be?" he snapped.

"We can't release that satellite information to non-government agents; i.e., you and your friends."

"*What the fuck?*" he exploded. "You know we're on the same team here."

"Try telling that to the people I work with—the people who control things such as satellite feeds. Anyway, my boss and I came up with an easy solution."

"And what's that?"

"I come along as guardian of the information."

"Emily," he groaned. "That's really a shitty idea. This isn't like handing out clean water and food to hungry children. These are really nasty people who'd love to get their hands on someone like you."

She bristled at the put-down. "I can take care of myself, thank you very much," she snapped emphatically. "I'll see you in Cyprus with the satellite feeds." She ended the call abruptly.

"Good call, was it?" Davies asked innocently.

"The good news is we get the pictures. The bad news is she's the one who's bringing them to us. She says she has to be part of the plan if we're going to use classified NSA information."

Davies didn't seem upset at the news. "She's smart and can handle herself. If that's the deal, that's the deal. We'll just work with it."

Viktor didn't think it was that simple at all, but he knew Davies well enough to know when more discussion was a waste of time. "Fine, but I really do hope the good Lord is listening when you call about getting into Syria."

Before Viktor could add anything, Davies suggest they go back inside and boot up Viktor's computer. Once they'd done so, and after pulling up a map of the area around Crac des Chevaliers, Davies spent the next several minutes explaining to a stunned Viktor just how he and Arlo were going to make their entry. When he'd finished, Viktor just sat back in his chair and whistled quietly. Then he laughed.

"You know this is nuts, but it certainly has the surprise element. I'll give you that."

"Well, now that that's settled." Davies chuckled. "All you gotta do is round up the delivery system."

***

Alexandria, Virginia

Emily's call to Telos was followed almost instantly by a call from the contractor's NSA contact to the anonymous office in Alexandria. That call was in turn instantly patched through to a retired colonel working for Cougar, who was told about the request to reposition a satellite over the Crac des Chevaliers.

"Son of a bitch," he exploded. "Who in Christ's name requested this? And who in hell approved it?"

The NSA contact said the request had come from an agent named Emily Wilkins and was approved by her boss, John Shepherd.

"Shepherd, I know about. Who the hell is Wilkins?"

"One of Shepherd's people. Promoted way above her station and sent on all sorts of special missions all over Africa. Before you ask, I have no idea how she stumbled on to the operation at the Crac," the contact preempted.

"OK," the colonel answered tersely. "I'll deal with this. You keep your mouth shut. Say nothing to anyone. Understand?"

When the NSA contact murmured his understanding, the colonel placed another call to his boss, who was working in Cougar's office.

"How the hell did this happen? You were supposed to have all that information locked tight," General Meadows fumed. "Any way you can stop that repositioning without calling too much attention to the area?" When told it was too late to cancel the satellite move, the general sat back in his chair and drummed his fingers on the thick wooden arm as his expression darkened.

"I hope you appreciate, Colonel, that this is a major fuck-up and a real threat to everything we've planned. How they found out is irrelevant. We have to stop it—now." He rubbed a big hand over his craggy face. "It gets worse, Colonel. This Shepherd guy you mentioned, well, it turns out one of our contacts on the staff of the Senate Intelligence Committee says Shepherd is due to testify in a closed hearing sometime next week. That will blow everything wide open. I want you to deal with this problem, you understand?"

The colonel paused, realizing the implications of the general's words. "Yessir, I understand. Any preferences on method?"

"Do what you always do, Colonel. Adapt and improvise. But," he added, "no trails. Nothing leading anywhere near us."

"Understood. What about the girl?"

"Nothing for now. Shepherd's the real threat. Just follow her and make damn sure she don't cause any more problems."

CHAPTER 13

Jerusalem, Israel

The midday sun was just warming the courtyard of the American Colony Hotel in Jerusalem, which wasn't far from the Damascus Gate leading through the walls of Suleyman the Magnificent into the old city. Mulberry trees were dotted around the courtyard. Sitting at one of the corner tables was a thin man wearing a thick, brown tweed coat whose shoulders were dotted with dandruff. A woolen scarf was draped casually around his thin neck, and he pulled the coat tighter around him—like someone still not used to the chill that can descend on Jerusalem at this time of year. His face bore the scars of childhood acne, and his prominent nose hooked over his thick mustache. With his thick, black glasses and very old flat cap, he looked like a recently arrived refugee. If the eyes are indeed the window to one's soul, the shutters on Benny Perlman's windows were tightly closed. His dark eyes constantly scanned the immediate environment like a mini radar screen—only receiving information and transmitting nothing. His wide mouth was downturned in the permanent skepticism of one who's witnessed—and often participated in—just about every sort of deceit, ignorance, and brutality that men—and women—can inflict on each other. Nothing much surprised him anymore. But then, that small piece of the world he'd known—and in many ways, helped to shape—had left him without much optimism about the future.

Binyamin—"Benny" to his very few friends—Perlman had been hearing those comments about his appearance since arriving in Israel from Baghdad in the 1950s. He still thought Moses had played a cruel trick on Jews by calling this rocky, unproductive outcrop the Promised Land. "Forty years," he'd often lament to himself. "Forty years of wandering in the fucking desert, and the best you can come up with is Jerusalem? Promised Land? Who are you kidding? Barren, rocky, and cold in the winter. What was wrong with Baghdad?" he'd ask anyone who'd listen.

The weather was better, and compared to what they called food in Israel, the Iraqi cuisine was heaven on earth. What Benny may have lacked in dress sense and personal charm, however, he more than made up for in a rare combination of intelligence, cynicism, pragmatism, curiosity, and sheer guile. He was a loyal Israeli but a very secular Jew. Growing up in Baghdad, he'd lived with and played with too many Muslims and followers of the other diverse ancient religions that populated pre-Saddam Iraq to agree with the rigid Ultra-Orthodox Jews so prominent in modern Israel.

He also got annoyed with those Israelis who thought the country was merely an eastern appendage to the culture and lifestyle of Europe or the United States. "We are not Frenchmen or Americans," he'd insist. "We are Middle Eastern! If you really want to protect the State of Israel, you *must* understand that. *Understand* your enemies. I'm not asking you to invite them to your kid's *bar mitzvah,* but you *must* understand them. Think like someone from this area, act like someone from this area, and for God's sake, speak like someone from this area." He'd drum this into the heads of new recruits into Israel's intelligence agency, Mossad, in which he'd risen to become deputy director.

Despite, or perhaps because of, his Arab background, Benny had proved invaluable in confronting Israel's enemies over the years. "It takes an Arab to think like an Arab," he'd declare with a laugh.

Now in semi-retirement—though you never really retire from spy craft—he was sitting there in a chilly courtyard, smoking his *hookah*, because he smelled trouble. His famous large nostrils were twitching, and he was just now starting to try to put all the subtle, wispy hints together in some sort of order. Unofficial contacts he'd developed over the years had recently been in touch with vague warnings. Any halfway competent intelligence agent gets such hints every day, and most of them are just someone trying to inflate his own importance with tales of imminent horrors not seen since the destruction of the Temple. But this time, Benny sensed real danger and couldn't pin down where it was coming from. There wasn't yet enough to take to Mossad. He needed to know more. From time to time, he'd glance at a ragged piece of paper and thin package of photographs in his hand and frown in concentration. He was of a generation that hated computers and had never had an email address. He'd never heard of Instagram, Facebook, or any of the other means of instantly communicating useless information. No, he was a paper-and-pencil man. The spoken—whispered—word was best of all. That way, you can see the guy's face, read his eyes, and tell how much is bullshit and how much just might have a figment of truth. But in this case, the spoken word wasn't possible, and electronic communication was just an invitation for every snot-nosed kid from here to Los Angeles to learn what you're saying. So this crumpled piece of paper, passed through several hands, and the photographs were the best he was going to get. Still, it was enough to worry him. Sometimes in this business, things don't go smoothly from one step to another. You never have 100% knowledge. But at least he could try to reduce his ignorance.

Avram Bronstein entered the courtyard and was surprised to see Perlman sitting outside. Where Perlman was rumpled and haggard-looking, Bronstein was tidy and clean shaven, wore a handmade black suit, starched white shirt, and had short, brown hair parted neatly down the right side. His one concession to fashion was to wear a light-blue tie with white dots on it. Being thin and a little on the short side, Bronstein had a pale face with expressionless eyes that gave nothing away. Essentially, he looked like a very successful accountant—which in fact he was. Trim, with concise movements that never drew attention, he was also essentially anonymous. That's what endeared him to Perlman because he sometimes ran errands for the old man when someone discreet with no official ties to Mossad was required.

Perlman acknowledged his presence by lifting his chin and motioning to the empty chair at the table. Bronstein walked quickly over to the table, used his pocket handkerchief to wipe dust off the chair, and sat down. He noticed Perlman was bundled up. "Always a pleasure to see you, Benny, but why are you freezing your ass off out here? Let's go inside."

Perlman pointed to the *hookah*. "Fucking Nazis won't let you smoke inside." He leaned over the table and almost whispered. "Besides, who the hell knows who could be listening in there. I counted at least three spooks from different agencies in there."

Bronstein thought the old man was exaggerating, but then again, with his record, maybe not.

Perlman gestured with his hands toward the lobby of the hotel. "See if those *Gauleiters* in there can scare up a couple of decent cups of coffee. Not the shit that comes out of those machines," he insisted. "I mean real coffee—Arab coffee—with lots of cardamom. Ask the Arab kid, Khalid. He knows what he's doing." As Bronstein headed for the door, Perlman shouted after him: "*Don't be tight. Give the kid a decent tip.*" He laughed.

A few minutes later, a beaming young Khalid came out with

two steaming coffees balanced carefully on a swinging copper tray. He placed them gently on the table along with two bits of *lokum*.

Perlman smiled and patted Khalid on the arm. "Şukran, Khalid. You didn't forget the *lokum*. Remember me to your parents."

The boy grinned widely and hustled back inside.

"Good kid," Perlman said to no one in particular. "He'll go far… if we can keep this fucking place from exploding."

He fumbled inside his voluminous overcoat and brought out three photographs, which he held against his chest like a card player. Before starting the discussion, Perlman savored the rich coffee and took a sip. He grunted in satisfaction. "That shit will raise the dead." He gave a dry chuckle. "At least we're in the right place for that. Anyway, Avram, I didn't call you out here to enjoy the charms of chilly Jerusalem in April. I'm hearing things I don't really like from Syria and Cyprus. And by the way, I don't much like some of the shit I'm hearing from some of our own people, but more on that later."

"So what's new, Benny? Those assholes in Syria are always up to something." Bronstein had worked with Perlman long enough not to immediately question the last part of his comment about problems at home.

"No, this seems different. Nothing I can put my finger on yet, but I don't like the vibes I'm getting." He touched his prodigious nose to emphasize those mysterious *vibes* and then pulled one picture from the three he was holding and dropped it on the table. "Know him?"

Bronstein blinked in surprise. It was a front-on picture of Viktor taken in Cyprus. "Yeah. That's Viktor Lipsky. We've done a few deals together. He's a relatively straight shooter—pardon the pun—for a gunrunner. From time to time, we put up the money, and he supplies weapons to enemies of our enemies all over Africa. It's worked out fairly well so far. No blowback on us. He's part of a small organization run by a very smart, very determined woman out of Addis Ababa."

Perlman sat up in surprise. "One of ours?" he asked, meaning one of the Ethiopian Jewish tribes.

"No, no," Bronstein assured him. "Orthodox Christian. Simply someone who got sick and tired of seeing her people gunned down by roving bands of thugs. She married a former Delta Force guy who kept his squad together after he left the service. They do the heavy lifting on some of the 'defense' operations." He paused for a minute as if trying to decide whether to share the next piece of information.

Perlman grew impatient. "Out with it, Avram," he urged. "What's bugging you about this picture?"

"Actually, I just had a call from this guy earlier today. He'd been in Cyprus and mentioned that he might have another "project." He's proven reliable in the past, and I thought it was worth the effort to go and meet him. To see what's on his mind."

Perlman sputtered in excitement. "You're damn right it is! I knew something was up." He slapped the table almost upsetting the small coffee cops. "You say this guy Viktor is on the level. Find out what the hell he knows or suspects and get back to me." Next, he slapped down another picture. This one was of Emily.

Bronstein shook his head. "Never seen her in my life."

"Well," Perlman grunted. "We know something about her. Her name is Emily Wilkins. Apparently, she's very smart and works for the NSA."

Bronstein had been around long enough not to even ask just how Perlman knew anything about Emily Wilkins or the inner workings of the National Security Agency. "OK," he said warily, trying hard not to show his surprise. "What next?"

Perlman ignored the question. "Who's this guy?" he asked as he put down a picture of Oleg Yushenko.

"No idea." Bronstein looked more closely at the picture. "From the look of him, I'd say he's Russian. Probably military."

"Humph, you should know. It wasn't that long ago that you were in the same position. It takes a Russian to smell a Russian." He laughed.

Bronstein shook his head, mystified by what Perlman wanted him to do. "So what's the story? Why do you have these three pictures? What's the connection?"

"That, my friend, is what you're going to find out. These three pictures were taken in Larnaca, Cyprus, last week—outside some church called the Church of St. Lazarus. They were sent to me by someone who thought I might be interested."

Bronstein didn't bother asking exactly who on Cyprus took the pictures. He knew Israel had a large intelligence operation on the island, which took an interest in anything that remotely concerned Israel—such as a Russian officer suddenly meeting with two Americans. He also knew Perlman had his own network. "What exactly do you have in mind, Benny?"

"You'll go to Cyprus to meet this guy Lipsky—off the books. Quietly. Which is something our guys have trouble doing these days. Renew your acquaintance and remind him of what we've done for him in the past. Time for a little return on our investment, don't you think? Also, find out what the hell the NSA is doing on the island. I doubt she's there just to be arm candy for this guy Lipsky. And look, Russian is your native language, so learn more about this Russian soldier. Why the hell is he getting close to the Americans? What's a Russian soldier who's supposed to be in Syria doing on Cyprus talking to those two? If they're just planning summer holidays, fine. But I somehow doubt that very much." He reached into another pocket of his overcoat, pulled out a thick envelope, and handed it to Bronstein, who looked inside.

He raised his eyebrows at the wad of euros. "There must be €10,000 in there, Benny. How the hell did you swing this?"

"Slush fund, Avram. A generous slush fund. Untraceable. You could be on that fucking island for several days trying to find these people." He leaned over, smiled, and patted Bronstein's arm. "And Avram, forget the fucking receipts and expense forms you love so much. OK?" Then he leaned back, took long pull on the *hookah*, and eyed Bronstein carefully. "Now about this other problem."

"Our own people?" Bronstein asked.

"Yes. Something strange is going on. People who normally can't shut up are unexpectedly quiet. They won't tell me anything. I'm getting cut out of some stuff. All I seem to get are fucking lunch menus. I know I've got one foot in the grave, but this isn't normal. Before, they were at least polite about it. You know the drill: 'Benny we'd love to include you, but...' Now I don't even get that. Reminds me of the days before the 1967 war. No one said a goddamned thing for fear the Americans or Europeans would get all excited and try to stop us. I don't like it."

He leaned forward and slapped a thin, spotted hand on the table. "I've been in this business a long time, Avram, and learned to trust my gut. And right now, my gut is telling me that some of our people—people who seem to live in the ancient past—are about to do something very, very stupid. They want more than the West Bank. They want the whole fucking Middle East. They're forgetting one simple fact: there are a hell of lot more Arabs around here than Jews. They have this pipe dream that the Americans will join them in this folly. They forget Benny's first rule: *Never. Trust. Another. Country. To. Save. You.* Do they think anyone else really gives a shit about Israel? I want you to keep your eyes and ears open, but for God's sake," he warned, "don't take any risks here or in Cyprus."

He reached over, grabbed Bronstein's arm, and looked him straight in the eye. "No heroics, Avram. I mean it. If you smell trouble, you get the hell out. We'll send in the hard boys. I do not want to say *kaddish* for you on Mount Herzl."

CHAPTER 14

Larnaca, Cyprus

The beach at Larnaca hadn't changed much in the time Viktor had been away. There was the same deafening music, the same smells of suntan oil and same cigar smoke mixed with a little light grass, and the same slightly desperate women with heavily sculpted, surgically reduced semi-naked bodies fishing for evening companionship. Viktor had been nursing a beer for the last half hour, fidgeting with his watch and wondering when Emily would show up.

Davies was relaxed, soaking up the local atmosphere. "Goddamn, Viktor, us poor ol' field hands could get used to this. And to think someone's payin' us!"

"Ricky, do I have to remind you? No one is paying us so far. We'll be lucky to get lunch money out of this one."

Davies scoffed. "Don't be such a pessimist, Viktor. The Lord usually provides. Have a little faith." He looked over his shoulder and laughed as he saw Emily sashaying her way through the array of beach umbrellas and ogling Russians. "As I was saying, the Lord has supplied at least part of the answer."

When Emily arrived, she nudged Viktor's legs over and sat

down on the edge of his lounger. "Nice to see you boys. Even better to see that you haven't started World War III yet."

"Actually, we were waiting for you. Wouldn't want to start anything without our paymaster's approval… and the pictures," Viktor said snidely.

She patted him on the leg. "Now, now. Be nice, Viktor. After all, I did get the support —and the pictures—you wanted." She turned to Davies. "You must be Desta's husband. I've heard a great deal about you."

"Any of it good?" Davies asked with a laugh.

"Some." She smiled, then she changed the subject. "Any word from Oleg yet? And how do we explain Ricky's sudden inclusion? Hope that doesn't spook him."

Davies dismissed those concerns: "This here Oleg should be grateful for the help. With me and Arlo, y'all have a chance to get outta that place with your asses intact. Without us, you might as well just stay right here on this nice beach and enjoy the sun. And by the way, this Russian's kid is probably gonna be dead within the month if he don't get serious help right now. We ain't got a lot a time for pissing contests about who does what and when."

Viktor recognized the changed tone of voice and body language that indicated Davies was deadly serious. He stood up, dusted the sand off his pants, and nodded toward the small taverna that had just opened up. "I suggest we head over to that little restaurant and take a look at the presents you brought, Emily, without showing the world and its mother what we're up to."

At Viktor's suggestion, the trio made their way over to the restaurant and sat at a table toward the back, out of the sun. Then Viktor had a few words with the owner, ordered a few beers, and gave him a wad of cash to encourage him to move the surrounding tables as far away as possible. This was Cyprus after all, and the owner was used to such very un-Greek requests for privacy. He appreciated the extra tax-free cash and nodded his agreement before he moved the surrounding tables to the veranda.

Emily smiled sweetly as the cold beers arrived and poured hers into a chilled glass, while Viktor and Davies settled for drinking theirs out of the bottle. Then she reached into her backpack and pulled out a think manila envelope that she handed to Viktor. "These were taken three days ago and should give you a good shot of the inside of the fort and the immediate surrounding area," she said in a low voice.

Viktor glanced around to make sure there were no overly curious bystanders and started to pull them out, but an impatient Davies grabbed the top three and spread them on the table. He pulled a small magnifying glass from one of the pockets of his cargo pants and studied each image carefully, going back over them several times. Finally, he looked up, smiled, and turned the pictures over. "These ain't half bad, Sarah or Emily or whatever the hell you call yourself these days."

Emily just blushed a little and raised her hands in a you-got-me surrender.

Davies tapped the pictures with his forefinger. "Just as I expected. Them boys got themselves a helo, an old Russian Mi-8, right square in the middle of the fort. Mostly used for transport these days. Then there's a half-assed windsock stuck up on the west wall. Maybe your new best friend Oleg can give us some idea of its schedule? We need to make sure it's there before we start all this." He took a swig of his beer and gently put the bottle down.

"I've spotted about eight guys just sorta hanging around. Sloppy as hell. Shirts hangin' out, laundry on a line, and their weapons just sorta piled against one of the walls. Bet they haven't fired those things in months—if at all. Looks to me like they're just sorta waitin' for their next meal, rather than really expectin' any trouble from the outside. These sure as hell ain't no frontline troops. Probably sent here because they fucked up somewhere else. Whatever real talent's here is most likely out of sight. Them Koreans are tough motherfuckers who know what they're doing. Don't know how many of 'em are inside. Could make things interesting."

"Glad you like the pictures," Emily said. "But I still don't see what good they'll do. You still have to get inside the place. Exactly how do you plan that? And what's so important about the helicopter?"

Viktor let out a small laugh. "This is where it gets *really* interesting."

Davies leaned back in his chair and held his right hand up above his head and made a downward gesture. "See, we ain't goin' in the front door. We're gonna drop in from the sky and then move up them skinny little tunnels." He moved his hand rapidly downward and flattened it out just about the table and pointed to a field at the bottom of the hill by the fort. "We're gonna jump right into this here field and go up the tunnels. Then we'll pop out like fuckin' rabbits—heavily armed fuckin' rabbits. They'll never know what hit 'em."

Emily's jaw dropped, and she looked at each of them as if they were nuts. "*That's a plan?* That's why I used up so many chips just to get those satellite pictures? Sweet Christ, I'll be the laughingstock of the agency," she moaned. "Parachute drops are inaccurate at the best of times. How the hell are you going to hit something smaller than a football field? Oh, and while I'm at it, where are you going to drop from? The United States sure as hell isn't going to provide a plane." She put her head in her hands and muttered, "Amateur hour, that's all this is."

She'd hit Davies's red button with the word "amateur." He sat up straight and gave her a searing look.

Viktor knew the warning signs and sat well back out of the way.

"Lady, we're many things. *Amateur* ain't one of them. *Amateur* is when you desk jockeys back in the U.S. think you can fight these brushfires with satellites, drones, and all them other electronic toys way the fuck away from the real action. We"—here, Davies pointed at himself and Viktor—"are still alive because we know what the hell we're doin' at the very sharp end—where the shit really hits the fan." His eyes narrowed in a way Viktor had often seen just before a firefight. "Lemme tell you somethin' else. Ol' Arlo may not be *summa-what-the-fuck* from some fancy school that costs more than I make in 10 years, but he's the best damn helo jockey I ever did see. Now that takes balls, lady—big balls. Ain't a helo in the world that Arlo cain't fly. Shit, he'll land one in your back yard if you want."

He cooled down by taking a long pull from the beer bottle and then offered the sergeant's view of warfare: "Plans are just that, plans. Things officers dream up. Just an idea of how things *might* turn out if everyone acts like you think they will. Sounds great at briefin's, but all turns to shit when the shootin' starts. Then you're on your own. You deal with what's in front of you, not what's on some piece of paper somewhere." He turned to Emily and spread his hands over the pictures to demonstrate the point. "You ever heard of a HALO jump?"

"No," she confessed.

"Theory's simple. A high-altitude low-opening parachute jump. Jump outta a plane at 30,000 feet, drop like a fuckin' brick until 700 feet, then pray the 'chute opens. Actually"—he scratched his ear in a self-deprecating sort of way—"when fallin' at 120 miles per hour, you ain't got much time to pray. If that 'chute don't open, you'll be strawberry jam all over someone's cornfield 'fore you can get a word out. Now the important part's for Viktor here to give us the exact—and I mean exact down to the last foot—coordinates of where he wants us to land."

"OK," she said, "let's say you actually land in one piece just outside the fort. Then what?"

He smiled. "Well, this is where the rubber hits the road. We know the goal: destroy the cultures and the lab where the Koreans are working. Exactly how we get there depends on what we find on the ground. To a certain extent, we gotta play it by ear."

"That sounds like a brilliant way to get yourselves all killed."

Davies smiled. "Always a risk," he acknowledged, "but we been doin' it a long time. And we're still here. Look" —he gestured at the pictures—"from what we've seen, they ain't got but eight, maybe 10, people on duty at ground level; less at the time we plan to land. They sure as hell ain't gonna be expectin' anyone to pop up outta them tunnels. Before they figure out what's happenin', they're down, and we've opened the main gate for Viktor and his friends. Arlo stays behind to get the chopper ready to go, cuz we ain't gonna have a whole lotta time to get out of Dodge once we take care of business down below."

"You'll be hopelessly outnumbered."

"*Outnumbered*, maybe. *Hopelessly*, no. We know what we're doin' and where we're goin'. They don't. That is a huge advantage. Plus, I'll bet this Oleg character can handle hisself just fine."

Emily knew when she was beaten. "All right, all right. I get the point. But," she reminded them, "there are a hell of a lot of holes."

Davies leaned back and spread his arms like a proud parent showing off his kid at the school nativity play. "Well, that's where ol' Viktor comes in. He's been real good at fillin' holes like this, ain't you, Viktor? Trick is to fill 'em faster than the other bunch can dig 'em."

Emily turned to Viktor with a skeptical look. "You can actually do this?"

"Maybe," he answered simply. His cell phone beeped, and he dug it out of his pocket to glance at the text message. "Actually, someone's just arrived who might be able to help." He stood up and gestured for the others to follow him, which they did.

Emily struggled to keep up with Viktor's long strides. "Hang on just a minute. Who's this mystery guy? What are we letting ourselves in for?"

"Relax. You'll find out soon enough."

They crossed Piale Pasha and walked down the broad

sidewalk toward the string of anonymous, indistinguishable hotels that lined the broad road. They passed groups of sunburned Northern European tourists dragging their reluctant kids away from the beach and back to the hotel. Hawkers pushing trolleys filled with tourist souvenirs worked their way slowly down the street, hoping to find customers willing to buy duck-shaped inflatable swim rings or sunhats bearing the logo of a famous Spanish football team. A guy selling what he called "*gelato*" was doing good business across the road.

Finally, they came to some broad steps leading up to a three-story rectangle that called itself grandly the Poseidon Resort Hotel. The front rooms each had a small balcony with a sliding door leading to the bedroom. Water dripped from the air-conditioning units tacked on to the outside of the windows. When they passed through the automatic doors leading to the lobby, they were greeted with a blast of frigid air conditioning that made Emily wish she'd brought a sweater. Most of the wall space on the left was filled with a long reception desk manned by a harassed concierge, who was doing his best to assure an irate British couple that their unfortunate experience the previous night with a large family of cockroaches in the bathroom wouldn't be repeated. The rest of the lobby was filled with three groupings of chairs and sofas covered in a hard, red faux-leather that really didn't encourage much lounging around. A sign above a door leading off to the right advertised the "all-inclusive, all-you-can-eat breakfast."

Seated against the far wall was the impeccably groomed Avram Bronstein. Everyone else may have been dressed in what could be charitably described as "holiday casual," but Avram—as usual—was wearing a perfectly pressed suit, a light-blue shirt, a darker-blue tie, and New & Lingwood shoes from London. His one concession to the location was exchanging his dark suit for a beige one. He glanced up from the newspaper he was reading and saw Viktor, Emily, and Ricky Davies striding across the polished-concrete floor. A thin smile crossed his face as he rose and folded the paper neatly in half.

There was no preamble as he greeted the group. He shook Viktor's hand warmly and addressed him in Russian: "I got your message. I must say it was intriguing—so intriguing that a good friend suggested I come here to meet with you as soon as possible." He turned to Ricky Davies. This time he spoke English: "Ah, the very capable Mr. Davies. Now this really *is* getting intriguing. I can't wait to hear what brings you all the way from darkest Africa." Finally, he focused his steady gaze on Emily. "And here we have Ms. Emily Wilkins from, if I'm not mistaken, the famed National Security Agency. This should be a very interesting discussion. Why don't we all sit down and complete the introductions?"

Emily was taken aback by his familiarity with Viktor and Davies as well as his knowledge of her role in the NSA. Determined to get back in the game and demonstrate her own *bona fides*, she answered him in Russian—just so he got the point. "I'm sorry," she said in a tone indicating more anger than sorrow, "I don't know whom I'm speaking to."

Viktor could sense this meeting was getting off on the wrong foot and jumped in to make the introductions. "Emily, this is Avram Bronstein, the person who—more than anyone else—has been responsible for our work defending several vulnerable groups in Africa. He's a good friend who often manages to find the necessary funds to keep us going."

She peered skeptically at Bronstein, only partially mollified. "And do we know, or care, about the source of those funds? Who exactly do you represent, Mr. Bronstein?"

Bronstein gave her a small smile, and—this time in English—said vaguely, "The funds come from a wide variety of sources who believe in Viktor's work. As for who I represent—right now, I simply represent myself. Someone I trust a great deal told me Viktor and I might have a serious mutual problem close to home—one that requires some delicacy—so I thought the least I could do is get on a plane to meet Viktor to learn more about this problem. I'm also intrigued by the NSA's interest in this problem. Is this a prelude to the 101st Airborne dropping in uninvited?"

She ignored the question and, thinking of her boss's worries, asked provocatively, "So the State of Israel isn't involved?"

"No. Right now," he said pointedly, "the State of Israel is not involved. And they'd like to keep it that way." His tone of voice indicated that the patience of the State of Israel wasn't infinite.

Emily looked nervously around at the growing crowds of tourists filling the lobby with their bags, beach toys, and tired children. "It may be better if we had this discussion in your room," she suggested.

Bronstein gave her a pitying you-think-I'm-actually-staying-in-this-dump look and declared he had a better place in mind: a small, discreet restaurant on a backstreet, which was run by a "friend of a friend." "Unfortunately, the restaurant just happens to be closed to the general public for a couple of days, but the owner has graciously offered to let us use it this afternoon. His wife Sarah has even agreed to cook for us."

The trio agreed to this alternative suggestion, and they all exited the hotel. A short cab ride took them to the door of a restaurant called Parea—which can be roughly translated as "group of friends." When Viktor had paid the cab driver, and they'd all got out of the car, Bronstein knocked on the door of the restaurant. The door was opened, and he was greeted warmly by a bear of a man with a full, dark beard that only partially hid the vivid scar running down the right side of his face. He also walked with a noticeable limp as he led them to their table, which was already set up for four guests. Bronstein didn't bother with introductions, and the knowing look from the owner said he was perfectly happy not to know who his friend's guests were.

Once they were seated around the table and the owner had

retreated to the kitchen, Bronstein noticed their curiosity about the location. "Eli is an old friend. He did good work in some of the more unpleasant places around here. He barely escaped the last time after an RPG hit the truck he was in. As he's too good a man to lose to retirement, he was set up here as sort of an unofficial listening post. He speaks Greek, Russian, English, Arabic, and even a little Turkish. Fortunately, many of our enemies combine a love of eating with love of talking. Sarah is a very good cook, and after the *meze* and a few glasses of *ouzo*, they start gabbing. You'd be surprised what an attentive waiter can pick up."

He picked up a napkin and shook it out over his lap just as Eli brought out a huge tray of *meze*. After everyone had filled their plate, Bronstein interrupted the meal. "Enough background," he said decisively, "what the hell's going on here? And why is a very, very smart person in Jerusalem getting nervous?"

Emily and Davies looked at Viktor, who cleared his throat and ran through developments up to this meeting in Cyprus. Bronstein said nothing, he simply sat and listened, giving nothing away. A raised eyebrow was the extent of his facial reaction to the news of the disease culture being prepared in Syria. It was as if a client were telling him about inventory problems in a distant factory. "It's quite clever actually," was all he calmly said when Viktor had finished his story. "I wouldn't have thought Assad had the brains to think of such a thing. Far too subtle for him." He carefully dipped some bread in the olive oil and took a delicate bite, making sure none of the oil dripped onto his suit. Then he turned to Emily. "And your people at the NSA buy this theory of a plague of rats about to infect the entire region? To infect people with a disease for which there's no known cure?" he asked incredulously. "And the North Koreans are involved. This sounds just weird enough to be true. No wonder Benny is worried," he added almost to himself.

"Benny? Who's Benny?" Emily asked.

"Just some guy I know. Before your time," Bronstein said dismissively. "By the way, do you have any solid proof, or is this merely the result of some half-cocked game theory back in Washington?"

"Look"—Emily was getting defensive— "we *know* the North Koreans have developed this culture. We *know* a lot of people in Syria are dying from something that looks a lot like this disease. We *know* Assad has been in touch with North Korea. We know *something* is going on at the Crac des Chevaliers. We don't know for certain *exactly* what they're cooking up, but no one wants to take the chance that it's benign. We *also* know the Russians are aware of what's going on, but they feel powerless to stop it. They don't like it, but they say their hands are tied."

"And your people, why don't they just blow the hell out of that place?" Bronstein asked.

"The real answer? Internal politics. Our somewhat-knowledge-deficit president doesn't like to make difficult decisions, especially ones that will drag the United States further into the Middle East quagmire. And the so-called 'intelligence agencies' seem to spend more time fighting internal battles and spreading the blame than solving real problems."

Bronstein sat back and steepled his fingers. "So let me try to summarize: We know—or think we know—that the Syrian regime is developing a particularly virulent biological culture with the potential to cripple large parts of this region's population. Something like a modern version of the Black Plague. The people who know, or suspect, this is true can't or won't act for fear of triggering a bigger war in the Middle East. Thus, they don't want any official Israeli military involvement for fear this would tip the entire region into an uncontainable war. Right so far?" he asked looking around the table.

Everyone else nodded.

"So people want this problem dealt with, but they also want deniability—they want the blame to fall elsewhere if everything goes wrong. Interesting but not entirely new conflicting goals," he mused. Then he turned to Viktor. "And this I assume is where you and Ricky Davies come into it?"

"We're certainly deniable." Davies laughed. "Ain't nobody gonna claim us if this thing goes tits up."

"That basically sums it up," Viktor confirmed.

Bronstein shook his head as if he didn't quite believe what he was hearing. "Let me make absolutely sure I have this right. Your small group thinks it can get into the bowels of this impenetrable fortress, eliminate the guards, destroy the lab beyond repair, *and then* escape. And in the more likely scenario that you all get wiped out, then and only then—as a last resort—do the big boys go in with the drones, smart bombs, and everything else in their armament to eliminate this menace." He looked slowly around the table as they all nodded their agreement.

Then he reached into his inner jacket pocket and pulled out his slender notebook and pen. "This is totally nuts," he said with a laugh. "Benny will love it. Right, if this insanity is to have any chance at all, what do you need from us? Unofficially, of course."

Davies rearranged the cutlery and used the salt and pepper shakers to demonstrate their plan. "We ain't got but one hope— and that's surprise. All them big-deal military operations you talked about take time. And sure as God made little apples, in that time there'll be a leak somewhere. Folks will be waitin' for you. They'll probably move the that damn lab before your planes even take off." He moved the salt shaker aggressively in a downward motion toward the plate. "See, the last thing they'll be expecting at 3 a.m. is a couple heavily armed crackers coming out of holes in the ground. They won't hear or see a thing till it's too late." He grinned at the thought of that surprise. "Then we gotta move fast—real fast—to do the job and get the hell outta there. I figure we got 20 minutes, half an hour tops before the cavalry comes." He pulled from his pocket a crumpled piece of paper covered with scribbled notes and tried to smooth it out on the table. "Basically, what we need from y'all is transport, a few bits and pieces of firepower, and maybe some help on the way out. Cain't be sure that chopper's gonna make it all the way to friendly dry land—of which there ain't a great deal in this part o' the world."

Bronstein didn't respond to any of this. He merely neatly wrote a few notes in his pad. "I assume this transport you speak of cannot be seen to come from Israel, officially that is?"

"That's probably best. Otherwise, it could generate a lotta excitement we don't need."

"And the equipment you need for the jump? It will be about -50°C at that altitude, and there won't be a lot of oxygen. I suppose parachutes are specialized? I'm not sure we have a lot of that lying around. You have all that equipment?"

"Not now, but we were all trained in them jumps and keep in touch with them boys in special forces. We're still considered 'family.'" He nodded at Emily. "With a word from her in the right ear, I believe we can get all that gear."

Bronstein looked carefully at Emily. "You can arrange this?" he asked, dubious that it would be so simple. "Your people will allow such a thing? In my experience, they don't like to share their toys—or information."

Privately, Emily shared his doubts, but she put on a brave face and assured everyone that the United States wouldn't let them down.

"There's one piece of this puzzle that's not here." Bronstein reached into his pocket and pulled out the picture of Oleg. "Exactly how does this Russian fit into this operation?"

Viktor coughed, trying to cover his surprise at Bronstein's knowledge of Yushenko. He took another sip of the *ouzo* before explaining how they found the former soldier and what role he could play.

Bronstein picked up on the "could."

"Only *could*, Viktor? You're not sure?"

"He wants assurance that we can get him and his family out of Syria and arrange good medical care for his son. Emily assures us that that can be arranged…"

Bronstein looked sharply at Emily. "Is that right? Your agency has agreed to that? For sure?"

She nodded her head. Bronstein had serious doubts that the American administration would ever let the NSA honor that deal. But for now, he kept those doubts to himself. At least Israel has good medical care, so maybe they could be a useful backup—and extract a few more favors from the United States in return.

"As I was saying," Viktor continued, "Oleg plays a critical role in getting me into the Syria and then down to his wife's village by the fortress. We'll guide Ricky and Arlo to the opening of the old water tunnel beneath the fort. As far as the local Syrians are concerned, I'll simply be another Russian officer visiting an old comrade who's spending time with his wife's family." He paused for a minute. "But tell me, how do you know about Oleg?"

Bronstein allowed himself a small smile of understatement. "We do have a few resources in Cyprus and even in the great Russian army. They give us some idea of what's going on." Then he changed the subject. "Tell me, what will you do if the tunnels you're counting on are blocked up and you can't get in them? What then?"

Davies looked at Viktor and answered. "We improvise. May have to land right inside the fort. Riskier, but doable. Viktor here will be in the town for a couple days before the operation. He'll have chance to scout out those tunnels and let us know one way or the other. It'll still be a helluva a surprise for those boys when we land on top of 'em. Now you tell us—what do you know about this Oleg guy?"

"When we spotted Yushenko in Cyprus, some of our people got interested and dug a little deeper. Your story is accurate—as far as it goes. You missed a bit, however, on his army story. He was a highly regarded soldier who really did slug a superior officer—someone most people regarded as a complete idiot. But the army is the army, and rules must be followed. So Yushenko leaves, and the idiot officer is sent to a new assignment: somewhere in the Far East along the Manchurian border. The point is Yushenko isn't forgotten and still has a lot of friends in the army. They want to help him without being too obvious about it." He lifted his finger and pointed to each of them in turn. "Your little plan could be just the answer they're looking for."

"What do you mean?" Emily blurted out. "All of a sudden, we're to play nice with the Russians?"

Bronstein gave her a pitying look. *These Americans,* he thought, *are always going in straight lines. They never really appreciate the complexities.* Out loud, he said, "You told me the Russians suspect what's going on in Crac des Chevaliers, but they feel powerless to do anything about it. Well, turning a blind eye to what Yushenko might do could be their way of actually doing something—killing two birds with one stone, as it were—without doing much of anything."

The others were looking confused puzzled at this bit of Talmudic hair-splitting.

"It's very simple. They help Yushenko and his family *and* they screw up Assad's great infected-rat scheme—without a single trace back to them. It's brilliant, actually." Bronstein moved some of the small tea glasses around the table to demonstrate his point. "See, let's assume this glass is the fortress and that glass a little way over there is the main Russian naval base at Tartus or the air base just up the coast. Now, let me ask you something. Under normal circumstances, what are the chances of a plane—even one at 30,000 feet—getting into even a small amount of Syrian air space without the Russians noticing?"

Davies nodded his head deliberately. "Man's got a point. We could do it, but some bright spark at the base would probably pick up the change in routine. If he has any interest in movin' to the day shift, he might just tell one of the officers. Might not, but"—he raised his chin toward Bronstein—"the man's right. It's a risk. One we don't need."

"Ah," Bronstein pronounced, trying to keep the triumph out of his voice, "but what if our young Russian radar technician decides to go for a coffee break around 2.30 a.m. on the morning of your little parachute exercise? Then that little blip on his radar screen showing up where it shouldn't show up is like a tree falling in the woods. Who knows about it? And in about 15 seconds, it's gone anyway."

"The Syrians," Viktor shot back, "are not complete idiots."

"That's debatable, but let's say they do notice something at that hour of the morning. What are they going to do? The Russians would check and double-check. But the Syrians?" he asked rhetorically, dismissing the very idea that the Syrians would check anything. "It's along the coast, headed north, and gradually swinging west nowhere near any major Syrian city. They'd probably assume it's a passenger flight that's gone slightly off course. They might call the pilot and tell him he's wandered off course and should leave their air space immediately. When the pilot, speaking Arabic, apologies profusely and replies that he's just an unscheduled cargo flight from Amman to Istanbul that got a little careless, they relax and wish him a pleasant trip. If they're really diligent, they might check with the Russians to see if they spotted anything unusual. If the Russian were to say what he really thinks, he'd reply that everything in that godforsaken country is 'unusual,' but he restrains himself in the interest of fraternal relations and says they haven't noticed anything at all. Even if they're extremely diligent and call Amman air traffic control for confirmation of the 'cargo' flight, they'll speak with someone who says such a flight did in fact recently depart from Queen Alia Airport."

No one said anything for a minute, then Davies broke the silence: "Could work, I suppose. But" —he smiled— "even if they get real excited and send up a fighter to check, we'll be long gone by the time they pull alongside for a look-see. It'll take several minutes to get word to a pilot, get him into the plane, and get it in the air. Then it's another bit of time for him to get to 30,000 feet. The chances of 'em picking up two specks plunging toward the ground in HALO suits ain't real high. Besides, by that time, the 'cargo' plane is way over the Med and we're on the ground."

"And the Jordanians," asked a still-skeptical Emily. "Are we sure they'll cooperate with this little scheme?"

"They'll cooperate," Bronstein answered firmly, as if they had no choice. He pushed back his chair and stood to leave. Then he ripped a page out of his notebook and wrote a short message on it before handing it to Viktor. "I'll be in town for a couple of more days. Let me know how your conversation with Yushenko goes. You can reach me on that number." Then with a nod to Eli he headed toward the door. Abruptly, he stopped and turned back with a smile. "Don't worry about the bill for lunch. It's taken care of." With that, he was out the door.

"Well," Davies said, "nice to know someone has our backs—maybe."

Viktor moved quickly to reassure them. "Look, if Avram Bronstein says he'll do something, he will—if only because it's in his interests and the interests of his backers to do so. As long as the people behind him think we can solve this problem for them, they'll be our new best friends. If they doubt us for one minute, they'll drop us faster than you can blink and go to their own plan B."

"Which may or may not involve our survival," Davies suggested.

"I doubt they'd think that's a very important factor in the scheme of things." Emily checked her watch and signaled that they should make a move. "Oleg's probably waiting for us by the church. We should get moving."

CHAPTER 15

They found Yushenko in the same dark church, sitting near the front with his head bowed and his hands clasped in prayer. Emily tapped him gently on the shoulder, and he looked around warily. She nodded toward the door where Viktor was standing and then stood back to give him room to get out of the small chair and into the side aisle. As she followed him past the rows of icons and candles toward the dimly lit door, she noticed he was carrying a bulky parcel wrapped in brown paper and tied loosely with string.

He nodded a small greeting and lifted the package to show that, at least for now, he was going along with their plan. It was the time of day, between a late lunch and early evening, when most Cypriots take a nap to prepare themselves for the long hours of sitting around small tables drinking coffee and/or *ouzo*, and swapping tales about the day's conquests, the follies of their leaders, or the antics of the many foreigners attracted to island's lax attitude toward taxes. The broad square around the church was empty, and one of the few shops open at this time was the café where they'd met the last time.

Yushenko drew back when he saw Davies sitting at the table. He grabbed Viktor's arm and whispered angrily into his ear. "Who's this guy? What the hell have you done? I said no complications. Do you have any idea of the risks I'm taking? Get him the hell out of here or I'm gone." He started to pull away back toward the street.

Viktor tugged at his sleeve. "Calm down, Oleg, for Christ's sake," he spat out through gritted teeth. "This just happens to be the guy who's going to make this plan work, make sure you and your family get somewhere safe, and—most important—make sure your son gets the right medical care. Do you begin to understand?"

Yushenko took a deep breath and grudgingly turned around. He tapped his forefinger hard into Viktor's chest and looked him coldly in the eye. "If this doesn't work, my friend, I will find you. We will settle accounts."

Emily noticed the flare-up and stepped between them, smiling brightly. "Well, now we're all friends again, I suggest we move on. We don't have a lot of time to waste on pissing contests."

Yushenko stalked over to the table and, for several minutes, stood eying Davies, who calmly returned the gaze. His hands were carefully placed on the tabletop in a sign of non-violence. Emily and Viktor held their breaths while the two alpha males worked out who the leader was going to be.

Finally, Yushenko sat down and dropped the bundle next to him. "You a soldier. Some kind of special forces," he said to Davies in broken English. It was a statement of fact not a question. There's something frontline soldiers recognize in each other: the air of being a tightly coiled spring, calmness in the face of hostility, the chiseled face and hard body, the undefinable air of martial competence, and—perhaps most of all—the casual acceptance of war and violent death as their inevitable end created a strong bond among real soldiers around the world.

"Was, Lieutenant. Was," Davies answered. "Sergeant Richard Davies, formerly of the United States Army, Delta Force. Now retired."

Yushenko cracked a smile. This was someone he could deal with. "Lieutenant Oleg Yushenko of Russian Federation army. Also special forces: Spetsnaz. Like you, retired—only not voluntary. Now, seems we go back into action," he said, almost happy at the thought of gunfire and explosions.

The same young waiter as before was watching this interplay with his jaw hanging down. He wasn't sure what was going on, but it didn't seem like the usual discussions of women, booze, Rolex watches, fast cars, and drugs. They didn't look like Turks from across the island—he rapidly fingered his worry beads, muttering, "God help us all!"—but they looked like they could do someone some serious damage. He crossed himself for protection, and then, almost holding his breath, edged up to their table to take their orders. *What is the woman doing here with these three tough men talking as an equal?* he wondered.

Once the coffees had come, Emily explained what had happened since they last met—albeit leaving out the connection with Avram Bronstein. She wasn't sure how that would go over right now.

Yushenko nodded and opened the bundle at his feet. Turning to Viktor, he said in Russian, "Congratulations. You're now a captain in the Russian Navy. This should fit."

Viktor looked down into the bundle and saw the jacket and pants in basically the same camo pattern as used by the U.S. Navy. The small shoulder patch with the three stars identified him as a captain.

Then Yushenko reached into his jacket, took out a thick sheaf of papers, and handed it to Viktor.

"These are your papers, Kapitan Boris Nemstov. You're with navy intelligence and had an emergency meeting on Cyprus, plus"—Yushenko smiled—"your honeymoon. Now you're returning to your base near Tartus. The papers are real, but try not to talk too much. These," he cautioned Viktor, tapping the papers, "are enough to get you into the country, but don't press your luck. Your Russian is good, but you use too many old words. You're returning to Syria with your new wife—a French woman who doesn't speak Russian"—he waved toward Emily—"after a short honeymoon on Cyprus. You got married just after the meetings."

"This is gonna be fun," Davies chimed in.

Emily's face reddened, and she asked if this was totally necessary.

"Absolutely," Yushenko said seriously. "It makes the trip to the village much more credible. You"—he nodded at Emily—"traveling with my wife makes sense. A fellow Russian officer on his own makes no sense. People will talk."

"OK, OK; I get the point," she conceded. "But just out of curiosity, where's the real Kapitan Nemstov? Anything bad happen to him?"

Yushenko laughed. "No, no, nothing like that. Boris is a good friend. I gave him a story about a joke I wanted to play on his stupid commander. He didn't really believe it, but he's now sitting on a beach with a girl I got him from Damascus. So don't worry about Boris; he's OK. He owes me."

Davies, who had been sitting quietly during this interplay in Russian, spoke up. "Look, before this goes much further, let's make sure that ol' Oleg here is up to speed on just what we're plannin'. He's got any problems, we need to hear about 'em now—not when me an' Arlo are droppin' outta the sky like a ton of shit."

Viktor spent the next half hour telling Oleg what they knew so far and what they'd planned. He emphasized Oleg's critical role in both getting them into the country and hosting him and Emily in his wife's village near the fortress. "That's the whole thing. My visit has to appear entirely natural. Just an old army buddy visiting his friend at his wife's hometown. We walk around, let everyone get used to us, and settle down."

"Couple things we need to know," Davies added. "One, what's the schedule, if any, for the chopper to show up? Once a week, a couple times a week? When we know that, we can time our move. No chopper, no move."

Yushenko looked confused. "What's the chopper got to do with anything?"

"That's our way—and your family's way—outta there. My buddy, the one who's droppin' with me was one of the best helo jockeys in the army. So, above all else, we keep him healthy if we wanna see home again. Second, we need to know the exact, and I mean exact, GPS coordinates of the two possible landin' areas: one outside the fort and one inside. If it's outside, you and Viktor meet us at the landin' spot and guide us to the mouth of the tunnel. Then the two of you get Emily, your wife, and your son and then get up to the main gate. If the tunnel's still there, you give us half an hour to get up the damn thing, take care of business ,and get that gate open for you. If we have to land inside, we get the gate open first and then take care of the lab. We ain't got a lotta time to get this job done. The only things we got going for us are speed and surprise. We hang around too long, and we're gonna face a lot more than a few sleepy guards."

Yushenko moved his head from side to side indicating he wasn't totally sold. "Risky. You sure about the tunnel?"

"Ain't sure about anythin'. That's why you and Viktor have to do a little scoutin' around. Let me know what's really on the ground. Whole fuckin' thing is risky, my friend. But if you've got a better idea, I'm all ears."

***

Amman, Jordan

A few days later, Major General Fawzi Zuhair Hashem, director of Jordan's General Intelligence Directorate—otherwise known by its Arabic name Mukhabarat—sat at his large desk, gazing idly through the bulletproof and bombproof windows onto the hot streets of Amman, where ordinary people were scurrying about their daily tasks. Most of those pedestrians gave the large, sand-colored building a wide berth, even crossing the street in a vain attempt to avoid the scrutiny of the heavily armed guards and the powerful electronic surveillance equipment. Many of those pedestrians had friends or relatives incarcerated in the interrogation cells of the Mukhabarat, and they—wisely—had no desire to join them. The main function of the Mukhabarat was to protect the throne of the Hashemite Kingdom of Jordan. The major general reported only to the king, and his budget was a closely guarded state secret. He was all too aware that he sat on top of an active volcano of simmering political, religious, and ethnic hatreds that could erupt any day. As if the domestic troubles weren't enough, Major General Hashem had to worry about the even more sensitive international situation. Right now, it was—as usual—the Syrians who were the problem. With the endless war, thousands of refugees—many of whom he considered serious threats to Jordan—were pouring into his country and disturbing the delicate social and economic balances. Added to all this was the fact that the country's economy was floundering. Its only natural resource was dust, and the kingdom had to rely on the generosity of wealthy neighbors such as Saudi Arabia or patrons such as the United States to keep things going.

Powerful patrons are fine, but their patronage comes with a price. In the case of the United States, that price was expressed in its 14-acre embassy compound, which had become its center for intelligence activity throughout the entire Middle East. The darker side of that partnership was using Jordan as a location for the so-called "renditions"—a fancy name for anyone deemed an enemy of the United States being grabbed and sent to an unnamed site for some vigorous interrogation.

None of this bothered Major General Hashem very much. Weak countries, after all, can't be too fussy about the nature of alliances. Besides, Jordan and the United States—for the time being anyway—were more or less on the same side. Both of them detested *jihadis* of any type, and neither of them had much use for the Palestinians. And if the Americans were willing to pay a great deal of money to use his jails cells, who was he to complain?

But he was getting a little annoyed by the silence from his counterparts at the embassy. Intelligence was a two-way street, but the flow had recently been all in one direction. He was getting disturbing calls from some of his sources about unexplained activity near one of the crossing points into Syria, but he couldn't get any confirmation from the Americans. Either they really didn't know anything, or more likely, they simply weren't sharing. He'd heard one story about a very sick Syrian refugee who was hustled off to an American doctor at the embassy. "Who was this refugee?" and "Why did the Americans think it was so important to treat him?" were questions that needed an answer?

He needed to think. Rather than merely pressing a button and ordering a coffee, he got up from his desk, went over the heavily armored door, and pressed the switch to open it. As it swung sluggishly back on its hinges, the guard always on duty just outside jumped to his feet and buttoned his jacket hastily. As usual, he missed a button, and consequently, the jacket hung unevenly off his shoulders. Hashem smiled at the guard, who was from the same Bedouin tribe as the major general and would consider it an honor to sacrifice himself for his clansman. He told the guard to relax and said he just wanted a coffee—a real Bedouin coffee. The guard understood and swiftly passed the order to the coffee boy—yet another clansman.

The steaming coffee, together with the *lokum* and glass of water, arrived within minutes. Hashem smiled as the rich aroma wafted up from the small cup. "If this won't clear my head, nothing will," he muttered to himself. He gave a regal nod of appreciation to the coffee boy, who almost skipped out of the room, pleased to have performed this small service for his illustrious clansman.

A thought struck Hashem as he sipped the coffee. He knew just the person to call. He opened the bottom desk drawer and pulled out one of his several encrypted phones—one that even the Americans didn't know about. He allowed himself a small chuckle as he punched in the number he knew by heart. Israel and Jordan had been locked in an uneasy embrace since the State of Israel was founded in 1948. Jordan had long ago given up the fantasy of "driving the Jews into the sea," but it had to keep a respectable distance to appease the large Palestinian population in Jordan. That distance, however, didn't prevent quiet, close cooperation on issues of mutual security.

After a few rings, a gruff voice answered in Hebrew.

"*Salam alaykum*, Benny. How are you?" He could sense Benny Perlman brighten at the other end of the line.

"*Alaykum salam*, you old camel trader. Good to hear you're still in one piece," Perlman answered in Arabic. "You know, I was thinking of you a couple of days ago when drinking some of the shit this office calls coffee." He paused for a minute. "Don't tell me. You're sitting there with a cup of the real stuff in front of you, and you called just to piss me off."

Hashem laughed. "I do have a cup of the real stuff in front of me, but I didn't call to piss you off."

Perlman was instantly alert. "Can our people or your friends hear this call?"

"Doubt it. We've got some very smart encryption guys. We like to keep some things to ourselves. What are you up to these days? Anything we should know about?"

"Idiots have pushed me into semi-retirement," Perlman answered angrily. "They're as bad as the Americans. They depend almost entirely on so-called 'electronic intelligence gathering.'" His deep disdain for those methods came through loud and clear. "What about you? You keeping busy? And your family? Are they well?" This was a standing joke. Perlman knew very well that Hashem slept about four hours at most, smoked three packs of cigarettes a day, and his family had moved to Austin, Texas, for safety.

"Well, you know"—Hashem shrugged—"we manage to keep busy. The bad guys haven't disappeared." He abruptly shifted into a more serious tone. "Actually, Benny, I need to pick your brain."

"Not much left to pick my old friend, but you're welcome to it."

"Something's going on next door that's spilling over here. Our 'friends' say they don't know what—if anything—is happening. They may not, in fact, know anything, but that doesn't explain why very sick refugees are being taken to the embassy."

Perlman paused for a minute, wondering just how much to share with his Jordanian friend. Quickly, his mind played over the shifting regional scenarios, and he realized they both had more to lose than gain by failing to cooperate. There are times when national interests, however seemingly different, coincide quite nicely. Perlman decided this was one of those times. "Actually, Fawzi, I'm glad you called. I should have been in touch earlier. My mistake."

This time, it was the major general who sat up straighter in his chair. Old professionals like Benny Perlman don't often acknowledge mistakes, so something big must be developing. "You sure Big Brother up the road from you can't listen in to this call?"

"Very sure. What's up?"

"One of my guys just came back from Cyprus with the strangest goddamned tale you ever heard. I'd laugh if it weren't so fucking frightening. Tanks, planes, and soldiers we can deal with, but fucking infected rats? How the hell do you stop them?"

The major general wasn't sure he'd heard right, but he decided not to interrupt the Iraqi—he still considered Perlman an Iraqi instead of Israeli. You can change nationalities like nightshirts, but you can't change the character and traditions you were born with so easily. He thought he'd heard all the bizarre schemes dreamed up in the terrorist petri dish of the Middle East, but diseased rats? That was a new one.

Perlman spent the next several minutes relaying what Bronstein had told him about the meeting on Cyprus and the plans to destroy the lab in the Crac des Chevaliers. He also spent some time on the complications of involving the big powers or Israel at this time.

Hashem just listened until Perlman had finished. "You think this is real, Benny?"

Hashem heard Perlman take a deep breath that set off a fit of coughing. "Fucking cigarettes. One of these years I'll cut down," he finally croaked out. "Anyway, yeah; yeah, I do unfortunately. My guy was impressed with this small team. He says they're solid, no bullshit. They might just pull this off."

"What do you want me to do?"

"Look, Fawzi, I'm in no position to offer advice to the director of the Mukhabarat. You don't need my advice, but I may have to ask a small favor. An unmarked plane may have to take off late one night from one of your airfields deep in the desert."

"Will it attack anyone? That would be a problem. We don't need any blowback from our more unstable neighbors."

"No, no. It won't even be armed, and it certainly won't frighten anyone. In fact, it will be in Jordanian air space for only about 15 minutes. We simply need it to fly northwest over Lebanon and then 'mistakenly' enter Syrian air space at 30,000 feet for about two minutes. It will be logged as a routine cargo flight to Turkey."

"The Syrians will bitch like hell."

"Maybe not. First, it's the Russians who'll pick it up, and they won't do anything. Second, even the Syrians know that fighter aircraft seldom go above 10,000 feet. They shouldn't get too excited about a careless commercial pilot at 30,000 feet."

"I need to think about this Benny. It should be OK, but I need to check a couple of things. Also, I have to tell the king about the rats. Wouldn't do my career any good if he hears about it from someone else."

"Understood. Listen, this whole thing is going to happen sooner rather than later. Let's hope it works. But we—I mean the IDF—have to be prepared to go in heavy if these guys can't get it done. It'd be nice if they could knock this shit out without torching the whole region, but we can't afford to make that assumption. We'll be ready with plan B."

CHAPTER 16

Outside Crac des Chevaliers, Syria

The few houses huddled at the base of the Crac des Chevaliers didn't even have a real name. Nothing official was listed on the maps of Syria—if you could get one these days. There were a couple of dusty streets with a crude, worn channel in the middle to handle rainwater runoff and any other liquid sludge that flowed to the barren fields outside the settlement. The houses might once have been white, but after years of being blasted by the constant west wind and dust, they were now deep beige in color. Why bother repainting them when they'll just be covered in dust again in a few days? The few remaining scraggly trees had long ago given up the battle against the wind and were now bent over—almost prayer-like—to the east. There weren't many people going about their daily business. With every available boy and man called up for the war, there weren't many people left to start with. But mainly it was the oppressive presence of the fortress that encouraged people to stay indoors. Looming over the small settlement, it cast a gloomy literal and figurative shadow on the houses. In certain weather conditions, the old-timers swore they could hear the screams and moans of the original Crusaders as they defended the fortress against the Saracens.

A few stray goats wandered up and down the streets in search of food, but most found much better pickings near the rivulet that emerged briefly from the ground just by the rear wall of the fortress before petering out. There, the goats munched happily on the thin green shoots springing out of the damp patch between two big rocks. At one time, there must have been a real stream bubbling out of the ground, but centuries of neglect had left just this small damp area. Still, the goats were happy enough—especially in the summer when a cool breeze whistled down from an old, disused tunnel that disappeared deep inside the fort. Sometimes, the young shepherd Ali would find his goats huddled under this refreshing breeze and then he too would make a comfortable spot by the wall and pass the long, hot summer days enjoying a cool draft. At first, the place frightened him because he could hear sounds from inside the fort, and he swore the place was filled with *jinns*. His grandmother had told him all about the power of these creatures, and the first time he heard the noises, he ran away as fast as he could. He'd tried to be brave, but the fort itself terrified him, and the mysterious sounds only increased his fear. He'd never been inside the fort, and given the frightening stories his parents and grandparents told about the place, he had absolutely no interest in entering its massive gates. The goats, however, were undisturbed by the *jinns* or the imposing walls, and they continued to enjoy their refreshing location. Over time, Ali concluded that, because his goats didn't run away and were unharmed, these must be friendly *jinns* that didn't mind him getting out of the sun for a short while.

***

Deep inside the fort, two levels down from the surface, Kim Jung-Woo didn't share Ali's comfortable experience. He'd been stuck in this small, dank room—which was once probably a storeroom—for the better part of four months with three other monosyllabic North Koreans. Two of them were supposed to be biochemists, but Kim had rapidly concluded they knew much more about martial arts than chemistry. As fervent supporters of the North Korean regime, they were sent to Syria more as a "favor" than in any hopes they'd help Kim produce anything. The other member of the North Korean team was a badly disguised security agent. Kim was sure he was there to make sure none of them wavered in their devotion to the Supreme Leader back in Pyongyang, rather than defending them against any attacks from the outside.

His colleagues' lack of conversational skills really didn't matter very much anyway because the constant drone of the large generator that supplied power to the lab and their small living quarters made any conversation difficult. Besides, they weren't there to talk. It had been made clear to them before they arrived that their one job was to create this deadly culture that their new "ally" Syria could use against its multiple enemies.

Kim stared blankly at the rows of petri dishes, vials, chemicals, and all the other top-of-the-line laboratory equipment the regime had acquired from reputable Swiss and German firms, who had no idea their cultured Asian customer was in fact a front for North Korea. But the money was good, and they saw no need to ask embarrassing questions.

Until the age of 14, Kim was just another California kid, a little brighter than most, who spent a lot of time in the skateboard parks, surfing the gentle waves off Santa Cruz, or combing social media for information on that hot girl who sat in front of him in his algebra class. His Korean heritage was no big deal because over half his class were from Korean, Taiwanese, or Japanese backgrounds.

Then one day in the spring, all those dreams of endless waves and dealing with the rampant hormones rushing through his brain and body came crashing down. That was the day his "parents" sat him down and told him of the new reality. Everything he'd been living up to that time was a complete fraud. Whether he knew it or not—or liked it or not—he was now an official servant of the North Korean regime. His so-called "parents" were long-time North Korean agents who'd been ordered to take an unnamed infant and bring him up as an American child. Now it was time for him to fulfill his duties. From then on, his life would be choreographed by his agents/parents: his education, his professional career, his social activities—everything. His goal was ultimately to infiltrate one of the biggest and best U.S. biotechnology companies and basically steal every secret he could find. A powerful stick encouraged obedience. Failure to achieve any of this would result in the U.S. authorities being informed of his status as an enemy agent. Given the choice of obeying his new masters or spending the rest of his life hounded by the U.S. security services, he chose to obey.

By the time he'd finished his Ph.D. in biochemistry at the California Institute of Technology, the screws began to tighten. His North Korean handlers told him exactly where he'd apply for a job. With his grades, it was easy to find a job at one of the world's leading biochemistry research companies, where he specialized in virology.

The path from the rarefied atmosphere of a leading research institute to a dim room in an ancient Crusader castle had been surprisingly simple. Too simple from Kim's point of view.

One day, he was working in a high-tech lab. Then, after "compassionate" leave to visit an allegedly dying relative in Seoul, he was bundled on to a plane and sent to Pakistan. From there, another plane took him to Dubai and then finally Damascus. A long, dusty truck journey brought him to the Crac des Chevaliers. It was here he was told to develop a deadly virus—one that had no vaccine. His employers in California were told that, unfortunately, young Kim had been in a serious car accident and wouldn't be returning.

CHAPTER 17

Annapolis, Maryland

It was a Sunday morning in Annapolis, and John Shepherd allowed himself to sleep in a little: he got up at 5 a.m. instead of the usual 4.30 a.m. His wife of 20 years, Helen, smiled slightly and rolled over. As a leading trauma surgeon, she was used to the odd hours both she and her husband kept. The sun had just begun to hit the dome of the Naval Academy chapel as he opened the kitchen window of their condo by the harbor and took a deep breath of clean air—so different from the literal and figurative mixture of poison gasses that seemed to envelope the country's intelligence agencies. He thought it a perfect day to go out on Chesapeake Bay with his wife for a picnic on their lovingly converted 35-foot Maine lobster boat *Caroline*—named after their daughter who'd died during birth. Being unable to have other children, Shepherd and his wife lavished their attention and care on the boat. No detail was too small: neither the brightly varnished handrails, the spotless cockpit, the immaculate small cabin, nor the carefully maintained engine.

Shepherd decided to go to the boat to make sure everything was in order for their outing. He knew everything was always in perfect order, but he just liked being on the boat, drinking a cup of black coffee in the quiet of the early morning. It gave him a chance to think. He was worried about Emily and hoped she wasn't getting in over her head. He shook his head to clear that thought. *She's a big girl who can handle herself.*

As he sat on the engine hatch, he noticed a small, dark smudge by the hatch opening. He frowned at this slight imperfection and quickly wiped it off with the rag he always carried. Normally, he would have checked for the source of the mark, but he was distracted by a flock of noisy seagulls that tried to land on the bow. After chasing them off, he decided to warm up the engine and make sure everything was running smoothly before returning to the condo for breakfast. He took the key out of his pocket and put it in the ignition. As he pushed the starter button, the boat erupted in a loud explosion and ball of flame that left the *Caroline* and several nearby boats nothing more than smoldering bits of wood and fiberglass on the oily waters of the harbor.

***

Larnaca, Cyprus

Viktor stood with a cup of coffee in his hand, gazing out the large plate-glass window in the arrivals section of Larnaca Airport as the small Gulfstream g650 circled over the calm Mediterranean Sea for its final approach. As the pilot banked sharply to line up with the main runway, Viktor noticed the German markings on the tail. *Nice touch*, he thought. *No entry issues with an EU plane—or at least one that said it was from the EU.*

He crushed the empty coffee cup, threw it into a nearby trash can, and signaled for Davies and Emily to join him near the small door leading out to the tarmac. Emily had used her

NSA pass and connections to clear their entry into the restricted area. Once outside, they stood in the shade of a jetway as the small plane made a smooth landing. Airport personnel guided the plane to a stand about 100 yards from the jetway and signaled the pilot to wind down the powerful twin Rolls Royce BR 725 engines. Viktor, Davies, and Emily left the shade of the jetway and walked over to the plane as an attendant opened the door and lowered the short stairway. The first person off was a shaken Avram Bronstein, who was still immaculately dressed in a lightweight, dark-beige cotton suit and a blue silk tie, along with wearing a deeply puzzled expression on his face. Viktor walked over and offered his hand, which Bronstein grabbed the way a drowning person would grab a life belt.

"What's wrong, Avram? Rough flight?" asked a worried Viktor.

Bronstein waved away the suggestion of rough flight as if the quality of a particular flight was of no importance. "No, the flight was fine. For the money I'm paying," he said somewhat irritably, "it should be."

"OK, then. What's up?"

Bronstein gestured agitatedly back toward the plane. "I just spent four hours in close quarters with someone who didn't utter a word—not a single word, mind you—that I understood. I speak five languages well, but I've never heard anything like what came out of his mouth. When he did try to speak, it was in some unintelligible language that's probably never been written down. All he did was drink quantities of Coca-Cola and eat every single sandwich on the plane, along with bags of potato chips."

"Ah," Viktor said with a smile. "Glad to hear you spent some quality time with Arlo. Speech may not be his strong point, but then most of what he does very well doesn't involve a lot of words."

At that moment, the subject of Bronstein's irritation edged out of the small airplane door dressed as usual in a white T-shirt and cargo pants, which were tucked into his combat boots. He was carrying two large, heavily loaded duffel bags. When he saw the small group meeting him, his thin face broke into a gap-toothed grin that spread from one jug-ear to the other. A thatch of red hair that no comb could ever control sat on top of his head.

Viktor and Davies stepped forward to help with the bags. Viktor winced as he hefted one of them onto his shoulder. "Goddamn it, Arlo; what the hell did you bring with you?"

"Just tools of the trade, Viktor; tools of the trade."

Bronstein and Emily looked at each other, not really understanding.

Davies came to their rescue with a translation and explanation. "He just brought along some tools for our job. See, Arlo here is from the Arkansas hill country. He spent a helluva lot more time huntin' and fishin' than goin' to school. Fact of the matter is he lied about his age and joined the army at 15. Figured it was better than wastin' his time in some schoolroom. College was never part of Arlo's life plan. Him and the army was made for each other. The physical trainin' was a piece of cake." He pointed to Arlo, who'd put down the bags and was standing at ease. "I mean look at him. All muscle and sinew; not an ounce of fat on him. The only one I know who can keep up with the Ethiopians on one of their jaunts over the hills. He mastered every type of weapon the army handed to him. Didn't take even them dumb shits long to recognize they had somethin' special, and they moved him to Ranger trainin' right quick. Then he volunteered to become a helicopter pilot. Ate that right up and soon found himself in Afghanistan. With his crazy daredevil flyin', it ain't clear who he scared more: the troops flyin' with him or the Taliban. Anyways, he wound up with my unit in Africa and stayed with me when Viktor here introduced us to free enterprise and capitalism."

Emily was trying to usher them inside toward passport control when Bronstein grinned and pointed to black SUV parked nearby. "Cyprus isn't a place, my dear Ms. Wilkins, where formalities like passport control stand in the way of making a little money."

She gave a what-the-hell shrug and followed them to the car. "By the way, where in Germany did you pick up Arlo? I thought he was in Africa."

Bronstein gave a little cough. "Actually, we never went near Germany. We picked up Arlo in Nairobi. Given the nature of Arlo's luggage, we didn't think he'd make it on to most normal airlines. We simply thought we could avoid unnecessary questions by filing a flight plane from Munich rather than Kenya. Tonight, the German markings will come off and the plane will return to its Israeli nationality."

They finally exited the airport and headed to the car park to pick up their vehicle. Once loaded with people and gear, they set off. Viktor was rummaging around in the duffel bags as Davies drove the car through the perimeter gate and onto the slip road. The guards stood up straight and almost saluted. They had no idea who was inside, but they'd learned the hard way to treat cars with dark-tinted windows and access to the airport apron with great respect.

Viktor lifted out two Uzis and two H&K MP5s with the retractable stock. "Good job, Arlo. I see you also brought along some silencers and some flash-bangs. Let's see, what else? Plenty of ammo, plastic ties, and a first aid kit. That should do it."

"Shit, Viktor, if we're gonna do this, we may as well do it right. Don't pay to go in half-cocked." Arlo grinned.

"What's in the other bag?"

"The 'chutes. Don't let no one else pack my 'chutes. Or Ricky's. Seen too many boys make a hole in the ground cuz some peckerhead fucked up the packing." He tapped Emily on the shoulder. "What about them HALO suits and the rest of the equipment? You got them, right?"

Emily hesitated slightly before nodding and checking her

watch. "They should be there by now," she said in way that sounded as if she weren't really sure.

Viktor picked up on the doubt in her voice. "Is there a problem? That equipment is critical. No suits, no jump."

She sighed in frustration. "My contact at the embassy is a real asshole. He wanted to know just what was going on and got really pissed when I told him that information was above his pay grade."

Arlo leaned over to Davies and said something in his peculiar military/Ozark patois. Emily asked for a translation.

"Ol' Arlo here's got a point. He's gotta go with you when you get the gear. To check it over. There's damn few people he trusts with his jump equipment—least of all some suit that ain't never been near a jump. He's gotta check everythin': from the helmets to the altimeters. Too many things can wrong—things normal people don't really think about. For example, someone messes with the oxygen or the oxygen pre-breather, and you wind up with nitrogen in your blood stream. Can cripple you in seconds."

"Oxygen pre-breather? What are you talking about Mr. Davies?" All of a sudden, Bronstein was alert to the fact that a last-minute detail could derail an already complicated plan.

"No big deal, Avram," Davies tried to reassure him. "Just that me an' Arlo here have to get all the nitrogen out of our systems. The way to do that is to breathe pure oxygen for about half an hour before the jump. One whiff of atmospheric air, and we're fucked up real good." He gave Arlo a nudge. "Ain't we, Arlo? Fucked up, I mean."

Arlo gave one of his comic-book, Tom Sawyer grins. "Got that right, Sarge. But, shit, you've always told me I'm a little fucked up anyways. Don't see how a little nitrogen can change that."

Bronstein was beginning to look a little worried about this small team.

Viktor told him, "Relax, Avram, and trust me. These are

the guys you want next to you when the shit starts flying. Then they're as calm and collected as your basic librarian—at least those librarians that carry machine pistols."

"I hope you're right."

"I am."

Right then, Emily's encrypted satellite phone buzzed. She pulled it out of her pocket, read the message, and turned to Viktor with a bewildered expression.

"What's up?" he asked.

"I'm supposed to call my boss's office before going to the embassy. That's very weird. He's never asked me to do that before."

Before anyone could respond, she punched in the long number and waited impatiently while the connection was finally made. Shepherd's assistant answered the phone.

"What's going on, Martha? What does John want?" As Emily listened to the long answer, her face darkened and tears welled up in her eyes. "*No!*" she wailed. "That's not possible. I just saw him a week ago. He was planning to go to the senate hearing in a day or two." She held the phone tightly to her ear as Shepherd's assistant continued.

Martha let slip that she was now reading from an internal memo sent from the office of the deputy director of operations. "Due to the untimely death of John Shepherd, Agent Wilkins is to cease any current operations and return to base as soon as possible. Under no circumstances is she to offer any assistance from the U.S. government to non-American or non-official personnel."

Emily clicked the end-call button and let the phone drop onto the seat. Everyone turned to her as she stared blankly out the window.

"John Shepherd—my boss who authorized this little venture—is dead," she intoned in a dull monotone. "They say someone put a bomb on his boat in Annapolis. It blew up when he tried to start it. Nothing was left except some cinders. Now I'm supposed to stop what I'm doing and go home. All official American support has been pulled."

Davies was about to say that this torpedoed their plans when Viktor put up a cautioning hand and turned to Emily. "Any speculation on who planted bomb?"

"No need to speculate," she spat out. "The idiots in Washington will never admit it, but it's the people he warned *me* about. The ones you can't see. The ones behind you in the shadows. They're all looking for an excuse to start WW III in the Middle East, and Assad's rat program gives the perfect excuse."

"Wait a minute," Viktor said with some skepticism. "You're telling me that some unknown person possibly connected with the NSA killed Shepherd? That makes no fucking sense. Why would anyone go to that trouble? Is there something you didn't tell us?"

Emily's eyes were flashing in anger, and her fists were clenched tight. "You don't get it, do you, Viktor? You think everything is so straightforward. Good guys on one side and bad guys on another. You go in and wipe out the bad guys. Everyone is on the same page." She took a deep breath. "Don't be so naïve. In any organization bigger than your little troop, very few people are on the same page. I'll guarantee that any investigation will be superficial at best. It will even disappear from Twitter in a day or two."

No one in the car said anything, sensing there was more to come.

"You see," she continued more calmly, "John approved our plan on his own authority. He warned me there were others in the Agency who were completely against the way we operated. But his real warning was that there are some—inside the Agency and in some bizarre fringe groups—who were looking for an excuse for a real war." She shook her head ruefully. "He was supposed to testify in front of the Senate Intelligence Committee this week about his concerns. I never thought they'd go so far as to essentially assassinate one of the few really good people we have so as to stop that testimony."

"That's the goddamnedest tale I ever did hear," said Davies. "I knew we had some seriously fucked up people, but killin' your own to set up a real war? That's plum crazy."

"But not beyond the realm of possibility," stated Bronstein, who'd listened impassively without any visible reaction to Emily's tale. Having been born in Russia and then having lived most of his life in the Middle East, he was all too familiar with betrayal in all its forms. Killing Shepherd was something the Russians would have done without batting an eye. The only surprising thing was that it had taken the Americans so long to catch on to this way of "discharging" problem employees. It eliminates those always awkward termination interviews. "In its own twisted way, it makes perfect sense. We're trying to do two things: eliminate the very real threat of a devastating biological attack, while simultaneously removing the excuse for an all-out war with unknown consequences. The United States will escape this folly with limited consequences, but those in the region will pay a heavy price, I fear. Put another way, we've become a serious threat to their plans."

"I don't wanna be pessimistic or anythin'," Davies interrupted, "but what the fuck do we do now? Without them HALO suits, ain't no way Arlo and me is jumpin' outta some plane at 30,000 feet. Besides, we got another problem in case you hadn't noticed. We gotta assume that Emily's a target now. Killin' her boss is only part of the solution. They cain't let her run around out of control." He turned to Emily. "Just how far off the books are you willin' to go? This could get real ugly real fast."

"Don't you worry about me," she said with deadly calm. "They'll find they're fucking with the wrong person. I'll get my revenge—and it won't be with a long spoon."

Davies grinned. "My kind of woman. Now that's settled, whadda we do now?"

"We think," Bronstein answered simply.

"Thinkin' is real good, Avram. But we ain't got a whole lotta time if we're gonna stop this shit. It's one thing to go up against a few dopey guards, but I ain't real sure we got much chance against the whole fuckin' U.S. army."

At that moment, Emily's phone buzzed again. She looked at the caller ID and gasped. "It's John's phone. Who the hell is using it?" She gently pushed the receive button and held the phone slightly away from her ear. "Yes," was all she said.

"Emily Wilkins?" asked a firm, unfamiliar female voice.

"Yes."

"This is Helen Shepherd." No preamble. No tears. Just cold determination. "John spoke highly of you and had your number on his speed dial. I'll get right to the point. He liked and trusted you, Emily. Find out who killed him and deal with them." She paused for half a second. "Understand me? It's not for me. Arrange their permanent termination in John's memory."

Emily understood perfectly. "I will find them. And they *will* be dealt with."

"Thank you," Helen Shepherd said and ended the call.

Emily continued to stare out the window. The others in the car had seen enough grief and anger to realize empty words of comfort were useless—even offensive.

Bronstein acknowledged this with a small nod and turned to Viktor. "Remember that operation in Chad?"

Viktor gave a small smile, knowing what was coming next.

"Time to call in a favor, don't you think? Meanwhile, I'll call someone who won't be totally surprised at this development. There may well be a connection with something closer to home. If anyone can throw a wrench in these plans, it's Benny Perlman.

"Actually, I suspect he'll be delighted at this turn of events. It will—as you put it—get him out of the pasture and simply confirm his already jaundiced view of humanity."

"Aren't we forgetting something?" Viktor asked. "What about

Yushenko? We promised him the moon to get him to cooperate. Without the American guarantee for him and his family, he's not going to lift a finger."

"Don't worry, Viktor," Bronstein said. "He'll get his help. But he may have to learn something besides English. I think it's best if we get to the restaurant. Eli has secure communications we can use to rearrange the chessboard."

"This is going to be a game for the books, Avram." Viktor chuckled.

Davies laughed along with him. "Well, shit, Viktor. This is right up our alley. Fuckin' plague-ridden rats in front of us and heavily armed maniacs behind. Nuthin' to it!"

***

The crowds on the sidewalk in front of the restaurant were a little puzzled when five grim-faced people piled out of an SUV and went quickly into the restaurant, despite the prominently displayed "Closed" sign. Eli took one look at their faces and led them silently to the large table where Yushenko had already started on the *meze*.

Yushenko gestured toward the huge bags Arlo was carrying, but then he too sensed the situation had changed. "What happened? Do we still have an operation?"

"Yes," Viktor answered, "but the ground rules have changed." He then explained what Emily had learned about Shepherd's death and the likely existence of groups that wanted to see them fail.

Yushenko was quick to get to the thing that concerned him. "And the agreement about my relocation and medical help for my son? What happens now?" As a career Russian army officer, Yushenko was familiar with the games that military leaders and their political masters play with each other. The true objectives remain carefully hidden in all the misinformation and half-information that passes for communication. He let out a big sigh. He'd always thought this deal with the Americans was too straightforward to be true. No Russian would ever act like that. However, now he had a problem. Once he'd started down the road with this unlikely group, it had become increasingly difficult to pull out. And what was the point if he couldn't get his family out of Syria and find medical help for his son? He liked these people well enough, but he wasn't sure how much longer he could hang around.

It was Bronstein who broke the ice. "First things first, Lieutenant," he answered in his native Russian. "Even if the Americans back out of their agreement, I can assure you we'll bring you and your family to a place with good medical facilities."

"Who's 'we'?" Yushenko interrupted.

"Someone who wants to see this project succeed."

"OK," he answered slowly, not quite trusting this newcomer—a Russian at that. "How exactly? It seems all our earlier plans have been flushed down the toilet."

"Not completely." Bronstein nodded toward Viktor, who was busy on Eli's secure phone. "Why don't we all sit down and enjoy some of Sarah's delicious food while we—what do the Americans say?—*wait for the cavalry*." He grinned at his memory of American cowboy shows on TV.

While the food was being prepared, Yushenko unzipped Arlo's bag and let out a low whistle at the contents. He picked up an H&K 433, inspected it, and stripped it in less than 10 seconds. Arlo's eyes widened in admiration.

"Not bad," Yushenko muttered, "ours was better, but this will do." He rummaged around in the bag some more. "What else do you have in here?" He smiled as he held up and examined a compact Israeli-made rocket launcher. "Very good. It will go through anything. Ammunition; you got ammunition?"

Arlo pointed to another bag, and Yushenko grunted with satisfaction. Satisfied, he carefully replaced the weapons in the sack. Viktor and Davies breathed a sigh of relief. Apparently, they'd passed some kind of test.

"Your plan is still nuts, but with these"—Yushenko patted the two bulging bags—"maybe it's not completely impossible."

"We still have to fill a major hole," Viktor cautioned. He looked at his watch. It was lunchtime in France. He took a chance and dialed Phillipe de Villers's cell phone. He could picture Phillipe fumbling around in his pocket for the phone, annoyed that someone would interrupt his lunch.

"Allo," Phillipe answered in a tone that indicated he'd much rather be tucking into his *poulet au pot* than answering his phone. He brightened immediately when he heard Viktor's voice. "Ah, Viktor, if you hurry, we may still have enough of Suzanne's special *poulet* left for you. But," he added when he heard Viktor was calling from Cyprus, "I think this call isn't about luncheon recipes and wines to accompany them."

He listened intently about the developments at the Crac des Chevaliers and motioned for Suzanne to bring him a pad and paper. He cupped the phone under his ear and wrote down Viktor's requests. He let out a small gasp when Viktor told him their plans. "This is an ambitious plan," he declared with Gallic understatement, "and something that Bernard would love. His only regret will be his inability to join you personally," he said referring to the former commanding officer, now Général de Division Bernard Lecount, of Phillipe's parachute division. "He's a good man; as tough as nails and not one to forget a debt. He remembers Chad very well and speaks highly of you when we meet. He always wants to know what you're up to."

He listened some more and smiled broadly. "You're in luck, my friend. He stopped in here a few days ago on his way to Cyprus—to the British bases to be exact. There's some sort of joint command meeting, and he was told to go and represent France. He hates those things and was moaning about wasting three days. He'll no doubt welcome your call as an excuse to get out of another pointless meeting. Oh, and nothing gives him more pleasure than running circles around the so-called 'intelligence agencies'—especially American ones." He looked at the list Viktor had read to him. "I don't see a major problem with any of this. We use the same type of equipment. It should work well with a few minor adjustments." He gave Viktor the general's private cell phone number. "Give me a few minutes to brief Bernard, then call him. You'll make his day."

Viktor put the phone down and went back to the group waiting anxiously around the table. Only Davies, Arlo, and Yushenko were sampling the many different dishes—following the soldier's mantra of eating and sleeping when you can. Viktor helped himself to a small *dolma* and said the first step had been taken.

"*And?*" Emily demanded in frustration.

"Perhaps I have to make one more call," was all Viktor said. He looked at his watch and then moved into the back room.

As Phillipe predicted, General Lecount was pleased to get Viktor's call. "I'm grateful you called, M. Lipsky. If I had to listen to one more talk about 'field rations', I'd have shot someone."

From the sound of his voice, Viktor wasn't entirely sure he was joking.

"Now, what can I—or the Legion, I should say—do for you? Phillipe explained some of it, but it sounded so bizarre I think it would be better if we met to discuss this matter."

Viktor replied, "That's a good idea. I'll be bringing Ricky Davies, who has a better idea of exactly what's needed."

General Lecount smiled. "Ah, the estimable Sergeant Davies. My men remember him well. In that case, I'll also bring my own estimable sergeant, Said Chakroun. You and Sergeant Davies may remember him from that incident in Chad."

Viktor did indeed remember the wiry, tough Foreign Legion soldier—the French equivalent of Ricky Davies. He and the general agreed to meet in a fish restaurant in the Old Port of

Limassol, about half an hour's fast drive on the motorway from Larnaca.

After ending the call, Viktor gathered up the keys to car and signaled for Davies to come with him.

Davies rose to follow him, but before they got to the door, Davies pulled him aside. "Ain't you forgettin' something?"

Viktor looked puzzled.

Davies sighed in exasperation.

"Jesus Christ, man! If them bastards got to Emily's boss, exactly how long d'you think it's gonna take 'em to come after her? I know she's a tough lady, but them boys play for keeps. They ain't no time-servers like Balko's men."

"Oh. Yeah, you're right. What do you propose?"

"We let Arlo and the Russian start earnin' their keep. They keep a close eye on her. Gimme a minute."

He walked back to the table and sat between Arlo and Yushenko. Emily was busy talking with Bronstein. Davies whispered his concerns and nodded slightly toward Emily. Both got the message.

"Don't you worry none," Arlo answered. "Me an' Oleg here will make damn sure she ain't got a scratch on her when you come back. Won't we, Oleg?"

Yushenko only half understood Arlo's accent, but he got the drift and nodded his head in agreement—almost eager to try out some of the equipment in the bags.

"OK, then, boys; we're off. Keep your eyes open and fingers on triggers," Davies ordered.

CHAPTER 18

Limassol, Cyprus

General Lecount may not have been in uniform, but Viktor had no trouble picking him out of the crowd in the restaurant. Standing at a little under 6' tall, he had the hard, lean body; weathered face; and sharp, wary eyes of an army officer who's spent a great deal of time fighting real rather than bureaucratic wars. Seated next to him was the French/Algerian equivalent of Ricky Davies—a tough, gnarled package of energy. Viktor could sense the easy, informal relationship the two had, and he noticed the only drink on the table was a bottle of mineral water.

Davies's face broke into a wide grin when he spotted Said Chakroun. He walked quickly to his table and slapped his friend on the back. "Well goddamn if it ain't my favorite Ayrab. How you doin'?"

Chakroun returned the grin and jumped out his chair to grab Davies around the shoulders. "Allah be blessed! My favorite cotton-picking infidel, still alive and in one piece," Chakroun replied in heavily accented English.

Viktor observed this exchange with some reserve, not quite sure how a general of the French army would react to the seeming disregard for the protocol appropriate to his rank. He shouldn't have worried; this wasn't a man who worried about protocol.

The general merely smiled and motioned for Viktor and Davies to take seats at the table, which had been pushed away from the others. He reached over to shake Viktor's hand. "Phillipe—and Said—have told me much about you and Sergeant Davies. I'm glad to finally meet you and offer my thanks for getting him and his men out of that mess."

A waiter approached the table and hovered over them, waiting for their order. The general scowled at the interruption and showed why he was a commanding officer. Rather than wasting time on everyone placing individual orders, he fired off instructions in decent Greek for their food and drinks. That done, he sent the waiter on his way.

"My mother," he said by way of explanation, "is Greek. She insisted I learn enough of the language to at least order food." He looked closely at Viktor. "Now, about this impregnable fortress in Syria; what can you tell me?"

Viktor then spent the next half hour—interrupted only by the delivery of an enormous sea bass and salad—explaining what they knew about the Crac des Chevaliers, plus the plan to produce a virus with no known antidote and spread it through infected rodents. General Lecount and his sergeant listened without interruption as Viktor went through all the complications about involving the major countries for fear of igniting a much larger regional war. The general merely nodded his agreement with that assessment and suggested they eat the fish before it got cold.

"That much I understand," he said when only the bones were left, "but why do you need us?"

Davies took a deep breath and turned to Viktor to explain this wrinkle, which he did: "This is where it gets interesting, General. For reasons I don't really understand, there are people in our own agencies who seem to want this experiment in biological warfare to succeed. They've canceled all official assistance to us. And the one senior intelligence official who agreed to help us was killed a few days. One of our group, an NSA agent herself, is convinced he was murdered by people on our own side. And now she's probably a target too."

Chakroun sat up straight and turned to Davies. "This is true?"

"Looks that way," Davies sighed.

General Lecount regarded Viktor and Davies for a long time without saying anything, assessing this information. "And you, M. Lipsky—do you believe her version of events?"

Viktor shrugged his shoulders. "In a twisted way, it makes perfect sense, General. I'm sure there are people back in Washington who'd like nothing better than an excuse to exercise massive military power. They tend not to care very much about thousands of ordinary people dying."

"Pardon the interruption, General," Davies blurted out, "but it's tough enough facin' people in front of you. And it don't get any easier when they're behind you as well."

A grim smile creased General Lecount's face. "We aren't entirely unfamiliar with such a situation, Sergeant." He looked over at Chakroun, who nodded his head vigorously in agreement. "In my experience, politicians have their own agendas, which may or may not include people like us"—he waved his hand to include everyone at the table—"who are too often considered 'acceptable' sacrifices." He paused for a minute. "One thing puzzles me. What about the Israelis? Surely they won't let this biological warfare happen on their doorstep?"

"Officially, no, General," Viktor answered. "But from our information, they'd like it solved without starting World War III." He glanced across the table at Davies. "That's where we come in."

"Yes," the general acknowledged. "Exactly what are you planning? And, unofficially of course, how can the Legion help?"

Viktor breathed a sigh of relief and outlined their plans. He explained that the whole operation depended on high-level parachute equipment that the Americans were no longer providing.

The general once again turned to his sergeant, who merely nodded his head as if to say there was no technical problem with what Viktor needed. The general placed his knife and fork carefully on his empty plate and took a drink of water. "You know, M. Lipsky, the Legion is famous for acting independently. Sometimes, we go where our political masters don't wish to be seen and do what they don't wish to be seen doing. I believe this might be such a time. Sergeant Chakroun has indicated that we do indeed possess the NATO standard HALO kits, and I'm sure we can arrange to lose three of them in a training exercise in deepest Africa where no one will ever check..."

"Three?" Viktor asked. "We only need two, sir. It's just Ricky and one of his soldiers who'll be making the jump."

"I think not, M. Lipsky." The general laughed. "From a professional, classical military point of view, what you're proposing is idiotic. Suicidal even. But Sergeant Davies is right. With surprise and a few very good men, it might just work. In my experience, sometimes too few men are better than too many. Moreover, if France is going to provide the equipment, France must monitor its correct use." He turned toward his sergeant. "And I can think of no one better than Sergeant Chakroun to do that monitoring. He has some leave coming up and he's certainly familiar with this type of jump."

Chakroun's face lit up at the prospect of getting back into action.

Davies chuckled. "We're happy as hell to have Said on board, but it ain't exactly my idea of 'leave' to go jumpin' out of some plane at 30,000 feet into what could be a big mess."

"Don't worry, Sergeant Davies," the general interjected. "Said has what's called a 'very low threshold of boredom.' He has months of leave accumulated over the years because he has never, in my recollection, taken any." He looked at Said for confirmation.

"*Rien, mon général,*" Said responded defiantly. "*C'est ennuyeux.*"

Davies looking questioningly at Viktor.

"He just said he hasn't taken any. Considers leave boring," Viktor said.

Davies clapped the Frenchman on the shoulder. "This sure as hell ain't gonna be borin'. I can promise that much."

The general quickly brought the discussion back to the point: "Viktor, do you have any solid information?"

Viktor patted his backpack. "I suggest we continue this discussion in the car."

The general nodded his agreement and started to leave money for the bill.

Viktor shook his head and grabbed the bill with a grin. "This is the least we can do for the Legion's support."

He and the general exited the restaurant together, leaving the others to finish their meals.

***

Once inside the car, the general pored over the maps and came to the same conclusion as Davies. "*Mon Dieu.*" He whistled softly. "My ancestors built very well. Sergeant Davies is right. The tunnels are your best—your only—way in. He's also right that the only people who'll fit are him, his comrade, and now Sergeant Chakroun." He turned to Viktor. "You can arrange the transport to the drop site?"

"It's being taken care of by people who've helped us in the past."

"*Bon,*" was all Lecount said. Sometimes, it's better not to know too much.

He scanned the piece of paper Davies had handed him with their requirements for the HALO equipment. He then handed the list to Chakroun, who checked each item meticulously before nodding to the general and whispering something in French military shorthand that Viktor couldn't understand.

General Lecount translated: "The equipment is now on one of our bases outside Marseilles. We can arrange for it to be shipped here to arrive"—he checked his watch—"late tonight' time. Satisfactory?"

"More than," Davies answered. "Where should we pick it up?"

"Don't trouble yourselves. Sergeant Chakroun will bring it to you. It will give him a chance to meet the rest of your team." As he shook Viktor's hand in farewell, Lecount said, "If I were 20 years younger, I'd be the first out of the plane."

***

Larnaca, Cyprus

Emily had been toying with her food at the restaurant, pushing the food around on her plate and eating only small bits. Shepherd's death bothered her more than she was letting on, and she decided she wanted some time alone. She slid the plate away, stood up, and said she was going back to her hotel, and she'd wait for Viktor and Davies in the lobby.

Yushenko sat up abruptly and looked over at Arlo. Both of them nodded their understanding that this wasn't a good idea.

"Actually, Emily," Yushenko said, trying to keep the tone light, "Arlo and I would like to take a walk ourselves. Wouldn't we, Arlo?"

Arlo was caught out only momentarily and realized quickly what was expected. "Absolutely, Oleg. All this sittin' around don't do my legs no good at all."

Bronstein was quick to add his support to this plan. "Given what's happened, I think that makes good sense. I'll stay here with Eli and wait for the others to get back from Limassol." He glanced at the two bulging duffle bags. "Something for the road, gentlemen?"

At first, Emily was annoyed that anyone would think she needed bodyguards. She'd been looking after herself for a long time, thank you very much. However, she was also touched by their concern and conceded as gracefully as she could. "That would be nice, boys. I'd appreciate the company."

Arlo unzipped one of the bags and rummaged around inside until he found what he was looking for. He gave one of his gap-toothed smiles and held up two H&K 30 semi-automatic pistols. Yushenko took one of them and stripped it swiftly, just as he'd done with the H&K 433. "Almost as good as our SR-1," he concluded.

"Well, hell, Oleg. This ain't no pissin' contest. Someone gets hit by either one, they drop like a sack of shit. Ain't that the point?"

Yushenko chuckled as he quickly reassembled the pistol. "Yes, my friend. That's the point."

Emily stared as they loaded the pistols and grabbed some extra magazines. "For Christ's sake! We're not going to a war."

"No, Emily, we're not," Yushenko agreed. "But we need to be ready if the war comes to us—uninvited."

They were heading out the door when Bronstein spoke up, shaking his head almost sadly. *Soldiers can be very useful people,* he said to himself, *but they're too quick to rush into gun fire. Sometimes, it pays to do a little planning.* "Aren't you forgetting something?" he asked gently.

"Like what?" Arlo answered with a quizzical expression on his face.

"A plan. If Miss Wilkins actually is in danger on this island, where's the threat likely to come from? Any close-in attack would most likely be suicide, and I don't think the people who meticulously planned the murder of her boss go in for suicide attacks. My guess is that any attack will be from a distance and create enough confusion for the gunman to walk away calmly."

Yushenko and Arlo gave each other a sheepish the-man's-got-a-point look and returned to the table.

Bronstein turned and said a few words in Hebrew to Eli, who left and returned in a few minutes with a shiny, new Mac laptop. He opened it swiftly, punched a few keys, and a map of Larnaca appeared with much more detail than anything Google could generate. Exact distances; building heights; locations of businesses, shops, parking garages, and hotels; and every street and alley were highlighted in a wide variety of colors.

Yushenko stared at the screen in awe. "Where did this come from? I have never seen anything this detailed."

Bronstein gave a thin, enigmatic smile. "Not every Israeli who visits this island is a tourist. Any information, even about today's friends, is useful." He brushed aside any further questions. "Anyway, let's see what we're dealing with." He focused a laser pointer on the hotel where Emily was staying. "Oleg, what strikes you about this location?" he asked rhetorically.

"Four-story building, wide sidewalk, busy street, and low-rise buildings all around." He paused for a minute. "Not an ideal place for an ambush," he concluded.

"Exactly." Bronstein beamed. Then he moved the computer image out a little. "Now what do you see?"

Yushenko gave a now-I-get-it grin. "Taller buildings, five to six stories, and about one to one and a quarter miles from the hotel." He peered closer. "A parking garage, another hotel, and a semi-finished building with some reinforcing rods sticking up from the roof."

"In your professional opinion what does that tell you?"

"A shooter can set up right there," Arlo chimed in, jabbing his finger at the semi-finished building and running it along the screen until it came to the road leading to the hotel. "Clean line of sight from the roof right along this street. Unfinished empty building. Easy shot for a halfway decent shooter. Emily would be toast, and the guy long gone before the cops even got to the hotel." He shook his head in admiration. He turned to the others. "What do you think the odds are that he's there right now, just waitin' for us, knowin' we have to go back to hotel sometime, and trainin' his scope on the crowds?"

"I don't know," Yushenko answered. "but they're probably pretty good."

Suddenly, Arlo was in attack mode. All the good-ole-boy antics were over.

"OK. We're dealin' with a pro; no fuckin' suicide jockey." He pointed to Yushenko. "Oleg, you go with Emily. You're a big bastard, and no one on the street is gonna mess with you. I'm gonna circle around these backstreets here and make my way up this here buildin' to get to the roof. Give that fella a little welcome."

Bronstein turned to Eli, who gave a "better than nothing, and it could work" shrug. "All right. Off you go. Emily with Oleg; Arlo to the building. I hope all this precaution is a complete waste of time, but… but…" he stammered looking for the right words. Not finding any, he simply said goodbye.

CHAPTER 19

Arlo only had to glance at the map once to know precisely how to get to the unfinished building where, if he were the sniper, he would set up. His uncanny sense of direction led him through a series of small alleys and courtyards until he came to the construction site. The ground was littered with piles of rebar, cement mixers, and planks used to make forms. The hoist that was used to haul material to the upper floors was now being used to suspend the big generator in a vain attempt to stop it from being stolen. What he didn't see were any workers, but then he remembered this was a Saturday afternoon in the spring, and no one would be around. This was perfect from the shooter's point of view: an open field of fire, isolated, and with lots of cover.

Arlo was convinced he'd found the right place. He picked his way carefully around the detritus of the construction site to reach the back of the building, where he found an entrance and some crude, unfinished stairs. While leaning against the wall, he took off his shoes and left them just inside the opening before taking out his pistol and chambering a round. He then approached the steps, and as he did so he noticed fresh footprints that had picked up the cement dust all around the building. Now he was sure he wasn't alone.

Silently, he crept up the rough steps, thankful they were

solid concrete and not wood, which would give warning creaks to anyone there. As he started up the steps, all the instincts from his hunting days back home and in the mountains of Afghanistan came back to him. He was in his element. His breathing automatically slowed, his eyes swiveled constantly to search out potential threats, and each movement of his arms and legs was made with exaggerated slowness. Silent foot by silent foot, he made his way up the stairs to the roof.

Finally, he peered around the corner of the stairwell at the roof of the building, which had several half-finished pillars, more piles of rebars, and more general construction trash. He couldn't see the entire roof, so he duckwalked very carefully over to one of the pillars. Using that as a vantage point, he scanned the entire roof. He'd been wrong. There was nothing and no one. "Motherfucker's gotta be here somewhere," he whispered to himself.

Cautiously, he inched over to the edge of the building that was facing the town, being careful not to let his shadow give away his presence. He could see Yushenko and Emily making their way warily toward her hotel. Then he glanced down. "You clever cocksucker," he muttered. Marginally sticking out of one of the windows on the floor beneath him, he could see the thin barrel of a weapon he knew well—the army's M107 sniper rifle. "Of course, you're down there where no passing helicopter or some kid's drone might spot some guy with a rifle on top of an unfinished building."

***

The streets were more crowded than Yushenko liked. A few puffy clouds did little to hide the brutally hot sun. Crowds of sunburned tourists were clogging the sidewalks as they ambled along, stalling at every stand selling souvenirs and Chinese-made "I Love Cyprus" T-shirts. They grudgingly gave way as Yushenko strode along like a human snowplow. After one look at his size and the determined expression on his face, the tourists edged off the sidewalk and onto the small street, where small delivery trucks blasted their horns for everyone to get out of their way.

Emily was no help. She hated the idea of a bodyguard and thought the whole thing was an embarrassing waste of time. She tried to explain this to Yushenko, who only growled at her in Russian to shut up and do what she was told for the first time in her life. This didn't go down well and earned him a slap on the arm. He was constantly scanning the streets, alleys, and doorways for potential threats. Occasionally, he'd turn around and make sure no one was following them. After about 20 minutes, as they were approaching the hotel, they passed the glossy, black marble wall of a new office building. The wall was polished to the smoothness of a mirror, and Yushenko glanced at it. He was about to pass by when he jerked his head around and took another look at the wall, in which he spotted a small glare—a reflection of something bright shining off a piece of glass somewhere off to the side. Without thinking, he grabbed Emily, threw her to the hard ground, and covered her body as something shattered the shiny wall just where her head had been. The nearby tourists were focusing on their smart phones or looking at the souvenir shops, and they only noticed flakes of marble dropping down on their heads. They shook their heads in annoyance and glanced angrily at Yushenko and Emily for blocking the sidewalk. A Syrian kid pushing a food trolley down the street knew exactly what the sound was and instantly dove under his trolley.

***

Seconds before, Arlo had heard the soft pfft of a silenced high-powered bullet and saw the thin trail of smoke from the end of the barrel. "Fuck, fuck, fuck. Too fucking late," he growled to himself. Then he looked toward the hotel and saw the chipped marble and Yushenko and Emily crawling toward a nearby doorway for protection. "Ha, asshole, you missed!"

***

The shooter cursed silently and was about to load another round when he thought he heard an unexpected scrape on the roof above. He rapidly pulled the rifle back, took out his Sig Sauer pistol, and peered out the window toward the roof. He saw nothing, but he decided to take no chances and headed toward the staircase.

***

Arlo heard him coming and felt a little unprotected with just a pistol against a pro with a sniper rifle and God knows what else. Then he remembered the hoist holding up the heavy generator and jogged back to the edge where the bracket was fastened. It was time for the hunted to become the hunter. After grabbing the rope, he dropped off the roof and slid down the rope until he came to an empty window on the floor below. A kick of his legs got the rope swinging just enough to get him close enough to drop through it. From there, he ran over to the stairs, on which his bare feet made no sound as he moved toward the roof. Once there, he picked up a piece of half-inch rebar about the length of a baseball bat in case he ever got close enough to take a swing at the shooter.

In the end, it wasn't necessary. The shooter had seen nothing on the roof and was now peering over the edge, wondering what had made the noise that distracted him. He never heard Arlo creep up and start to take a vicious swing with the rebar. The shooter must have sensed something at the last second because he turned around with a stunned expression on his face a moment before the heavy metal smashed into his head, sending him over the edge. He plunged soundlessly for six stories onto the hard ground and now lay in a crumpled heap by one of the cement mixers.

As Arlo looked down at the body, his face was calm with no expression of remorse or guilt. He'd long ago accepted that, for a soldier, there was only the thinnest of lines between life and death. It wasn't worth worrying about. That's just the way it was. No, his one concern now wasn't with the obviously dead. It was the with living—especially any living person who might have witnessed what happened. After glancing around, he was relieved not to see any casual passer-by with a cell phone stuck to his ear calling the cops. That wasn't unusual on a Saturday afternoon in a construction zone.

Arlo examined the rebar in his hand and was relieved there was no blood on it or on the roof; there was nothing to encourage the notoriously incurious local cops to regard this as anything more than a tragic accident—even if they couldn't explain exactly why some foreigner was on the roof of an unfinished building in the first place. To be on the safe side, he took the rebar with him to drop by some distant half-finished building. The rifle and pistol had flown out of the shooter's hands as he was hit and had landed near one of the unfinished pillars on the roof. *Nice pieces of work,* Arlo thought as he picked them up. He climbed down one floor and went to the shooting nest, where he found the sniper's accessories: water bottle, pee bottle, and a bag of sand to rest the rifle on. The real treasure trove was the backpack that contained a couple of passports: one American and one Spanish. The Spanish passport was in the name of Gerald Delgado and the American one was Thomas Stapleton. He stuffed them back in the backpack and dug around until he found the latest model iPhone, which was still on. After cutting the bag to empty out the sand, he broke the rifle down, put it back in its case, and took everything with him.

***

Once back in the hotel room, Arlo dropped the backpack and rifle in front of Yushenko and Emily, who had by this time replaced her initial shock with sheer fury.

"Those bastards," she spat. "Those stupid, stupid bastards. They're going to have to work a lot harder and be a lot smarter to stop me. There's no hole big enough for them to hide in."

There was a soft knock on the door, and Yushenko pulled Emily to one side while Arlo cautiously drew his pistol and went to the door. He gestured for Emily to answer.

"Who's there?" she asked.

"For Christ's sake, Emily, open the goddamned door. It's just me and Viktor. We got some interesting news," Davies chided.

"And so do we," Emily replied as she opened the door with a smile of relief.

At one glance, Davies took in the expressions on Arlo's and Yushenko's faces, as well as the rifle case and the backpack. "OK," he said slowly, "looks like you should go first."

Davies and Viktor could only nod in admiration as Arlo and Yushenko relayed what happened.

"Quick thinking, Oleg; very quick. Goddamn glad you were there. And, Arlo, that was real good; real, *real* good. That bastard ain't gonna be botherin' anyone again. The question is what now? What do we do with this here phone? Probably encrypted seein' as how whoever don't like us went to so much trouble to give this guy a fancy piece of hardware," Davies declared as he picked up the iPhone.

Viktor took the phone from him and looked at it closely. "Nothing I can do with it, but we know someone who can." He used his own phone to call the Parea and ask to speak to Avram Bronstein. After quickly giving Bronstein an edited version of the events of the last couple of hours, he said there was an encrypted phone that might hold some answers as to what was going on. He listened for a few more seconds and then hung up. "Avram said he might just know some people in town who can solve this phone problem. He'll send them right over. Oh, by the way, he said good news about the French helping. He wants to see us back at the restaurant as soon as we're finished here. He says there's someone we should meet."

"The French? What about the French? Where the hell did they come from?" Emily asked.

Viktor smiled at her annoyance at bringing in yet another country. "Relax, Emily. Take a breath. They're friends. More important, they've agreed to supply the equipment that *your* one-time friends have refused to give us. On top of that, one their people is going to join our little group."

"*What?*" she exploded.

Before she could go off on a tirade about the French army, Davies cut her off. "Don't you worry none about Said Chakroun. We been in some tight scrapes together, me 'n' him. He's one tough sumbitch. Good man to have on our side. Besides, he's gonna bring the equipment we need in a couple days. No French, no operation—it's that simple."

At that moment, there was another knock on the door, and they all reached for their weapons.

Emily opened it cautiously and saw a thin, nervous pizza delivery boy in the hallway. "Who ordered the pizza?" she asked.

They all shook their heads and leveled their pistols at the delivery boy whose eyes opened wide in fear as he dropped the pizza box onto the floor. "Avram," he squeaked, "Avram Bronstein sent me."

They all put their weapons away, and Davies grabbed the kid's shirt and pulled him swiftly inside. "Take a deep breath, son. Nuthin's gonna happen. You're safe."

The kid's eyes said he really didn't believe that.

Viktor gestured for him to sit down and showed him the phone. "We *found* this phone on someone. It appears to be encrypted, and we'd really like you to try to unravel this little puzzle for us. Understand? You speak English, right? By the way, what's your name and why the pizza routine?"

"Of course I speak English. I'm from Minneapolis. Otherwise known as Silicon Tundra. The pizza was Avram's idea. It appears you people aren't universally popular. He thought it would reduce suspicion about so many people coming to this particular room. Anyway, here I am. Can I have a glass of water before getting started on this phone?"

"Couple of questions," Viktor said. "Are you part of Mossad? Where's this information going to go? Oh, and how did a kid from Silicon Tundra wind up in Israel?"

"One thing at a time," the boy answered. "Gideon, Gideon Rubin's my name. And no, I'm not part of Mossad—not directly. I do some jobs for Avram from time to time. My information distribution stops with Avram. What he does with it…" He raised his hands in the universal "who knows?" gesture. "As for the other part, well, living in the land of giant, blond Swedes who actually like sub-zero weather and mounds of snow is nice, but it gets old fast. The Jews up there had a special name for themselves: the Frozen Chosen. Anyway," he said, dismissing the recollection of frozen winters, "let's figure this fucker out."

He opened his backpack, took out a slim computer, and attached some cables between it and the phone. Then his fingers danced over the computer keyboard faster than anyone could follow.

Davies raised his eyebrows at Viktor, asking if he understood what was happening. Viktor shook his head. Not a chance.

After a few minutes, Rubin stopped and looked up at them with a worried expression.

"Somethin' wrong, kid? Somethin' you cain't figure out?" Davies asked.

"No," Rubin answered, "it's not that. It's actually fairly simple. It is, after all, based loosely on the latest Pentagon/NSA encryption schematics. It's a poor man's substitute. The actual Pentagon/NSA encryption program is a real ball-buster. It's almost impossible to crack. This, however, is pretty straightforward. It's enough to fool most hackers but not good enough to stop a pro. It's as if someone tried to copy the real thing in a hurry and missed a few key steps."

"*What?*" they all said at once, not quite believing that a skinny kid from Minneapolis could break something like that.

"What are you talking about?" queried Viktor.

"Who, exactly, did you piss off? Because whoever sent this really wants to shut you down." Rubin looked at the screen again. "Anyone ever hear of a Thomas Stapleton, also known as Gerald Delgado? It seems they wanted him to fulfill a contract."

All eyes shifted to Arlo. He gave a small cough. "That person met with an unfortunate accident not long ago."

"Industrial accident, was it?" Rubin asked with a knowing smirk. "Mossad generates a lot of those."

Viktor turned toward the kid. "Is there any way for you to track who actually sent those messages?"

"Unfortunately, no. They never use names, but I can probably track IP addresses and give you a general location. I think it's somewhere around Washington, but I'll need to do some more work to get more accurate."

Viktor was about to ask another question when the iPhone started to vibrate. They all looked at each other, not knowing what to do.

"Pick it up, for Christ's sake. It's not going to bite you." Rubin laughed as he unplugged one of the cables and handed the phone to Viktor who delicately pushed the receive button. He didn't have to say anything as an angry voice boomed out of the phone.

"Where the hell are you, boy? What kind of game are you playing? You were supposed to contact us hours ago. That was an order, soldier. Did you complete the mission? Did you put the broad's body where we told you? Sitrep now, soldier!"

"Hello to you too," Viktor responded.

"Who the hell is this? Where the fuck is Stapleton?"

"He's indisposed right now. Is there anything I can do to help?"

"Who are you?"

"Room service."

"*Don't get smart with me, boy,*" the caller yelled.

Viktor could just picture the type of man on the other end of the line getting redder and redder in the face, close to a stroke.

Before the conversation could continue, the phone was yanked out of the caller's hand. "Don't say another word," they heard someone order in the background.

Rubin glanced at his screen, alarmed at what he saw. "We got a problem. Someone's erasing everything instantly." He looked at them helplessly. "It's gone goodbye."

"Can't you do something? Can't you retrieve any of that data?" Emily pleaded.

Rubin merely shook his head sadly, like a surgeon coming out of a failed operation.

"Goddamn it," she wailed. "Just when we were getting somewhere. Now we've got nothing."

Viktor told her, "Calm down; we've actually learned a lot."

"Such as?"

"Such as whoever is behind this may not be active military, but they have close ties—not just with the military but with your bunch. Close enough to get some pretty good encryption—not top of the line maybe, but close enough. The top-of-the-line stuff would have taken even Gideon a bit longer to crack."

Davies, who'd been sitting on the sofa with one ear cocked toward the small phone, stood up and moved to the center of the room. "I'll tell you somethin' else we ain't got—and that's time. This call and the shooter's presence here in Cyprus where no one is supposed to know we're at both tell me we're up against some heavy opposition with a shitload of resources."

"So what are we supposed to do?" Emily demanded. "Just close up shop and go home?"

Davies sighed in exasperation. "Jesus Christ, woman. Hold your horses. I didn't say nuthin' like that. What I was tryin' to say, before I was interrupted, was that we're outta time. These boys, whoever the hell they are, are movin' fast." He turned to Viktor and Yushenko. "You two gotta get to Damascus as fast as you can and work your way down to that village by the fort. What I suggest we do right now is get back to the restaurant and see what Avram's got for us." He turned to Rubin who was packing up his computer. "You too, kid. No tellin' when we're gonna need some of your magic."

CHAPTER 20

Alexandria, Virginia

General Meadows drummed his fingers on the expensive leather blotter that covered most of his desk as he recalled some of his earliest training: *"Improvise, son; improvise. Adapt and control. Shit happens. Deal with it."* It didn't matter *how* those people had dealt with Stapleton. The fact was that they had. It was time to focus on what to do now. He turned to his two senior aides. "Move up the timetable, boys. Tell them folks in Israel to get word to their Syrian contact to pull his finger out before some uninvited *guests* crash the party. They don't need to know specifics. Just tell 'em it would be smart to take some extra precautions."

The general got up and started for the door saying he had to get in touch with his people at the NSA and the Pentagon. Instead of leaving the building, he went into an empty office and pulled out a highly encrypted satellite phone that no one in the company knew he had. He could never remember the long string of numbers required and relied on some ancient technology—a piece of much folded paper tucked deep inside his wallet. Holding the phone in one hand, he laboriously punched in 12 numbers and listened impatiently to the multiple squeaks, squawks, and beeps of an international call. He wasn't even sure exactly where he was calling, but he hoped his contact would. "Son of bitch could be anywhere."

Finally, a deep, guttural voice gave a loud grunt as an answer. There was no need to give away even the language that might identify him until he knew who was on the other end.

Meadows felt no such constraints. "Dmitry, is that you? For Christ's sake, answer."

Dmitry Utkin, the head of the Russian military contractor Reinhard, secretly thought Meadows was a fool but one who could possibly deliver some serious firepower. "Stanley, you should be more careful. You can never tell who's listening."

Meadows told him, "Relax. We have all those security issues in hand. There's no problem there, my friend; we got people all over the listeners."

Utkin wasn't impressed. "What happened in Cyprus and Annapolis were serious errors. Very messy. Now they've been warned."

A thin bead of sweat broke out on Meadows' brow. There weren't many people who made General Stanley Meadows sweat, but Utkin was one of them. He'd met the tough, battle-scarred ex-Spetsnaz commander with the dark, emotionless eyes of a real killer for the first time in a glitzy Hong Kong restaurant. He didn't remember much of the actual conversation, but he was left with the overall impression that this man of very few words—he didn't need many—played by a different rulebook. Without saying a word, he'd made it perfectly clear that anyone who crossed him would encounter some serious pain. How the hell did Utkin know about Cyprus so quickly? Meadows knew the Russian had people on the ground there, but this was ridiculous. He'd only found out about it a few minutes ago. Had he underestimated the guy? His first thought was to try to bluff his way out of it, but on second thoughts, he realized that was a bad idea.

"That was a little hiccup, Dimitry, but the plan is still on track. Now we've shut down their supplies and information flow, there's not a helluva lot they can do."

"Let's hope so," was the less-than-wholehearted response.

"Look, just in case it wouldn't be a bad idea to take some precautions."

"Like what?" Utkin snapped. He really didn't trust Meadows and was worried that the American would pull the plug at the last minute.

"Those Syrians at the fort are useless. And who the hell knows what the Koreans will do? Sending 10 to 15 of your people down to the fort would ensure that nothing happens to blow this program off course."

Utkin mulled this idea over for a couple of minutes and realized that Meadows just might have a point. He could spare that many people for a week or two. They'd bitch like hell at being sent to that dump, but the extra money in their accounts would ease the pain. "OK," he finally said. "I'll send Ivan Balko and some of his people. They need the work after their fuck-up in Africa."

"That should take care of it," said a relieved Meadows.

"But Stanley," Utkin continued ominously, "no more screw-ups. OK?"

"Absolutely, Dmitry," Meadows gushed. "It's all smooth from here on out."

"I hope so," said an unconvinced Utkin. Left unsaid but understood was the rest of the sentence: "… for your sake."

***

Parea restaurant, Larnaca

When Viktor and the others returned to the restaurant, they were surprised to see a thin, seemingly frail old man with hooded eyes and a sardonic smile sitting across the table from Bronstein. They wondered who the hell he was. Since when did Eli open the place to the general public? Bronstein grinned at their surprise and explained that he'd taken the liberty of calling in an old friend from Israel.

Emily gave a short laugh and filled in the rest of the team. "Let me guess. This is none other than the famed not-quite-out-to-pasture Benny Perlman. I've heard a great deal about you, Mr. Perlman, but what brings you out of retirement to this island paradise?"

"Retirement, my ass," he snapped. "You're right, Avram, she does have a mouth on her."

Everyone took this opportunity to sit down and start to pick at the food Eli had placed on the table.

"Actually, I wanted the chance to finally meet Mr. Lipsky and his team—people we've been supplying a great deal money to over the years." Perlman looked carefully at each member of the team and held up a hand before Viktor could say anything. "Money well spent, I must say. Mr. Davies you do very good work."

Davies looked surprised that this old man knew so much about him, but he merely nodded in acknowledgment of the praise.

Perlman took another pull on his cigarette, coughed up some phlegm, and continued, "But I'm mainly here to make sure your latest little project doesn't go too far off the rails. Your chances of success are slim enough without fools from our own goddamned countries trying to fuck you over." Once again, Emily was about to say something, but Perlman cut her off with a wave of his hand. "I understand from Avram that you've already seen how far those idiots will go to stop you before you even set foot in that godforsaken country. I know about our own nutcases and can only guess that they have lots of company in the United States."

He spent the next 20 minutes giving them a summary of the "unofficial" far-right groups within Israel that are supported by some members of the military and parliament. He concluded, "We pretty much know what they're doing." He paused to look at each of them carefully. "But make no mistake, they're powerful and will stop at nothing to create what they consider to be the Greater Israel. I don't know so much about the U.S., but I can easily imagine there are enough 'super patriots' in the intelligence agencies, the military, and private contractors who'd be very happy when Armageddon comes to the Middle East. The ones in Israel, we have some control over. The ones in the United States…" He raised his hands in the "who knows?" gesture. "Bottom line, as we saw from today's action, is that you have very little time."

Davies shook his head. "Fuck, this makes Africa look like a walk in the park. Look, Mr. Perlman—"

"Benny, please."

This got a grin from Davies. "OK, Benny, we got the pieces of a plan, but that's all. I hate goin' into somethin' bare-ass naked where I don't know all the players."

"That's where we come—"

"Who's this 'we'?" Emily interrupted. "The State of Israel?"

Perlman grinned in a way that said there were games within games, and few were better at playing such games than Benny Perlman. "No, Miss Wilkins"—he was old-fashioned enough to avoid the odd-sounding "Ms."—"The State of Israel isn't officially involved, for now. When there's to be a general war in the Middle East, the State of Israel would prefer to be the one to set the terms, not"—a sharp edge of iron and anger had edged into his voice—"some half-assed group of fuck-ups who think they can create the ancient Kingdom of Israel by driving the State of Israel and, I might add, the United States into a regional war with disastrous potential."

This got everyone's attention.

"I know about the American groups," Emily said, "but what are you saying about the Israelis?"

"I've always known we had disgruntled ex-this and ex-that who thought we should have finished the job in 1967 or 1973—taken Damascus and Cairo." He shook his head sadly at the folly of such an idea. "The trouble that would come with our small state ruling over about 100 million very pissed Arabs never seemed to dawn on anyone. They have good connections inside the intelligence and military operations, but because they're outside the official system, they can operate pretty much independently. I was getting weird signals from various sources about some operation in Syria. I checked with our people. We were just doing the usual snooping—nothing dramatic. Then a friend in Amman picked up the same thing you discovered, Miss Wilkins, and gave me a call. By this time, I'd learned that you" —here he pointed to Emily, Viktor, and Yushenko—"were all on Cyprus, and I decided to learn more by sending Avram to see what the hell was going on."

"And," Emily prompted, "just what did you find out?"

"Enough to scare the shit out of me and bring me here. Up to now, we just had the fucking rats. The game has ratcheted up—as you recently found out earlier today. Whatever American group is involved has learned of your activities and is determined to stop you. Thus, the murder of your boss, Miss Wilkins, and the attack on you today. We have a strong suspicion that they're linked to a group in Jerusalem. We know some of them, but they're too well protected to do anything—right now at least."

"Damn," Davies uttered. "We're goin' out on a limb bare-ass naked."

Perlman held up one gnarled finger. "Not exactly, Sergeant. We aren't friendless or powerless ourselves. From what Avram tells me, you and your friends have actually created a workable plan. And to keep you from going out 'bare-ass naked,' we've created a small team to help." He saw Emily about to interject, so he motioned for her to wait. "Before you ask, Miss Wilkins, the State of Israel isn't officially involved in this effort. I called a few very trustworthy friends in Jerusalem and Amman to help. They too realize the grave danger of a wide conflict. Jerusalem has too many people listening in, so we'll operate out of Amman."

This raised a few eyebrows.

"Don't worry," Perlman added with a chuckle. "The Jordanians have as much to lose as we do. They'll do what they can to help."

"OK," Davies said. "Exactly how does all this work out? Once we drop outta that plane, we'll lose all contact with your group."

Perlman dug around in the shapeless shoulder bag he was carrying and pulled out a very small device. "We have some very clever people who prepared this device for just such a situation. I haven't got a clue how it works, but"—he turned to Gideon Rubin—"young Gideon here can explain the finer points. Basically, it lets you remain in touch with us at all times. You need to know if the situation has changed at all, and we need to know what's going on inside the fortress." His expression turned grim for a moment. "Because if you fail, my friends, we'll send in the full power of the Israeli Defense Force and wipe that fortress off the face of the earth before letting the 21st century version of the Black Plague loose on Israel—even if that sparks the wider war we're all trying to prevent." He didn't have to add that, in "wiping the fortress off the face of the earth," the Israelis would also be wiping out Viktor and his team. Perlman looked carefully at each of them to make sure they understood the consequences of failure. Satisfied the message was received, he continued, "Good. We understand each other."

He looked at his watch. "From the information I've received I figure we have a maximum of four, maybe five days"—he waggled his hands back and forth in uncertainty—"before those buffoons in Syria are ready to release those rats right at our front door…"

"That's cutting it very, very tight. We don't even have the HALO suits yet," Viktor reminded him.

Perlman laughed. "You did well to contact the French."

"How the hell do you know about the French help?" an exasperated Viktor asked.

Perlman gave him a pitying look. "The waiter at the fish restaurant in Limassol is ours. Besides, we've known General Lecount for a long time. We have some mutual enemies in Africa."

"Of course." Viktor chuckled in spite of his annoyance that their plans were so widely known.

"Anyway," Perlman went on, "Sergeant Chakroun should be here sometime this evening with the HALO suits and a few additional items you might find useful. But"—he looked at his watch again—"we're running out of time. Mr. Lipsky, I suggest that you, Lieutenant Yushenko, and Miss Wilkins head to Damascus no later than early tomorrow morning. We've got to learn the situation on the ground. I've checked, and there's a flight leaving at 6.30a.m. I've booked three seats."

"Wait a minute, wait a minute," Yushenko cut in angrily. "You can't do that. What about the medicine for my son? I can't go back without that."

Perlman reached down and grabbed a large plastic bag emblazoned with the logo of the largest Cypriot pharmacy. Medicines don't weigh very much, and he was able to lift it easily onto the table. "It's all there, Lieutenant. Three months' worth. I checked with some of our people at home and made sure these are the latest, most effective treatment. All with Swiss labels. Nothing to be traced back to us."

Yushenko let out a sigh of relief. "You just guaranteed my enthusiastic membership in this little group. But" —he smiled and turned to Viktor—"we still haven't solved his hair problem."

Bronstein looked around and called out for Eli, who held up a large pair of scissors and some clippers and then waved Viktor back into the kitchen. "Turn our friend here into a Russian soldier," Bronstein requested with a laugh.

A few minutes later, a shorn Viktor emerged scratching his head in irritation. "Christ, no wonder so many people are deserting," he muttered.

"At least now we have a chance to get past the VP in Damascus," Yushenko said. "Let's go back to the hotel, get you into the uniform, and make sure the paperwork is good."

"Hang on a second, Lieutenant. Aren't you forgetting something?" Perlman asked.

"Like what?"

"Like how in hell is Miss Wilkins here going to get through the controls with her nice American passport—not to speak of her wardrobe that looks more suitable for an African safari than lounging around a pool in Cyprus looking for a 'sponsor.' If she's supposed to be arm candy, make her look like arm candy, for God's sake. When she goes though those controls in Damascus, I want the guards focused so much on her ass—which is a nice one, by the way—that they barely look at the paperwork—even if it is pretty good," Perlman told them.

Emily shot him a look as if to call him a dirty old man and was about to object loudly in her best professional woman's tone when Viktor put his hand on her arm.

"Look, if I can get shorn like a spring lamb, you can gussy yourself up a bit." Then he smiled. "The original is pretty damn good, so they can't do too much damage."

She gave him her best pout, but she agreed to make the changes.

Bronstein asked, "Eli, will you get your wife to take Emily on a little shopping trip and to visit the hairdresser?"

As they turned to leave, Perlman held up a hand to stop them. "One more thing."

"What now?" Emily exploded. "You've already making me into a cheap hooker. Well, maybe not cheap, but still a hooker."

Perlman reached into his jacket pocket and held up a black

passport. "This should clear you in Damascus. A valid South African passport made out in the name of one Emily de Groot. It has all the proper stamps and visas."

Emily grabbed it and riffled through the pages. She gasped when she got to the picture. "The picture! How the hell did you do that?" she asked.

Perlman merely smiled as if to say this was something his people had done many times. She gave the passport to Viktor who looked at the picture of Emily and almost laughed. Instead of the stern-looking intelligence agent, it showed a tanned, vivacious young woman with a broad smile and spiky, blonde hair. He was about to tell her he was looking forward to meeting this woman when she grabbed the passport back.

"Bastard! Not one word," she warned him. "Not one word."

"Don't forget," Perelman called after them, "to let us know what the hell is happening on the ground. Use that transmitter as soon as you can. As Sergeant Davies put it so well, we don't want to be 'goin' out on a limb bare-ass naked.'"

Davies coughed loudly. "Speaking of limbs…"

Perlman glanced at the clock over the kitchen door. "Don't worry, Davies. Sergeant Chakroun should be here soon, then we're taking a little trip."

Davies and Arlo looked at each other quizzically. "Where to exactly? Israel?" Davies asked.

"Not exactly. Jordan. We're heading to small airbase in southern Jordan, not far from the Saudi border."

"You boys take over Jordan while I wasn't looking? What the hell's goin' on?"

"No, no." Perlman smiled. "The Hashemite Kingdom is still independent—sort of. It's just that the king and my good friend Major General Fawzi Zuhair Hashem, who runs their version of Mossad, also think that an invasion of infected rats would be very bad for Jordan as well as Israel. They're doing us a little favor."

"Such as?"

"Such as lending us an airfield as well as an old, modified cargo plane that will deliver you, Arlo, and Said Chakroun over that damned fortress in a couple of days' time."

"OK," Davies said slowly, "and this is all happenin' without the Americans—the official Americans, that is—or the official Israelis knowing anythin'. That's a real good trick. Them boys like to think they know everythin.'"

"Not everything, Sergeant. Not everything. Some things we keep to ourselves. Can't risk telling anyone official in the United States. Don't yet know how deep the rot goes. If they found you here, they already know too much. No, this little venture will remain well below their radar. We've won a little time because they think whatever you were planning is dead in the water without the HALO suits. So far, they know nothing about the French. Let's keep it that way. Now enjoy your food while we wait for Sergeant Chakroun."

***

Two hours later, there was a knock on the door. Eli peered out the spy hole, did a double take, and cautiously opened the door just enough to allow the wiry form of Said Chakroun into the room. He wore his civilian 'uniform' of a scruffy pair of jeans, running shoes, and a loose, gray shirt. Wrapped around his neck was a long, red-and-white *keffiyeh*, which was often worn in Jordan. Chakroun laughed at the astonished looks on Davies's and Arlo's faces as he came over to give them big hugs.

"Jesus Christ, Said," Davies growled. "You had me goin' there for a minute. I thought we was gonna be blown all to hell. Didn't know who's side you was on."

"Perfect," Perlman beamed. "You'll fit right in. Where's the equipment?"

Chakroun said, "I've parked a van loaded with the HALO suits and a few extra items right outside the door."

"Bring the truck around to the small alley in the back, just in case there are watchers in the crowds of tourists out front."

"On it."

***

When they'd arrived at the small private airfield, Davies and Chakroun started to load the boxes into the plane.

Arlo was counting the boxes carefully. "Wait a minute. I gotta check these things now, not at 30,000 feet. You boys have yourselves a cup of coffee. This is gonna take a few minutes."

One by one, he meticulously went over the HALO suits, checking all the fittings and making sure he understood perfectly that the French system was the same as the American. Arlo finally gave his approval, and the suits were loaded into the plane.

He tried to pick up another large duffel and could barely get it off the ground. "What the hell's in here?" he asked Chakroun.

Said opened the bag to reveal a large, oblong cannister. He unclipped the locks and lifted the heavy lid.

Davies looked in and whistled softly as he lifted out some machine pistols, RPGs, and hand grenades. "Son of a bitch, Said; there's enough in here for a decent little war." He picked up three folding climbing axes. "What the hell are these for? We ain't goin' up some mountain."

Chakroun merely lifted his eyebrows fractionally. "And how do you expect to get up that small tunnel? Doubt they have a lift. Better to be prepared, no?" He turned to Arlo. "Can we handle this extra weight on the drop?"

Arlo ran through some calculations in his head. "Yeah. Once we split it into three and make some adjustments for the extra weight, we should be OK."

"Only *should*?"

Davies chuckled. "Look at it this way, Said: if it ain't OK, you won't have enough time to worry."

CHAPTER 21

The Damascus-Aleppo Road, Syria

The so-called "M5 highway" leading north from Damascus was filled with potholes and exhaust-spewing army trucks carrying a mixture of Syrian and contract troops toward the hellhole of Aleppo. Expressionless and blank-eyed, like soldiers everywhere headed toward combat, they stared at the dull countryside, which featured little except a few shrubs along with scrawny pine and oak trees coated in a film of dust and leaning eastward under the relentless pressure of wind pouring through the gap between the Lebanese and Turkish mountains. Here and there, hulks of destroyed buildings were scattered in the fields. Only the sight of Emily jammed into the back of a small Datsun got their attention. A few of them stood by the tailgate and made unmistakable gestures as to what a "real" man would do with her. The gestures stopped abruptly when Viktor stuck his uniformed arm out the window with the clear markings of a senior Russian naval officer. One of the soldiers even threw him a mock salute as the Datsun whined its way past the lumbering trucks.

That same uniform and Emily's figure had also helped them with the military police and customs officials at the airport.

Yushenko was known to many of the soldiers lounging around the arrivals terminal, and so he passed through with merely a nod or two. By the time "Kapitan Boris Nemstov" came through, all eyes were focused on Emily as she teetered along on spike heels while clinging to her companion's arm. One of the guards looked casually at the Nemstov papers and joked about the good things you could pick up in the Cyprus duty free shops. As she handed over the South African passport, Emily smiled broadly and made a desperate attempt to pull down her knock-off Hervé Léger bodycon dress that barely covered her ass. It had the desired effect, as the passport official was focused entirely on Emily's ass, and he hit his own thumb with the stamp. Once through the formalities, they went over to the Russian army reception desk, at which Captain Nemstov commandeered a car to drive back to the base at Tartus and drop his good friend Oleg Yushenko off at this wife's village on the way.

A few minutes later, the small Datsun appeared by the door, and Yushenko pushed Viktor into the driver's seat. He slid into the passenger seat while Emily was crammed into the rear of the two-door car. The only way she could fit was with her back against the side and her legs stretched across the seat. This earned a smart salute from the guards outside the terminal.

Viktor was about to start the car when he turned to Yushenko. "Where am I supposed to go? The roads are a mess and most of the signs have been shot up or torn down."

Yushenko just pointed straight ahead. "Get going before anyone gets suspicious. Look, we're southeast of the city, and we've got to get on the main road north, toward Homs and Aleppo. For now, just follow the traffic toward the city. Sooner or later, we'll pick up a sign."

In the end, they found a small Russian military convoy to follow.

Viktor looked carefully into the back of one of the troop carriers and did a double take. "They're not regular soldiers, are they?"

"No," Yushenko said through gritted teeth. "They're contractors—real scum that come from all over. Look at them. Most of them aren't even Russian."

Emily squirmed around until she could more or less lie on her side facing the front. "Next time, Oleg," she suggested, wincing, "do you think the great Russian army could spring for a decent car with four doors?"

"Maybe, but I'm counting on there being no next time." He grinned widely. "The next car I drive better be one of those monster American pickup trucks with lots of chrome and a gun rack. Of course," he added, "that assumes we live through the next few days."

"Anyway, as I was saying," Emily continued, "the Russians aren't the only ones using contractors. That clown in Cyprus was one of our very own contractors. That voice on the phone sounded vaguely familiar. Unless I'm totally off base, he's some sort of retired general who runs a big contracting group. I can't remember his name, but he stands to make a bundle if there's another big war over here. He's probably connected with some of those loonies in Israel that Perlman was talking about."

Viktor twisted his large shoulders around so he was at least talking sideways instead of to the windshield. "Maybe," was all he conceded. "Even wild conspiracies can sometimes be true, but let's not leap to conclusions until we know a little more."

The convoy finally had reached the turn for the M1 north, and Yushenko pushed the small car to pass one of the trucks. Only then did he realize that the highway was filled with nothing but convoys. If you passed one, another one showed up—some with soldiers, some piled with weapons, and others pulling artillery pieces. "Someone's going to catch it," Yushenko said to no one in particular. "Give the boys a break, Emily; show them a little more leg."

"Bastard," she muttered. But she flashed her legs provocatively and got a huge round of applause. The soldiers roared even louder when she wrapped her arms around Viktor and kissed him loudly on the cheek.

"We've got a long convoy ahead of us. This could get fun." Viktor laughed.

"Don't get your hopes up, big boy."

When they'd finally passed the last truck, Emily couldn't restrain herself. "How much further, for God's sake? Any more of this being crammed in like a sardine and I'll never walk again."

"Another hour or so to the turn off, and then it's about 45 minutes to the village—assuming no roadblocks," Yushenko confirmed.

"When can I change into some real clothes?"

"Not yet. You need to play your party-girl role if we hit any patrols. Remember, this is the main road to the Russian naval base. They patrol it carefully."

They hit the first patrol about half an hour after they turned off toward Tartus. There were six Russian soldiers in battle kit, sitting at a long table by a guard hut. A thick, red-and-white striped pole blocked the road. One of the soldiers stood up, adjusted the machine pistol across his chest and signaled for them to stop. He sauntered over to the car and, after taking one look at Viktor's uniform, gestured for his lieutenant to come over. Emily was trying hard to breathe normally, and Yushenko gripped Viktor's arm tightly signaling him to be very, very careful.

"At least they're Russian and not contractors," he whispered to Viktor.

The young lieutenant came up to the car, noticed Viktor's uniform, and saluted smartly. Trying hard not to stare at Emily, he told Viktor, "We have orders to check the papers of anyone coming toward Tartus."

"Of course, Lieutenant. You're just doing your job," Viktor said magnanimously. He reached into his jacket to pull out his packet of identity papers and orders. He handed them to the lieutenant, along with Yushenko's identity papers and Emily's passport.

He scanned the passport. "Who's with Miss de Groot?"

"She's with me, Lieutenant." Viktor smiled. "We met on Cyprus, and I wanted to show her a little Russian hospitality."

Lucky bastard, the lieutenant's expression seemed to say. Then he looked at Yushenko's papers and walked rapidly around the car to the passenger's side.

Emily held her breath, wondering if they now had a huge problem.

The lieutenant stopped by Yushenko's window and compared the identity papers in his hand to the real thing. "Oleg Yushenko. *The* Oleg Yushenko? The famous lieutenant who flattened that asshole senior officer—the so-called 'colonel'—with one swing?"

Yushenko bowed his head and grinned sheepishly. "The very same. Now just former Lieutenant Yushenko."

"Not to us you're not. We're proud of you. About time someone stood up to those people. They just give us a bad name." He handed the papers back and reached to shake Yushenko's hand. "Where are you heading now? Is there anything we can do to help?"

"Thank you, Lieutenant, but my friends are just dropping me at Al-Narish, where my wife and son are staying with her parents." He held up the large bag of medicines. "I had to go to Cyprus to pick up medicines for my son."

"Of course. We've all heard about that. Please give him our best. By the way," he added as he ordered the soldiers to lift the bar, "I should warn you that a group of about 15 contractors from the Reinhard group came through here earlier today. Arrogant pricks didn't say where they were going, but I overheard one of them talking about that famous fortress somewhere over there." He gestured vaguely to the west. "If you run into them, give them a shot from all of us."

Yushenko forced a smile on his face and waved goodbye as the car rattled through the guard post. "That certainly changes things. You still want to go through with this now it's no longer just sleepy Syrian guards we have to worry about?"

"Not necessarily," Emily said. "These guys aren't exactly frontline troops, and we still have the element of surprise on our side. Let's just contact Ricky when we get to the village and see what he has to say. He may want to bring a few extra bits of equipment."

***

The small town of Al-Narish was on the side of a hill facing Crac des Chevaliers about three miles to the south.

"My God!" Viktor exclaimed as the fortress came into view. "No picture or diagram does that thing justice. It's massive. Right on top of a hill with perfect fields of fire in all directions." He shook his head in admiration. "Those boys knew what they were doing back in the day."

"Getting cold feet, are we?" Emily quipped.

"No, just realistic feet. I hope that damn tunnel is still there. It's supposed to be around the other side, where a small river used to run. You see anything that looks like a river, old or new?"

Yushenko pulled out a pair of binoculars and scanned the area in front of the fortress. "No. Nothing from here. We'll have to figure this one out on foot."

"Exactly how are you planning that? Even those guards would spot us a mile away," Emily said.

"Carefully, very carefully," Yushenko suggested.

Little one- and two-story preformed concrete buildings lined the half dozen streets of the small town. There were a few stores whose window displays held motley collections of all types of products—from light bulbs to four-day-old bread. Some of the homeowners had made the effort to whitewash their homes, but most had simply let the dust and constant wind control the outside decoration. Thin, beige curtains hung in most windows, and a few had even tried unsuccessfully to plant a small garden in front.

Emily turned and glanced out the window. "Where is everyone? I don't see a single person on the streets."

"What are they going to do on the streets?" Yushenko answered. "There's nothing to buy, and no one feels like socializing. These days, you don't say anything unless you know which side your neighbor is on. Staying inside with your own family is the safest bet."

Viktor turned down a street at the edge of the town and came to an unusually well-maintained two-story house that had recently been whitewashed and even had an air-conditioning unit hanging out of one of the downstairs windows. As Yushenko pulled up alongside it, they noticed a real garden in the back, which had a couple of pomegranate trees and a struggling lemon tree.

Before Yushenko opened the door, he turned to them. "My wife's parents are expecting you. I told them I was bringing a friend and his fiancée."

"*Fiancée?*" Emily erupted. "That's a bit much."

Yushenko waved his hand to stop her in mid-flow. "Look, this is a very Christian family. When you live in a place surrounded by Islamic fanatics and genocidal rulers, you have to cling to something. And they cling to their faith—strongly. Outside the house, they're just good little Syrian civilians who keep their mouths shut and their beliefs tightly wrapped up. Inside, they keep their sanity with their Christianity. And that means"—he grinned—"no living in sin. Besides, there's only a pullout sofa for you to sleep on."

"This will be fun," Viktor declared with a smirk.

Emily punched him in the back and told him not to even think about it—but in a tone of voice that suggested she really wouldn't mind that much if he did actually think about it.

Just then, the door of the house flew open and a thin, haggard-looking woman with long, dark hair rushed toward the car with her arms wide open and a relieved smile on her lips.

Yushenko pushed open the car door and greeted his wife

with a bear hug as he stroked her hair. "It's OK, Anne Marie. It's OK. I'm home." He reached back into the car and pulled out the large bag of medicines. "See, I even brought more medicines. Some of these are new and are supposed to be more effective than the old ones."

Her head sank in relief and tears began to fall down her thin cheeks as she crossed herself discreetly. "Thank God, thank God. He's been getting worse and could barely breathe these last couple of days. I was going out of my mind with fear." Then she remembered that her husband had brought some guests. She straightened up, wiped the tears away, smoothed her hair, and walked over to the car in a dignified manner as Viktor and Emily climbed out. She may be poor with a very sick child, but she was still proud and would welcome her husband's friends.

Emily was embarrassed by her clothes and tried unsuccessfully to pull the hem of the dress down. Anne Marie paid no attention to that, clasped Emily's hands in both of hers, and said in fluent Russian that she and her "fiancé" were welcome. Then she sized Viktor up and down, nodded affirmatively, and said she was glad that Oleg had such good friends.

The introductions finished, they all went into the house. The inside of the house was spotless, and the front room held a sofa and three chairs arranged around a round table covered with a lace tablecloth. Sitting on top of the table was a bowl filled with fresh fruit and a jug of cold water. While Yushenko took the medicine and rushed up the short stairs to see his son, Anne Marie's parents appeared from the kitchen, carrying a tray loaded with sweets, cups, and a pot of tea. They urged Viktor and Emily to make themselves comfortable on the sofa. Given the food shortages, these may have been their last bits of tea and sweets, but they were going to make sure it was given to the guests.

Her father was thin, of medium height, and had a thatch of thinning, white hair. His face was drawn, but his soft, brown eyes radiated intelligence and curiosity. His clothes were immaculate and perfectly ironed—soft cotton pants and a fine linen shirt. Her mother was pleasantly plump and wore the apron of a house-proud wife. No one would find dust on her table or stale bread in her kitchen, regardless of general food shortages. The expression on their faces asked a thousand questions, but the rules of hospitality forbade them from asking direct questions.

Despite the uniform, they both had their doubts that Viktor was in fact a Russian officer. But rather than expressing those doubts directly, Anne Marie's father chose the oblique method common in the Middle East. The truth, whatever that was, would emerge in the course of the conversation. Politely, he asked about their trip. He apologized for not speaking Russian, but he said he hoped his French-accented English would do. He smiled and explained he and his wife had been educated at one of the French Catholic schools in Beirut and that he'd learned English in his years in the textile trade. Finally, he asked where they'd met Oleg.

Viktor stole a brief glance at Emily, and they came to same quick conclusion: they were going to need this man, and there was no point in starting off the relationship with a pack of lies.

Viktor took a deep breath, coughed lightly, and carefully placed the uniform cap on the floor—a sure sign he was no Russian officer. "We met on Cyprus a few weeks ago, where we discussed some, uh, mutual problems and how we might solve them together."

This brought a thin smile to the father's face.

Viktor waved his hands at the uniform and smiled. "That's why the uniform doesn't really fit."

"I thought the Russians had better tailors than that. And this—this subterfuge—was a necessary part of that solution?"

"Unfortunately, yes, but we have no intention of deceiving you, your wife, or your daughter."

The father lowered his head and thought for a minute or two before responding. "And these problems you mention have something to do with the fortress behind us?" He gestured with his head toward the Crac des Chevaliers.

Viktor was saved from answering when Anne Marie's mother remarked that they must be hungry and passed them a plate of *baklava*. Emily took this opportunity to ask if she could take her small bag and go into one of the side rooms. The mother nodded graciously and indicated the way to a small back room. Emily swiftly disappeared inside it.

A few minutes later, she emerged wearing her customary khaki trousers and shirt. A pair of comfortable running shoes had replaced the spike heels. The hair would have to wait.

The father gave a short laugh and inspected the clothes with a professional eye. "Good; almost American military grade. I somehow didn't think you were someone who had been picked up on a beach in Cyprus. But tell me, who are you exactly?"

At that moment, Anne Marie and Oleg came down the stairs carrying a small bundle wrapped in a white blanket. "We can talk about that later, Papa. Now let's introduce our friends to Yuri."

Emily never thought of herself as being particularly emotional. Her work in Africa had exposed her to most of the horrors that mankind can inflict on itself, and her well of emotions had pretty much run dry. However, the sight of that tiny, helpless creature gasping for air melted her reserves. She let out a gasp as Anne Marie turned the blanket toward her, and a small, very pale, blue-tinged face peered out with half-opened eyes. She grabbed Viktor's arm for support as tears swelled in her eyes. "It's so small, so helpless," she whispered into his ear. Suddenly, the real reason for this mission—one far removed from public health or geo-political maneuvers—became crystal clear. She vowed to herself that no more harm would be inflicted on this particular innocent.

Yushenko took the blanket-wrapped infant from his wife and was almost able to hold his son in one of his large hands. "Now you see why I agreed to help. Those medicines I got in Cyprus are much more powerful than the ones we were using earlier. I can only guess where they came from, but if your friends can really come through with better care for our son, I'll do anything to help."

Anne Marie's parents shared worried glances as they both thought, *What help? What problems? Who are these people? Just what are they planning?*

Anne Marie, who'd heard the story from her husband while upstairs, motioned for her parents to relax and have some tea. "It's complicated, but Oleg's friends—Viktor and Emily—are trying to stop an even worse war and, at the same time, save your grandson."

Her mother gave a nervous flutter of her hands, and her father gave his wife a reassuring pat. "Let's listen," he told her. "This could be interesting."

It took over an hour to explain the entire situation with all its multiple moving parts. Anne Marie's mother alternately covered her mouth in horror and shuddered at the implications of what they were being told. Her father didn't move during the entire explanation—feeling almost numb at what he was hearing.

"I thought I'd seen and heard all the horrors this region had to offer. But this, this…"—he struggled to find the right words—"this is a new level of barbarity in a region that sets a very high standard for barbarity." He wiped his hands across his face. "In the old days, you could tell who was fighting whom. It was fairly easy. Now? Who knows? Israelis and Syrians, I can understand. People used to be on one team or another. Now it's all mixed up. 'Good' Americans; 'bad' Americans. 'Good' Israelis; 'bad' Israelis. North Koreans." He thought for a minute. "Oh, and let's not forget the Russians and now the French." He turned to Oleg. "And you and your friends are going to stop them?" he asked dismissively. "Oleg," he pleaded, "I know you're a soldier—a good soldier—but this is madness. Don't make your wife a widow and your son fatherless."

In the end, it was Anne Marie who brought them around by reminding them that the real person they were trying to save was their grandson. "If we don't do this, Yuri will surely die—and soon. Even with these new medicines, he doesn't have much of a chance. He needs real medical attention from doctors who know what they're doing. I don't know how long he has anyway, but I'll be damned if I'm going to give up," she said with real steel in her voice.

Her father slumped in his chair and gripped the armrests tightly. "You're right, of course. We don't have a choice. We have to try." He looked at Oleg, Viktor, and Emily with new determination in his eyes. "What can I do to help?"

Emily and Yushenko nodded at Viktor to take the lead.

He was happy to oblige. "We have friends in Jordan waiting to hear from us. The first thing we must do is let them know about the contractors inside the fort. We'd been expecting to face only second-line Syrian troops. Nothing we can't deal with," he said more confidently than he felt, "but we need to know exactly what we're facing. I know we can't actually get into the fort itself, but the town will be filled with gossip. Even second-line soldiers don't like getting pushed aside—especially by a group of mercenary thugs from some of the worst places in the world." He paused to let that sink in and then asked Emily to demonstrate the small communications device Perlman had given them in Cyprus.

Anne Marie and her parents stared in wonder at the device, which was smaller than a Post-it note. Emily took a short lead and plugged one end into the device and the other end into her phone. Then she pushed the small power button and was rewarded a few seconds later with a steady, green signal from one of the tiny LED lights embedded in the device. Using the keypad on her phone, she punched in the long series of numbers and characters she'd memorized. Once the required authorization came through, she typed a short message saying they'd arrived but the situation in the fort had changed, with the arrival of about 15 contractors, and they'd find out more shortly. The device, acting as both a scrambler and transmitter, sent the message in a micro-burst up to a very secret Israeli satellite that relayed it securely to the team now waiting on a seldom-used airstrip in southern Jordan.

It didn't take long for a response to come. It was short and to the point: "Not a deal breaker, but we need to know more. Especially about the tunnel."

Emily grinned and turned to the others. "Looks like we're taking a little stroll through that village at the base of the fort to see what we can pick up."

***

The only thing that had changed in the small group of tired buildings, which looked much older than they were, was the addition of a few more disgruntled Syrian soldiers from the fort. The Reinhard contractors had told them to clear out of the best rooms and find places to stay outside. The few remaining villagers were careful to remain indoors in fear of the heavily armed, bored, undisciplined soldiers, who were scrounging around for whatever scraps of food and shelter they could find.

As the four of them entered the hovel of buildings, Viktor could sense trouble building. The soldiers paid no attention to his uniform rank and leered openly at Emily and Anne Marie. Yushenko was about to pound one of the leering soldiers when Anne Marie smiled sweetly and told him to relax. She'd had a better idea and pointed to large basket she'd brought that was filled with produce from her last visit to Tartus, where she still had a pass to the Russian commissary. She spread a blanket over the remains of a dried-up fountain and began to lay out the fruit, fresh bread, meats, and cheeses. Then she asked some of the nearby soldiers to come over and share the bounty. From that moment on they reverted to the young boys they were and regarded her as their older sister, instead of an object of their lust. Viktor and Yushenko smiled at this victory of smart diplomacy over power.

As they ate, the young soldiers complained to her about the conditions in the fort—about how the contractors and the Asians had taken all the best rooms and provisions. The Syrian soldiers had been left with scraps. No one knew what the Asians were doing, but their area of the fort was strictly off limits. One soldier who'd dared to climb down to the second level near the rear, where the lab was located. was caught and sent immediately to northern Syria to face the *jihadis* and the Kurds. No one was hopeful about his return. It took a while for Anne Marie to translate all this for the others, but much of it didn't need translation.

Viktor and Emily took a short stroll to the bottom of the long entrance leading to the main gate of the fort. Viktor took one look at the massive wooden gate with its strong iron reinforcement bands and shook his head. "That's going to be a bitch to open," he mouthed.

Emily took a few steps closer. "We won't have to. Look at the small Judas gate right in the middle. It's hard to see because the wood has weathered to the same color as the stone. They probably use that most of the time and open the main gate only for cars and trucks. That smaller gate is all we need."

Further examination of the gate was cut off when one of the soldiers broke off abruptly and started laughing and waving his arms around—holding his hands together and making slashing motions with both arms.

"What the hell is he doing?" Viktor asked Anne Marie, who was having trouble following the boy's tirade.

Apparently, she explained, he was describing a scene inside the massive ceremonial hall when several of the contractors had gotten drunk on vodka and beer. During the time when tourists were still admitted, the hall had been decorated with replicas of Crusaders' shields and heavy two-handed swords, the latter of which were still razor-sharp despite being replicas. During one drunken incident, the contractors had decided to re-enact a battle. They took several of the swords off the wall and started swinging them around. One of them got carried away and took a slice out of his comrade's ear. The infuriated, now earless soldier came after him with every intention of taking his head off. Only the intervention of all the others prevented him from doing so.

"Well," Yushenko said drily, "that's what you get with contractors. Bunch of drunks. More dangerous to themselves than anyone else." He was clearly disgusted.

All of a sudden, the clatter of a low-flying helicopter heading for the fortress interrupted the conversation. Viktor ducked instinctively as the chopper flew overhead, but then he did a double take as he glanced through its open door. He couldn't believe his eyes. There, sitting astride the opening with one leg resting on the skid, was none other than Ivan Balko. There was the same bald head. The same sour expression. He was probably pissed at being sent to this nothing place, far from where any lucrative action might be. And he was no doubt complaining that there wasn't even anything worth stealing or bribing in this dump. Viktor motioned to the others to head back to Anne Marie's house in the nearby town. Emily looked at him, obviously about to raise a question on their sudden departure, but she quickly nodded her head in agreement when he mouthed, "Balko," and motioned toward the helicopter hovering over the fortress.

***

Southern Jordan

When seen from a miles-high surveillance satellite, the Jafr Sub-District in southern Jordan appears bleak and barren. When seen close up from the ground, it didn't get any better. Stretching for miles in all directions was only empty hardscrabble. There wasn't a tree in sight and scarcely any water. The only shade was under a once-green and now-mottled dusty, brown awning hanging between poles outside the small concrete building serving as an office, sleeping quarters, control tower, and maintenance shop for the unmarked planes that used the crude landing strip. These planes sometimes carried people who didn't wish to be seen talking to each other. Other times, they carried munitions or heavily armed men heading toward some distant war or insurrection. The Jordanians were well paid for their discretion in these matters and only requested that the origins of these flights remain secret—regional sensitivities being what they were.

A small group of men were sitting in rickety plastic chairs, doing their best to find some bit of shade under the awning. A couple of others were busy sticking decals from the commercial Royal Jordanian Airlines on the dark fuselage of a Royal Jordanian Air Force C-130 cargo plane.

Arlo was busy checking and rechecking the HALO gear and the four kilos of Semtex that Chakroun had brought, while Ricky Davies was trying vainly to wipe the sweat off his brow with a sodden bandanna. It didn't do any good and only succeeded in moving the sweat around. It had been three days since Perlman and his Jordanian counterpart had delivered them there from Cyprus via Tel Aviv and Amman—and they were getting bored. The Israeli and Jordanian had retreated to their respective headquarters, while Davies and his men were told to wait for news from the Crac des Chevaliers. They'd reviewed the Crac's plans until they'd memorized the exact layout and planned what each of them would do. Chakroun and Davies would handle the Koreans and the lab, while Arlo would hustle up to ground level and head for the gate.

"Ain't a great plan," Davies admitted, "but 'til we get there, it's the only one we got. Then it's adapt and improvise. We'll just have to wait and see what Viktor and Oleg can tell us about that damn tunnel."

Further conversation was prevented by the chirp of the telecommunications device. Davies hustled inside and connected his phone to the device. He signaled that he was ready and waited for the message. As the words began to scroll across the small screen, his eyes widened, and his mouth curled in a wicked smile. "Holy shit! Christmas has come early, boys. Guess who's at the fort?"

Arlo and Said shook their heads.

"Ivan fuckin' Balko, that's who. We gotta score to settle."

"Who else is there, Ricky? It ain't just Ivan and a bunch of fuckin' Ayrabs," Arlo said.

"Viktor says about 15 contractors from the Reinhard group have kicked the Syrians out of the fort. Good news is they're now very pissed and won't lift a finger to help the contractors. The Syrians say there are also four tough-lookin' Koreans guardin' the scientist. They don't say much, but they scare the shit outta the Syrians."

"At least we know what we're facing now," Chakroun said. "Fifteen isn't so bad—especially if they're the usual undisciplined rabble I've seen elsewhere. I think the Koreans will be the toughest part of our job."

Davies quickly wrote back, asking if they'd found the tunnel yet. Not yet, came the reply. They were going on a search mission that night after the moon had set.

"Just give us the exact coordinates and tell us when to be there. The sooner the better," Davies answered.

He was about to disconnect when another message came through: "Tell Arlo the helo has been upgraded. Balko is using the Kazan Ansat. Is Arlo OK with that?"

Davies asked Arlo if he could fly this particular model.

Arlo wiped his hands on an old rag and nodded his head. "All the same, basically, Sarge. Yeah, I can git y'all where you're goin'. Just make damn sure it ain't shot to hell before we get to it."

Davies answered the message and said Arlo could fly the

new helo. He turned to Chakroun and Arlo. "Not much longer now, boys."

Instinctively, they all went to their weapons to clean and check them for the umpteenth time.

***

Al-Narish

It was close to 1 a.m. when Yushenko and Viktor—their faces and hands blackened with burned cork—slipped out of the house and headed toward the fortress looming three miles ahead of them. For the first 45 minutes, they stuck to the empty road to make better time. There was no sign of any living creature for miles—no lights, no traffic, and not even animals. As they approached the town, they veered west off the road, around the houses, and into the fields filled with stubble. They slowed their pace and made use of old, disused irrigation ditches and folds in the landscape to shield their movements from any watchers on the ramparts of the fort. From what the Syrian soldiers had told them, it was unlikely that any of the contractors could be bothered to keep watch at that hour of the morning—even if they were sober.

A dog started barking in the distance until a rough voice in Russian told it to shut up or get shot. Yushenko pulled Viktor down into one of the ditches, where they lay for several minutes listening to the slight whispering of the wind across the plain. The smell of the earth reminded Viktor of the land around his house in Telos.

Then Yushenko reached for the bag on his belt, pulled a large slab of meat from the bag, and sliced it into several pieces. "In case a dog gets too close," he murmured.

As they slithered up and over the mounds on the once-tilled

field, they noticed the ground was getting damp. Then they heard the faint tinkling of bells ahead of them and froze.

"Fucking goats," Viktor whispered. "They could wake the dead if they sense we're here and start to panic."

Yushenko rolled silently over the small mound of dirt and down into the shallow gully. He landed on something soft, which was curled up in the depression.

Suddenly, the small bundle sat up, wide-eyed at the sight of two huge figures with blackened faces. *Surely these are the jinns my grandmother warned me about?*

The young shepherd Ali struggled to get up and was about to let out a loud scream when Yushenko's large hand clamped firmly over his mouth. "Stay still. We're not going to hurt you," he managed to say in his limited Arabic.

Ali, who was too frightened to move at this point, merely nodded his head in agreement.

Yushenko relaxed his grip and reached into his pack for some food, which he offered to the boy. The shepherd, who was dressed in a torn shirt and ragged pants with flip-flops on his feet, was more used to abuse and kicks from other people. He stared at the offering, not sure what to do. He was starving, but he was afraid of getting beaten if he took the food. Cautiously, his hand reached out and hesitated for a few seconds before grabbing the food and stuffing it into his mouth. Reassured when fists and boots didn't hammer into him, he signaled for some more.

"Are you from here?" Yushenko asked.

The boy shook his head and waved vaguely in a westerly direction. "I follow goats. Stay away from this," he said gesturing fearfully at the fortress behind him.

"Ever been inside?"

The shepherd gave him an "are you crazy?" look and shook his head vigorously. "Very bad people in the fort. But," he added slyly, "I've seen a back door." He pointed around a corner, where the field sloped away from the wall.

"OK," Yushenko continued cautiously. "Can you show us this back door?"

The boy nodded slightly and held out his hand for some more food.

"Natural born trader, this kid." Viktor chuckled as he handed over the last of his supplies.

By this time, the moon had settled beneath the horizon and the area around the back of the huge fortress was draped in total darkness. Ali, who knew this area like the back of his hand, led them silently over the uneven ground, around piles of loose stones, and toward the shallow gulley where a stream had run more than 1,000 years ago. The goats, reassured by their shepherd's familiar smell, didn't make a fuss, but one of them came over and nudged the boy just to make sure everything was all right, despite the presence of two strangers. Ali sent the animal away with a soft pat on its head.

They put their backs to the massive wall and felt their way gently down the slope and around the corner. Viktor could only shake his head in admiration of the fort's construction. No way was any assault going to get inside this place. Once around the corner, Ali held up his hand and motioned for them to look a few yards ahead. At first, they saw nothing. Then a black hole seemed to appear gradually in the stonework. They could even feel a draft coming out. Yushenko cupped his hands and whispered to Viktor that this must be the opening. As they crept closer Viktor could see Davies's point about the size of the entrance. He could barely get his head through the opening, let alone his shoulders.

His nose wrinkled. "Christ, this place stinks."

"That's what centuries of garbage and shit will do for you." Yushenko grinned. He held out his GPS device and waited impatiently for it to acquire enough satellites to give an accurate position. Finally, the right number of satellites was acquired, and he created a way point with their exact position. He also looked around and made a mental note of the surrounding land.

There was a slight slope to the west, then it was more or less level. It would be easy enough for experienced jumpers. He also made a note to tell Davies to bring strong bolt cutters. There was a good chance some clever defender had put a metal grate over the hole—maybe even a metal cover.

As he was putting the GPS device back into a pouch, something—another animal, a snake perhaps—spooked the goats. They all started bleating and took off down the hill toward the south. The noise of the bleating and bells aroused a couple of guards on the ramparts. They flicked on powerful searchlights and shone them on the fleeing goats. Viktor heard drunken laughter, and then he pulled Yushenko next to him tight against the wall as the unmistakable sound of automatic weapons being cocked came rattling down to them. The guards wanted a little entertainment and started firing at the goats, laughing in triumph and collecting bets as their shells tore into the animals. Ali gave a loud cry and started to run after them. Yushenko was too late to grab him and could only watch in horror as Ali ran down the hill, trying to round up his goats. The guards thought this was great sport and took turns spraying bullets all around the boy caught in their spotlights. He dodged vainly as the ground burst in front of him. One of the guards soon tired of this game and rested his weapon carefully on the rampart until the back of Ali's head appeared in the cross hairs of his telescopic sight. One smooth pull of the trigger was all it took. Ali's head exploded like a watermelon dropped from the roof of a building. Once the sport was over, the guards shut off the lights and went back to drinking. Ali and the goats were left for nature to deal with.

Yushenko gave a soft cry and started to rush toward the boy, but Viktor grabbed him and held him down. "Soon enough, Oleg; soon enough. We'll get those bastards. That boy will be avenged."

***

The sky was beginning to lighten when they got back to the house, where they collapsed in exhaustion just outside the front door. They sat there panting until the door opened a crack and Anne Marie stuck her head out.

"Inside, quickly," she said softly.

Right before entering the house, they remembered to take off their filthy boots before making a mess of the front room. The women registered the angry, haggard faces of the two men and understood that something ugly had happened. Exactly what, they didn't know, but they assumed it had something to do with the faint sounds of gunfire they'd heard earlier. Emily, annoyed with herself for not going along, was about to say something when Anne Marie motioned for her to wait. In their own time, she seemed to say.

After they'd drunk some of the strong, dark tea, Viktor explained what had happened: how they found the tunnel, and how the drunken guards had killed the young shepherd. "Just for fun, you know. No reason at all. Just for fun," he said shaking his head. "He was a good kid. All he wanted to do was look after his damn goats."

Anne Marie started to weep softly. "This country is cursed, Oleg. Assad is bad enough, but now we have these pigs and the Koreans trying to kill us all. We have to get out." She looked hard at her husband and Viktor. "Just do what you have to do, but get us out of here. And," she added, "that includes my parents."

CHAPTER 22

Jerusalem, Israel

Benny Perlman sat at his government-issue metal desk in a non-descript office in a non-descript office building just outside the walls of the old city and twirled a pen through his thin fingers in distracted manner. It was a trick he'd learned from a friend in his early schooldays in Baghdad. Now he did it unconsciously when he was deep in thought. Over the years, people watching him weave a pen back and forth through his fingers had tried to copy the trick, but they only wound up picking their pens up from the floor. If you asked him about the habit, he'd look astonished that he was actually doing it.

Right now, he was thinking about what to do with the information that was coming to him from various official and unofficial sources. Some of this information involved the identities of people in the group within Israel that wanted the infected-rat program to succeed as a prelude to a major war, during which Israel would dramatically expand its borders. Other information had to do with the small group hoping to destroy the rat program before it started. He stopped twirling the pen long enough to look at a small piece of paper on his desk that had one name written on it: "Myer Hirschon." Perlman smiled. It was people like Hirschon that made his job easier. Myer Hirschon was a very small player, but in most conspiracies, it was the small people—the peripheral players—who talked too much. Maybe they were trying to impress someone, overstate their importance, and puff up their usually deflated egos. Perlman really didn't care. He was just glad that they talked and were careless where they talked.

In this case tubby, balding Myer Hirschon was in a bar, trying desperately to prove his manliness to a well-built girl wearing a stretch T-shirt. Not only did he tell her he was involved in some top-secret, *hush-hush* program to "save" Israel, but he also made the serious mistake of giving her his cell phone number. The young woman artfully shook off Hirschon and soon contacted her uncle, who'd been a close associate of Perlman until he retired a few years ago. Her uncle straightaway passed on details of the meeting and the phone number to his good friend, who immediately set up intercepts of Hirschon's cell phone. From then on, it was just a short wait until other names, including Uri Abramov, crossed Perlman's desk. A little checking revealed that, while Hirschon was basically a *gofer* with an inflated sense of self-worth, Abramov was the one with the contacts in disgruntled parts of the Israeli political and military establishment, as well as with key American contractors. An ex-army captain, Abramov was known to a few people in the security services as a loud—but up to now, an impotent—supporter of "Greater Israel." He was another Odessa native.

What is it with these fucking Russian Jews? he wondered. *Is this payback for getting the shit kicked out of them for centuries?*

Whatever the reason, they'd helped change the image of Israel from a bunch of socialist *kibbutzniks* with vegetable gardens into fierce commandos with atomic weapons. Perlman twirled the pen some more. Now, perhaps, this guy Abramov required a closer look.

The more disturbing news was that, according to more phone intercepts, the American contractors wanted the rats released as soon as possible. Perlman wasn't sure exactly when they had in mind, but he believed it was days, not weeks. Maybe even hours. *Should they be rounded up now? Or should I let them run, and then see who else comes into the net? That depends on Bronstein's little group. Can they actually pull this off? Are they ready?*

He put in a quick call to Bronstein who was getting ready for another trip to southern Jordan. "What's the story, Avram? Your boys ready to move? More important, do you really think they can pull this off?"

"If anyone can do this, it's those guys. They're pros." Bronstein filled Perlman in on developments at the fortress and the replacement of the Syrian guards by the Russian contractors: "Yushenko and Lipsky found the tunnel right where it was supposed to be. Apparently, Lipsky and Sergeant Davies have a score to settle with the leader of the contractors. I'm also planning on delivering the last of the equipment Davies asked for—the bolt cutters."

"What the hell are those for?"

"Lipsky's taking no chances, just in case someone's put a metal grate over the tunnel entrance."

"Smart kid," Perlman grunted.

"There is one other thing," Bronstein added.

"What?" Perlman demanded, well aware of how many of his operations had been scuttled or ruined because of "one other thing" that no one had mentioned earlier.

"Yushenko's parents-in-law."

"What about them? Where do they fit in?"

"In the helicopter, to be precise. They're coming along. Yushenko told Davies they can't be left behind to be butchered by Assad's people."

There was no point in fighting the obvious. Perlman conceded, "He's got a point. What does Davies say? Is this going to threaten the operation?"

"Apparently not. Davies says there's plenty of room in the

helicopter. However, the main thing they've learned is that they don't have to open the big gate to get into the fort. They've found a small door built into the larger gate, which should be opened fairly quickly. Once inside, he's confident Lipsky and Yushenko can handle themselves. Oh, and for the record, he says the girl's not a bad shot herself. Evidently, she saved Lipsky on that little island paradise of his."

"OK, but remind them that the mission comes first. The only thing that matters is getting rid of those fucking rats and that lab. When does Davies say they'll be ready to go?"

"In a day or two at most. There won't be any moon tomorrow night. Furthermore, they're afraid someone might notice them down at that camp if they wait much longer. All it takes is some shepherd or a hot air balloon filled with tourists coming over from Wadi Rum."

"Let's plan on tomorrow night. I need to check with Fawzi and make sure he clears everything on his end." Just before he hung up, he himself added one thing: "Avram, make sure they understand the protocols. There can be no blowback to us or the Jordanians. They either succeed or they don't survive. Do what you have to do. They're big boys. They'll understand."

***

Southern Jordan

Davies heard the clatter of the helicopter and motioned for the others to stay out of sight inside the building. He focused his army-issue binoculars on the whirling, hazy image coming over the ridge and told Arlo and Chakroun to grab their weapons just in case they had an unwelcome visitor. They stayed ready to defend themselves as the chopper descended in a cloud of dust and bumped down about 100 yards from the building. Only when they saw the familiar figure of Avram Bronstein climb out of the unmarked helicopter, vainly trying to wave away the dust storm, did they relax.

"Avram, goddamn it, man!" He laughed. "You've gotta be the only person within 200 miles wearing a suit and tie."

"My point, precisely, Sergeant Davies. This suit and these shoes," he said, pointing to the now dust-covered handmade New & Lingwood shoes, "were made for civilized places with paved roads and sidewalks—not the likes of this… this wilderness." He waved his arms around at their desolate surroundings.

Arlo grabbed the bag from the hold of the helicopter, tested it for weight, and carried it inside the building. He looked at Chakroun and gave him a thumbs-up that the weight wasn't going to be a problem on the drop.

While Arlo was testing the weight, Davies ushered Bronstein into the building. Once inside, Davies handed Bronstein a mug of tea. As they sat in the folding canvas chairs, Bronstein took a drink, grimaced at the sand that went down with the liquid, and pulled out his ever-present notebook from an inner pocket. He opened it to a well-marked page in the middle and ran his finger down a list he'd prepared. "First, any more news from Lipsky and the others?"

Davies shook his head. "None since yesterday. They're ready to go any time we give the word. Don't wanna wait very long, however."

"Neither do we. How does tomorrow night suit you?"

Davies looked at the others. Chakroun nodded his agreement.

Arlo, who was checking the equipment Bronstein had brought, also nodded. "The sooner the better, Sarge. The HALO gear is good, and the Semtex is gonna make a helluva bang."

"Good. We have information that the opposition also wants to move up their schedule for releasing the infected rats. So sooner is better. Now," Bronstein continued, "what exactly is your plan? Benny, and his friend in Amman, would like to know. They have to be ready for any fallout."

"Ain't real complicated, Avram," Davies said. "We got the coordinates from Viktor. The three of us start our jump at 03:00. With all the gear we're carryin', we'll probably get down faster than normal. Anyways, Viktor'll be at the drop site on the northwest side of the wall—away from any watch tower. Once we're down, Viktor'll grab the weapons and flash-bangs from the cannister we brought and then head back toward the main gate while the three of us start up the tunnel. I'll clear any obstacles. Said here will move out as fast as he can and find that lab, while Arlo makes his way to the surface and opens the small gate. Said and me will eliminate the Korean guards—quietly if possible—and set the Semtex in the lab with a 15-minute timer."

"Fifteen minutes!" Bronstein exclaimed. "That doesn't leave you any time."

"If we ain't out of there within 15 minutes after setting the bombs, we're fucked anyways. Let's just say the timin' will encourage us to move right along. We're countin' on most of the contractor guards being drunk or asleep. The main problem is the Koreans."

"And what do the others do?"

"After openin' the gate, Arlo'll run like hell for the helicopter with Yushenko's wife and her parents. Then he'll get the chopper ready to go. The others'll take care of anyone in our way."

"And the girl, Miss Wilkins?" Bronstein asked.

Davies chuckled. "Don't you worry none about her. She can handle herself. Besides, I would *not* wanna be the one to tell her to run for cover. No, she's been well trained. She'll do fine."

Bronstein ran his finger down the list to one of the last items. "And all this is coordinated with the team at the fort—what time you leave here, and what time you jump out of that plane? And the equipment's fine?"

"Equipment's good, Avram. We been around the block a few

times and know the drill. Said brought us the best gear goin'. We figure it's gonna take about 45 to 60 minutes to get to the jump zone. We'll aim for wheels-up from here at 2 am. If we're early, we'll circle in Jordanian air space before headin' for the jump zone. Don't want Viktor waitin' too long by that tunnel. Plane is headin' for Adana, Turkey, but it'll stray off course for a minute—just long enough to drop us. Pilots'll apologize and get the hell out of Syrian air space. Then they'll fly some lazy circle patterns over the sea and head toward Israel and home. Just be damn careful not to shoot 'em down," he cautioned.

"There's one last item," Bronstein brought up. He really didn't want to, but Perlman was right. There could be no blowback.

Davies beat him to the punch. "Figured there might be. We took all the labels out of our clothes. The weapons are from a mix of places. They won't even be able to trace the jump suits. They'll know they weren't from Syria, but beyond that, they won't have any real evidence. Said has done a real good job removin' all the source material. Hell, even the instructions are in three languages—includin' Chinese."

"That's good, Sergeant, but there's still one other thing." He reached into his pocket, pulled out three small bronze pill cases, and handed one to each man. "You cannot be captured alive."

Davies flipped the case open and saw the small pill. "Relax, Avram. We figured that was part of the score. We knew the risks before signin' on." He turned to Arlo and Chakroun. "Didn't we, boys?"

They nodded agreement.

"Besides, we're lookin' forward to a few days of beach time once this gig is over. Seriously, we got speed and surprise on our side. Unless there's some huge unknown inside that damn fort, we should be in and out of there within half an hour. As soon as we've lifted off, we'll send you a message. Just make damn sure your fighter planes don't mistake us for a hostile. I'd hate like hell to get shot by our own side. Arlo figures we can make it out over the sea before folks know what's happenin' and react. That chopper does about 170 miles per hour, so we should be over friendly waters fairly soon. Then we run like hell for some nice soft landin' in Israel."

"It sounds too simple. An awful lot can go wrong," Bronstein protested.

"Most good plans are simple. Leaves room to improvise if everythin' goes to hell."

"Well then, I'll leave you to it. Good luck. We'll do everything we can to get you back safely." He shook hands with each of them and headed back out to his unmarked helicopter for the ride back to Jerusalem.

Davies broke the solemn mood by telling everyone to pick up the gear and load it onto the plane. He walked over to where the pilots were resting in the shade of the wings and told them they'd be leaving early the following morning. The pilots were officers, but they stood up out of respect for the sergeant—a fellow professional. Davies rummaged around in his backpack until he found the charts of the drop area that Bronstein had given him. The pilots examined them closely and said they'd been briefed by the head of the Jordanian secret service.

One of them clapped Davies on the back. "Don't worry. We'll get you where you need to go, Sergeant. We hope you kick the shit of those bastards," the captain said in perfect American English—the product of four years of training in Texas and Arizona.

***

Crac des Chevaliers, Syria

Kim Jung-Woo seldom got to leave the lab, but even though he was two levels below the surface, he knew something had changed earlier in the week. For one thing, the language he distantly heard was no longer Arabic. He could identify the Russian, but he wasn't sure about the others. Then there was the drinking. The Arabs may have been sloppy, but they never drank that much—if at all. These new people drank all the time—and were loud about it. He'd also heard a new helicopter come in. The engine had a slightly different pitch and was clearly well tuned compared to the old one, which sputtered and coughed every time it started up and was shut down.

Finally, there was the visit from the new leader of the guards. Soon after the new helicopter landed, a short, bald man with a permanently pugnacious expression on his face tried to enter the lab. He wrinkled his nose in disgust at the onslaught of the strong chemical odors coming from the lab bench. It wasn't just the chemical smells that assaulted him. Cages in the next room held hundreds of rats—rats whose cages hadn't been cleaned for several days, while they were waiting to be injected with the virus.

"*Jesus fucking Christ,*" Ivan Balko yelled as he grabbed a handkerchief to hold against his nose, "*what the fuck is that stench? Don't you fucking people ever flush the toilet?*"

The Korean guards leaped to their feet with guns drawn, and they barred his way before he could get near the testing area. He yelled at them—first in Russian and then in English—to get the hell out of the way. Stone faced, they didn't say anything, but they lowered their weapons until they were pointing directly at his heart.

Frustrated, he pulled out a small notebook with a calendar and jabbed his finger at a certain date. "*Two days from now, you fucking idiots! Two days, and you let those stinking little motherfuckers out,*" he yelled.

The guards were unmoved and only pushed their weapons closer to him. Kim, who was immune to the flood of smells coming from his lab and the cages by this time, stood up and tried to defuse the situation. He said something to the guards in Korean, and they made just enough room for him to stand in front of the newcomer.

"What do you want?" Kim asked wearily. He was tired and just wanted to get out of this dungeon.

"Who the fuck are you?" Ivan Balko barked.

"The person who's making this experiment work. Now, again, what do you want?"

"You got two days to wrap this up and get those fucking rats—along with whatever shit you're cooking up—out of here. This project goes live." He tried to jab his finger at Kim to reinforce the point, but one of the guards grabbed it and nearly broke it in two. Balko yelped in pain but didn't move.

"That's impossible," Kim said. "The program isn't ready yet. Some yes, but not nearly the amount that was ordered."

"Tough shit, kid," Balko snarled. "You better get your ass in gear then and finish it up." They could hear him cursing and moaning as he stomped up the stairs to the surface.

The guards returned to their posts without a word or a change of expression. Kim returned to his stool by the lab bench and sank his head into his hands, wondering just how in hell he was going to survive this mess.

***

Later that night, the sound of automatic gunfire woke him up and brought the guards to instant attention. One of them grabbed a weapon and slipped out of the lab to see what had happened.

A few minutes later, he returned with what passed for a smile on his face. "Drunken idiots shot up a herd of goats. Probably got the shepherd as well."

Kim rolled over and tried to get back to sleep, thinking that the shepherd was probably lucky considering what was about to be unleashed on this godforsaken part of the world.

***

Al-Narish—two days later

Viktor opened the front door a crack and was relieved to see that the night was pitch black. There wasn't a sound or a light anywhere. Even the goats and dogs seem to have retreated from the solid-black darkness. The road leading to the fortress was just a pale, dusty outline between the rocky fields.

The last few hours had been hectic, and he was anxious to get going. Two nights on the cramped, narrow bed had been bad enough, but now he had to deal with Emily and his changing feelings about her. Maybe it was her reaction to Yushenko's son, maybe it was her reaction to the strength of Yushenko's family struggling against impossible odds with a very sick child and an oppressive regime, or maybe it was something she missed in her own life—that touchstone of family that allowed you to keep going when the outside world was yelling at you to stop, but instead to struggle against what everyone else called inevitable. But whatever the reason, the hard shell of the NSA professional had begun to crack—and he found he liked what was underneath that shell. There was an appealing softness, a vulnerability there.

When he was twisting and turning during the night, trying to get comfortable, he'd volunteered to move onto the floor. Absolutely not, she'd said. To reinforce the point, she'd grabbed his arm and pulled it across her waist—as if to make him hold her on the bed. After a few minutes, her breathing had evened out, and she was asleep. Every time he'd tried to move his arm out of the way, she tugged it back. Finally, he'd given up and left it where it was, curled around her.

The message from Davies had come through late in the afternoon—the one giving the timing, the rough plan, and the equipment. His stomach had contracted at what they were about to do. It was one thing to talk about all this from the safety of Cyprus. It was quite another when faced with the reality of shepherding a group of people—including two reluctant, elderly people and a sick child—undetected to a rendezvous point and then assaulting a fortress that had withstood assaults from entire armies. It was idiotic really. *Don't think too much,* he told himself. *Maybe it's time to light a candle and avoid rational analysis.* He hated to admit it, but much depended on sheer luck. He had no doubt that Davies and the others could land where they said, but he had no idea what surprises the tunnel held. Was it open all the way to the top? Was it heavily guarded? Could they really destroy the lab? Could Arlo even get to the helicopter? There was no use worrying about all this. You just had to get on with it and make your own luck.

The whole plan had almost fallen apart when Anne Marie told her parents they had to come with them. At first, her mother flatly refused. "This is our home," she wailed. "Where would we go? How will we live?"

Her father was no more enthusiastic until Yushenko explained what would likely happen to anyone connected with the destruction of Assad's pet project. He reluctantly agreed at that point and tried to calm his wife, who was trying to jam everything they owned into two bulging suitcases. He wrapped his arms around her. "Our safety and the safety of our daughter and grandson are more important than anything you're stuffing into those bags. And they said we can take nothing with us, my dear. I think they mean nothing except the clothes on our back."

She collapsed, weeping, onto the floor and gently stroked all the items, all the pictures of their life, and all their the favorite clothes. "Where will we go? How will we start over again at our age?" she sobbed.

"I don't know, Mama, but wherever we go, it will be better than here," Anne Marie said, looking at Yushenko for confirmation.

He too wondered just where they'd wind up. But for now, he

simply nodded his confirmation. "Yes, it will be better. Nothing could be worse," he said soothingly.

While Anne Marie and her mother retreated to the kitchen to prepare some food, Emily pulled Viktor aside. "This plan, does it really have a chance?"

Viktor waggled his hand back and forth. "With a little luck maybe."

"What's the downside?"

"We all die."

Emily smiled despite the gloomy outlook. "Trust you never to sugarcoat anything."

"I never saw much point in that. It screws up reaction times, and that's all we've got going for us right now—we can react faster than those clowns in the fort. When we leave, I'll take point, and Oleg will carry his son and push the family along. You take the rear and watch out for anything that could cause a problem. Once we get to the fort and Arlo opens that small door, you grab the family and run like hell for the helo. He'll give you a weapon so you can stand guard while he tries to get that thing started. Basically, you shoot anyone who tries to get too close." He looked straight into her eyes and touched her hand gently. "You OK with that?"

She gave him a small smile and a quick peck on the cheek. "Fine. Remember Telos? You just take care of yourself."

He checked his watch nervously. "As soon as I hear Ricky's ready, we'll head out. It will take us about an hour to get into position. The timing is going to be tricky. Too soon, and we'll just draw unfriendly attention to ourselves. Too late, and Ricky will risk getting noticed."

At that moment, the transmission device vibrated gently in his pocket. He attached the cable to his phone, read the short message, and took a deep breath. "It's showtime. They're about to get on the plane. Round up the troops, Emily. We're out of here."

Emily sensed his tension and touched his arm reassuringly. "We'll be fine, Viktor. Don't worry about us."

***

Southern Jordan

The pilots lowered the ramp, and the three jumpers, with all their gear, waddled into the empty cargo hold and began to get into their cumbersome jump outfits. Meanwhile, the pilots went through their start-up routine, with one turbo-prop engine at a time coughing into life until all four of them were running smoothly. Satisfied with the synchronized rumble, the pilots looked back at their passengers for a final check and got a thumbs-up from Davies, who'd spent the last half hour with the pilots reviewing once again their flight path, altitude, and precise drop time and zone. He also checked the large altimeter on his wrist whose GPS was preset with the coordinates of the landing area. The hydraulic gear began to whine, the rear ramp gradually began to lift off the ground, and then it closed with a loud thump. The green light came on, indicating that all doors and the ramp were firmly shut, and the plane swung slowly around to start the short taxi into take-off position. The jumpers checked each other's gear—sometimes tugging to tighten a strap, and sometimes giving the oxygen valves a minute twist. No words were necessary at this point. They'd said all that needed to be said and were now purely focused on each step of the operation. Step one: make sure the gear is in working order. If that doesn't work, it's no use worrying about step two. Deal with one step at a time, with everyone doing their job, and the big picture will take care of itself. If Viktor's there to meet them, that's fine. If not, they'd carry on anyway. They looked at each other and gave a tight we've-been-through-shit-like-this-before-and-can-do-it-again smile.

The heavy plane started to gain speed, and Davies instinctively checked the second hand on his watch. He grinned as the plane lurched upward at the 15-second mark. He'd been on several C-130s in his career and always marveled at their use of short runways. "Fuckin' things can land and take off on a driveway," he muttered to himself.

As they were slowly climbing to cruising altitude, the copilot unwound himself from his seat and made his way back into the hold, hanging on to the overhead railing for support. He handed Davies a short message they'd just received. As the copilot made his way back to the cockpit Davies opened the piece of paper: "All the pieces are in place. We're standing by. Take care of yourselves. Avram."

"Good to know somebody's out there," Davies said to himself.

The pilot turned the controls over to the copilot, pulled out a thermos of tea, and looked back into the hold. He held up the thermos as an offering to Davies and his team. They shook their heads in a no. The last thing they needed at this point was an urgent need to empty their bladders. The pilot poured some of the tea into a small metal cup and screwed the cap back on the thermos. Jumping out of a plane at about 5,000 feet with a normal parachute, he could understand, but jumping out at 30,000 feet and dropping like some awkward bird until under 1,000 feet struck him as totally insane.

After about half an hour, he checked their position and announced they were now leaving Jordanian air space. Far below, at the powerful Russian radar station near the naval base at Tartus, the Jordanian plane showed up as a small blip on the outer ring of the screen. The technician tapped the screen just to make sure it wasn't a piece of dust. No, there it was droning on a northwest course. He checked another screen for scheduled flights that day and was surprised not to see anything listed for this time of the night or course. He twisted a few more dials, and the blip only stayed on its course—very close to Syrian air space. What the hell was going on? Could this be a problem? He was about to ask his supervisor about calling the Syrians to see if they'd picked up the same signal when he felt a heavy hand on his shoulder. He looked up and nearly fell off his stool in surprise. It wasn't just his direct superior officer squeezing his shoulder hard; it was the base commander himself. The technician was about to jump to attention when the pressure on his shoulder increased, keeping him in his seat.

"Relax, son. Why don't you take a break and come back in about 20 minutes?" the commander said in his deep, bass voice. "I'll deal with this." He gave the kind of smile that froze subordinates in their place and precluded any objections.

The technician slid from under the hand and made his way gratefully to the canteen. The commander moved into the seat, looked casually around the room, and nudged his knee toward the circuit breaker under the desk. Instantly, every screen in the room went dark. While the technicians were pounding their machines or cursing Syrian technical incompetence, the commander was looking closely at his watch. Ten minutes, he figured, was all it would take for the plane to swing slight east over Syrian territory before getting back on course—with loud apologies for the navigational error. With luck, the Syrians wouldn't notice anything. With all their air defenses rotated toward Israel, they sometimes never even noticed other flights. Or if they did, the plane would be long gone before they got off their asses and did something. In the meantime, he was daydreaming about how to spend the $25,000 that would magically appear in his Cypriot bank account. He could probably guess where it was coming from, but he really didn't see the point in pursuing that thought.

CHAPTER 23

Crac des Chevaliers, Syria

Viktor looked at the small group huddled out of sight by the long ramp that led to the main gate of the fortress and let out a silent breath of relief. It was a miracle they'd made it this far, and he was hoping that their share of miracles hadn't run out. They were going to need them. Thank God there was no moon. Their walk from the house to the village hadn't exactly been subtle, with Anne Marie's mother still weeping about leaving home, her father shuffling along slowly, and young Yuri letting out a few squeals from time to time. Only Oleg's steady presence gently nudging them along kept them going. Mercifully, this was Syria where no one—neighbors, friends, or perfect strangers—was encouraged to be curious about figures creeping down a dark road in the middle of the night.

Their first challenge was the scrawny dogs that roamed the area day and night in the vain search for food. If one of them picked up the group's scent, it would begin barking loudly. They were about half a mile from the village when one of the dogs saw them and was about to start barking. Just then, Anne Marie opened the food basket she'd prepared and held out a large piece of meat. The dog grabbed it out of her hand and sloped off quickly before any other dogs showed up.

The second challenge, which happened just below the fortress, was met the same way. One of the young Syrian soldiers who'd been thrown out of the fort earlier was sleeping propped up against one of the houses. Wakened by the sound of them shuffling past, he jumped up swiftly and grabbed for his rifle—more to protect himself than acting as any kind of guard for the fort.

As he crept forward with his rifle lowered in their direction, Viktor pulled out his pistol and held it by his side. Right then, Anne Marie stepped forward and motioned for Viktor to put the gun away. In the dim light, she'd recognized the young boy as one of the hungry soldiers they'd fed the day before. She smiled at the boy soldier and held out the basket of food she'd brought. As he saw the basket, his earlier suspicions evaporated, and he eagerly grabbed the food. He started to thank Anne Marie, but she put her finger to her lips urging him to remain quiet as they both sat down.

"Yes, yes, older sister, I recognize you. You were kind to us. What are you doing here at this time?" he whispered in between bites.

She looked at the others, who nodded that she should continue, rather than have this kid raise the alarm.

"Tell the kid to get as far away as he can," Viktor whispered to her.

Anne Marie nodded and started to explain about the people in the fort.

"The bad ones," the kid muttered. "The ones who threw us out onto the street."

She nodded.

"Yes, those ones. We have to stop them from doing something very, very bad to all the people in this area. They're making something that will kill many, many people."

The boy's eyes widened, and he looked questioningly at the

small group with her. "How are you going to stop them? You don't have many people."

"We have a plan," she said simply, and she gestured to the dark, empty sky, praying that the kid didn't understand much about parachutes. "Very soon, something will fall from the sky and help us deal with the people inside."

The kid's eyes widened in fear as he remembered stories about flying bombs that come out of nowhere. His body started to shake, and Anne Marie grabbed his shoulders to calm him down.

"He's thinking of drones," Viktor said. "Tell him his best chance of living until sunrise is to run like hell back up that road."

She didn't have to tell him twice. The last they saw of him was a small trail of dust heading away from the fort.

Viktor checked his watch again. He had to be by the tunnel in 20 minutes to meet the jumpers. The only warning sounds he'd hear would be the faint rustle of parachutes and the soft thump of feet landing on the rocky soil. They didn't have to worry about hiding the 'chutes or the rest of the gear. If they weren't in and out of the fort long before the 'chutes were spotted, they'd be dead anyway.

He motioned to the others that he was going to make his way around the fort and down to the opening of the tunnel. Oleg nodded and herded the others into the deep shadow by the ramp. With one hand on the rough stone wall to guide him, Viktor walked and slid down the long side of the fort. At first, he was worried about the sound of stones and small rocks rolling down the hill and waking anyone inside. Then he laughed at his own fears, realizing that, with walls so thick, the chances of anyone inside hearing anything were remote. And anyone inside who happened to hear something was wise enough to roll over and go back to sleep rather than investigate.

At the rear of the fort, the first hint that he was near the tunnel was the foul collection of odors from chemicals and rot, from ancient sources as well as modern rodents. His eyes began to sting from the chemicals as his hand at last found the opening. He stepped back, relieved to be in the right place with about 10 minutes to spare. *Armed guards will be the least of their problems,* he thought. *Who the hell can breathe in that place?*

He glanced nervously at his watch, as if suddenly aware of the million things that could go wrong with this plan: starting with jumping out of an airplane at 30,000 feet and landing next to where he was standing. *What if they jump in the wrong place? What if some of the equipment doesn't work? What if the GPS is wrong?* Then he realized who he was dealing with. He'd been in hundreds of tight situations with Davies and Arlo, and they'd never let him down yet. And Chakroun, of course. He also remembered how the tough Legionnaire had guarded his back during the long run to safety in Chad. *No,* he kept assuring himself. *They'll make it. They have to.* Still, he couldn't help checking as the second hand made its way ever so slowly around his watch dial.

***

Far above and slightly to the west of the fortress, Ricky Davies was also checking his watch. At a terminal velocity of about 125 miles per hour, he calculated it should take just under three minutes to free-fall from 30,000 feet. With arms and legs extended, he should be able to guide them to the precise drop zone next to Viktor. He gave a knowing chuckle. "There's that word 'should' again. Don't mean the same as 'will.' One little thing wrong, and we'll wind up in some Lebanese corn patch—as fertilizer. Don't pay to think about it. Let's just get this show on the road."

He turned on the comms system to check with Arlo and Chakroun. After they both gave a thumbs-up, he switched frequencies to talk to the pilot. "Open her up, boys; time we was leavin.'"

The pilot shook his head in disbelief as he pulled the switch to open the rear ramp. *These guys are nuts,* he thought.

Davies lived for these moments when all the preparations, plans, and contingencies disappeared in the face of action. It was a rush that no pill or powder could replicate. The time for doubts had long passed. Now you needed to focus 100% on only what's front of you. Don't sweat the other stuff.

As soon as the ramp had thumped down, he took one last look and then led the three of them into the void, his arms spread like some prehistoric bird zeroing in on some food far below. The pilots closed the ramp immediately and steered the plane quickly westward over the sea to avoid any angry questions from Syrian air traffic controllers. Somewhere between Cyprus and Turkey, they'd execute a few turns and then return to their base in Jordan.

Arlo loved the speed and grace of these free falls. They really were totally free: no bosses, no orders—only the sheer joy of gliding through the night sky. Encased in their jump suits and helmets, they didn't notice the speed and could simply enjoy the slight arm and hand movements where they turned in unison—almost like an aerial ballet—as Davies adjusted their course. Slowly, the pin pricks of light far below began to take shape and what had appeared to be completely flat land began to unfold into its ancient contours. Then, at about 5,000 feet, they could begin to make out the immense Crac des Chevaliers.

"Jesus," Arlo muttered to himself, "fucker really *is* big."

Davies made one final course adjustment and told them to get ready to open their high-performance Ram parachutes. They opened with a soft *pop* at just under 700 feet, and the specially designed rectangular 'chutes guided them silently to the rear of the fort, where they touched down as if stepping off a low stair. No noise, no fuss, no bother.

Dressed all in black and with black 'chutes they'd been invisible even to attentive guards, let alone the semi-sober, sleepy contractors on the towers. If the guards had heard anything, they probably thought it was just the sound of the west wind sweeping ceaselessly in from the sea.

Viktor let out a sigh of relief as the jumpers stripped off their gear and started to open their bundles. "Christ, that was perfect. You guys showed up just in time."

"We aim to please, Viktor." Davies looked up at the fort and whistled softly. "Big fucker, ain't it?" Then his nose began to twitch. "Sumbitch. Don't tell me that's comin' from that damn tunnel we gotta go up?"

"'Fraid so. Nice medieval sewage mixed with modern rat shit and foul chemicals. Look at it this way: it'll encourage you to be quick."

"If you say so," Davies retorted. Then he laughed and turned to Arlo. "Smells just like home, don't it Arlo?"

Arlo grinned. "Close enough. Now you see why I don't go home."

Davies double-checked the equipment they'd brought: a mixture of Uzis and H&K MP5 machine pistols, silencers, extra clips, bolt cutters, small headlamps, Semtex with the timing pencils, folding climbing axes, and some flash-bang hand grenades. He handed three of the weapons with extra clips to Viktor and reviewed the plan. "Me and Said are the first ones out of the hole. While we deal with whatever's in front of us, Arlo runs like hell for the front gate. Once he opens it, you and Yushenko fan out and take out the guards while Arlo and the others hustle over to the chopper. We'll join you as soon as we've set the timers on the Semtex. What d'you figure?" he asked rhetorically "Fifteen minutes?"

"Too long," Viktor answered. "I'll give you 10 minutes to get up the tunnel. A few more to deal with whoever is in the lab. Then set the timers. By that time, if we're not out of there in 10 more minutes, we're in trouble. Arlo, you know the course to get out of there, right?"

"Ain't real hard, Viktor. We just fly that baby west until we're over the sea, turn south, and run like hell 'til we see some help with a six-pointed star on it."

"Sounds simple enough—in theory," Viktor answered.

"Theory won't keep us alive very long. Let's get goin' before these dopey bastards sober up." Davies turned toward the tunnel, then stopped and unstrapped another small bundle. "One more thing, Viktor. Them Uzis is fine in close quarters but useless over more than 50 yards. You'll need this to deal with anyone on the upper ramps." He handed Viktor a compact rifle used by the British SAS soldiers, which carried a heavy .338 cartridge.

"Christ, Ricky. This is a sniper rifle. I'm not exactly going to have time to set up and take these guys out one by one."

"Don't have to. Just point in the general direction and pull the trigger. That cartridge makes a helluva bang when it hits somethin'. Them boys on the ramp will get the point even if you don't hit 'em. Help 'em keep their heads down."

Viktor strapped the rifle on his back and clambered back up the hill, taking the extra weapons with him.

Yushenko heard the scrape of a rock and turned just as Viktor came around the edge of the fort. He scrambled over to take the machine pistols and examined them closely, turning them over and over while checking the mechanism. "Good," he pronounced. He handed one to Emily and opened his eyes wide as she too expertly examined the weapon, tested the magazines, and flipped the safety off.

She turned to Yushenko and Viktor, smiling. "Not just a pretty face, eh, boys? They do teach us a few things."

Anne Marie's parents stared at them in disbelief and clutched each other tightly, wondering what they'd gotten into. Viktor told them that all they had to do now was wait for Davies and the others to clear a way to the gate. He made it sound routine, but he knew it would take a superhuman effort if they were to leave this place alive. If Desta were here, she'd tell them to stay calm and have faith. *She may have a point with her strong faith in the higher being of the New Testament,* he thought, *but right now, my faith is in ancient tunnel designs and the well-tested survival skills of Davies and his team. It's definitely time for some of that Old Testament righteous thunder and violence.*

The tunnel was indeed narrow, but the walls were rough enough to provide decent traction for the climbing axes and their feet. The generator and the squeals of the rats covered the sounds of their axes biting into the ancient stone and their grunts of exertion as they pulled themselves inch by slippery inch up the narrow tunnel. The malodorous cloud of chemicals and rat shit cascading down the tunnel was overpowering, almost suffocating, as Davies led his team foot by agonizing foot up through the foul-smelling darkness with their feet braced on each side. No one said anything, and the thin headlamps on straps wrapped around their heads gave just enough light to let him pick out the best holds. Then they came to their first obstacle: a rusted, ancient grate that some smart Crusader had put there hundreds of years ago to block exactly what they were trying to do.

Clever people, Davies thought as he examined it closely.

Fortunately, the metal had rusted with the damp and passage of time. He gave a strong tug on one of the bars, and it nearly crumbled in his hand as it fell loudly down the tunnel, just missing the other two men. They held their breath and unslung their weapons in case someone had heard them. Slowly, Davies peeled away the remaining bars and passed them to Chakroun, who in turn handed them down to Arlo, who tied them to a long piece of nylon line he was carrying and lowered them quietly to the bottom. Once they were safely on the ground, he untied the end of the rope from his waist and let it drop. He patted Chakroun's foot, who relayed a thumbs-up to Davies, who continued the climb.

After several more feet, he saw a dim light at what must be the opening of the tunnel. He turned off his headlamp and motioned for the others to do the same. As he came around the final bend, he gagged and nearly dropped his climbing pick. He understood why no one had heard them, or if they had heard something, they were in no hurry to investigate. The small, almost invisible opening of the tunnel was hidden by a large outcrop of rock, beyond which were dozens of wire cages stacked waist high and filled with hundreds of angry, squealing rats.

"Sweet Jesus Christ," Davies said to himself. "Emily wasn't kidding. Hope these little bastards aren't already infected. If they are, we're fucked. No time to waste."

The men pulled themselves out of the tunnel and fought through the eye-watering, throat-burning cloud of foul air. They sat panting after the effort of gettin up the tunnel. After seconds that seemed like hours, they got their second wind, and Davies padded quickly toward the bright lights, peering carefully around each sharp turn in the tunnel until they came into the wide space leading to the lab itself. They peeled off their headlamps and put them gently on the ground. Arlo and Chakroun were about to put their climbing picks down when Davies motioned for them to stuff them into their belts. They might come in handy later.

Davies's eyes widened in astonishment as they emerged into the lab, which was filled with long tables, testing equipment, and vials containing a vicious-smelling clear liquid. He saw two doors leading off from the lab into two side rooms. Then he spotted the stairs climbing toward the main hall and the courtyard. He motioned for Arlo to take the stairs as fast as he could. Chakroun guarded the other two doors while Davies unpacked the Semtex and timers. As he was fixing the bombs to the bottom of a table, he knocked a leg, causing an empty glass vial to crash to the stone floor. This sound brought one of the Korean guards rushing into the room, where he saw Davies and was just bringing up his gun when Chakroun fired a well-aimed burst of three shots into his chest, driving him back. Before the other guards could come out, Chakroun threw a flash-bang grenade into the room they were using as a barracks. One of the guards stumbled around holding his ears in pain, vainly trying to see what was in front of them. Before the guard could grab his weapons, Chakroun calmly walked out of the fog and delivered two kill shots into his head.

Chakroun came back into the lab as Davies was attaching the bombs. "We should move before any reinforcements arrive."

Davies said, "I have two more to attach in the lab and one by the rat cages. Can't afford to leave those little bastards around."

Suddenly, another Korean came staggering out of the other door with his hands waving in the air. "Don't shoot, don't shoot," he wailed in English. "I'm not with them. I'm an American. You've got to help me get out of here."

Davies and Chakroun exchanged "what the fuck?" looks.

"*Who the hell are you*?" they yelled in unison.

"Kim Jung-Woo," the Korean cried in desperation. "I'm the scientist they kidnapped. You *need* me."

"Sure we do. And I'm George Washington," Davies answered.

He and Chakroun were about to shoot when Kim looked nervously over his shoulder and bellowed a warning: "*Look out, there's another guard.*"

This gave Davies and Chakroun just enough time to duck as the third guard came surging out of a side room, expertly firing his machine pistol in short bursts. The guard grabbed Kim and roughly shoved him out of the way as he continued firing. Chakroun had slipped over to one side for a better angle and managed to fire a few rounds into the guard, which drove him back into the side room. No one moved for a few seconds, which seemed like hours.

Chakroun stood up and peered through the dust to find Kim cowering under a table and Davies slumped in a corner holding his left leg. He rushed over to help. "Sergeant, can you move?"

He winced in reply. "Not quickly. Ain't the first time I been hit. Fucker got me right through the thigh. Lots of blood, but no bones hit." He reached into his pack, pulled out a field-medic kit, extracted a compression bandage, and started to tie it around the wound. "I'll be OK, but you gotta get outta here with this guy. If he is who he says he is, we need him. If he's bullshittin' us, just drop his ass into the sea." He levered himself up and gave Chakroun a small push. "You git goin' now. I'll finish up with the Semtex and be along shortly." He glanced around the room and started to hobble over to the table. "*Kid,*" he yelled at Kim, "*them rats in the cages—they already infected with this shit?*"

Kim shook his head violently. "No, no. Not yet. I was supposed to start doing that later today. You're not infected."

"That's a relief," Davies said. "Means we only gotta worry about gettin' shot." He looked at Chakroun and nodded toward the stairs. "Get movin', *mon ami*. Ain't got much time."

Chakroun was about to argue, but Davies just shook his head and gestured toward the stairs. The Legionnaire wasn't happy, but he knew Davies was right. He grabbed Kim roughly and gave him a sharp push toward the stairs. "*On y vas—maintenant, pas demain,*" he barked at a shaken Kim.

***

Arlo could barely hear the muffled sounds of the fight in the lab two floors below as he ran upward through the labyrinth of passages and dead ends until he finally came to the main hall, whose walls were covered with ancient tapestries, swords, and axes. He glanced at them, but he was more interested in the opening that seemed to lead to the courtyard. He headed toward it, and once in the colonnade, he paused by one of the chipped pillars and broken arches to peer into the open space. There, about 50 yards away and bathed in the harsh glare of a strong spotlight, was the black helicopter with its drooping rotors, sitting in the middle of a large, whitewashed circle with a roughly drawn H in the middle. "Well, thank God for that," he whispered. "Now let's just hope the son of a bitch has enough fuel to get us where we want to go."

At that moment, he noticed a black-clad guard walking around the chopper. The guard must have heard some commotion from inside the fortress because he unslung his weapon and made his way cautiously toward the entrance. He never saw Arlo, who was well hidden in the shadows behind the pillar. Not wanting to alert the guards on the ramparts with the noise of a shot, Arlo silently took the climbing axe from his belt and adjusted it in his hand until he was satisfied that the balance was just right. The guard was about 10 feet in front of him and had taken a step inside the door when Arlo lifted his arm and threw the axe just as he'd practiced thousands of times with hatchets back home in Arkansas. He watched as the axe turned over once, then twice, and then the sharp end buried itself deep in the guard's unsuspecting back, severing his spinal cord just below the neck. He dropped without a sound, and Arlo scanned the ramparts for signs of activity. He was relieved to see that no one had been alerted. He then located the twisting passageway leading to the main gate, about 15 yards from where he was standing, took a deep breath, and started sprinting along the bottom of the wall, where it was still dark. A guard on the ramparts must have heard the noise, because one of the spotlights began to swing toward the opening just as Arlo ducked inside and skidded around the slippery corner. He stopped for a minute and leaned against the wall to catch his breath as the spotlight swept across the courtyard. Satisfied nothing was there, the guard returned it to its original position, shining directly on the helicopter.

He almost slipped on the steep path to the main gate as it rounded two more sharp corners. Finally, the massive gate was in front of him—its thick wooden planks held in tight iron bands. The only modern touch was a hydraulic ram used to open and close the gate. "Ain't no way I'm gonna move that sucker," he murmured as he fumbled around in the darkness, looking for the small door built into the main gate. Eventually, he found it on the lower-left side. Unlike the main gate, this door was opened and shut with just a latch and a light bar. He easily lifted the bar, set it down quietly, and pressed the latch. Letting out a sigh of relief, he opened the door and glanced left and right. It was pitch black. He could see nothing.

Where the hell is everybody? he wondered.

Just then, two large figures loomed out of the darkness beside the entrance ramp. Arlo grabbed his MP5, ready to fire, until he recognized Viktor and Yushenko. "Son of a bitch! How did you know it was me up here?"

"We didn't see you, Arlo. We could smell you from miles away." Viktor grinned. "Everything OK?"

"Don't know about Ricky and Said in the lab, but we got company on the ramparts and towers. Be good to take out them spotlights and the guard post."

All of a sudden, Viktor realized what the rifle was for. He turned and motioned for the others to climb up onto the ramp.

"This is gonna be fun," Arlo said when he saw the extra passengers. "Here's what we're going to do," he said, suddenly in helicopter command mode. "Once you get them spotlights, Viktor, then me and Emily—with the family between us—are going to run like hell for the helo. She'll provide cover as I jam everyone inside and try to start it up." He pointed to Viktor. "You *gotta* get them lights. Then you and Oleg, here, clean out the ramparts. Otherwise, we're just sittin' ducks down there. By that time, Ricky and Said should be on board. Just as I start to rotate out of here, you and Oleg jump on board, ready to provide covering fire."

Viktor nodded, and they all walked up to the gate. Once they were all inside the fortress, Arlo shut the small door, and they started up the ramp to the courtyard. By now, word of some disturbance in the lab had reached the contractors, and they were swinging the lamps around all corners of the courtyard looking for possible infiltrators. Arlo gestured for the family to stay hidden in the entrance passageway while Viktor crept around to the colonnade, where he found a shooting position by one of the pillars. Resting the rifle on one of the column bases, he moved the barrel around slowly until it was pointed at one of the lights. He took a deep breath, let it out unhurriedly, and squeezed the trigger. The light went out with a smash, and he heard the guards shouting at each other. Before they could do anything, he smoothly swung the rifle around and took out the three remaining lights. The guards responded by blindly spraying the courtyard with machine-pistol fire.

When the last light went out, Arlo shoved his small group out of the shelter of the entrance passage and ran for the chopper. Emily took up the rear, firing up at the ramparts. Yushenko ran over to Viktor, and they rushed up the steps onto the ramparts. In the sudden darkness, the guards still weren't sure what they were facing and were confused when Yushenko started barking orders in Russian. By the time they realized their mistake, it was too late, and they were cut down by short, lethal bursts of gunfire. Then he and Viktor methodically worked their way around the ramparts, cleaning out the few pockets of resistance. While they were clearing the ramparts, Emily dealt with the few who dared to venture into the courtyard from the safety of the rooms inside the fort.

By this time, Yushenko and Viktor could make out the whine of the helicopter starting up, and they rushed down the stairs, which were slippery with blood and broken glass from the spotlights. They got to the helicopter just as they saw Chakroun make a dash for the helicopter while firing and trying to shield someone.

"*Who the hell is this?*" Viktor hollered when Chakroun and Kim got to the chopper. "*Where's Ricky?*"

"Ricky's still inside setting the bombs. He was hit, but he's mobile." Pointing to Kim, he added, "Ricky says we need this guy. He's the scientist behind all this shit."

"Fuck him, I'm going after Ricky." Viktor remembered the promise he'd made to Desta about bringing her husband back in one piece.

"*Be real quick, Viktor,*" Arlo yelled, "*we ain't got but a few minutes before one of those shots cripples this bird.*"

Yushenko, Chakroun, and Emily assumed firing positions around the helicopter as Viktor raced back into the fortress, looking for Davies. From the diagrams they'd studied so hard a few weeks ago, he remembered that most of the stairs to the lower levels ran off the main ceremonial hall. He was about to choose one of the stairs when he spotted a bloody and battered Ricky Davies limping slowly, painfully, up the final steps into the hall. He waved Viktor frantically away. "Get out, Viktor! I set the timers early. This place is gonna blow any second now."

He took one more step and then the powerful concussion from four kilos of Semtex going off two levels below flew up the stairwell and drove Davies forward in a cloud of dust and stone chips. Viktor was blown off his feet and barely missed getting impaled by one of the ancient swords that was knocked off the wall. His machine pistol was sent flying, and his ears were ringing once the dust and rubble had settled around him, hiding most of his legs. One of his arms was caught behind a heavy table leg. He pulled it out slowly and wiggled his fingers to make sure they were still working. There was no sign of Davies, who must be lying under more debris. Viktor was about to try to stand up when he heard someone's foot scraping over the stone steps leading into the hall. Some inner instinct told him this wasn't the sound of friend, who—at the very least—would be shouting for both him and Davies. He stayed very still and blinked his eyes to clear the dust from them. After a few blinks, the image in the center of the room, a man with his back to Viktor, came into focus. He'd recognize that back and bald head anywhere:

Ivan Balko. The only thought going through Viktor's mind was the sheer insanity and unfairness of getting caught like this. *Goddamn it,* he thought, *the son of a bitch is going to win.*

Then he realized that Balko was focusing on something buried across the room and so hadn't seen him. Through the ear-splitting buzz inside his head, he heard Balko saying something about "finally settling scores." "Now you're mine, you little prick, Davies. You're done fucking up my life. I should turn you over to the Arabs, but then I'd miss sending you straight to hell."

Viktor was relieved by the next sound—a harsh cough, spitting out dust and debris, followed by an unmistakable southern drawl.

"You always were a useless sumbitch, Balko. Couldn't even guard a bunch of your own kind stuffed in cages in some old fort. Beaten by a handful of men—and a woman. Nice job, asshole," Davies said defiantly.

Viktor desperately felt around in the debris for a weapon—any kind of a weapon. "Keep him talking, Ricky. Keep him talking," he prayed. Then he felt the handle of something long and heavy under his fingers. Trying not to make any noise, he gently lifted what turned out to be one of the old medieval swords that had fallen off the wall. *Better than nothing,* he thought. *It worked several hundred years ago and should still work now.* He placed the tip on the floor and levered himself up on to his feet. His legs were weak, but he took a couple of deep breaths to steady himself, placed both hands on the long pommel of the heavy sword, and used every fiber of his strong shoulders to hoist it high above his head.

Balko was so intent on Davies that he never even noticed the dust-covered, sword-wielding apparition moving up behind him.

Balko raised his pistol. "It's going to be a real pleasure to shut that big mouth of yours, Davies." He must have sensed the swish of Viktor's backswing because he started to turn around just as the heavy blade was gaining maximum momentum toward his neck. Balko's eyes only had time to register complete surprise before the blade was driven by Viktor's massive shoulders and pent-up anger right through Balko's neck, severing his head in one blow.

Davies watched the head bounce a couple of times and looked up at Viktor. "Just like the old days. You do know how to make an entrance. Glad you showed up."

Viktor dropped the heavy sword with a groan and stretched his shoulders. "That damn thing weighs a ton. Can't imagine doing that all day. They must have had arms and shoulders like tree trunks." He reached down and hauled Davies to his feet. "Can you walk?"

"Not real easy. Gimme a hand, and let's get the hell outta here. I can hear Arlo gettin' anxious."

They headed out of the hall and emerged into the central courtyard as Yushenko, Chakroun, and Emily were keeping up a steady stream of fire against the few remaining contractors on the ramps. The helo's rotors were spinning, and Arlo was ready to lift off. Half carrying Davies, Viktor made it to one of the helo's doors, where Chakroun helped him push Davies inside before Viktor and Yushenko piled in.

Arlo motioned for Yushenko to sit beside him. "*All these dials are in Russian. You need to translate,*" he yelled.

Emily turned to let off one last burst of fire, and then she was thrown to the hard ground as a slug caught her high in the right side of the chest. She was lying face down, not moving, as the helicopter began to lift off. Three of the remaining contractors were racing down the steps toward Emily when Viktor jumped out of the chopper and dashed over to her, firing from the hip. One of his bursts of gunfire hit a contractor, who spun around and fell heavily.

Viktor reached down and grabbed Emily, who groaned as he lifted her up. "*Stay with me, Emily. Stay with me. You're going to be fine,*" he screamed. He was about to run toward the chopper when he saw it lift off at the far side of the courtyard pitched far forward, rotors just missing the ground, and heading right toward the two remaining contractors, who were concentrating on Viktor and Emily and never saw it coming. He could make out a grim smile on Arlo's face as he maneuvered the blades a little to the right, just enough to slice through the two gunmen, sending their blood and guts all over Viktor.

The chopper leveled off and hovered just off the ground as Viktor carried Emily to the door. Chakroun and Yushenko pulled her into the hold, and Viktor stood on one of the skids, looking for more contractors as Arlo lifted off as fast as he could.

"*Viktor, get your ass inside,*" Arlo shouted. "*You're screwing up the balance.*"

He hauled himself over the edge and fell heavily next to Yushenko, who was cradling Emily as gently as he could. A volley of shots from the ramparts raked the side of the chopper, barely missing everyone inside. Chakroun grabbed the RPG and loaded it in one smooth motion. He rapidly aimed it at the ramparts, pulled the trigger, and smiled bleakly as the stone walkway collapsed, taking the last remaining contractor with it.

Viktor looked anxiously at Emily, who was unconscious with blood pouring out of the wound. "*Oleg, where the hell is the medic kit on these things?*" he bellowed.

Yushenko gestured behind the rear seat, and his wife turned around to pick it up. Then she slid down next to Emily and pushed Viktor aside. "I'm a nurse, Viktor. Leave this to me." She cut away Emily's shirt, revealing the entry wound a little below the collar bone, and gently felt under her back. "There's no exit wound. The bullet is still inside." After putting compression bandages on the wound to stem the bleeding, she checked for vital signs. "Her pulse is there, but it's weak. Her blood pressure must be dropping. She needs a hospital fast." She rummaged around in the medical bag and gave a cry of relief. "Thank God!

They have a saline bag." She handed the bag to Yushenko and told him to find a place to hang it while she gently inserted the needle into Emily's arm. Satisfied she'd found the right vein, she looked up at the bag and twisted the slender butterfly valve as the fluid began to flow. "This should help with the blood pressure until we reach help." She glanced at Arlo. "When might that be?" she asked.

Viktor leaned forward over Arlo's shoulder and told him to go even faster. "Don't even think about Cyprus. We need to make it Israel. That's Emily's only chance."

"Goddamn it, Viktor. I'm doin' the best I can. This ain't no F-16."

At that moment, static and a short burst of command came over the radio. Yushenko leaned close to listen. "The Syrian Air Force has been alerted."

"OK, let the games begin." Arlo grinned as he drove the chopper even lower over the flat landscape, speeding southwest toward the Mediterranean coast. "Let's see now. We have a maximum speed of about 170 miles per hour," he calculated. "Them jets travel at about the speed of sound. This is gonna be fun." He turned off all the transponders and running lights, making it difficult for anyone to track them. Then he tapped one of the dials, which was wavering. "Oleg, that sucker what I think it is?"

"Yes. Fuel gauge," he confirmed.

The gauge was wavering wildly and rapidly declining from full.

"Fuck. One of them bastards at the fort must have put a hole in our tank. Don't suppose these babies have self-sealing fuel tanks, do they?"

Yushenko shrugged his shoulders and shook his head. "I only rode in them. Never flew them. Don't know."

Arlo's question was answered when the gauge steadied at about half full, and he let out a sigh of relief. "Well, that's better than nuthin'. But it still ain't enough to get us where we want to go." Then he brightened. "Hey, these have got to have at least two tanks," he said, more in hope than knowledge. "Oleg, can you look for the lever that'll switch the fuel from one tank to the other tank?" Both his hands were busy flying the chopper, and he gestured with his head for Yushenko to look by the side of the control panel between them.

Yushenko scrabbled frantically around the base of the control panel for a few anxious minutes before finding the small lever that might be the one to switch fuel tanks. He looked at Arlo for confirmation.

"Ain't got a lot to lose. Give it a flip."

Yushenko pulled the switch and held his breath until the fuel gauge registered full.

"Well, thank the good Lord for that. It's gonna be tight, but we might just reach friendly skies." Arlo glanced at the radar screen and saw two blips closing rapidly from the northeast. "We got company." He peered with a determined expression at the nearby mountains on the Lebanese border to the south. "Hang on, y'all. Let's make them suckers earn their money. We're gonna play dipsy-doodle for a bit. Hang on to Emily real tight." He nudged the cyclic to the left and slightly down, and the chopper veered toward the mountains at an even lower altitude.

"Jesus Christ, Arlo," Davies yelped as he saw the ground rush up toward them. "We don't need to trim the goddamned trees."

Arlo was focused on the rapidly closing blips of Syrian jets and the wall of mountains in front of them. "Gonna be close, real close," he muttered. "What comes first? Mountains or rockets?"

Yushenko, who wasn't convinced there was much difference, had begun involuntarily to push himself back into his seat, sure they were going to slam into the side of the looming cliff. Arlo saw the flash of something leaving the wing of one of the jets and violently shoved the cyclic to the right, just as a rocket flashed by and exploded harmlessly on the side of the mountains. "Shot too soon, you asshole," he said jubilantly—happy to still be in one piece.

Everyone in the back was tossed around as Ann Marie and Viktor did their best to cradle the still-unconscious Emily. Viktor was torn. His heart wanted Arlo to give them a smooth ride. His head said that Arlo's actions were the only way they were going to survive. At least Emily was unconscious and couldn't feel the twists and turns. He just hoped the bullet that was still in her chest wasn't dislodged and sent somewhere fatal.

Chakroun and Davies checked their weapons on the off chance one of the jets would come close enough for them to get off a shot.

There was more squawking on the radio as they came close to Lebanese air space. The gunners on the ground were confused because the helicopter was identified as Russian but was being chased by Syrian fighters. Rather than make a fatal mistake, they did nothing. Meanwhile, Arlo was racing through ravines and around mountain crags to evade the fighters, who surged through Lebanese air space, hunting them down. The bobbing and weaving helicopter was a difficult target, and their shots merely knocked off edges of cliffs rather than shattering the frail chopper. Arlo could see the plain extending south of the mountains and knew their protection would soon be gone.

"*Viktor,*" he roared above the scream of the complaining engine, "Now would be a real good time to tell our friends to send in the cavalry. Once we're over the water, we ain't gotta lick of protection."

Viktor pulled out his encrypted communications device, pushed the buttons, and hoped it worked. By this time, the Israeli air defense systems had detected unusual activity and were already on high alert. Orders had been issued for the northern fighter squadrons to stand by in case the Syrian jets approached Israeli air space.

Deep in Mossad headquarters in Jerusalem, Benny Perlman and Avram Bronstein were nervously pacing back and forth, waiting for word from Viktor.

"Benny, what do you think? Did they pull this off?" Bronstein kept asking.

Perlman tried to calm him down. "All we can do is wait." He checked his watch. "We'll know soon enough. Maybe all that noise up north is about them. Let's hope so."

They both jumped as the loud ring tone on Perlman's phone broke the tension. He grabbed it quickly. "Lipsky," he barked, "Is that you? Where are you?"

"In deep shit at the moment. Serious casualties on board. Just leaving the north Lebanon coast and heading out to sea—at about wave height actually. We've only got a few minutes before the fighters find us."

Perlman turned to one of the assistants next to him. "Get those fucking planes in the air. That helicopter you see on your screens needs our cover right now."

"But they've identified it as a Russian aircraft—not one of ours," the assistant protested.

Perlman rounded on him viciously: "I don't give a shit if it's Martian, you idiot. It has people we need—injured people. So get off your ass and do something. *Right now.*"

The hapless assistant punched a few buttons on his console, and the scramble alarm sounded in a key Israeli air base near Lebanon. Three F-16 Sufa fighters shot into the air within two minutes. The pilots were puzzled by their cryptic orders: go north along the coast until you spot a low-flying Russian helicopter being chased by Syrian jets and escort it home.

This is new, but orders are orders, the lead pilot thought.

It didn't take long for their radar to pick up the wave-hopping helicopter swerving frantically to avoid salvo after salvo from the attacking jets.

One of the shots had punctured a hydraulic line, and black oil was leaking along the side of the chopper's fuselage. The oil pressure dials were going crazy.

Shit, Arlo, thought as he manipulated the controls and flipped more switches, *we ain't got a lot more time.*

Yushenko pointed excitedly toward three streaks approaching

them fast. He saw them break formation and climb to confront the Syrian jets. The Syrian pilots cursed their old MiG-21s and decided this wasn't the day for a dog fight with the Israeli F-16s. They broke off at the last instance and headed home.

The helicopter's radio squawked into life. "Russian helicopter, Russian helicopter, this is the Israeli Defense Force. Can you read me?"

"Loud and clear," Arlo answered. "You took care of one of our problems, but we're leaking oil, and I don't know how far we can get. We got half the UN on board, plus some serious casualties."

"You're not Russian," the pilot observed.

"No shit. This here's Arlo, and I need a place to land real fast. I get this thing any lower, and we'll turn into a submarine."

"OK, Arlo, whoever you are. Keep going on this heading. You've just passed Beirut. Stay well out to sea, and you should be in friendly skies in a few minutes. We'll guide you to a landing spot."

"Don't forget the ambulances. We got people who ain't gonna make it much longer."

Bronstein and Perlman had been following the conversation and looked at each other in amazement.

"Did they by any chance do what I think they did?" Perlman asked rhetorically. "Who's wounded?" he wondered. Before answering his own question, he picked up another phone and ordered an army ambulance to race toward the coordinates the pilots had given Arlo. "And no fucking medic. I want the best goddamned doctor you've got. Understand me?"

Fifteen nervous minutes later, one of the IDF jets flew alongside the helicopter and the pilot pointed down to the beach, indicating that Arlo should land there. He gave a quick thumbs-up and peeled away to his base.

"Hang on tight, everyone," Arlo warned. "We're goin' down, and it may not be smooth."

Despite his words, he managed to spin the chopper expertly and bring it down on the flat sand with only a slight bump. His hands were shaking as he switched off the dials, and the rotors slowly wound down. Then he and Yushenko just sat there for a minute—numb, letting the tension escape, and not quite believing it had been less than 30 minutes since they'd left the Crac des Chevaliers.

Meanwhile, several vehicles were streaming toward them. The ambulance pulled up alongside, and the medics gently lifted Emily onto a stretcher and out of the chopper. They took her to the ambulance, where a doctor gave her a quick examination and ordered several more bags of intravenous fluids.

Ann Marie said, "Emily has lost a great deal of blood, and the bullet is still in her chest."

"You saved her life with that bag of fluid. At least she has some blood pressure to work with," one of the doctors told Ann Marie.

Viktor rushed up to the doctor. "Will she make it?"

"We'll do the best we can," was all the doctor could answer.

The medics also put a complaining Davies on a stretcher and hustled him into the second ambulance.

"*I don't need no goddamned ambulance,*" Viktor heard him shout as the doors closed, and the ambulances raced away.

Ann Marie turned to her parents, who were still in a state of shock. Her mother hadn't opened her eyes since leaving the fort and was scarcely breathing when they landed. Her fingers had made a permanent indentation on her husband's arm by gripping it so hard the blood flow had almost stopped. Young Yuri remained swaddled in blankets and was blissfully unaware of the last hour.

"Where are we?" her mother finally croaked. "Who are all these people?" Then she saw the blue and white flag with the Star of David and nearly fainted away. "Israel," she gasped. "Don't tell me we're in Israel! What will the Zionists do to us?" she wailed.

"Later, Mother; later. I'll explain everything later," Ann Marie answered softly, patting her mother's hand.

Any further conversation was cut off by the arrival of a senior-looking army officer, who strode up to Viktor and looked quizzically at the shot-up helicopter and the array of humanity in front of him.

"Can anyone possibly explain just what's going on here? Why were my fighters called out to escort you here? And why my best doctor was dragged out of bed and rushed here?" He moved in for a closer look. "Let's see. We seem to have two elderly people. One very young child. A civilian woman who'd presumably be the child's mother." Then he moved on to Kim. "Ah yes, and here we have an Asian—"

"Korean, actually; Korean American."

"Of course, how silly of me. Korean Americans drop on to northern Israeli beaches every day." Next was Chakroun. "Now you look like a real soldier. Are you?"

"*Oui, mon colonel.* Sergeant Said Chakroun of the French Foreign Legion. On leave."

"A French soldier. This gets interesting. *On leave*, no less. Sergeant, may I suggest some quiet island for your next 'leave'?"

Arlo had just climbed down from the cockpit and stood beside Viktor.

"And you must be the pilot who dodged three MiG fighters, weaving in and out of Lebanese mountains and flying so close to the water that fish are probably in the hold. My pilots are very impressed. They'd never seen anything like it."

Arlo was saved from answering when two more helicopters clattered down nearby. Benny Perlman climbed out of one and walked over to the group. His well-worn civilian clothes and air of weary experience immediately gave his role away. The colonel took one look at him and knew he'd learned as much as he was ever going to learn about this particular helicopter.

Before Perlman could say anything, the colonel smiled

wanly and held up his hands in mock surrender as Perlman led him aside. "I know, I know. You don't have to say anything. This never happened, and my fighters were simply called out on a routine night exercise."

Perlman smiled slightly and patted the colonel on the back. "You're right, colonel. One day, we might have a cup of coffee and talk about this, but not today. Just be aware that the State of Israel and several other countries owe this small group a huge debt of gratitude."

The colonel gave a smart salute and climbed into his jeep.

Viktor was standing by the tail rotor of the helicopter with his shoulders slumped from fatigue and his face twisted in anguished worry about Emily and Davies. Perlman took one look at him, with his shirt covered in blood, and realized he wasn't going to get much out of Viktor right now, but he had to know if the threat of biological warfare just across the border still existed. "I know this isn't the time for a detailed report, but did you manage to destroy the lab?"

Viktor nodded. "It's gone. Blown to hell. It was messier than we wanted, but the rats and lab are gone. The fort's still there," he said with some admiration for the 12th century craftsmen. "It will take a hell of a lot more than us to do any serious damage to that place."

"Well done, Viktor. Well done. Avram was right to trust you," Perlman said, smiling broadly. He gestured toward one of the other helicopters standing by. "Let's get all of you to some place that's safer and more comfortable than this beach. We'll sort things out in due course."

CHAPTER 24

Once they were back in Jerusalem, Viktor had remained constantly at the hospital demanding endless updates as the doctors flowed in and out of Emily's intensive care room. After receiving emergency treatment at a field hospital, she'd been transferred to a hospital in Jerusalem. He was given a chair and frequent cups of very bad coffee, but very little information. They'd taken the bullet out and stopped the bleeding. She was still in an induced coma to reduce stress on her body, and they'd bring her out of it as soon as they felt it was safe. An assessment of any permanent damage would have to wait.

On the third day, Davies limped over to say he was being discharged and Bronstein had arranged a flight to Addis Ababa for him and Arlo. Said Chakroun was already on his way back to Cyprus to meet up with General Lecount. Davies put a hand on Viktor's shoulder. "She's a tough lady, Viktor. She'll pull through. But I ain't so sure about you," he said in the tone of a drill sergeant barking at a raw recruit. "You look like hell, and you ain't doin' her much good if you don't shape up before she comes around. She don't want to see some half-assed, unshaven wreck in front of her. Go get yourself cleaned up. Get a shave and some decent clothes. And for Christ's sake, hang on to her."

Viktor stood up unhurriedly. "Thanks for all your help, Ricky. Hell of a mess, wasn't it? At least the diseased rats are gone. Sorry about the money. God knows when or if Uncle Sam will give us anything."

Davis broke into a wide smile. "Don't you worry none about that. Ol' Avram put his hand into the cookie jar and came up with a nice bundle. Sergei's as happy as a pig in shit, figurin' where to put it all. Maybe we can all take it easy for a while. Maybe Desta's right," he mused, "maybe I'm gettin' a little old for this crap." He chuckled and started to leave. "On second thoughts, not too likely, is it? Ain't no shortage of scumbags to clean up." With that, he waved goodbye and sauntered off.

Viktor smiled at the unlikely thought of a retired Ricky Davies. His phone buzzed, and he dug around in the deep pocket of his filthy cargo pants until he found it under a handkerchief that was still covered in some of the contractors' blood. There was a message from Bronstein to meet him at 4 p.m. in a place called the American Colony Hotel. After checking with the doctors that not much was expected to happen in the next few hours, he returned to his room to clean up.

***

Viktor stood at the entrance to the courtyard at the American Colony Hotel, scanning the space for signs of Avram Bronstein. A couple of tables were filled with tourists drinking heavily iced Coca-Colas while pouring over guidebooks for Jerusalem. Finally, he spotted Bronstein at a table in the far corner, almost hidden under a giant plane tree. With him were Benny Perlman, Oleg Yushenko, and his wife. They smiled and gestured for Viktor to join them.

Perlman put down his phone and smiled broadly. "Well," he began, "thanks to your efforts, we've begun to clear up our own mess. After a long talk with the prime minister last night to convince him of the dangers in playing with some of our own extremists, there was a raid on an office right here in Jerusalem this morning. Two irate citizens were picked up and bundled into cars to be taken to one of our discreet locations. They continued to babble about their *rights* until confronted with some of the evidence from their computers and hard copy from their files." He frowned deeply. "So stupid really. No," he corrected himself, "not just stupid. Arrogant. So arrogant about their connections to supposed 'power circles' within the government and military that they forgot the basic rule of conspiracies: never leave any evidence." He checked his watch. "As we speak, there should be announcements about sudden retirements from those same supposed power circles." He held his thumb and forefinger a tiny distance apart. "We were that close, you know. That close to another idiotic, needless war."

He stopped just long enough to let his favorite waiter Khalid put another cup of steaming, thick Arabic coffee in front of him. "Now this kid—a good kid—has a chance to grow up."

"What about the Korean kid? Did you send him back?" Viktor asked.

Perlman gave a loud laugh. "Are you kidding? He begged us not to send him anywhere. He said the North Koreans would shoot him on sight—if he were lucky. And he doubted the Americans would be too happy about accepting a known North Korean agent. No, he stays right here, working happily in one of our labs. In a few weeks, he'll just about double the number of Hebrew speaking Koreans."

"And the Americans? Any word there?"

"That's a little more complicated," Perlman answered. "Of course, they were *shocked* at the information we gave them and claimed they'd take immediate action. But it's going to take some testimony from Miss Wilkins to close that particular barn door. Apparently, the Senate Intelligence Committee is waiting as anxiously as you are for her recovery. As soon as she can travel, they want her back in Washington to help untangle this mess. In the meantime, we've heard that one retired General Stanley Meadows has been persuaded to really retire and disband his contracting company. And the FBI is looking for a certain retired colonel who seems to be implicated in the suspicious death of a senior NSA officer named Shepherd." He took a sip of his coffee. "Better than nothing, but they still need Miss Wilkins."

Viktor nodded toward Yushenko and his wife. "What about Oleg and his family?"

"There, I'm glad to announce that the State of Israel has gained a new family," Bronstein stated in Russian, smiling broadly. "They'll be resettled here. We can always use someone with Oleg's skills, and Ann Marie has several offers for nursing positions at leading hospitals. Their son is receiving the latest treatments for cystic fibrosis as we speak."

"And her parents?"

Bronstein laughed. "Once they got over the shock of being in Israel they seem to be settling in very nicely in a flat near Oleg and their daughter." Then he looked at Viktor. "And you, Viktor, what will you do?"

He blew out a breath and shrugged. "I don't know. Return to the island, I suppose. See what happens. Try to pick up some pieces..."

Just then, Bronstein's phone buzzed. He answered it, annoyed at being disturbed. He listened for a few minutes and then thanked the caller. "That was the hospital. They just brought Miss Wilkins out of the coma." He grinned. "She wants to know where you are."

Yushenko also smiled as Ann Marie looked sternly at Viktor. "I think one of those pieces you were talking about just fell into place. Go. Now, Viktor. The island can wait a day or two," she ordered.

September on Telos, Aegean Sea

It didn't take Viktor long to fall back into his old routine—only it wasn't so comfortable this time. The olive trees were heavy with fruit and it would soon be time to organize the harvest. He checked in the storeroom to make sure the nets were ready to unfold under the trees. After checking the other fruit trees for the umpteenth time and picking up tiny bits of rubbish from an already immaculate house, he sat down with one of his favorite books. That didn't work either. Frustrated, he picked up his backpack, containing his binoculars and handgun, and went down to the port where a ferry was due to arrive in a couple of hours.

The news from Washington was dramatic. Congressional hearings on the misuse of private military contractors had provided the best daytime TV since the O.J. Simpson trial. Congressmen who'd previously supported these contractors suddenly became defenders of liberty and transparency once the cameras were turned on. No one really paid much attention when senior Pentagon officials testified that they were forced to use these contractors because of repeated congressional budget cuts.

General Meadows was called to testify, and he didn't make many friends when he waved a piece of paper with dozens of names on it, bellowed something about "traitors" and that many Congressmen who'd previously supported him were nothing more than "weak-kneed, leftist commies." Great TV.

***

The general ultimately retired to his home in South Carolina, which was near several military installations. One of his habits was to walk into the small town every Wednesday for a shave and haircut. One particular Wednesday, he was surprised to see two new barbers in the shop—barbers who looked surprisingly like some of his former Delta Force soldiers. They explained that the usual barber had been called away on a family emergency and they'd be pleased to serve the general. As he made himself comfortable in the chair, he never noticed that they turned the "open" sign in the window to "closed" and locked the front door. One of them wrapped his face in a warm towel and began to strop the long razor on a piece of leather attached to the chair.

"You boys any good with that razor? I hate them nicks you sometimes get," Meadows murmured from beneath the warm, damp towel.

"Oh yes, General," the man assured him in his thick Appalachian twang, "we're real good with all sorts of knives and sharp blades."

The other leaned close to the general's right ear and whispered the name of John Shepherd.

General Meadows tried to sit up in alarm and whip off the towel, but a strong arm kept his head back against the chair while the other arm took the razor and sliced cleanly through his neck, almost to the spine. Blood spurted out in front of the chair, and the general tried uselessly to stem the red flood before collapsing in a heap on the floor. The two soldiers threw mock salutes and retreated through the rear door, never to be seen again.

***

If the Washington press corps was on a strict news diet, Viktor was starving. Once Emily had recovered enough, she'd been interviewed at length in Israel by an endless stream of American intelligence and military officials. They'd bristled at being required to go through Benny Perlman to get to Emily, but they were told bluntly that, because Emily was only a *former* NSA staffer, they'd get nothing from her without his participation.

They listened open-mouthed to her description of what had happened and repeated several times, "*You've gotta be shitting me.*"

Details of exactly how the infected-rat program was stopped were kept vague.

Viktor was constantly by her side at the hospital and during her initial convalescence. The doctors had warned them both that the damage had been extensive and the road to recovery was going to be long and painful. They warned that, at best, she'd regain about 80% use of her right arm. When she got tired and depressed after the first therapy sessions he was there to encourage her and tell her to keep the faith. Since they both were essentially emotional mutes, very little was said about their growing personal relationship. But others noted how irritated and truculent Emily became when Viktor wasn't around. They also saw how distracted Viktor was when he was away from her.

Yushenko and his wife spotted the connection, but they *wisely* decided that their intervention would only make things worse. "It will take time, but they'll work it out," was what they told each other. When it became time for Emily to return to Washington, the best they could manage was an awkward hug at the airport and a vague promise to stay in touch.

Once Emily had been taken into protective custody in Washington, that vague promise remained even more vague. Shortly after arriving, she received a two-word note from Helen Shepherd: "Thank You." Beyond that, she was forbidden all contact with the outside world, as before disbelieving senators, she unraveled exactly how far the American intelligence and military agencies had strayed from the theoretical congressional oversight. While the American public just might understand the misdeeds of some misguided officials, it was decided that the public could be spared information about the roles of Viktor, Davies, and Arlo—let alone the inclusion of a French Foreign

Legionnaire and a former Russian Spetsnaz officer. It was also deemed wise not to mention the role of an American citizen who happened to be a North Korean agent and who now was working happily in an Israeli research lab.

Viktor was growing increasingly frustrated during this radio silence. The judge even beat him a couple of times at their regular chess games. He tried to get rise out of Viktor by obliquely bringing up the congressional hearings he'd been following on the internet. "Quite a mess in Washington, eh, Aleco," he probed.

There was no response except a grunt and nod.

The judge tried again. "And Syria, what won't they try next?"

Again, just a grunt, followed by, "Terrible place," which was all he could get out of Viktor.

"And that lovely girl who was here for a few days. What happened to her?" the judge persisted.

"Don't know. Haven't heard anything," Viktor answered as he made the unlikely mistake of exposing his queen to attack from one of the judge's bishops.

"Not like you, Aleco. Check," the judge said quietly as he captured the queen.

"Oh Christ. Sorry, your honor," Viktor apologized. "I can't seem to concentrate these days."

Just then the ferry blasted its horn as it started its maneuver to moor. Viktor glanced up, as he always did, to check the disembarking passengers. The usual elderly ladies with their huge shopping bags were the first off. Then one or two tourists and the very few cars got off.

The captain was about to order the ramp raised when there was a loud shriek from the inside the hold: "Put the damn thing back down!"

Viktor got up so quickly he spilled the chessboard all over the ground. He started grinning broadly and jogged toward the pier. He could think of only one person with that type of commanding roar. The ferry nudged back toward the pier, the ramp slammed angrily down once again, and he could see Emily struggling to handle a heavy, wheeled suitcase with her one good arm. She made it to the pier and stood looking at Viktor hustling toward her. He stopped a few feet away not sure what to do.

"You bloody fool, is that any way to greet me?" She rushed forward laughing and threw her one good arm around his neck, hugging him as tight as she could.

Afraid of hurting her, he didn't squeeze her too hard. "Why didn't you let me know you were coming?"

"And give you a chance to get on the next boat out of here?"

"Not too likely." he smiled. "Now you're stuck here—way, way out of the fast lane."

"That's right where I want to be."

The judge and Maria exchanged knowing looks. "Guess I've won my last chess game," the judge commented wryly.

Maria cuffed him lightly on the shoulder. "Idiot. Looks to me like you better start brushing up on some of your civil marriage ceremonies."

This book is printed on paper from sustainable sources managed under the Forest Stewardship Council (FSC) scheme.

It has been printed in the UK to reduce transportation miles and their impact upon the environment.

For every new title that Troubador publishes, we plant a tree to offset CO_2, partnering with the More Trees scheme.

For more about how Troubador offsets its environmental impact, see www.troubador.co.uk/sustainability-and-community